Ruth Hamilton was born in Bolton and has spent most of her life in Lancashire. Her novels, *A Whisper to the Living, With Love From Ma Maguire, Nest of Sorrows, Billy London's Girls, Spinning Jenny, The September Starlings, A Crooked Mile, Paradise Lane, The Bells of Scotland Road, The Dream Sellers, The Corner House, Miss Honoria West, Mulligan's Yard* and *Saturday's Child* are all published by Corgi Books and she is a national bestseller. She has written a sixpart television series and over forty children's programmes for independent television. Ruth Hamilton now lives in Liverpool with her family.

For more information on Ruth Hamilton and her books, see her website at:
www.ruthhamilton.co.uk.

www.**books**at**transworld**.co.uk

The Corner House

Ruth Hamilton

CORGI BOOKS

THE CORNER HOUSE
A CORGI BOOK : 0 552 14567 X

Originally published in Great Britain by Bantam Press,
a division of Transworld Publishers

PRINTING HISTORY
Bantam Press edition published 1998
Corgi edition published 1999

7 9 10 8 6

Set in 11/12pt Baskerville by
Hewer Text Ltd, Edinburgh

Corgi Books are published by Transworld Publishers,
61-63 Uxbridge Road, London W5 5SA,
a division of The Random House Group Ltd,
in Australia by Random House Australia (Pty) Ltd,
20 Alfred Street, Milsons Point, Sydney, NSW 2061, Australia,
in New Zealand by Random House New Zealand Ltd,
18 Poland Road, Glenfield, Auckland 10, New Zealand
and in South Africa by Random House (Pty) Ltd,
Endulini, 5a Jubilee Road, Parktown 2193, South Africa

Reproduced, printed and bound in Germany by
GGP Media GmbH, Poessneck.

In memory of Dame Catherine Cookson, inspiration to so many, kindness itself to me.

Also Tom Cookson, husband of Dame Catherine.

May God bless and cherish these two fine souls.

Acknowledgements

Many, many thanks to the following:

Diane Pearson, my dear editor, who waited endlessly for this book while I went through a difficult year.

David and Michael Thornber, my two sons. Without them, recent months would have been impossible to bear.

Elizabeth Warmisham, who wrestled with my computer and my incompetence.

Ted Openshaw, whose knowledge of Bolton's fish-market was so valuable.

Sandra Heilberg and all the staff at Sweetens Books, Bolton.

Josephine Walker (researcher); David Rhodes of Yates Jewellers; also the staff at Whittle's Jewellers, all of Preston, Lancashire.

Eileen Weir (researcher) of Crosby, Merseyside.

In spite of a certain female critic who objects to my 'sentimentality' with animals, I say goodbye on this page to Benny and Scooby, two scruffy little mongrels aged sixteen and fifteen respectively. Both were humanely put to sleep on 1 July 1998 in the Corner House, which happens to be my home. They are so very sadly missed.

I welcome into my life Samson, two-year-old black Labrador with the sweetest temperament.

Also Fudge, chocolate Labrador aged three months, who has, in just over a fortnight, eaten his way through the bottom drawer of my bureau, some trainers with (according to my son) A Designer Name, the landing carpet, something called a joystick, a roll of sticky tape, two kitchen mats and a twenty-pound note. We all love him dearly in spite of his misdeeds.

NOVEMBER, 1964

It was a cold, grey morning with leaden clouds pressing down as if intending to impose their gloomy weight on the Mersey. The Liver Birds continued their eternal vigil; a tanker, its replete belly low in the water, drifted silently towards the next resting place. On the rail that divided land from water, several gulls cast beady eyes over flagstones in search of food.

Bernard Walsh, who was used to ice, did not even shiver as people hurried behind him towards buses with shopping, umbrellas and wailing children. He saw little and heard nothing, simply bowing his head and staring downward with the special passivity that visits the truly absorbed. She was dead. This morning, at the shop, the news had finally arrived. 'Oh, Katherine,' he whispered now. How could he tell Katherine that her mother's life was over?

He hadn't even managed to be at the bedside. His wife had died while he, Bernard Walsh, husband, father and fishmonger, had used his expertise to prepare and sell the chilled, glass-eyed fruits of Britain's coastal waters.

Urging himself to focus, he cleaned thick-lensed spectacles on a handkerchief, then watched the tanker drifting lazily into dock. He dragged his sad mind back into the present tense just as a female child screamed and complained about cold fingers. Katherine did not like the cold. She would be at work now, would be drumming facts into the tousled heads of thirty-four children at St Anthony's School on Scotland Road. Pretty, talented, happy Katherine, what a blessing she had proved to be.

Liz's sufferings were over. Liz was lying now beneath a snow-white sheet in the morgue at Walton Hospital. No longer would Bernard Walsh spend his evenings in the company of a comatose woman. In recent weeks, he had sat and watched the cruel and unforgiving disease consume his beloved wife. How on earth had he coped without her humour, her tenderness? Towards the end, Liz had drifted away into a morphine-induced retreat of her own, had been fed through tubes, had been bathed and tended by nurses like a helpless child. Even so, she had been alive. Bernard had half expected her to jump up and tell the nurses what to do with all their gadgets and needles, but Liz had remained a poor, crippled, ageing infant. He had never looked at another woman. He had been that rare beast: a happily married man.

Katherine. Newborn, she had been perfect, almost magical. A smile threatened to stretch his lips, and he refused to allow such an unsuitable expression to gain purchase. His wife was dead and, if he chose the path of righteousness, there was further heartbreak to come. The right thing. What was the right thing?

'Bernard?'

He sighed, and fixed myopic eyes on the man at his side. 'How did you know I'd be here?'

John Povey rested a hand on his friend's shoulder.

Since his arrival in Liverpool, Bernard Walsh had always visited the river in times of stress.

'I can't do it,' mumbled Bernard.

'Not today. It doesn't have to be today.' John trembled as a frosty wind sliced like a cruel knife through clothing and into his chest. 'Aren't you freezing?'

Bernard shook his head. The tall, rounded fish-monger seldom complained of cold, though the gradual erosion of his hair had driven him to wearing headgear: a trilby outside; a white hat while serving in his shop.

'I suppose you'll be used to it.'

'Aye, I am that.' For over thirty years, Bernard Walsh had worked with fish. The skin on his hands was so weathered that a clogger might have pinned irons to it without the need for anaesthesia. 'You've heard, then?'

John nodded. 'I popped up to Walton with some supplies, asked about Liz while I was there. A peaceful end, they said. Given her condition, that was a blessing, old son.' Liz and Bernard had been insep-arable. Like Darby and Joan, Laurel and Hardy, theirs had been a double act. He recalled some of the carryings-on, parties where Bernard had been foil to Liz and vice versa. The pair had prayed, played and stayed together. ' "I can drink any table under this man," ' said John softly. 'Remember her saying that while in her cups, Bernard?'

'Aye, she was well away that night. I think that was the first time she'd ever had vodka. Up till then, she'd called vodka a heathen drink, something to do with communism.' Bernard dropped his chin and pondered. 'Aye, vodka was her downfall that parti-cular night. Our Liz did her balancing act with the yardbrush and destroyed Dr Connor's chandelier. Austrian crystal. Cost me nigh on eighty quid to have it mended.'

'We'll not see her like again,' said John. 'That mould definitely got smashed.'

'Just like the bloody chandelier.' Bernard sniffed, exhaled, watched his foggy breath as it hovered for seconds in the chill November air. 'One off, was my Liz. She deserved some peace. What she went through was never deserved. I can't think of anyone bad enough to warrant pain like that.'

John thrust his hands deep into coat pockets, cursing himself for forgetting gloves again. 'Will you bury her in Bolton, then?'

Liz had left explicit instructions. Soon after the first operation, she had understood that she would not recover, because the voracious beast within her body had already sallied forth to sink its hungry, sharp teeth into most major organs. 'She's to be burnt – she didn't mind where.' The smile threatened again.

'You can put me on a bloody bonfire like Guy Fawkes for all I care,' Liz had said. 'Just make sure I get scattered properly and give Katherine all my jewellery.'

'Jolly Brows,' said Bernard.

'I beg your pardon?'

'North side of Bolton – that's where she's to be scattered. We used to meet there years back, before we were married. There was a little hillock with a pond nearby. In springtime, loads of baby frogs hatched out and jumped all over us.' Unlike most girls, Liz had taken the frogs in her stride. 'It was the frogs that clinched it at the finish, you see.'

John Povey scratched his nose, did a mental inventory of his famous herbal remedies. What could he brew up to ward off dementia? John, who had perfected the art of sartorial eccentricity, looked every inch the mad scientist: dishevelled hair; clothes which always managed to look like someone else's, seldom fitting, always creased. 'Isn't it enough that I'm daft?' he asked his friend. 'Do you have to catch the same bus as me? Don't start going soft in the head, lad. Don't start copying me.'

'She liked frogs,' continued Bernard. 'She liked most living things. I had to make a contraption when we had a mouse, a box with cheese in it and a door that shut itself once the creature got inside. She used to waltz off up to Blundellsands to release the bloody mice into the wild, as she called it. Any infestations in Blundellsands would be Liz's fault. I kept telling her they weren't field mice, but you know what Liz was like. She said if the mice insisted on living indoors, they'd get a better class of cheese in Blundellsands, a bit of Brie or Danish Blue.'

'She was a character, all right,' agreed John Povey.

Bernard nodded. Liz was a grand woman. Silently, Bernard corrected himself. She had been a grand woman, a lover of animals, a determined minder of wildlife, a protectress of all God's creatures. She had been, but she no longer was. Everything about the woman he loved was suddenly history.

John glanced at the Liver Building clock. 'Did you close the shop?'

'Henry's there.' Henry couldn't fillet a cod to save his life. Bernard Walsh followed the direction of his friend's gaze. 'The largest chiming clock in existence,' he said. Sailors from all corners knew the Liver Building, looked for its twin birds to mark the end of a journey. This, one of the most memorable buildings on earth, was often a sight for the sore eyes of a returning homesick traveller.

'How long are you planning to stay here?' John Povey asked.

'In Liverpool?'

'No. Here in the freezing cold.'

At last Bernard allowed himself a fuller smile. 'I'm thinking.'

'I know that.'

Bernard shuffled about, faced the river again. He remembered his days on Bolton's fishmarket, the wind blowing through those huge doors, lorries emptying their contents between stalls, early shoppers trying to get the pick of the catch before the market was properly opened except to wholesale purchasers. The rabbit man tramping in with a pole of rabbits; the chicken woman covered in feathers, a couple of sacks dragging from her hands.

He remembered the blue-misted moors, Sundays spent roaming across fields with Liz, evenings enjoyed at home with Mam and Dad. 'There's no going back, is there?' He had considered the possibility of returning to Bolton once before, after the discovery in Liverpool of a certain woman, but Liz had insisted on staying. She had been dug up once, and had declared her roots now to be settled. 'I shan't stand for another transplant, Bernard,' Liz Walsh had advised her husband. 'I'm all right. I've got friends and I'm used to the shops. Pull me up again and I'll perish like a dried-out bedding plant.'

'I don't know about staying, going, moving on or whatever,' mumbled Bernard.

John dragged reluctant hands from warm pockets and propped his elbows on the railing. 'Do the thing that seems best, Bernard.'

The fishmonger shifted his gaze to the left and looked at John Povey. With his over-long greying hair and intense hazel eyes, the chemist looked a bit like another Einstein. 'I've always done what's bloody best,' said Bernard Walsh, his tone almost snappy. 'And where did it get me? A lock-up on Scotland Road and a lie I've lived for twenty-odd year. There were times, you know. Times when I came near to telling Liz.' He swallowed a lump of pain. 'But I never did. Then, when she took poorly . . . Well, that's all over for her now, thank God.'

'Katherine isn't history, though.'

'I know that, John.'

'She's the future. She's a good girl and I know she'll take it on the chin.'

Bernard shook his head pensively. 'There's things I did that I never should have done, then there's other things I should have done that I never—'

'It's the same for all of us. Do you think you're the only sinner, the only chap who's ever made mistakes? You can't change the past, but you can make an effort for the future.'

Firstly, Bernard had to take himself back to Scotland Road, had to tell his one and only child that her mother was dead. Then there were insurance policies to wade through, people to be notified, coffins to pick and choose from. In his house, Liz's belongings would scream at him from every corner of every room. The house had caused him pain for many a month, but now, with Liz definitely gone, her trinkets and clothes would be angrier, louder, lonelier. And time would continue to tick on, marked by the Liver clocks and by the watch on his wrist, by the hourly beep-beeps on the radio, by the ever-turning pages of the kitchen calendar.

'Come on, Bernard,' urged John.

'Not yet. You go – I'll be all right.' He had thoughts to collect, phrases to arrange.

'Are you sure?' John Povey's face was furrowed by concern.

'I've never been sure of owt,' said Bernard, lapsing deliberately into the idiom that separated him from most of his fellows in this city. 'Except that I loved Liz and I love my daughter.'

John Povey shuddered again, trembling not only against the chill, but also because of a secret shared for more than a decade. Who could say what was right, what was wrong? Perhaps Katherine should not be told . . . and yet . . .

Bernard read his companion's thoughts. 'I shall have to work my way up to it, John. There's none but me shall tell the tale, because I know you'll say nothing.'

John nodded his agreement. 'I'll not push you any more, Bernard. You have my opinion, but I shan't force the issue. You know me well enough by now. I can offer pills and potions, but a cure's never guaranteed.'

'Thanks.' Bernard watched his friend as he made his way across the Pier Head and towards his car. 'What would I have done without that man?' he mouthed softly. For a long time, John had been Bernard's sanity. John Povey was a gentleman of principle, a genius with medicines, an unspoilt, down-to-earth bloke.

A gaggle of youths came into view, shaggy haircuts resembling what Liz had always termed 'tatty-'ead mops', the sort that got squeezed out in a special section of a bucket. Although the Beatles had moved on, the noise continued, bang-banging from the mesh speakers of portable radios, drumming its way through open windows in the summer months, escaping from coffee bars each time a door swung to or fro. And these young lads' heads seemed to warrant mowing, not cutting.

The boys stopped as if prompted by some invisible cue, drew combs from pockets and passed them through wild, abundant locks. Guitar cases leaned against blue-jeaned legs, while the omnipresent transistor radio sat silently next to a pile of sheet music. The group would doubtless be on its way to practise in the garage or bedroom of some tolerant or absent parent. These were the hopefuls, the also-rans who tried to pursue Ringo and the rest into lives of luxury and lunacy. 'Bloody daft,' muttered Bernard. They should be spending their time looking for a good job. The Beatles seemed to exist on the run, escaping from mobs of screaming girls and from the constant glare of scandal-hungry reporters. Aye, they'd all have been a damned sight better off in fish.

Katherine. She'd been to that last concert at The Cavern, had probably screeched with the rest while John Lennon played and sang in that wonderful, careless, I'm-here-to-enjoy-myself way, his head held up, notes pouring past adenoidal tissue and down a strangely aristocratic nose. Katherine had been through a few phases – pancake make-up thick enough to want scraping off by an interior decorator, white-as-death cheeks, eyes surrounded by spiky, false lashes, the upper lids painted as black as hell.

How could he tell her? How? And must she be told?

The chocolate workers had been sent home on that searing August day, the day of the last Cavern concert, because coffee creams and hazel fudge had melted around them in sticky, shapeless pools. In spite of the heat, Liverpool's young folk had squeezed themselves into that awful cellar, many fainting for lack of oxygen, some losing consciousness in the presence of their gods.

She had quietened, had attended a Catholic teacher training college in Liverpool, returning each evening to the bosom of her family. They lived in a nice big semi on the Northern Road in Crosby, had four bedrooms, a piano, a man who came round once a week to do the gardening, a lady who tidied up and cleaned the silver. They had a car, an automatic washing machine, a television set and a freezer. Carpets were top-grade Axminster; all rooms were centrally heated. And Liz was dead.

Majorca, Alicante, Venice, Rome – Bernard had taken his two girls on holiday in recent years. In Rome, Liz had discovered her lump, that tiny, hard pebble beneath sun-touched flesh. 'It'll be summat and nowt,' she had declared over a plate of pasta. It had turned out to be summat and everything, the very 'summat' that had finished her happy, selfless life.

A tear escaped and trickled down Bernard Walsh's ruddy cheek. With a numb hand, he dashed it away and steeled himself against its brothers. If he was going to cry, he would do it later, loudly and in private.

'You all right, mister?'

Bernard blinked. It was one of the mop-headed hopefuls, just an ordinary lad with longish hair and a few baby freckles lingering on his nose. 'Aye, I'll be better in a minute.'

'Can I . . . Do you want anything?'

He wanted Liz. He wanted his life back, wanted to be the same age as this copy-cat Beatle, wanted the moorlands, the camaraderie of Bolton market, a pie and a pint in the Wheatsheaf for his dinner. 'My wife died today,' he said. 'Thanks for being so kind.'

The boy frowned. 'You shouldn't be on your own. When my old gran died, we all stuck together. Have you got somebody?'

Bernard nodded.

'Do you want a lift? I can take you on the scooter – the lads'll look after my stuff. We were only on our way to practise, anyway.'

'My car's across the road, thanks.'

The boy continued to look puzzled. 'I've got you now,' he announced after a second or two. 'Mr Walsh – wet fish on Scotland Road.'

'That's me.'

The youngster grinned. 'Fridays, we always have fish.'

'Is that Jimmy Morris?' Bernard peered beneath the thatch and into eyes as blue as a June midnight. 'Well, I'd never have recognized you.'

Jimmy laughed, then remembered the sadness. 'Look, I'm sorry about Mrs Walsh. I met her the odd time—'

'Aye, it would be odd and all,' said Bernard. 'She hated the smell of raw fish. I had to go in the back way when I got home, then straight up for a bath. Even then, she'd tell me I stank like fifteen stone of cod.' He shook his head. 'No, she didn't often help in the shop. I had to be at death's door before she'd give me a hand.'

Jimmy reached out and touched the fishmonger's shoulder. 'If you ever want me, we still live over the barber's.' He wandered off to rejoin his companions.

There was hope for the future, Bernard Walsh decided. Jimmy Morris and his crew might look like a lot of big girls' blouses, but the heart was still there. Terry Morris was a barber. He and his wife had raised two boys in the rooms above what he called his 'saloon'. Terry was a good Catholic and a strong believer in cut-throat razors and hot towels. Terry Morris should pin their Jimmy to a chair and give him a short back and sides before the lad crashed his scooter due to impeded vision.

Bernard walked towards his car, waving at the disappearing would-be pop band. He sat for a while, fingers tapping the Rover's steering wheel, mind racing about as he worked his way through the list of things to be done. At the back of his conscious-ness, the truth kept its counsel, remained hidden behind names and addresses of those who must be invited to the funeral.

Liz hadn't wanted to come to Liverpool. She had pleaded to stay in Bolton, but Bernard, anxious to be away from the scene of other people's crimes, had dragged his wife and young daughter down the East Lancashire Road. And they had settled, had thrived on the Scousers' love of fresh and salt fish, had become comfortable members of the *nouveau riche* middle class.

And then, after a short lull of relative peace, the woman had arrived and Bernard had suggested an-other move, perhaps to Bury or Blackburn. 'I'm not going anywhere,' Liz had screamed. 'Why must we be forever shifting about? We've survived the bloody war, we're doing all right, so where's the flaming sense in taking off again?' Liz had made friends in Crosby, good friends, the sort she would not have left easily.

'I just feel like a change,' Bernard heard himself replying. The truth was unspeakable, so he could furnish Liz with no reason for his desire to leave

Liverpool, the city which had become the new love of Liz Walsh's life.

'Well, I don't. I'm changing no more than my underwear, you great lummox. I like it here. The shops in town are great and our Katherine's made a lot of new friends.'

They had stayed and had been lucky. The woman had moved to Waterloo, a mere couple of miles from the Walshes' house. 'God must have been on your side,' Bernard told his dead wife. 'Because you never knew.'

She knew now, though. Somewhere above these mucky clouds, a woman with a new halo was looking down on him. He should, perhaps, call in at St Anthony's, should get down on his knees and pray in the church before visiting his daughter's classroom. 'I did it all for you, Liz,' he said. And for Katherine. Yes, it had been for Katherine's sake, too.

He drove slowly through the city, as if trying to postpone Katherine's inevitable tears. Liz's death had been expected – even hoped for in the darker hours, but every child was shocked by the final disappearance of a parent.

Outside St Anthony's, Bernard turned off his engine and sat perfectly still. In ten or so minutes, the children would dash out of classrooms and Katherine would be free to talk and to listen and to weep.

The broader, merciless exodus from these largely Catholic streets had begun, leaving the area sad and much quieter. Families were relocating to pastures new, nasty little houses built on unloved land. The green that surrounded Kirkby was scrubby, pale and heartless, as if it had given up hope long ago.

'I might as well retire,' he whispered. 'There'll be

nothing much left here for me in a year or two.'
Katherine would get wed. She had been through so
many suitors that Bernard had sometimes considered making a rota just to have things fair and
square, equal time and attention for all comers.
But now, there was Martin, who had bought an
engagement ring, who would be Katherine's husband in a few months.

He entered the church, knelt and prayed for Liz's
repose. He prayed also for the woman he had feared,
that other poor creature whose soul had departed
some years ago. She had left her mark. Theresa
Nolan's mark had smudged its path right across
Lancashire from the inland foothills to the coast.
Her fury had destroyed families, had made grown
men cry, had affected innocent children. Yet she, the
truly injured party, had simply looked for justice.

'What's it all been about?' he asked his Maker.
'Did I do it wrong from the very start?'

Bernard Walsh closed his eyes. A knock at the
door; a woman standing in the street, a newspaper
parcel in her hands. Upstairs, Liz sleeping. Someone
else's sin. Fish scales beneath his fingernails, gas
lamps doused against possible invasion, silent skies,
no bombs yet. Liz too ill for air-raid shelters; instant
decision, instant lie.

His eyelids raised themselves. Were there good
lies, then? Were there degrees of untruth, some
types more acceptable than others? He blessed himself, heard the school bell ringing in celebration of
another finished morning.

Genuflecting, he turned his back to the altar and
walked slowly down the aisle. Soon, he would face his
living conscience.

ONE

By 1940, Bernard and Daniel Walsh were the last surviving remnants of a dynasty that stretched back through more than a century. Their father and grandfather had sold fish on Bolton Market for at least a hundred years, while the Derby Street shop had been in the hands of a Walsh since 1897.

Danny, older than Bernard by seven years, was a dyed-in-the-wool bachelor, unlovely of face, lean, sound in wind and limb. Although he remained blissfully unaware of the fact, Danny Walsh had a sweetness of nature that charmed many women into hovering on the brink of infatuation. But Danny knew exactly what he wanted from life. With a hoe, a rake and a bed of weeds, he was armed and in his natural element.

This older Walsh brother had chosen to live outside the town, in a place where the moors and fields could be viewed and appreciated. His back garden was bordered by a low privet hedge, but it seemed to continue onward and upward for ever, stretching through pasture and arable land, climbing softly, gently, eastward towards the Pennines. The weaver's cottage in Bromley Cross was small, yet its setting was pure magic to a man whose boyhood had been spent among factory chimneys and dark terraced streets.

With his pipe, his baccy pouch and his predictable life-pattern, Danny existed quite happily like a man twice his age. He went to the same public house each evening from nine o'clock until ten, then rose at the crack of dawn, travelling to meet the incoming fish trains or to run the Derby Street shop. Catholic to the core, he attended mass every Sunday and on most saints' days unless such items on the calendar of Rome interfered with the progress of business.

The brothers took life in their stride. As providers of essential services, they had been excused call-up, which fact, as each was wont to declare, was a definite plus for Britain, since both men were short-sighted and inclined towards the special headaches that often accompany myopia. 'Guns?' they ruminated from time to time. 'Guns? Our Danny [or our Bernard] couldn't hit a dartboard with a crossbow unless he had a guide dog and a papal blessing.'

During the early months of war, Danny Walsh spent many nights on a makeshift bed in a tiny room behind the Derby Street shop, returning to his cottage only when other duties did not demand his total attention. For five nights of every week, he and Bernard were stand-by firefighters. The blazes they had doused thus far had been caused by domestic accidents rather than by bombings, although both brothers had been mentioned in the press for extraordinary bravery. Bernard was the real daredevil. He had emerged from burning buildings on more than one occasion with his clothes on fire and a child or an animal in his arms.

As January drifted its snow-softened way towards the next month, Danny declared himself to be browned off. Sirens kept sounding, but nothing ever happened. He wasn't complaining about that, because he didn't want bombs, didn't want to be picking up the dead, but he could have been at home, could have seen the moors covered in blankets of silvery-white, could have been feeding his birds and providing water for them.

He sat in his smelly little room. The brothers scarcely noticed the odour of fish unless decay had set in. Danny was of the opinion that both he and Bernard carried cod liver oil rather than blood in their veins. An ancient clock ticked uncertainly; a thin, wartime version of the *Bolton Evening News* lay on the floor next to a faded rug. The unmistakable sound of Liz Walsh's carpet sweeper filtered through the ceiling. It was a waiting game – waiting for the baby, waiting for the Luftwaffe.

Danny checked the black-out, lit a candle, stretched out on his iron-framed cot and used a penknife to prise a few stubborn fish scales from the rims of his fingernails. Upstairs, Liz continued her relentless to-ing and fro-ing with the carpet sweeper. Seven months into her pregnancy, Liz refused to sit down and rest her legs. 'I'll rest when bloody Hitler rests in his grave,' the feisty woman had been heard to shout. 'And I've never sat down since I married yon daft ha'p'orth.' 'Yon daft ha'p'orth' was Danny's little brother, though 'little' went no way towards describing Bernard Walsh. Bernard, in spite of being an active man, was inclined towards rotundity. The general opinion of folk hereabouts was that Bernard was the full fish, while Danny, tall and skinny, was the fish after the cat had been at it – all skull and spiky bones.

The Walshes usually took turns, one remaining at the shop while the second man collected fish and then, after supplying the shop, going back to run Walsh's stall on the market. Lately, Bernard had stuck to the shop in order to keep an eye on his pregnant wife. As a result, Danny was often tired owing to constant early rising and an excess of responsibility, yet he remained even-tempered and benign throughout the most trying of days.

The door opened and Bernard stepped in. He wore the air of a man who had just decided on tactical retreat. 'She won't listen. If she polishes that sideboard again, it'll collapse into a heap of fire-wood, fit for nowt but kindling.' Because of his bulk, Bernard seemed to fill the space between bed and door, especially now, with his large arms akimbo.

'No fires so far tonight, thank God,' pondered Danny aloud. 'Nowt for the brigade to go out for.'

'Not yet.'

Danny placed his knife on a small table and waited for Bernard to let off steam.

'She's not stopped since tea-time.'

'I can imagine,' replied Danny. 'She's swept that carpet to within a hair's breadth of its hessian backing this past half-hour. She'll be coming through my ceiling in a minute. Happen you must nail her feet to the floor and chain her top half to the door handle.'

Bernard sat in an old kitchen chair. 'It's this baby. She wants everything clean and shiny before it arrives. I reckon she'd Mansion Wax me if I sat still for long enough. And she's going on and on about moving out, getting away from the shop. Says she doesn't want her kiddy going to school smelling like somebody's breakfast kippers.'

Danny raised his shoulders in a shrug. 'Please yourself. Once the war's over, we can turn this into a lock-up, let some young couple have the upstairs flat.'

Bernard mulled this over for the umpteenth time.

He didn't go a bundle on change for change's sake, wasn't really struck by the idea of moving. 'I like it here,' he said. 'Near enough to town, near the church and the school.' The quarters were a bit on the small side, but they had a decent living room, an adequate kitchen, a plumbed-in bathroom, a good-sized bedroom and a boxroom for the baby. 'We've even got the electric, but is she satisfied? Oh, no. She wants something better, she says.' Liz wasn't a shrew, wasn't a moaner, but she knew her mind.

'Children need grass,' offered Danny.

'Well, we never had grass. The only green we ever saw was Queen's Park or the Jolly Brows. Didn't do us any harm.'

'Country's healthier,' replied Danny. 'Fresh air, loads of space. A nice garden, flowers, grow your own veg.' Danny's garden, unlike his house, was meticulously groomed. He grew potatoes, cabbages, lettuce and carrots. In a small greenhouse, he produced tomatoes and propagated seedlings for his many flower-beds.

With regard to the inside of the cottage, Danny's strongly held and often stated belief was that dust settled after a while. Women tended to go into the business of shifting dirt, attacking the stuff with dusters, brushes and mops. Which was all very well, but the dust simply moved round the planet before blowing back to seek out its various sources of origin. Short of blasting the lot into outer space, there was no avoiding muck, therefore it should simply be tolerated. If a person never dusted or polished, things sorted themselves out after a year or two.

'That life's not for me,' sighed Bernard. He couldn't imagine scraping about with rakes and hoes, cutting and rolling a lawn into two-tone stripes, pruning roses, manicuring privets and declaring war on leaf-mould or greenfly.

'Well, you can't stop here for ever,' ventured Danny. 'When Hitler gets beaten up, things'll change. Folk'll likely expect more from life – only young ones setting up'll want to be living above shops. Progress, you see. Our grandad sold fish down Churchgate off a barrow, then in the old fishmarket. This shop must have looked posh to him. Expectations change with every generation.'

Bernard grunted his disapproval. 'They should take what they can get and be satisfied.'

Danny clicked his tongue. 'Listen, our kid. These last few months, women have started to do men's work as well as their own. They'll not step back easy into flowered pinnies and slippers. I know they've always worked in cotton, but they'll be setting their sights on nice houses, carpets, better jobs and better grub. Whether you like it or not, there'll be change coming.'

Bernard left his brother and trudged upstairs, happily unaware that Danny's warning about change was to remain in his mind for some time to come.

Liz was polishing brasses, her small hands scrubbing furiously at the surface of some inanimate and blameless object. 'You can see your face in this plaque now,' she told him.

Bernard didn't want to see his face. It was all right as far as faces went, but it was a round, very ordinary face. 'Will you leave well alone, Liz?' he begged.

She sniffed the air. 'Shut that door tight,' she ordered. 'I'm not having visitors complaining about the smell of cod.'

They seldom had visitors, though Bernard chose not to remind his wife of that fact. Liz's aversion to the odour of fish had increased in proportion to her girth.

With a seven-month belly on her, she could scarcely tolerate the scents that floated up the stairway from time to time. 'Thank God it's winter,' she continued. During the summer months, the stench of fish permeated everything – even her washing out on the line.

Bernard sat down and rattled yesterday's four-paged *Bolton Evening News* into some semblance of order. There was no peace by his fireside these days. He would have to give in gracefully once the war was over, he supposed. It would be Harwood or Bromley Cross, compulsory fresh air and weeding. Liz wouldn't want to stop here, not with a young one to worry about. But there was petrol to consider. Where would he get the extra fuel to drive to the shop? Would petrol rationing be cured as soon as the war ended? If not, he'd have to come down from the moors on buses and trams, he supposed, and leave the van here. What time was the first bus? Early enough to meet the fish trains? And what about the flat over the shop? What about Danny and—?

'Bernard?'

He sighed, lost the thread of his thoughts, and turned a frail page. 'Yes, love?'

'My waters have just gone. All over the rug and all. I cleaned it nobbut half an hour since.'

He jumped up. 'But you're only seven months.'

'Try telling the baby that! Look, send Danny for Mrs Harris on View Street. She'll have to hurry up.'

Bernard ran out, but returned when his wife howled in pain. 'Liz?'

'Are you still here?' she yelled. 'Get gone, tell Danny I've a baby coming.'

'Push,' ordered Eva Harris. She was a small woman with a voice that didn't fit her. The ringing tones seemed too huge for her reed-like frame and thin, prematurely greying hair.

'You should have been a sergeant bloody major,' breathed Liz.

And you should have taken things easy, thought the midwife, although she kept this thought to herself. 'Don't just lie there like a pound of wet tripe, Liz.'

'I don't like tripe. And as for fish . . .' Pain swallowed the rest of her words.

'I'm not here to talk about menus,' chided Eva. 'In case you haven't noticed, there's a baby's head trying to come out of a very small opening in your nether regions. If you'd just shut up and start fettling, we might get somewhere.'

Liz fixed her adversary with as hard a look as she could manage in the circumstances. 'It hurts,' she said.

'It's supposed to hurt. If it didn't hurt, nobody'd know they were having a baby. They'd be giving birth on bloody trams, in the Co-op divi queue and all sorts.'

'God should have organized things a bit better,' moaned the patient.

'Tell Him next Sunday,' snapped Eva. 'See if He'll swap nature round to suit you. Save me a job and all if kiddies gets flown in by stork.' Eva wasn't happy. If Liz Walsh's export department didn't do its job soon, a doctor would have to intervene. Eva Harris, midwife and self-appointed medical advisor of folk from the Daubhill end of Bolton, didn't hold with doctors. They were too happy with their forceps and knives. Such tranklements, as Eva termed them, did far more harm than good.

At last, the head crowned. 'I suppose we should be

thankful for small mercies,' muttered Eva. 'At least yon babby seems to have a bit of sense. Now, push when I tell you.'

'I'll push when I bloody well can,' replied Liz.

Eva, keeper of more secrets than any priest, deserted her post and arrived next to Liz's pillow. 'Any more trouble from you and I'll send for the fire brigade.'

Liz managed a watery smile. 'Oh aye? My husband is the fire brigade and you chucked him out of here hours ago.'

'An answer for everything,' complained Eva as she reclaimed her true position in life. Liz Walsh was having a rough time of it, poor soul. She was one of those deceptive women – rounded on the outside, but with a small skeleton. This one wasn't really built for child-bearing, which was a shame, because the Walshes would make good parents.

The child seemed to be stuck. Panic fluttered stupidly in Eva's breast. There was nothing else for it – she would have to send Bernard Walsh for the doctor. The daft lump was just outside the bedroom door – Eva could all but hear him breathing. This was a seven-month pregnancy. Still, better the seventh than the eighth. Eva, like many of her generation, preferred prematures to arrive before lulling themselves into the long, lazy sleep usually enjoyed by the unborn just prior to full term.

As Eva prepared to throw in the towel, the child's head emerged. It was tiny, perfectly formed and with small tufts of brownish hair punctuating the baldness. Eva reached out, guided the shoulders and received yet another life into expert hands. But this was not another life. Liz Walsh's little daughter was not moving. Eva cleared air passages, slapped and cajoled, massaged the tiny chest, but to no avail.

Liz stared fearfully into Eva Harris's eyes. 'What's wrong?' she managed eventually.

'I'm sorry, love.'

'No,' screamed Liz. 'No, no, no!'

Bernard crashed his way into the bedroom. 'Liz?' he managed.

'Take the baby and put it near the living-room fire,' yelled the demented patient. 'Babies need warmth!'

Eva shook her head at Bernard.

'Do it!' ordered Liz. The chocolate-brown eyes were wide and fearful beneath a tangle of wet, dark hair. She pushed a lock from her forehead. 'Take no notice of Eva Harris,' she commanded. 'There's nowt wrong, nowt at all. Baby's resting after working hard, that's all there is to it.'

Bernard took the dead child in his arms.

'Go on,' yelled Liz. 'Plenty of blankets.'

When Bernard had removed the sad bundle, Liz turned her fury on Eva. 'What would you know? You're not a bloody doctor.'

For an hour or more, Liz Walsh ranted and raved about the various stupidities of humankind, then she settled down very suddenly and gazed in silence at the wall opposite her bed. Bernard came in a dozen times, spoke words of comfort, left without receiving a reply from his wife. Danny, who was easily as distraught as his brother, paid a short visit while the midwife brewed tea. But Liz sat perfectly still in her own little world. Her mind could not cope, so she had simply shut herself down.

In the kitchen, Eva took Bernard to one side. 'Listen, lad,' she whispered. 'If I were you, I'd not be in a hurry to put Liz through this again.'

Bernard swallowed a sob. 'You what?'

'She's narrow round the beam.' Liz might well need a Caesarean next time. In spite of mounting evidence, Eva refused to have any faith in the benefits of surgical intervention. Women's wombs were not meant to be hacked at; a man with a knife was all right as long as he stuck to carving pork or chicken. 'She'll get over it, Bernard. She'll be chattering away like her old self in a day or two.' The baby was downstairs in a shoe box. 'Give your Liz time,' said Eva.

The midwife bustled off, tears dampening her face as she closed the fish-shop door. They would have made a lovely mam and dad, Liz and Bernard Walsh.

Bernard entered his brother's little room. 'I think Liz is asleep,' he muttered wearily.

Danny placed a hand on the larger man's trembling shoulder. 'What do we do with . . . with her?' He pointed with the stem of his pipe.

Bernard lowered his head and stared dully at the box containing his daughter. 'No ceremony, Danny. Eva Harris'll come back and do what's necessary.' He gulped, dragging a shirt sleeve across his face. 'She never breathed, so she never existed. I'd best get back to Liz.'

'Like a perfect little doll,' whispered Danny, his eyes fixed to the makeshift coffin. The box had 'SIZE TEN' and 'MADE IN ENGLAND' printed on the end. 'God, I'm sorry. So bloody sorry.'

Bernard climbed the stairs and entered the bedroom. 'Liz?' She hadn't moved, was still propped up as still as a rock on the pillows, eyes closed, chest moving in time with slow, even breaths. 'Liz?'

She opened her eyes and moved her head a fraction of an inch. 'What?'

'Are you all right?' That, thought Bernard, was the daftest question of all time.

'Is the baby still asleep?' asked Liz.

He cleared his throat of emotion. 'She's dead, Liz. She was born dead.'

'Make her a bottle, will you? I've no milk yet, so use that National Dried in the kitchen cupboard. Keep her well wrapped up, too. It's very cold tonight.'

Bernard left the room again, closing the door softly in his wake. Danny was halfway up the stairs. 'She's gone crackers,' mumbled Bernard.

'It happens,' replied his brother.

'Not to my wife.' Bernard sank onto the top step. 'No, I can't let Liz go crazy.'

The night dragged on. Bernard and Danny sat in the first floor kitchen, ears straining towards the silent bedroom. Liz was asleep. Perhaps she would be all right in the morning? 'She won't,' whispered Bernard.

'Eh?'

'Liz. I don't think she'll come round in a hurry, not after this shock. She was putting all her energy into getting the nest ready. We've even bought a cot.'

'You must move,' replied Danny. 'Get away from Derby Street, let these rooms, go for fresh air and a fresh start.'

Bernard pondered. It was three o'clock in the morning. Neither man had bothered to report for duty at the fire post. Everybody knew about Liz's pregnancy, so Bernard's absence might be accepted. But Danny hadn't wanted to leave his brother alone with an unbalanced wife and a pretty little waxen doll in a shoe box. 'You should have reported in, Dan.'

'Sod it.' Danny stirred his umpteenth cup of tea. At this rate, there'd be no tea coupons left. 'Shut the shop tomorrow,' he suggested. 'I'll meet the train and see to the market.'

36

Bernard shrugged. If he shut the shop, there'd be customers kicking the door down. He couldn't even manage to worry about that, seemed unable to fret about anything except the state of Liz. He cocked his head to one side. 'Did you hear that?'

'What?'

'Like a tapping sound.'

Danny listened. 'It's not your Liz. That's from downstairs. I'll go. There must be a fire.' He left the room and crept downstairs, anxious not to wake the sleeping Liz.

Fingers rattled the letterbox.

'I'm coming,' he hissed in a stage whisper. He opened the shop door, his jaw dropping when he saw Eva Harris. 'Hello,' he began uncertainly.

She thrust a package into his arms. 'Take that,' she ordered abruptly. 'I'll go and get the . . . the wotsit. The box with the . . . I'll get the box.' She bustled off to pick up the dead baby.

The parcel moved, causing newspapers to rustle. What was this? A kitten, a puppy? Was it some hastily wrapped child substitute?

Eva returned with the shoe box. 'It's a girl,' she said, her head nodding in the direction of Danny's parcel. 'Same as the one poor Liz lost, God love and keep the little lass.' She nodded in the direction of Danny's wriggling parcel. 'Yon kiddy's full-term, but underweight, needs looking after. She could easy be a prem, so the two babies aren't that much different from one another. There's a bit of blanket round her, but newspaper's nice and warm. All the tramps wear it between their layers, especially in winter and—'

'A child?'

Eva nodded.

'But it's not . . . I mean, whose is she?'

37

'Never mind that. Just tell Liz that her baby warmed up near the fire. Tell her that's her own baby.' She stepped closer to the astounded man. 'Just do it, Danny. It's for the best all round, I'm telling you.'

Danny gulped. 'But the real mother?'

'Enough on that family's plate,' answered Eva. She paused. 'Have you told anybody about the stillbirth?'

He shook his head. 'I've not been out. Neither has our Bernard.' The second baby mewled in its cocoon of cotton and newsprint.

'Then say nowt, Danny Walsh. Liz'll rear that child without knowing the difference.' She paused. 'Look, your sister-in-law's in shock. I've seen it all afore. I bet she still thinks her own baby's warming up near the fire. Am I right or what?'

Danny gulped noisily. 'Aye, Liz seems to be a bit strange, but what if—?'

'And Bernard – well, he'll do owt to keep Liz happy. I'll have to go, because I'm needed. Tell them I'll call in first thing tomorrow. If Bernard doesn't want that sad little scrap, I'll find somebody who does.'

Danny stood and watched the midwife as she bustled off to her other business. He removed one hand from the living, breathing package and scratched his nose. This was a right bonny state of affairs and no mistake. The real little Miss Walsh had gone away in the clutches of Eva Harris. This imposter was supposed to be registered within a few days as the daughter of Bernard and Elizabeth Walsh. The whole thing seemed sinful, heathen.

'Danny?' Bernard was still sitting on the landing.

'I'm thinking. Stop where you are,' Danny ordered his brother.

'Bernard!' screamed Liz from the bedroom. 'Bernard? Where's my baby? I let you mind her for two minutes, that was all. Bring her here, I want to nurse her.'

Danny went into his cold little room and peeled back a few sheets of the *Bolton Evening News* Saturday Green Final. She was beautiful. His heart turned over when he realized that this was his first contact with a recently emerged living soul. As long as he lived, Daniel Walsh would not forget this precious, hurtful, joyous moment. Tears welled in his eyes. He thought about this little mite's overworked, poverty-stricken and possibly dead mother, about the rest of that unknown family.

Determinedly, the new Uncle Dan cleared his clogging throat. 'You've come to the right place, sweetheart,' he told the newborn. Her face was streaked with birth fluids. He imagined the sight of poor Eva Harris as she placed the child on one side in order to fight for the mother's life. Or had the mother deliberately given away an unwanted daughter? 'You'll be loved, I can promise that much. Aye, you'll have a cracking mam and dad, you will.' He set his mouth in a hard, straight line and forgot about being a Catholic. If this was a sin, then it was a good sin. Wasn't it?

When the child was wrapped just in the blanket, Danny carried her up to his sister-in-law's bedroom. 'Here she is,' he called with forced cheeriness.

Bernard's jaw sagged.

'She's on the small side,' added Danny.

Liz beamed. 'I told you she'd warm up, Bernard. Look at her. She's the image of my mother, God rest that good woman's heart and soul.'

The brothers' eyes met across the counterpart

that covered Liz Walsh. Bernard asked silent questions while Danny nodded his willingness to give answers when an opportunity presented itself.

Liz crooned and put the child to a breast. Bernard looked at the tiny head, noticed the absence of patchy brown hair. He dragged his brother out to the landing. Liz, too engrossed in her daughter, perceived nothing amiss.

'What the flipping heck—?'

Danny dragged Bernard into the kitchen.

'Where did you get her? It's not ours come to life, Dan. Ours had bits of hair. Ours was bigger—'

'Eva brought her.'

'You what?'

'It's probably a little orphan, likely from a big family. Eva took . . . she took the shoe box away. There's only thee, me and Eva knows about what happened here last night.'

'So this is . . . Whose baby is it? What if they want her back? I mean, folk don't go about giving kiddies away, do they? This is bloody lunatic behaviour, our kid.'

Danny raised a shoulder. 'Too late if they want her back now. Liz gave birth last night and she has a baby girl. Do you want to be the one who takes the child away? Eh? Is that what you really want to do to your wife?'

'But it's not right—'

'It's not right that your baby died, Bernie. It's not right that some little orphan child shouldn't be given a chance. This is a miracle. So shut up and get on with it. Look on it as fate or the will of God. Remember Moses in the bulrushes, Bernard.'

Bernard Walsh sat for a while in the kitchen while his brother grabbed some sleep. He was a father to a child who wasn't his child. Liz was mother to a dead child, mother to a live one. 'Yon baby needs us,' he said finally to the empty room. 'And God above knows we need her. So we'd best just get on with it.' This was too big for confession. This was a matter that could not be discussed with anyone, even a priest; not yet anyroad. Were commandments being broken? Was this theft, mendacity, greed? Bernard shook his head. 'And the greatest of these is charity,' he muttered aloud. Then, after a few seconds, he begged God's forgiveness for a sin that had simply happened.

There were few secrets among the stallholders on Bolton fishmarket, though customers were often kept in the dark. Gossip seemed to transmit itself by some osmotic process from stall to stall, so, under the dark curtain of a dim winter dawn, Danny Walsh told his big lie just once. Later, as the day lightened, he was forced to add a little embroidery, but the die was cast once the tidings had travelled from Ashburner Street right through to New Street.

Between these two thoroughfares the fishmen spent their days, hands deadened by ice, fingers almost too numb to behead, fillet and arrange their wares. This was their own pungent little world, their private domain. They thrived together and suffered together, shared sorrow and joy, understood each other at that special level which needs no explanation.

The day brightened slowly, as if begrudging the earthbound even the slightest glimmer of hope. Lorries, single-filed in the market's central aisle, coughed, spluttered, then followed their leader towards one of the huge doors. The rabbit and chicken vendors came and went, those with fish-and-chip shops collected cod and plaice. Then, in that short

41

lull between wholesale and retail, the shouting began. Chants of 'Elrig, elrig,' attacked Dan's ears. Jim Brocklehurst, who had run a book throughout Liz's pregnancy, paid out on the *elrig* list, and coppered up his winnings under *yob*.

Backspeak was the official language of Bolton's fish-traders. When a word could not be reversed perfectly, it was bastardized into as near a representation of backspeak as was possible. This clever method of communication meant that prices could be stated and adjusted without the customers' knowledge. A few Boltonians had struggled hard to understand the strange jargon, but most had given up after a few wearisome attempts.

To the rhythm of 'Elcun Nad Shlaw', the new Uncle Dan Walsh set out his stall. Bernard was open for business as usual on Derby Street, while Liz, tired from birthing and flushed with new motherhood, remained in the bedroom with another woman's daughter. The baby was to be christened Katherine Jane Walsh, thereby becoming the physical embodiment of human dishonesty.

'Danny?'

He lay down a thin, keen knife and blew into icy hands.

'A word,' commanded Eva Harris.

He followed the quick-footed woman into Ashburner Street.

Eva wasn't looking forward to what was about to happen. Bernard Walsh was her usual companion on such unsavoury expeditions, but Bernard was unavailable. She could have gone on her own, she supposed, but the presence of a man was always a good thing, a sort of lubricant that oiled the wheels of negotiation.

'Well?' asked Danny.

'Theresa Nolan had a daughter in the early hours,' she stated without preamble. 'I think just about the whole blinking world went into labour yesterday. Anyroad, there's business wants doing. I reckon your Bernard'll be tied up, what with one thing and another.'

'So am I,' answered Danny. He didn't fancy bearding any of the lions, not today, not after such a harrowing night.

'Peter Nuttall can man your corner.' It was a well-known fact that fish-traders went out of their way to stand in for one another whenever necessary, often selling an absent colleague's wares in preference to their own. The art of fair play had been truly mastered on Ashburner Street. 'This lot knows as how your Bernard's a dad, don't they?' continued Eva, a crooked thumb pointing towards the fish-sellers.

Dan nodded resignedly.

'Then get your stall sorted,' continued the midwife. 'I've jobs to get to, babies as wants visiting. You can say you're going on an errand for Liz and the kiddy.'

Danny thrust chilled hands into his pockets. 'Look, I wasn't a witness to . . .'

'To the rapes?' Eva was not one to bandy words. 'Nobody said you were a witness. I wasn't there, neither, but I made bloody sure I met the buggers after Theresa Nolan came to me. Oh aye, they got their membership cards stamped all right, once I got hold of them filthy rotten devils.' Her nose twitched, then the already thin lips set themselves into a narrow line of fury.

Danny shuffled about, wondering what the hell to

43

do next. 'Look, our Bernard went round to see all of them the day after . . . the day after he saw them attacking her—'

'Then I put me oar in once we knew the lass was pregnant. You don't have to draw me no pictures, lad. As for the fathers of them three hooligans, they'll not be surprised that your brother told you what he saw. Main thing is, we've to make sure Theresa and her baby's cared for proper.'

Danny was flummoxed. It was nothing to do with him. Their Bernard hadn't been the same since witnessing that terrible sight in the spring of 1939. 'Our Bernard's acted like a bloody lunatic ever after,' he said, almost to himself. 'First into a burning building, last out. As if he's trying to make up for not being able to help that night, forever going on about if only he'd arrived a few minutes earlier. Riddled with guilt, he is. And it wasn't down to him, because he did nowt at all to hurt that poor girl.'

Eva pulled up the collar of her coat. A bitter wind was promising snow, and she wanted to get out of the cold as soon as possible. 'If it hadn't been for me and your Bernard, Theresa Nolan would have starved. I'm not feared of any of them, even if they are rich. Such upstarts still wear underpants like the rest of us, you know. A jeweller, a tanner and a bloody furniture-seller? They're nowt a pound, Danny Walsh. And while the rapist sons are away fighting for King and flaming country, it's up to us to deal with them as fathered the three blasted musketeers. Theresa gets the best – that's the top and bottom of it. If you're too scared, I'll go and see the buggers on me own. Call it blackmail, call it what you like, they'll pay up and shut up, or my name's not Eva Harris. Only I'd be happier if you came as a witness, like.'

Danny returned to the market and made his arrangements. Eva Harris, all four feet and ten inches of her, was not an item to be trifled with. She and Bernard had already managed to frighten the living daylights and a lot of money out of three eminent business families. With dragging feet, Danny Walsh forced himself to play his brother's part. 'A damned understudy, that's what I am,' he mumbled to himself. 'And all I set out to do this morning was to sell a few pounds of cod and hake. I haven't even learnt me pigging lines.'

'Did you say summat?'

Danny eyed Eva. 'If I did, it wasn't fit for a lady's ears.'

Eva laughed. 'You should hear the so-called ladies in the throes of labour,' she told him. 'They come out with stuff fit to cook a prize-fighter's cauliflower ears, I can tell you.'

They sat in the van. 'Who died?' Danny asked as casually as possible.

'Eh?'

'The baby. The little girl you wrapped up like a bag of chips for our Bernard and his Liz. Who was her real mam?'

Eva shook a tiny fist at him. 'For goodness' sake, Danny. I called in at Derby Street early on, and Liz looked a picture of happiness. Does it matter? One human being needs another, and I only—'

'Acted like God.'

Eva sucked in her cheeks, exhaled slowly. 'Happen I did and happen somebody needed to. And happen I'll tell you in time. Well, I might let your Bernard know at some stage. Liz is best in the dark. What she doesn't know won't plague her, 'cos she's got a baby and the baby's got a mam. The rest we can leave to nature.'

Danny stared through the windscreen.

'I'm tired,' moaned Eva. 'Four births I saw to last night.'

'And one of them births came to nowt.' What had this woman done with that perfect little body? He mustn't think about that. 'So you pinched another kiddy and brought it to us. There's summat wrong with your way of thinking.'

'That's just your opinion, Danny Walsh. Now, get a flaming move on, will you? I'm that clemmed, me stomach thinks me throat's healed over.'

If only her voice-box would just heal over, the world would be a sight more peaceful. Danny started the engine. The van probably stank of fish, though Danny scarcely noticed. Liz and Bernard had done some of their courting in this very vehicle and, as far as Danny knew, Liz hadn't complained about the smell then. Women were very strange animals – especially this one here. A diminutive figure, she was probably capable of frightening the skin off a rice pudding and the devil off his horse.

'Will they be stopping on at Derby Street, or moving?' asked Eva as the van pulled away from the market.

Danny shrugged, turned the corner. 'I've no idea. Liz is for moving, he's for staying put.'

They travelled in silence for a few moments along Deansgate and in the direction of Maurice Chorlton's jewellery store. Danny, who had managed thus far to stay out of this particular piece of trouble, drove like a dying snail.

'Is there summat wrong with this here van of yours?'

'No.' Their Bernard had never recovered from the shock he received April '39. To this day, Danny's younger brother could not quite explain himself. 'I can't say I was frightened,' Bernard was wont to ruminate, 'but I was stuck. You know, as if both me feet had got glued to the cobbles.'

The van drew up outside the jeweller's. 'Anyroad,' continued Bernard inside Danny's head, 'they'd very near done with her when I came on the scene.' Danny Walsh swallowed audibly. 'They're all serving now, aren't they?' He referred, of course, to the cowardly brutes who had inflicted pain and indignity on Theresa Nolan.

Eva inclined her head. 'Lancashire Fusiliers. If they've had leave, they've kept well out of the road. I hope they get shot and all once they arrive over yonder.' She jerked her thumb towards where she imagined Europe to be. 'Castration'd be too bloody good for them. They want a few bits of lead between their ears.' Since last August, when poor Theresa Nolan had arrived penniless and pregnant at Eva's door, the midwife had hated four people: Theresa's father, a bigoted loudmouth, and the sons of three prestigious tradesfolk, who were lower than cockroaches in Eva's scheme of things. Never one to hide her light under a bushel, Eva had gone forth and created mayhem, making sure that Theresa received regular amounts of money from the relatives of her attackers.

'We'll not be welcome.' Danny rubbed a fish-oiled hand down a jacket that had seen better days.

Eva chuckled. 'Nay, lad. Maurice Chorlton knows which side his bread is salmon-pasted. He pretends to be a Methodist, which makes him the sort as doesn't want no scandal.'

47

Danny turned off the van's engine. 'You know, Eva, I blame Theresa Nolan's dad and all. She must have told him it was rape.'

'She did. Even her sister pleaded with him, and I've never had much time for Ruth Nolan-as-was. But no. Michael Nolan threw Theresa out without a rag to her back or a penny to her name. I wouldn't care but their Ruth's wedding was on the hasty side. She chased yon Irish feller till he got her pregnant, then it was up the aisle in a pale blue suit, butter wouldn't melt. Little Irene turned up six months later, and I can tell you now she was a full-term baby. Mark you, Danny, there's nowt worse nor a cocksure, two-faced Irish Catholic, and that's Michael Nolan to a T.' She patted her hair. 'Come on, let's be having you.'

It was plain from the display in the window that business was not exactly booming. There was a tray of five-quid wedding rings, a few strands of seed pearls and half a dozen watches. The shop's main area of trade was round the corner where a small, unmarked gate led into a paved, sloping cellar yard. Through a window in the rear of the shop, Maurice Chorlton paid out money and took in valuables. A miser to the core, Maurice was taking full advantage of the war.

'Front or back?' asked Danny.

Eva straightened her short spine. 'There's nowt second-hand about thee and me, lad. We use the gentlefolk's entrance.'

Maurice Chorlton was in grumbling mode. Like a small, plump rodent, he bustled about his shop, making his assistant's life an absolute misery. He had a bring-me, fetch-me, carry-me policy, which, together with his tendency towards displaying eternal displeasure, wore down his staff with monotonous frequency. Rumour had it that Chorlton changed shop assistants more often than he changed his shirts and socks.

As the talented designer and manufacturer of his own very exclusive jewellery, he was not pleased about Britain's eagerness to leap into war. Even though the war had only just begun, the rich could no longer afford good jewellery. Of course, there was some money around, the sort that stayed in banks or went into war bonds, but people were holding on to their cash.

Maurice pushed a strand of oily hair away from a temple. He had a widening, hairless track that ran from forehead to crown, and he compensated by growing the side hair long, then plastering it over the baldness with hair cream. He glanced at his helper in case she had noticed the movement – where hair was concerned, Maurice was extremely touchy.

Pauline Chadwick, who had noticed, kept her head down. For two pins, she would tell him where to stuff his job, but Mam wasn't getting any better. Pauline couldn't work in a factory, couldn't do shifts, so she served this miser for six hours each day, and the resulting pittance just about kept the wolf from Pauline's door. Maurice the Mole was a necessary evil for the time being.

'Get some work done,' he snapped.

Pauline smeared a blob of Mansion on a shelf, then attacked the length of wood with a yellow duster.

The jeweller stood near his front door and stared along Bradshawgate. For the present, he seemed to depend for his living on desperation and crime. In the cellar below the shop, ornate clocks were stashed in the company of Dresden figurines, ornamental screens, paintings and valuable gems set into a variety of precious metals. Some had been sold to him by decent people whose times were suddenly hard; other items . . . well, it didn't do to dwell too much. The point was that Maurice was paying money out and taking little in. Come the war's end, he might be rich, but no-one would want to buy much while hostilities were still ongoing. He was comfortable enough, he supposed. He could afford to sit on his assets and wait, just about, if hostilities didn't go on into the next decade.

He swivelled. 'Put some weight behind the cloth, woman.'

The woman, a childless widow with a fractious mother, rubbed a little harder. She hated the Mole with a passion too deep to be immediately accessible. In his perennial black suit, he looked just like a burrowing, troublesome animal – alert, greedy, fat, oily, fussy. She finished the shelf and ran a chamois across one of the glass-topped counters. If and when Mam died, Pauline would be out of here like sugar off a shiny shovel.

'I'm just going downstairs,' said Maurice the Mole.

'Yes, Mr Chorlton, no, Mr Chorlton, three bags full of horse manure, Mr Chorlton,' she grumbled quietly as he left the room. He would be tunnelling again, she supposed, wandering within his catacombs and counting his assets, those valuable objects acquired by him via other people's misery and deprivation. Well, he would get what was coming to him, Pauline mused inwardly. Anyone as self-engrossed as Mr Chorlton was bound to receive his comeuppance sooner or later.

Down in the vaults, Maurice thought about better days when he had worked from dawn to dusk with gold, silver, palladium, rhodium. His mouth almost watered when he thought about gold. He hadn't laid eyes or hands on a decent amount for ages. The war effort. Everything was blamed on this bloody war. The government hung on to its precious metals like a limpet sticking to the bottom of an old ship. The nearest Maurice had come of late to jewellery manufacture was when mending broken brooch fasteners or resetting loosened stones.

As he stood near the bench, his hands itched to pick up the tools, while his dark, bulging eyes ached to suffer once more the pleasurable pain caused by sharp bolts of colour emanating from a naturally formed, white, preferably octahedral diamond. Cut, polish, polish again. Set it in platinum or gold, lay it on a pad of blue velvet, display it in his window. Whatever folk thought about him, he didn't care. As a designer of jewellery, he had no equal outside London.

Depressed beyond measure, he sank into his work seat. Bench brush, grinders, polishers, jewellers' rouge and flex shafts lay like a row of idle soldiers mocking a general with no battle to fight. He picked up a ring clamp and a pin vice, wondered whether or when he would ever use them again. Twelve sets of pliers hung on a board alongside hammers and files. It was like looking at a graveyard, a place where humanity's brief visits to the planet were marked by rows of dead, useless markers.

Roy. He sat back and thought about the lad. Roy had done his best to stay out of the army, but his sight had been judged adequate for the mowing down of enemy gun-fodder. So he had gone to training camp. Mind, Roy wasn't much when it came to jewellery. Maurice's son was happiest when positioned behind a pint glass in the King's Head.

He took a gold hunter from his waistcoat, marked the time, glanced over his shoulder before turning the dial of a walk-in safe. Once inside, his spirits lifted. Glorious ornaments fought for space on high, cramped shelves. Flawless pearls, rubies, sapphires and diamonds nestled beneath thick plate glass, while linen-shrouded paintings stood guard around the walls. He dipped a hand into a box of sovereigns, let their silken surfaces pour through his fingers. 'To hell with the war effort,' he mumbled. 'This lot's mine, Mr Churchill.'

Pauline called down the stairwell. 'Mr Chorlton?'

He stepped out of the strongroom. 'Yes?'

'Customers, sir.'

There was no respect in the 'sir'. If she didn't buck up, Mrs Pauline Chadwick could get on her broomstick and bugger off into munitions. A customer? At worst, it could be someone looking for a new watch strap; at best, there just might be a club card to be updated. Many locals paid into the all-the-year-round club as a way of saving towards the bigger of life's punctuation marks: silver and golden anniversaries, a christening, a special birthday.

But the more useful type of client came to the back door. At the top of the cellar steps in the rear yard, a bell summoned Mr Chorlton himself. No mere assistant was ever allowed to respond. Maurice asked few questions whenever a grimy, beer-soaked tramp exchanged a silver tea-set for ale money. A person who made no enquiries got told few lies. With a world war on the go, who was going to worry about a few missing sugar bowls?

'Coming,' he answered eventually. He closed the thick metal door and spun its dial.

Halfway up the stairs, an odour floated down,

causing him to widen, then pinch his nostrils. Fish. He stopped in his tracks. Fish: Bernard Walsh. Bernard Walsh and Eva somebody-or-other, one of those self-appointed busybodies. April. January. About nine months between those particular markers of time. Fish. Bernard Walsh and Roy Chorlton. Rape.

Maurice entered the shop. 'Would you like to run your errands now?' he asked Pauline.

She froze for a second, then grabbed her coat from a hook, picked up her purse and scuttered out of the shop.

Maurice Chorlton shot a bolt home and pulled down the window blind. 'Well?'

Eva Harris placed a shopping basket on one of the glass counters. 'Theresa Nolan survived the birth,' she announced. 'Which was a miracle, what with her heart being poor.' She sniffed, looking the jeweller up and down. 'It was surprising when she recovered from what your lad and his friends did to her.'

Chorlton fiddled with his gold albert and fixed his gaze on Danny. He had not dealt with the man before, not with regard to this particular business. 'Walsh,' he stated flatly. 'Brother to the so-called witness, I suppose. I think I've seen you on the market – first stall on the left near Ashburner Street.'

Danny allowed a beat of time to pass. 'Our Bernard saw what he saw,' he whispered. 'No more and no less. He's not one for making up tales, Mr Chorlton.'

'And neither is Theresa,' snapped Eva. 'A more honest young woman I'd defy you to meet. And your Roy was the ringleader, all right.'

Maurice Chorlton gritted his teeth and waited. When the silence became unbearable, he spoke up. 'What do you want this time?'

'In case you're wondering, like,' said Eva, 'it's a little girl. Jessica, she's to be called. Theresa's mam was Jessica, God rest her soul. Anyroad, it's a right bonny little lass. So get your mates round the table and cough up a bit extra for the child's needs.'

The jeweller contained himself, just about. He, George Hardman and – sometimes – Alan Betteridge had been coughing up thirty bob a week for months, while their respective sons, the supposed rapists, were playing soldiers somewhere in Cheshire. And now, the blackmailers had arrived to ask for more. 'How much do you suggest?' he managed through a rigid jaw.

'Extra pound a week should do it,' replied Eva.

Maurice Chorlton paid lip-service to Methodism. He attended chapel each Sunday and, as a lay-preacher, delivered the odd sermon. He liked being holy and noticeable on Sundays. When Monday arrived, he slipped easily into his other role and received goods whose origins were sometimes uncertain. His flawed philosophy was simple: God came first on Sundays and business ruled for the rest of the week. Unfortunately, these two people were bringing God into the shop, trying to prick his conscience on a day when principles were determinedly dormant.

'Well?' Eva tapped an impatient foot.

The shopkeeper sighed inwardly. Roy Chorlton, motherless son and heir to Maurice, had kept bad company since leaving school. The minister at Maurice's chapel was of the opinion that the sudden death of Roy's female parent was the cause of the temporary delinquency, but Maurice knew better. The boy was a weak character, one who, when drunk, would follow his companions wherever they led. Not to put too fine a point on the issue, Roy was a failure.

Driven off track by his peers and by drink, Roy had raped a slut called Theresa Nolan. Who else but a slut walked the streets after dark? The terror of scandal drove Maurice to provide compensation for a chit of a girl who had been left bruised, bloodied and pregnant. 'Any one of them might be the father,' he said now.

'Exactly.' Eva nodded her head jerkily. 'So it's up to you to get money out of Betteridge and Hardman.'

The jeweller shook his head wearily. Getting cash out of Hardman was one thing, because the tanner had a reputation to consider. But Betteridge, comedian and purveyor of furniture, didn't manage to care too deeply about his son's escapades. 'I'll do what I can.' He pushed back another string of greasy hair that had loosened itself.

Eva smiled. 'See, we know you're an honourable man, Mr Chorlton. You're a decent, churchgoing soul.' She had no time for Methodists; a sober-sided, miserable lot of grey folk, they were. But at least this fellow went to some sort of church.

The jeweller was not taken in by Eva's unheralded flattery. The woman wanted extra money. She always wanted something for Theresa Nolan. 'There's been a fair few bob paid out up to now,' he grumbled.

'Children is expensive,' replied Eva quickly. 'And a scandal could shut your shop good and proper. His brother' – she jerked a thumb in Danny's direction – 'is a highly respected man, so if he tells the world what happened, he'll get listened to and believed. And he knows for himself about the cost of babies, because Bernard's wife gave birth within hours of Theresa Nolan. Remember, if Bernard opens his gob too wide, you, the tanner and that good-for-nothing chair-seller won't hold your heads up again. As for your sons . . .' She pulled a face, as if an acid taste had entered her mouth. 'Least said about them three, soonest mended,' she concluded.

Inwardly, Maurice Chorlton agreed with the midwife. His son Roy was what locals might call nowt a pound, while George Hardman's lad, too, was a waste of space. As for the furniture-seller's son – well, that boy wasn't worth the paper his birth certificate was written on. 'I don't know why it has to be down to me all the time,' said Maurice.

'Because you can be trusted.' Eva's tone was saccharine sweet.

Danny felt like a bit of a spare part in all this, as he had not been involved before. He watched Eva, the expert in negotiation, manipulating, hooking her fish, reeling it in. He guessed that Eva might have done very well with the Fleetwood fishermen, because she wasn't one for letting go.

Chorlton opened the door and ushered the unwelcome guests into the street. While Eva muttered a few final words of wisdom into the jeweller's ear, Danny leaned against the window.

'Have you finished?'

Danny turned his face to the right, saw Chorlton's assistant hovering near the wall. 'Just about,' he replied.

Pauline smiled nervously. She hadn't done any shopping, because the money had run out yesterday.

The fishmonger was at a loss for words. He wasn't one for small talk, especially when in the company of a young woman. 'Cold,' he managed finally.

'Aye.' She fastened the top button of her serviceable grey coat. 'More snow, I reckon,' she offered belatedly.

Danny noticed the pinched cheeks and that special pallor born of undernourishment. 'Call round at our stall some time,' he said with a degree of nonchalance. 'I'll find you a bit of fish for a good price.'

'Ta.'

He watched Eva as she finally let go of the jeweller's sleeve, thereby allowing him to return inside and attend to business. 'Don't forget,' Danny told Pauline.

'I won't. Me mam likes fish.' Pauline scuttled off to join her master.

Eva eyed Danny. In Eva's opinion, Danny was wasted. 'She lives at three hundred and one, Tonge Moor Road.'

'What? Who?'

'Pauline Chadwick. The woman you've just been talking to. Her husband died down the gasworks, got himself blew up. Her mother's all right as long as you show her who's boss, and they own the house outright. Pauline's dad had a good job on the railway, engine driver or some such fancy title. She's a nice woman, is Pauline. Make somebody a good wife, she will.'

Danny shook his head. Bolton was an enormous town, yet Eva Harris probably knew every flea on every dog's back. 'What's all that got to do with me?' he asked impatiently. The midwife was matchmaking again. It was something of a hobby, an activity reserved for leisure hours when no babies were being born and no bodies wanted laying out.

Eva smiled as sweetly as her premature wrinkles allowed. 'She needs somebody. You do and all, so—'

'Playing God again, Eva?'

They sat together in the van. 'You're blushing.' There was amusement in Eva's tone.

57

'I'm frozen stiff,' replied her companion, who seldom felt the cold. 'And mind your own business, Mrs Harris.'

Eva smiled all the way back to the fishmarket. Danny Walsh and Pauline Chadwick were going to make a lovely couple.

Maurice Chorlton returned to the table. He had ordered drinks, and was awaiting the arrival of George Hardman and Alan Betteridge. They were both late, of course. Hardman would be in the bath, scrubbing himself until his epidermis shone, as the tanning of cowhides was not the most aromatic of businesses. Even those who worked in offices at Hardman's Hides needed Lady Macbeth's perfumes of Arabia to cover the various stenches that hung and clung in the oily atmosphere of stripped animal fats. As for Betteridge . . . well, Betteridge was Betteridge, a clown, a loose cannon, a blot on mankind's vast landscape.

Maurice tugged at his collar, then drew the valuable gold hunter from his breast pocket. It was half past seven. He had a sermon to prepare, a small homily on the subject of pride, that deadliest of sins. Of course, some pride was necessary. There was the pride that arose from the joy of a job well done, the pride folk felt for their families . . . He paused. Roy was certainly nothing to write home about. Rape? The jeweller shivered, felt shame tainting his cheeks. His son had abused a woman, as had Teddy Betteridge and Ged Hardman, the offspring of the men for whom he waited now.

'All right?'

Maurice Chorlton glanced up. 'Hello, Alan.' He was not particularly happy to be seen with Alan

Betteridge. Betteridge was comfortably off, was reasonably dressed, but he was no gentleman. He had a reputation for acting the buffoon, especially when in his cups. Betteridge had been known to dance on the Town Hall steps, to climb drunkenly onto the back of one of the twin lions couchant that guarded Bolton's municipal centre. He was an ass, a thoroughgoing idiot.

'Cat got your tongue?'

Maurice pushed a pale imitation of brandy under Alan's nose. 'Drink that,' he said.

'Ta.' Alan poured the amber fluid into his mouth, choked slightly, then reached for George Hardman's drink. 'Happen the second'll mend the first,' he announced. 'Let George buy his own, he's wealthy enough.'

The Hen and Chickens was not busy, since most decent citizens would be at home with their families, probably messing about with black-outs and indoor shelters. Maurice coughed. 'The child's arrived,' he said softly.

'Eh?'

The jeweller leaned across the small, circular table. 'Theresa Nolan. She's had a girl.'

'Oh.' Alan Betteridge rooted about for a Woodbine, lit it, leaned back in his seat. 'What's that to do with the price of Magee's Ale?' he asked. 'I've done my paying. That stupid sod can do his own coughing up when he comes home a hero.'

Maurice Chorlton sighed heavily. The 'stupid sod' was Alan Betteridge's son, Teddy. Teddy was a loud-mouthed coward, the sort who ran with the hare and hunted with the hounds. 'We want Theresa Nolan to keep her mouth shut, Alan.'

The furniture salesman shrugged. 'I'm paying no

more. I've nowt to lose if they all open their gobs and scream blue murder. We weren't there, remember. It was your Roy, our Teddy and Ged Hardman that did the damage.'

Maurice nodded thoughtfully. 'Watch yourself, Alan,' he said quietly. 'Once the fighting's over, the Merchants will get back on a normal footing.'

'What?'

Excellent, thought Maurice. A raw nerve had been discovered, plucked at, irritated. 'You want to get on in business, don't you? You'll be waiting to hear your name going in the lists when a new Merchants' Club committee's chosen. Well, just mark my words, because I carry a lot of clout in that particular area, as does George Hardman. We keep our sons' nasty mess among ourselves. One foot wrong and that midwife'll make mud of all our names. You'll sell no more sofas if that happens.'

Alan Betteridge grinned. 'Me? On the committee?'

Maurice suppressed a shudder. Installing Alan Betteridge in a position of authority would be like training a chimpanzee to make the King's dinners. 'There are more influential bodies in the Merchants' Club than there are on Bolton Corporation, including the mayor and his merry band of aldermen. It's based on interdependence, you see.'

'It's what?'

Maurice smiled encouragingly. 'For example: say I've a family with a wedding pending – engagement ring, wedding bands and so forth. I might ask them where they were thinking of buying their furniture. I might send them to John Willie's or Boardman's.' He paused for effect. 'Or I might persuade them to step along to Betteridge's if they want quality and a good price. Merchants take care of one another.'

Alan Betteridge laughed aloud. 'Now you're talking.' He slapped a five-pound note onto the table. 'Stretch that as far as you can, then get back to me. Only I've got to go home,' he said.

Maurice Chorlton stared hard at the self-made idiot. Betteridge played the clown because he was stupid and because he wanted to be liked, valued as a 'card'. His wife had left him, his son was another damned fool, so Alan smiled, joked and laughed his way through life, using jollity to paper over the fissures.

'I've a chap coming round with some house-clearance bits,' continued Betteridge. 'If there's owt in your line, I'll see you get it.'

'Thank you.'

Alan Betteridge winked at his companion, blew a kiss at a fat barmaid, then left the pub.

Maurice closed his eyes for a few moments. There were times when life didn't seem worth living, and this was one of them. A bloody war on, everything running short, folk too timid to invest in the finer things. Betteridge expected to see little normal furniture for the duration. Once current stocks became depleted, a new breed was promised, articles thrown together with indecent haste and with Utility printed onto unvarnished rear panels. Bedroom suites were going to be made of cheap and nasty wood with thick layers of lacquer failing to conceal poor timbers. Meat was on ration, so cows and pigs stayed alive longer – where was Hardman going to get his hides? As for jewellery – well, that didn't bear thinking about.

'Hello, Maurice.'

Maurice smiled. After Alan Betteridge's hunched shoulders and not-quite-correct clothing, George

61

Hardman was a sight for sore eyes. One of the richest men around, George was slender, elegant, yet undoubtedly masculine. Grey from the age of twenty-five, the man had always looked clever and eminent. 'Betteridge has gone. I got you a whisky, but he drank it,' explained Maurice.

'Of course.' George repaired to the bar to buy drinks.

Fascinated, the jeweller watched as a group of newcomers stepped aside in the tanner's favour. George Hardman had everything. He had a fine house, servants, a healthy bank account. And he had a wife who behaved like a trollop. In spite of Lily Hardman's meanderings, Hardman continued to be admired, courted, listened to. No-one ever questioned George; if anyone considered him a cuckold, the opinion was not voiced, or not in public company, at least.

George planted a Scotch in front of his companion, then sat in the chair recently vacated by Betteridge. 'Is the child born?' he asked.

Maurice Chorlton nodded.

'I thought that might be the case.' The newcomer sniffed at the contents of his glass. 'Not a bad Scotch,' he announced. 'Did she have a boy or a girl?'

'A girl. And the blackmail continues.' Maurice stared into the tanner's pale green eyes. 'The fishmonger and the midwife, of course, demanding money with menaces. An extra pound a week.'

George twisted the glass in his hands. 'Mother and child must be cared for.' The voice was low and steady. 'Our sons were lucky to avoid imprisonment. They were also fortunate not to have received a dozen lashes from me. We do manufacture the odd horsewhip, Maurice.' He paused for a second. 'Betteridge? Will he pay?'

'Yes.'

'Then we continue as before, but with another pound.' With the air of a man competing with time and against a multiplicity of pressures, George Hardman left the Hen and Chickens.

Maurice Chorlton remained in his seat. Life was a mess. Ellen was long dead. She hadn't been much to look at, but Ellen Bradbury had known how to run a house, how to keep a gardener and a daily in order, how to present a meal, how to deal with company.

The jeweller glanced at a clock on the wall, then drained his glass. Roy, Teddy Betteridge and Ged Hardman were training to be soldiers. They would go to war, they would live or die, they would be heroes whatever happened to them. But Roy had let his father down. By becoming a rapist, Roy Chorlton had besmirched the family name.

As he made his way home to compose a lecture on the subject of pride, Maurice Chorlton gave no thought to Theresa Nolan and her bastard. Rape was ghastly, of course, but the woman had come out of it very well. With a quieter conscience and hooded headlights, the master jeweller began to recite his sermon. 'Pride cometh before a fall,' he said aloud. Yes, that was a good beginning.

TWO

Jessica Nolan was three days old before her mother managed to feed and dress her properly. Under the watchful eye of Eva Harris, Theresa Nolan struggled with nappy and pins, with hooks, eyes and the many loose ends that seemed to accompany the garb of a newborn human.

'That's better,' said Eva, lifting the baby from her exhausted mother's arms. 'It'll get easier.' The result of rape was a contented little soul, a quiet child who fed readily, brought up wind obediently and cried only when hungry.

Theresa sank back into a mound of pillows. Eva had enlisted the services of several miners who had been passing on the morning following the birth. At the risk of reporting late for their shift, these gentlemen had brought Theresa's bed into the kitchen. 'Will it really get easier?' she asked the midwife. 'I feel as if I've spent half my life in bed.'

Eva nodded, but made no reply. Theresa, a victim of infantile rheumatic fever, was not the healthiest of Eva's clients. The disease had left its fingerprints on Theresa's heart, had weakened her body and her soul. It was as if the girl had lost the will to live long before coming of age, Eva mused inwardly. That father of Theresa's hadn't been much use either, cursing mankind for the premature death of his wife, trying not to curse God for the same reason. And yet . . . and yet there was something different about Theresa today, a glimmer of hope, a tiny spark of not-quite-ripe energy.

'I mean, will I still have to work?' asked Theresa. People had to work during a war. Even the women – especially the women – were forced into factories to spin, to weave, to make bullets and bombs.

'You'll not be expected to do anything while this one's so young,' replied Eva. When the child became old enough for school, Theresa would probably be excused on medical grounds. 'You've done your bit.' Surviving the birth had been more than a bit. It had been closely related to the miraculous.

Theresa sighed. She didn't know how to thank Eva Harris. Months earlier, when Theresa had been forced by her father to leave home, Eva had come to the rescue, had sheltered Theresa, had eventually found this house for her. The midwife had also intervened on Theresa's behalf to extract money from those who had created so much pain and sorrow in Theresa's life. 'Do they know?' the mother asked quietly.

'Your dad and your Ruth?' The woman in the bed was almost transparent, so worn out was she, yet she seemed angry. Was angry the right word?

Theresa shook her head. 'No, not him and Ruth.'

Eva sat at the table with Jessica in her arms. Theresa's mother had been Jessica – it was a lovely name for a perfect child. 'Aye, I know who you mean, lass. I paid a visit on yon Chorlton feller in his fancy shop, told him to meet his mates and come up with a few bob for this baby.'

65

'And?' Theresa's heavy eyelids closed themselves. 'They'll pay. Oh, they'll pay all right.'

Theresa sighed. 'But it was their sons who hurt me, Eva. The fathers did me no harm.'

'Sons takes after their dads,' snapped the tiny midwife. 'That's a well-known fact. If you find a bad girl, look at her mam. A bad lad nearly always has a rotten father.'

Theresa had no axe to grind with the tanner, the jeweller or the furniture man. They hadn't raped her, hadn't left her bruised, pregnant and crying on Bernard Walsh's broad shoulder. 'I still think what we're doing is wrong, Eva.' Her eyes opened. 'We shouldn't be taking money from the parents. Especially Mr Hardman.' The owner of Hardman's Hides was a true gent, the sort of exception who proved, perhaps, the rule so loudly uttered by Eva. 'They don't always take after their dads,' she said. 'And it's the sons I want.' The voice remained low and even.

Eva saw the cold lights flashing, almost sparking from Theresa's eyes. Had the desire to live been born with Jessica? Theresa no longer seemed quite so vulnerable or powerless, was suddenly more alive. 'Getting yourself worked up won't do your heart any good.' The girl wasn't worked up at all. She was exhausted, but she was on a very even keel; too calm in fact.

'It's my own heart and my own temper. You know, I bet I'll stay alive for as long as necessary.'

'Eh?'

'Till I've got them. Till they've paid back – and I don't mean money. They owe me more than money. A lot more.'

Something in the new mother's face sent a shiver down Eva Harris's short spine. 'How do you mean?'

Theresa's mouth shaped a smile, though the expression did not reach those frigid eyes. 'That's for me to know and for you to wonder about. I had to take what they did to me lying down, because that was how they held me, pinned out like the skin of a stripped cow at Hardman's Hides. Anyroad, things have changed and I shall be back on my feet soon.'

Their names were indelibly printed at the forefront of Theresa's brain. Roy Chorlton, son of Maurice, Ged Hardman, son of George, Teddy Betteridge, son of Alan. These heirs to jewellery, tanning and furniture businesses were Theresa's molesters, her targets. The victim would soon become the perpetrator. 'The fox'll catch the hounds,' she muttered under her breath. 'If the fox's heart will just keep ticking long enough.'

'Theresa, what . . .?'

But Theresa had decided to be deaf. 'One by one, they attacked me. One by one, they'll suffer.' The new mother nodded thoughtfully. 'I'll have to see to Jessica first, get her started in life, make sure she's all right. Then I'll find her a nice family who'll look after her and give her all she needs—'

'Theresa! Stop talking like this, stop—'

'Everything she needs,' repeated Theresa. 'Once that's sorted out, I'll do what wants doing.' She blinked rapidly, as if clearing her mind. 'I've no intention of showing them the other cheek,' she told her companion. 'As far as I'm concerned, one bad turn deserves another.'

Eva looked down on the child's downy head. 'You'll give her away?' she managed finally, tears threatening to choke the words.

Theresa inclined her head. 'Yes.'

'But . . . couldn't I look after her? Just while

you're . . .' Just while Theresa Nolan committed three murders? Was manslaughter on this young woman's agenda? 'Just till you've done whatever you plan to do? See, if you give her to a family, you might not get her back.'

Theresa lifted a shoulder. 'I might not want her, Eva. Have you not thought? Has it not come into your mind that this baby's a constant reminder of what happened to me?'

'That's not the child's fault.'

'Did I say it was?'

'No, but—'

'No, but I could do without looking at her and remembering how she was made. I'll keep her till she goes to school, then . . .' She looked at the midwife's prematurely old face. 'Then I'll leave her with you.'

'Promise?'

'I promise.' Theresa noticed her companion's unhappy expression. 'You've been so good to me,' she murmured. 'I'll never forget what you've done.'

Eva sniffed back a mixture of emotions. 'She's a beautiful child. She's took after you for looks.'

'Good. I'd hate her to favour one of them three ugly buggers.'

'She's just a little scrap of innocence.'

'I'll try to remember that.' There was no sarcastic edge to these words. Theresa would try, because Jessica Nolan had not asked to be dragged into a cruel world.

Eva placed the child in the drawer that filled a new role as temporary cot. 'I'll have to be going,' she said.

'Up to the fish shop?'

'That's right.'

'And how is Mrs Walsh?'

Eva thought about the dead child, about the child she had 'found' to act as replacement. Had she done the right thing? Of course she had. Little Katherine Walsh would be doted on, treasured. 'Doing all right,' she replied eventually. 'Danny came with me to the jeweller's. Bernard's all wrapped up with his wife and baby, then there's the shop to run.'

'They've been kind to me, the Walshes,' mused Theresa. 'Good when it happened, cheap fish ever since.'

'They're great people. There is some gradely folk in this world, you know.' Eva gazed down at the contented child in the dresser drawer. 'Make sure you look after Jessica.'

'I will.'

'Because you'll have me to answer to if owt goes wrong with her.'

Theresa stared at her visitor. 'I like to think of myself as one of the good people,' she said softly. 'I'll do what's right by my baby. You don't need to go worrying over me or mine. And she is mine.' Sometimes, Eva Harris stepped over the mark by an inch or two – on this occasion, she had taken several paces too many. 'I'm grateful, Eva. To you and to the Walshes. Without you and them two brothers, I don't know what might have happened to me. But I've a lot of thinking to do, stuff I can't talk about. That doesn't mean that my daughter will go without.'

'I'm sorry.'

'Forget it.'

Eva left the kitchen and picked up her coat from the front room. As she layered herself against the weather, she shivered, but not from the cold. She trembled because the woman in the next room had changed. Pregnant, Theresa Nolan had been quiet,

69

almost biddable. She hadn't become noisy, hadn't started shouting the odds, yet here came a different Theresa, still weakened by many wounds, yet beginning to emerge all new after the shedding of her little burden. Life was a mystery, and no mistake.

The midwife opened the front door and looked out into Emblem Street. Steam rose above Kershaw's mill, a turbaned woman stoned her step, another nipped into the corner shop with an empty basket. A pungent smell emerged from a building just a few strides from Theresa Nolan's house. God forbid, but if a bomb ever dropped on Emblem Street, the whole community might well be destroyed. Munitions were manufactured round the clock, seven days a week, right in the middle of an area so built up that daylight was almost a luxury. 'Should be making bombs in the bloody countryside, not here,' she muttered. 'Flaming lot of them wants talking about, not a brain cell between them.'

Eva adjusted her scarf, waved at the woman with the scrubbing brush and donkey stone. 'Stupid sods,' she continued under her breath. Thus she dismissed the government, the Germans and Bolton Corporation before hastening towards her next patient. Eva was in the business of bringing new life into a world that courted disaster, and she nursed little respect for those stupid men who threatened humanity's safety. With her head bent against a bitter wind, the midwife walked towards Derby Street and a stolen child in a pretty, lace-trimmed crib.

Theresa squeezed the last drop of tepid tea from the pot. Thoughtfully, she chewed on fishpaste sandwiches prepared by Eva Harris, then poured water from a bottle to slake her thirst. Breast-feeding was a nuisance, because it required a degree of liquid fuel, but she did not want to lose her milk. The money remained untouched thus far, and mother's milk came free and involved no expeditions to shops.

Something was happening to Theresa, something she hadn't bargained for. She had fallen head over heels for the child in the drawer. Jessica. Despite her weariness, the mother's arms ached to hold her baby. 'I could do without this, you know,' she advised the sleeping infant. 'You weren't supposed to be a point of interest on the map, Jessica.' Pregnancy hadn't been about a particular person. Theresa had never imagined the end product, had not even chosen names. Pregnancy had been tiredness, swollen ankles, a big belly. This situation was one for which Theresa had deliberately neglected to prepare.

She swung her legs over the side of the bed and stood up with the aid of a chair. It was time to get a move on, time to start going down the yard again. Buckets were all very well, but the lavatory was preferable.

With shaky knees, Theresa dragged herself along, fingers trembling over the buttons of her coat, legs stiffened by several days in bed. She edged past the lidded pail that used to be her toilet, then looked back at little Jessica.

All that had mattered so far was the money: pounds, the odd fiver, some ten-bob notes and a pile of silver. She wasn't quite sure why she'd saved so assiduously, but she suspected that the motive might well be revenge. What was that saying about revenge? And where had she heard it? It was something to do with vengeance needing an extra coffin, because it often finished off the perpetrator as well as the target. Theresa shook off a sudden chill and tried to concentrate on the matter in hand.

But even as she staggered towards the door, Theresa's brain remained in gear. How was she going to drag herself away from her daughter? So far, Jessica was a warm, mewling infant whose needs centred on a full stomach and a clean, dry body, but she would develop a personality, would become interesting, would turn into a person. As Jessica grew, would the love keep pace?

It was freezing outside, and the cleared area of yard was slick with a thin layer of new ice. Snow piled against the walls looked grey and crusty, as if the miners who had shifted it had brought their trade onto Theresa's flags. She must not fall. Remaining upright was important for . . . for Jessica's sake.

White distemper was peeling off the walls in the lavatory shed. She wanted better, better for Jessica's sake. A nice house with an inside bathroom, a bit of grass at the back, even a tree or two. Privet hedges, a blue front door with a brass knocker, carpet in the living room, a red Axminster runner up the stairs with white paint at its edges. For Jessica's sake. But no, she had to stop thinking like this. There could be no house, no neatly trimmed privet hedges, because she would have to leave Jessica behind in a safe place until . . . until all the other business had been concluded.

Jessica's fathers' fathers all had nice houses, two up Chorley New Road, lap of luxury, red-brick boundary walls and wide pavements where no-one threw empty beer bottles or cigarette packets. Even Alan Betteridge had a decent enough home, though it wasn't as well placed as The Villa and Holden Lodge. The Betteridges had a great big place up

Deane Road, not as fancy as the others, but worth a few bob all the same.

The rapists all enjoyed three meals a day cooked in proper gas ovens and served at decent tables onto good plates. When they were at home, that was. They were all in the army now, all carrying guns and piking about on parade grounds in big boots and daft hats.

She let herself into the scullery, turned on the single brass tap and forced herself to let the scalding cold burn into her fingers. She had to be clean, had to keep the germs at bay with carbolic and a stiff brush. The pain didn't matter. Just now, the money didn't matter either, because the child was the pivot, the centre of Theresa Nolan's universe. The three men could wait, she supposed. Perhaps the Germans would get them. If the enemy didn't manage it, then Theresa would. When she was ready. In her own good time.

The King's Head was filled with chatter, smoke and the scent of Magee's Ale. The hostelry's landlord, a placid man with a large belly and very little hair, was doling out drinks and keeping a weather eye on three rowdy soldiers who sat at a table just inside the door. Had it not been for their uniforms, he would have asked them to leave an hour ago, but the country needed its heroes. 'She'll bleed us bloody dry.'

The trio of champions supped another pint of ale, arms raising in perfect unison, glasses returning simultaneously to the scarred top of a metal-legged table. 'I imagine she'll forget it in time,' replied Roy Chorlton, the lie sliding past slightly crooked teeth. She would never forget. In his heart of hearts, Roy knew that the girl's life was ruined for ever. Still, he shrugged off the guilt and straightened his tie.

'She'd better forget, all right,' belched Teddy Betteridge.

Roy Chorlton's father was the spokesperson, the one who dealt directly with the Walshes, so Roy took it upon himself to calm the lesser beings with whom he kept company. 'She'll have the baby to think about.' He smoothed a slick of short black hair, wiped the resulting deposit of oil on a sleeve of rough khaki. If Teddy Betteridge didn't shut up about Theresa Nolan, Roy might just crown him with his beer glass. 'Let's change the subject,' he suggested for the third time. Things had become very heated a few minutes earlier, and the landlord was watching. Also, something akin to conscience had begun to stir in Roy Chorlton's breast. Perhaps it was the war that had made him sensitive, the knowledge that he might easily be dead within weeks or months.

Teddy Betteridge shrugged. After three or four jars of ale, he scarcely knew what day it was. 'She'll forget it,' he agreed drunkenly. He always agreed with Roy Chorlton, because Roy was quality. The Chorltons had a jewellery shop on Deansgate and a detached mansion at the best end of Chorley New Road. 'I wonder where they'll send us?' The short sentence was punctuated by several more loud belches.

Roy gazed at his companions, wondering how the hell he had managed to fetch up in such glorious company. Ged-short-for-George Hardman had a face that resembled the surface of a full moon, round and deeply pitted by years spent picking at abundant acne. His father, the unabbreviated

George Hardman of Hardman's Hides, was a man of influence, a major employer in the township of Bolton. The son was a mess.

Teddy Betteridge, who sat opposite Roy, broke wind, guffawed and lit a Woodbine. 'Could be posted anywhere, I suppose.'

'It's nowhere yet,' snapped Roy. 'The fighting's hardly kicked off. This isn't embarkation leave.'

Teddy inhaled and blew out a couple of smoke rings. 'We should tell her to bugger off,' he declared drunkenly. 'She were asking for trouble wandering about in back alleys.'

Roy Chorlton bit back a quick retort. He didn't like to think about his crime, hated to be reminded, wished he had joined a different regiment. He didn't fancy digging himself in with these two, German bullets flying towards him, Teddy Betteridge going on about that bloody girl. According to a certain shrunken midwife, the victim had been returning from an errand of mercy when she had been pounced on and raped.

Ged Hardman leaned back against the wall. Life hadn't turned out as expected; it wasn't what he had imagined for himself. He should have been working with his dad at the tannery, should have had a car, a nice girl, a future, a decent skin. Hardman Senior had taken a tough line with his son, had belted Ged across the face after hearing about Theresa Nolan's ordeal. That had been a frightening day, because the suave, perfect gentleman who had fathered Ged was not given to displays of strong emotion. 'I'm fed up,' declared Ged now. 'Bloody war, bloody Nolan whore.' Mother believed in him; Mother swore that her son was incapable of rape.

Teddy Betteridge grinned lewdly. 'I doubt you're

the father of that kiddy, anyway,' he told Ged. 'You've not much lead in your pencil, lad.'

Sensing more trouble, Roy Chorlton left his companions and wandered into the gents'. He shut himself inside the single, evil-smelling cubicle and sighed deeply. Had he seen a picture of himself in that moment, shoulders slightly hunched, hair threatening to thin, eyes bulging slightly, he might have realized how similar he was to his father.

Betteridge. Like the Chorltons, Teddy Betteridge's family were tradespeople. Unlike the Chorltons, they were not particularly well thought of. Betteridge Fine Furnishings sold stuff that often fell to pieces after a year or two. Alan Betteridge, Teddy's father, didn't seem to care. With the threatened advent of Utility items, he might begin to sell something almost decent at last, though he would no doubt be admonished from time to time about overcharging. Yes, the Chorltons and the Betteridges were traders, but they shared no common ground beyond that simple fact.

Roy closed his eyes and tried not to breathe too deeply while keeping company with unsavoury odours. He had never drunk brandy after last April's fateful occurrence. But the beer had loosened his mind tonight and was allowing unpleasant thoughts to invade the forefront of his brain. It was his fault. He had been the instigator, the first rapist. The child was probably his, born out of lust, greed and several glasses of cognac.

Ged Hardman, the unlovely by-product of a handsome father and a beautiful, wayward mother, had simply taken his first chance, his first woman. With a skin like his, Ged got few opportunities where females were concerned. Inflamed by Roy's actions, the tanner's son had enjoyed a very brief moment of sexual gratification.

As for Betteridge, he was a pig. Like his uncouth father, Teddy Betteridge acted first, thought later – if at all. 'One more brain cell and he'd be a dandelion,' Roy muttered to himself. Betteridge was incapable of remorse. Betteridge was probably devoid of pity, forgiveness, charity or any other form of sensitivity.

He thumped a closed fist against the wall. Something had to be done. Roy Chorlton, son of a two-faced and money-grabbing jeweller, had discovered a sense of morality. It had arrived late, but it was here and it was screaming to be heeded. But why should he carry the weight of all this? The answer came swiftly. He had been pickled in brandy. He had raped a woman. And someone was banging on the door.

'Hast tekken root i' yon?' shouted a rough voice. 'I don't want th' urinal, I need a sitting-down job.'

Roy pulled the chain and emerged to face an old man with an apoplectic complexion. 'It's all yours,' he said.

'Aye, well tha'll get no lavvy in a trench, lad. It's a case of drop it where you must in battle.'

Roy stared at the closed door. The hidden man carried on, told his invisible companion about trench foot, the trots, fleas. For good measure, he threw in scabies and a bit of gangrene before settling down in the small cubicle.

Roy re-entered the bar, saw Betteridge and Hardman being removed by two policemen. Near the door, tables and chairs were overturned and sharing floor space with broken glass and spilled beer. Teddy Betteridge's loudly expressed opinions on the subject of Ged Hardman's sexual inadequacy had brought forth yet another fight.

'Friends of yours?' asked the publican.

Roy shook his head. 'Not really,' he replied. 'We just happen to be in the same regiment.' He had outgrown Betteridge and Hardman, he told himself firmly.

'Another drink?'

Roy shook his head. 'No, thanks,' he answered. 'I have an appointment.'

'You the jeweller's lad?'

'Yes.'

'Ah well. Good luck to you when you get thrown into the thick of it. I got a bellyful last time. Shot twice, I was.'

It had occurred only recently to Roy Chorlton that he might actually die. His father had wanted him to become an officer and a gentleman, but Roy hadn't been keen. 'This will be different from the Great War,' he replied now with a confidence that was not really felt. 'Should be over by next winter.'

Having heard it all before, the tenant of the King's Head got back behind his bar. Hitler would take some shifting and, even if he did give up the ghost, the nasty bastard would take a few British lads with him.

Outside, Roy Chorlton stood with his back to the pub, legs set wide, each foot itching to take off in its own direction. Chorley New Road or Emblem Street? Head in the sand, face up to responsibility, run away, run towards? There was nothing to lose. He could take a brisk walk, clear his head, go home later. But as he followed his right foot, Roy knew exactly where he was going. Like a magnet drawn to iron, he pursued his own undeniable destiny.

* * *

She cowered in the bed, coverlet clutched in taut fingers, the hand drawn up against her throat. 'Don't touch me,' she managed. Nobody locked a door in Emblem Street, not before bedtime. It was only a quarter to ten, and Eva Harris had promised to return. 'You've no right to come in here,' she added with a coolness that belied inner terror. For the baby, she must remain calm. She looked hard at the man, the beast she had feared, the nightmare whose features had occupied so many dark dreams. He was smaller than she remembered, less muscular. He was tense. He was afraid of her. 'Get out of my house,' she said, her voice steadier. 'This is my house, my home. You've no right to be here.'

'My dad owns most of the street,' came the swift reply. Roy Chorlton wished that he could bite back the words. He hadn't meant to sound aggressive or threatening. He hadn't even wanted to come here, but his feet had travelled up Emblem Street of their own accord, had forced the rest of him to follow. If only Father hadn't given Roy the address. But Maurice Chorlton made sure that his son felt every needle of pain, every pang of guilt. 'Sorry,' mumbled Roy. 'I didn't intend to . . .' The words died in his mouth. 'But my dad does own property round here.'

Theresa swallowed noisily. 'Oh, does he?' No wonder Eva Harris had hung on to the rent book, then. 'Well, the rent's paid, so it's my home.'

'Rent free. That's part of my punishment. He takes the rent out of my inheritance.' God, was there to be no forgiveness? One mistake, one drunken night, and the girl in the bed would probably hold that against her attackers for all time.

Theresa glanced down at the sleeping babe. She had not expected to see Roy Chorlton again, especially here in her own place. Bumping into him outside would have been bad enough, but here? Righteous anger collided with fright, the resulting tremor causing Theresa's frail heart to chatter drunkenly behind its cage of ribs. 'Get out,' she begged.

'I won't hurt you. I mean you no harm.'

'Then go. If you don't want to hurt me, just go.'

The baby was very tiny. She lay in her drawer, body wrapped in a pink blanket, mittened fist pressed against a cheek. 'A little girl, then.' He stepped nearer to the child. 'Why does she wear gloves?'

'To stop her scratching her face.' Theresa bit down on her lip, ordering herself to answer no more questions from the unwelcome guest. 'If you don't go, I'll scream,' she informed him. Eva would be here shortly. Barring emergencies, Eva always made her last visit between half past nine and ten.

Roy backed away, hands held up, palms facing her in a gesture of submission. 'I came simply to offer you marriage,' he told her, the skin of his face tightening beneath a blush. 'I was the one . . . the first . . . The baby is probably mine. I'm on a five-day pass, so we might just manage a special licence in the circumstances.'

Theresa felt the blood draining from her brain. She must not pass out. The fainting fits were never welcome, but now, while she and the child were so defenceless, Theresa Nolan was determined to remain alert. She gripped the quilt, inhaled deeply and stared at the intruder. 'What?' She could not believe her ears, didn't want to analyse such nonsense.

'To give the child a name, a father.'

'You?' The ensuing laugh was hollow.

'The world doesn't like illegitimates, especially in

80

these parts. She'll need a dad. I could change your life.'

Theresa's hackles rose, and all thoughts of fainting were banished. 'You've done that already,' she replied smartly. There was no need to be afraid. This man was pathetic, stupid, awkward.

'But I want to make it right,' he said. 'I'm offering a solution.' He swallowed, gulping noisily. 'If I get killed, a wife will inherit my money, the shop and . . .' His voice faded to nothing.

Theresa glowered at the man. Like his father, he was about five feet six inches in height. Like his father, he was oily, dark, almost creepy. She could imagine him serving at a counter in a few years' time, hands rubbing together, demeanour obsequious as he pandered to the buyers of gold and gems. 'You can't put anything right,' she said softly. 'You can't buy back time. You can't wind the clock the wrong way and stick back all the missing pages from last year's calendar. You're just a big bully. A bully and a coward.'

He held his ground, but allowed her to continue.

'There's no way of unraping me.' Shocked by her own words, she shook beneath the bed linen. 'Yes, you were the first, but Jessica's no child of yours. She's mine. You and the other two pigs aren't good enough to be in the same room or the same town as Jessica.' Theresa nodded, the movement quickened by a rising bubble of hysteria. Was the man mad? Was she, too, insane? With deliberation, she chose her words carefully, kept her voice steady. 'I hear you've all joined the army, so happen a few bullets will sort you out. Because I'm telling you now, Roy Chorlton, that if the Germans don't get you, I will.' She could not bite back the threat, was unable to retrieve words that seemed to hang in the air like the threads of blue smoke from a just-fired pistol. Theresa calmed herself and fixed her eyes on Roy Chorlton. He would not attack her or kill her, because he was absolutely terrified.

Riveted to the spot, he saw the icy chill in her grey-blue eyes, the furious set of her lovely mouth. She was beautiful, tiny, with strawberry-blonde hair and delicate, childlike hands. Hatred seemed to glow from every pore, stiffening her body and hardening those wide-set, unavoidable eyes.

'Did you hear me?' she asked.

A shiver began at the base of his spine, an unstoppable, ice-cool thrill that climbed stealthily, cruelly, touching each separate vertebra until his scalp seemed to crawl with guilt and fear. 'I heard.' In that moment, Roy Chorlton understood the true nature of terror. The woman in the bed was closer than the enemy; she was real, visible, alive.

'Do we understand one another?' Her tone was conversational now. 'I hope we do, Mr Chorlton.'

She was clever. She had prettiness and brain cells, a lethal combination. 'At least I offered,' he said lamely.

'Don't expect gratitude. I took bread and milk that night, carried food to a poor family. After meeting you, I got home with a great deal of pain, and blood on my clothes. You are the scum of the earth.' Suddenly, she didn't care. He was frightened of her, was standing like a rabbit in the glare of searchlights. 'And your dad's a joke. Your mam died on purpose, just to get away from him. Greasy, you are, both of you.'

'I can't undo it,' he said lamely. 'It was the brandy. My offer of marriage was genuine.'

'No-one will marry you.' This felt like a prediction, like something she foresaw in a crystal ball or in a pack of ugly tarot cards. 'Now, get out before I scream the place down.'

A draught swept into the house, followed by the sound of a slamming door. 'Brass monkey weather.' These three words heralded the entrance of Eva Harris.

The jeweller's son breathed deeply. When the small woman entered the kitchen, he took a step back and rested a hand on Theresa Nolan's time-scarred dresser.

'What do you want?' asked Eva.

'He wants to marry me,' replied Theresa. 'Full blessing, white frock, a bit of a ring bought cut price off his dad. Fancy that, Eva. A three-course dinner afterwards in the Commercial, free ale, even a drop of wine. I can't wait.' Relief flooded Theresa's chest. Eva was here. Everything could go back to normal now, because Eva was the very personification of normality.

He glanced at Theresa, realized yet again what a looker she was, a woman any man might be proud to call his own. He cleared his throat. 'I was just trying to . . . to make it right, to do the decent thing.' He wished with all his heart that he had not developed a conscience of late. It was the war's fault, he told himself determinedly. Well, the war and his father going on at him about endless blackmail, endless payments. Oh, he didn't know what he thought, couldn't work out why he was here.

Eva's chin had dropped, and she closed her gaping mouth with a loud snap of porcelain dentures.

As he looked at the girl in the bed, Roy realized that he could do no right in this house. Theresa

83

Nolan was beautiful and she was furious. 'I'll go,' he mumbled. Indignation brewed and simmered in his chest. She was a mill girl, an urchin; she should have been grateful for his proposal.

Eva retreated, allowing him to leave the room.

'And don't come back,' called Theresa just before the front door slammed.

Eva Harris sank into a chair. 'Well, I'll go to the foot of our stairs,' she said softly. 'What were all that about?'

'You tell me,' answered Theresa. 'And I'll give you a medal.'

Danny Walsh's breath preceded him by several inches, iced air hovering like a single plume of cloud in the dark frost of a February morning. At six o'clock, stallholders and shopkeepers stood around the railway sidings, some battering arms across chests to keep the blood moving, others hunched over the meagre glow of a hand-rolled cigarette. The Fleetwood train was late, was probably floating about on ice-scalded tracks somewhere between the coast and Bolton.

'All right, then, Danny?' Bob Hewitt stamped across the goods yard, a balaclava drawn low over his eyes, high beneath the end of a frozen nose.

'That you, Bob?'

'Aye, who did you think it were? Jack the Kipper?'

Danny shrugged. It could have been the abominable snowman, because the only recognizable parts of Bob Hewitt were his voice and a pair of hairy nostrils. 'Train's late,' commented Danny unnecessarily.

'How's yon babby of your Bernard's?'

'Fine. Coming on a treat, she is.' The cuckoo in the nest was beginning to thrive.

'We'll need no ice today for keeping fish,' grumbled Bob. 'Blood's fair froze in me veins – I can hear it cracking every time I shift. Any colder, they can shove a stick up me nethers and sell me as an ice lolly.'

'Not sweet enough,' chuckled Danny.

A rumble heralded the advent of a fire-breathing monster with its cargo of fish and ice. The sidings came to life, LMS fish porters leaping forward to jump aboard as soon as the train ground to a screeching, slippery halt.

Danny and Bob Hewitt, whose fish stall was a few feet from the Walshes', claimed their prizes, heavy wooden crates bound by metal bands, each container weighing at least ten stones. 'Jesus,' cursed Bob through the wool of his balaclava, 'I don't remember putting me name down as a pack mule.' He rubbed his back with a gloved hand. 'I thought I were that cold as I'd feel nowt, but me back's fair shattered.'

Carriers struggled past the two men towards a convoy of vehicles, everyone moaning and puffing against the weight of their burdens. Lorries piled high with boxes shuddered to life in preparation for delivery rounds covering shops all over Bolton and its surrounding villages.

Danny and Bob sat in the van. Bob, a well-known character, continued to live up to his reputation. 'I feel like retiring,' he grumbled. 'Too hot in summer, fish going off, ice melting. And winter's like a bloody life sentence. I fancy a nice little village pub, good ale, cheese butties, meat pies, no fish.'

Danny shifted into first gear and drove slowly out of the sidings. Bob Hewitt and fish were like salt and vinegar – doomed to a lifetime partnership. 'Listen,' he said. 'You and Ernest Openshaw won't get buried.

You'll end up pickled like a pair of giant mussels. We'll keep one jar at the Ashburner end and the other in the New Street doorway.'

'I'd rather get cremated,' laughed Bob. 'Or buried in a nice plot up Heaton, couple of rose bushes, a gradely marble headstone.'

'With a cod's head carved in it,' concluded Danny. He couldn't imagine Bolton fishmarket without an Openshaw, a Hewitt or a Walsh. Year in and year out, the same families collected, delivered, filleted and sold tons of fish. Kids left school, joined their fathers' firms, became absorbed into the daily routine in the twinkling of an eye, or so it seemed.

'I see you've had an elrig hanging round your stall.' Bob Hewitt's tone was deliberately casual, while his eyes seemed to be concentrating deeply on the architectural merits of Bolton's deserted heart.

'She's not a girl, she's a woman,' replied Danny.

'How old?'

'Thirty.' Danny turned a corner rather quickly, causing Bob to rattle slightly in his seat.

'All right, a namow,' answered Bob once his equilibrium returned. 'Not bad looking if you like 'em thin. I hear as how meat's sweeter near the bone. What's her name?'

'Pauline Chadwick. Works for Maurice Chorlton. And don't start asking stupid questions and jumping to daft conclusions, because there's nowt going on.'

'I never said there were.'

'Right.' Danny steered the van through a slight skid and towards their destination. 'We'll have to keep an eye on the lads today,' he advised his passenger. Danny was referring to the younger members of fish dynasties, boys who served their time by unpacking and preparing cod and hake for elders and betters. 'One twist of a gutting knife, they could lose a finger and feel nowt.'

Bob sighed heavily, then rubbed the resulting steam from the windscreen with a gloved hand. 'Change the subject if you must,' he invited pointedly. 'Who cares about you and your new lady friend, anyway?'

Danny ignored him and thought about the long day ahead. There was just one hot water tap in Ashburner Street Market, a single outlet at which young men queued with buckets to obtain a mere gallon of insurance against frostbite. In weather such as this, the buckets' contents would cool within minutes. It was a hard life, yet Danny had known no other. 'We should have more hot water,' he commented gruffly. If he talked about water, Pauline Chadwick might just escape without further discussion.

They pulled into the market's huge doorway, waited until Bolton Refrigeration and Palatine Dairies had unloaded blocks of ice whose usefulness was questionable on this occasion.

Bob Hewitt beat his hands together. 'You know, Dan, there's been more women had their eyes on you than I've had cod-and-chip dinners.'

Danny tapped the steering wheel.

'Have you never noticed?'

'What?'

'The road they look at you.'

'Can't say I have.'

Bob chuckled. 'Have you got your name down for a dog and a white stick?'

'No.'

Bob shook his head. 'As old as you are and you still

don't notice the come-on even when it bites you on the nose.'

Danny turned his head and looked at Bob Hewitt. 'You worry about your dripping nose and I'll see to my own.'

The passenger sniffed. 'She likes you. She flutters when she sees you.'

Pauline Chadwick was not a flutterer. Pauline Chadwick was a nice young woman who worked for a Scrooge and looked after a virago called Edna Greenhalgh. In spite of the cold weather, Danny tugged at his collar as if seeking cool air. Tonight, he was going to walk into the spider's web; tonight, he would be sitting down at a table on Tonge Moor Road with a decent woman and an unknown quantity whose reputation preceded her like the stench of rotted mullet.

'Danny?'

'What?'

'Are you blushing?'

'Shut up, Bob.'

Bob shut up.

Number 301, Tonge Moor Road was a mid-terrace with a tiny front garden, an iron gate and a square-panelled door from which the number three hung drunkenly next to its two companions. A cut above the warrens of Daubhill and Deane, Tonge Moor houses had decent red-brick frontages, reasonable curtains and bits of leaded patterns on windows. As well as these privately owned homes, the road boasted a library, a cluster of presentable council dwellings and a corner Co-op next to some smaller shops.

Danny stopped at the gate. Behind the door, a

promise of poached egg and haddock beckoned, but his mouth was not watering. 'She doesn't take to people easy,' Pauline had informed him. Why was he here? Why hadn't he made an excuse?

He bit his lower lip. Taking Pauline to the Man and Scythe for a shandy had seemed innocent enough. In fact, she had instigated that first expedition, had asked him bold as brass while he was busy wrapping two steaks of silver hake. Was he being introduced as a prospective replacement for the dead husband? Danny swallowed and felt the Adam's apple rasping against his inner throat. Marriage. Now, that was a big step. Women wanted things. They wanted talking to, wanted fussing, bunches of flowers, ironing boards, new blouses for Christmas and bonnets for Easter.

Daniel Walsh sidled off towards the corner and sheltered in the doorway of Lever's Grocery. If Pauline came through to her front room, she would doubtless see his van, but he needed to think. He should have thought before setting out, should have thrown their Bernard out of the little room behind the fish shop to give himself a chance to consider his position. Bernard had laughed his socks off, of course. 'Bring her home, our kid. Let's be having a look at her before you take the plunge.'

'Excuse me, I want to get in.'

Danny flinched. 'Sorry, I thought the shop was shut,' he said to a little woman in curlers and a dark coat.

'Black-out,' she snapped. 'Lever's never shuts.'

The shop bell clattered. Danny, feeling totally foolish, clutched at a couple of cod in his overcoat pocket. He would have to go into the shop, because he couldn't stand here like cheese at fourpence.

Spuds. Aye, he'd buy a couple of chipping potatoes to go with the cod. That should give him an extra few minutes . . .

'He's no right coming here in a van. Vans is for business purposes.' Edna Greenhalgh sucked her few remaining teeth and cast an eye over her willowy daughter. 'His journey is not really necessary. He could get arrested if somebody clocked him using petrol for courting. There is a war on, in case he hasn't noticed.'

Pauline raised her face to the ceiling. Mam was a pain – not just in the neck, either. At sixty-four, Edna carried on like an eighty-year-old, always ill, often complaining, usually as petulant as some unfortunate soul locked inside a second infancy. But Mam was not as frail as she liked to make out. She was cunning, manipulative and extremely clever. 'He's not coming courting, Mam,' replied Pauline with exaggerated patience. 'He's been good to us, and you know it.' She liked Danny. He wasn't all over her like a rash, didn't take liberties. He had kind eyes behind the thick lenses, a lovely smile and—

'And once he's got his feet under yon table, we shan't ever see the back of him.'

'We're eating his fish,' said Pauline, forbearance still etched deep into the words.

'You paid for it. And what about the eggs you're cooking? And you've nobbut known him a couple of weeks. Why the heck are you fetching a man to see me when you've met him just days since?'

Pauline didn't know why. Yes, she did. She had invited Danny Walsh because he was ordinary and nice. He knew all about people, was an expert when it came to truculent old women, because he dealt with them day in and day out. With Danny, she wouldn't need to be ashamed of Mam, wouldn't have to make excuses.

She smiled to herself as she set the places. He had told her a story or two in the Man and Scythe, had related some of the market's ongoings. 'Her elastic went just as she left the stall, so we all stood round her in a close circle with our backs towards her. Once the safety pin was in, she pushed her way through and demanded a penny change because Bob Hewitt had just reduced his prices. Folk. There's nowt as queer, is there?'

'What are you smiling at?' asked Edna Greenhalgh.

'Nothing, Mam. And you'd better be nice.'

'Or what? The workhouse?'

Pauline placed a spoon on the multi-coloured tablecloth. 'Worse than that. I'll send you to live with Cousin Betty.' Cousin Betty was the only woman in Christendom who could manage to be as abusive as her Aunt Edna.

The doorknocker fell, was lifted, fell again. 'He's here,' sighed Edna. 'I suppose you'll please yourself as always.'

Pauline, who could not remember pleasing herself ever, left the room, walked down a narrow lobby and opened the door. 'She's all fired up,' she whispered.

Danny winked. 'Leave her to me,' he mouthed with false confidence.

Edna was all frowns and folded arms when the couple entered the living room. She cast beady eyes over the newcomer, judged him to be as thin as a rake and not particularly handsome, especially with those bottle-bottom glasses. Once introduced, she gave a terse nod and offered no hand to the man.

He removed his coat, sat opposite the old lady and warmed himself at the bungalow range fire. It was a nice enough house: big dresser, fancy mirror with a painting round its edges, a few ornaments, a photograph of Pauline and her husband on their wedding day.

'Are you owt to do with gas?' snapped Edna. She knew the answer, but she wanted her oar in right from the start.

'I've still no electricity up in my cottage,' he replied.

'Cottage?'

'Bromley Cross. Nice big garden, grow a lot of my own veg.'

Edna sniffed. 'I thought you lived up Daubhill?'

'We've a shop. My brother lives there, then I stop a few nights for auxiliary fire duties.'

Pauline spoke up from the scullery-cum-kitchen. 'He's been in the paper, Mam. Saved some lives, he has.'

'And my brother. Bernard's a fireman, too.'

Edna sniffed again. 'Her husband got blew up with gas. He was a foreman at the gasworks, very well thought of. As long as you're not going to get yourself blew up—'

Pauline put her head round the door. 'Mam? Will you behave yourself? I warned Danny. I told him you'd think we were courting. Well, we're not, so shut up. He's nothing to do with the gasworks.'

Danny smiled at the face in the doorway. When Pauline's retreat had been accomplished, he stood up, walked over to the sofa under the stairs where he had laid his greatcoat, and took out of the pocket the parcel of fish and the potatoes acquired at Lever's. 'For your dinners tomorrow,' he advised the old lady. 'Good chippers, them spuds.'

'I don't like chips.'

'They'll mash.' He returned to his seat after placing his offerings on the dresser. Completely unimpressed by Edna's animosity, he spoke about the weather, fish trains, a sudden shortage of cod and a trainee who had finished up at the infirmary. 'You tell them a dozen times a day to watch out for sharp knives, then this daft lad goes and skids along New Street, breaks his leg and finishes up in plaster. He'll be doing no filleting this side of Easter.'

In spite of her better judgement, Edna found herself almost smiling. Her mind raced ahead towards the future, forcing her to face her biggest fear, the prospect of Pauline entering a second marriage. John Chadwick had been a decent, quiet bloke, had lived here with Pauline, had never complained about sharing his home with Edna. How many John Chadwicks were there?

'His mam went with him to the hospital and he got no sympathy. She clocked him across his head with her handbag when she found out about his leg being fractured. He was lucky to finish up without concussion as well.'

Edna nodded. 'He'll be all right. It's folk my age as has to watch for broken bones.'

'You're not old,' answered Danny. She was lazy. He could tell from the way she was sitting that she'd scarcely shifted a muscle all day. 'You carry on moving about,' he advised. 'It's them that sit still who suffer. I can see you're very fit, Mrs Greenhalgh.' A muffled giggle from the kitchen was swiftly altered to simulate a cough.

'So you own a business, then,' said Edna.

'With our Bernard, yes.'

'Doing all right?'

'So-so,' he answered. 'With the war, we don't get as much fish from Iceland as we did, but there's plenty to sell.'

'Short-sighted?' she asked.

'We both are. Our Bernard's specs are thicker than mine.'

Edna was satisfied. He wouldn't be traipsing off to war, what with providing food and being myopic. He wouldn't get blown to shreds in a gasworks. 'You can come again,' she announced with the air of one giving an order. 'And ta for the fish.'

In the kitchen, an item of pottery hit the flagged floor and smashed. Edna scarcely noticed. She was busy doing a mental tot-up of her wardrobe. The navy suit would do. And Pauline could get wed in that little green two-piece.

Roy Chorlton's visit set Theresa back, made her linger in bed rather longer than expected. Jessica was doing well. After four weeks, she was robust and extremely contented. Eva Harris, who was fully aware of Theresa Nolan's medical history, continued to visit on a daily basis. The front door of number 34 was always locked, because Theresa could not bring herself to believe that Roy Chorlton was safely back at his camp. She was edgy and very thoughtful, turning over in her mind the man's words. He had offered marriage, had been willing to accept his responsibilities and shoulder the guilt caused by his terrible crime.

Why could she not forgive? Of course, she could never marry him, could not bear the concept of

94

living with the man who had stolen her virginity so viciously. She had been a mere toy, a recreation for three drunks who had wandered into the warrens between Daubhill and Deane. But why must she hate so strongly?

Theresa stirred the fire, let down the bars and planted the kettle in their centre. Her heart, always weak, had taken a battering with Jessica's delivery, but its irregularities were slowly correcting themselves. No black-outs for a week now, few palpitations and only one really bad headache.

Someone tapped at the door. She hastened down the narrow lobby and put her ear against a panel. 'Who is it?'

'Me. Let me in before I bloody well freeze.'

Theresa was the one who froze. Their Ruth? Ruth had been ordered to stay away from Theresa's house of sin. The last time the two sisters had met on Derby Street, Ruth had scuttered off towards the post office like a scalded cat. 'Does he know you're here?' The 'he' was Michael Nolan, father to Ruth, Theresa and several others.

'No.'

Theresa turned the key and opened the door.

Ruth, a pale-skinned, dark-haired woman, pushed her way into the house. 'He's dying,' she said without preamble.

'Dying?' Again?

'Pneumonia.'

Theresa didn't know what to feel, what to say. Her dad was a tyrant, but he was still her dad.

'Doctor thought he'd pulled him through, but there's been a relapse.' The visitor paused. 'Everybody's there, even our Frances.'

Theresa led her sister through to the kitchen.

With the bed against one wall and Jessica's drawer next to the table, the room was smaller than ever. But no room on earth could be large enough to contain Ruth's terrible and inexplicable anger. 'Sit down,' Theresa said.

Ruth cast a cursory glance over the baby before settling near the fire. 'Our Phil sent me, said as how you might want to be there before Dad goes.'

Theresa sat in the opposite chair. She couldn't go. She couldn't walk about in all that ice, dare not expose herself to the wintry winds. 'Who'll mind Jessica?'

Ruth raised a thin shoulder. 'I'll stop till you get back.'

Theresa suppressed a shudder. She would not leave a dog with Ruth, would certainly not place Jessica in the dubious care of this sister. Ruth's daughter, Irene, was turning out to be very strange. She was strange because Ruth was strange. Right from the start, Ruth had disliked Irene. Irene was ugly, and Ruth stated her opinion about the child's appearance whenever she had an audience. For almost eight years, Theresa had shared a home with Ruth and Irene, had watched the child's face growing old and far too wise, too resigned. Irene had never winced, had never reacted at all to her mother's words. 'Eeh, Dad, isn't she ugly . . . ?'

'Well?'

Theresa braced herself. 'I've to stop in,' she said. 'Dr Clarke says I've not to go out till the weather gets better. Eva does my shopping.'

Ruth bridled. 'He's your dad.'

'Yes. And he threw me out. He wouldn't even listen, wouldn't believe that I'd been raped.'

The visitor lit a cigarette. As long as she had her

smokes, she was almost bearable. Almost. On tobac-
coless days, Irene suffered immeasurably. 'Bonny
baby, anyroad.' Ruth nodded in the direction of
Jessica's makeshift cot. 'At least she didn't come
out looking like that one of mine.'

Theresa sighed. 'Irene will turn on you one day,
Ruth.' Irene would probably turn against the world
in general.

'Oh aye? Her and whose army? Bad little bugger,
she is. Sly. Always up to no good, always missing
school and pinching stuff.'

Theresa nodded. 'Being bad gets her some attention. She'd sooner be thumped than ignored.'

'Then she'll have to be thumped, because I've had
enough, I've lost interest.'

There had never been any interest to lose.
Theresa watched her sister covertly. Ruth had
dark, curly hair which she wore at shoulder length.
When her hands were not engaged in smoking, the
long, slender fingers were used to twist the healthy
mop into ringlets. Her brown eyes were not quite
true, one wandering off towards the nose unless
her spectacles were in place. She hated everybody
and everything; she was always right, always top
dog, first in a queue, last to offer help. Ruth
commanded attention at all times, no matter what
the cost. She resented her own child, because
Irene might have stolen a little limelight had Ruth
not doused it.

'Well?' Ruth's dark eyebrows were raised above
the glasses' upper rims.

'No,' said Theresa quietly.

'So, I've come all this road for nowt.'

'I suppose so.'

Ruth, in judgemental mode, stood up and towered

over her seated sister. 'Nowt good'll ever happen to you in this world,' she said.

'Yes, I can believe that,' replied Theresa. 'Up to now, I've had a lousy dad, then I've had to watch you torturing that daughter of yours. The way I got Jessica was no piece of cake, either. So if knowing I'm miserable makes you happy, go and have a party.'

Ruth glowered. 'Listen here, you. Five or ten years from now, you might need me—'

'Nobody will ever need you, Ruth.'

'Just you wait, lady. You'll get what's coming, believe me.'

Theresa folded her arms. 'Get out, Ruth. You make me sick and tired. Go and pull wings off flies.'

'There is none. It's winter.'

'Soon be spring,' answered Theresa smartly. 'Shut the door on your way out.'

THREE

All the bad things lived in the coal hole under the stairs. There were giant rats, ugly-featured goblins, huge monsters with fiery breath and purple eyes. In the darkest part, where the staircase met the kitchen floor, the devil himself had his own special playground. The devil was as small as he wanted to be, as large as he needed to be. In the night, he crept out and ate all the bits of mouldy cheese in Mam's mousetraps. He mingled with cockroaches at the midnight hour, disappeared with the silverfish as soon as dawn arrived, shrinking back and back, down and down until he managed to fit himself into that small, secret place in the narrowest, squashiest part beneath the stairs.

Jessica Nolan had not seen the devil, had glimpsed none of his more exotic playmates, but her knowledge of their existence was rooted deeply within her four-and-three-quarter-year-old brain. The cockroaches were just the visible signs of Satan's malicious presence in her home. Sometimes, when she rose early, she heard the swish of the Dark Master's cloak as he glided cleverly past the meagre store of coal and wood. As long as she failed actually to see him, she was safe. Soon, Jessica would be five. After her fifth birthday, she would be old enough and brave enough to fetch the wood and coal. The devil would not tackle a great big five-year-old.

She sat in the kitchen where gas mantles had glowed for what seemed like endless nights. With just one penny left for the meter, the fragile globes would soon cease to glow. 'Don't break the mantle,' Mam was always saying. 'They don't grow on trees, love.'

Oh, where was Lucy? Lucy, Jessica's special friend, was invisible to all other people. Lucy, with blond hair like Jessica's and blue eyes like Jessica's, had abandoned her creator, had disappeared without so much as a goodbye. Mrs Harris, who held strong opinions on the subject of Lucy's existence, had not visited for a while now, was probably helping more babies to be born. 'Lonely children with good imaginations often make up invisible friends,' Mrs Eva Harris had been heard to opine.

On the hearth, a blue-rimmed enamel mug held water, while a small bowl contained a few unsavoury crumbs of stale bread. The wireless had given up the ghost, its spent accumulator standing uselessly beside it. In the scullery, milk had soured in the jug, cheese had hardened until it looked like cracked yellow soap. But she would have to eat the cheese, because there was nothing else.

The fire had gone out ages ago. Mam would wake soon, the child insisted firmly. Mam would come down and do the magic, rattling old ashes into the pan, crumpling paper, building a little house of firewood and balancing coals on the structure until the flames licked and took hold. Mam was clever. She could make pies and cakes, could fry an egg so that it was all soft in the middle, but brown and crispy-laced round its rim. Mam was so quiet, so cold.

Jessica had slept with Mam, had piled blankets and coats on the bed, had snuggled close so that the German aeroplanes, if they came, would not find her. But Mam was so quiet, so cold.

No-one had come to the door for ages. There was no jug on the step, so Mr Jones had not stopped to pour milk and replace the saucer-lid that was usually left by Mam outside the front door of number 34. Mrs Kershaw at number 32 was in. Mrs Kershaw was rattling her poker in the fire, was preparing food for her family.

The child's stomach groaned. She imagined the smell of frying bacon, remembered sausages, black puddings, toast. Even a dreadful concoction involving dried egg would have been welcome.

The clock had stopped ticking. It sat in the middle of the mantelpiece looking down on her like a dead thing. She knew about dead things. Dead cockroaches, dead mice, dead rats. They were always stiff, those little mice, with strange mouths that seemed to set in a very unhappy, thin line.

She was sitting with her back to the window so that she could keep an eye on the coal hole. If she stared hard at it, nothing would happen. Only if she dozed off in the horsehair rocker would the things come out and get her. What would they do if they did get her? Would they make her dead and stiff, would they leave her with her mouth set in a sad, thin smile? She recalled sitting on the stairs while Mam had listened to Valentine Dyall. 'Do you believe in ghosts?' Valentine Dyall always asked, his deep, dark voice booming all the way from London to the wireless on the dresser. Jessica was not supposed to listen to the Man in Black. The Man in Black was for grown-ups who could make fires and turn great big keys in doors, folk who could collect coal without fearing the devil.

Her feet were going numb again. She lifted them up and screwed her legs beneath the navy blue dressing gown. She was wearing three jumpers, two skirts, two pairs of socks and this boy's dressing gown that Mam had picked up at a jumble stall. Jessica had sworn that she would never need the item, but it was useful now because it was big enough to fit over all the layers of clothing. Her hands were encased in another pair of socks.

Something was wrong. She leaned back and looked at the washing on the pulley line, everything arranged in order, Mam's things, her own things, sheets, pillowcases and towels. Two flat irons mocked a fireless grate next to the mug of water. There was an ironing blanket in the dresser, an old brown thing from the army. If she closed her eyes, she would be able to see Mam spitting on the iron, but Jessica's eyes were on point duty. Even the blinks were rationed, because things under the stairs moved as quickly and as silky-smoothly as the voice of Valentine Dyall. 'Lucy?' she whispered. Why had Jessica's special friend chosen to leave at this terrible time?

She had tried to turn the heavy door keys, had tried to go outside to find Mrs Kershaw or Mr Moss from further down. Mr Moss from further down kept pigeons and breathed sneezing powder up his nose. The little hairs that grew out of his wide nostrils had turned brown with the snuff. He had three snuff tins. One was plain black and for everyday use, one was silver and for Sundays. The third had a picture of an eagle on it, a gold-coloured eagle that stuck up a bit and could be enjoyed by small fingers. That was his weddings and funerals tin.

Mam's mouth was set in a thin line. Mam was cold and stiff like the little mice who ate the special, tasty poison in the night. The poison was in a green tin behind the curtain that hung like a skirt below the scullery slopstone. The back and front doors were closed tightly, each with a four-inch key sticking out of its lock. Jessica could not manage to budge the keys, had been unable to get out to the lavatory in the yard. Her toilet was an enamel bucket in the front room. Soon, she would die.

She wondered about dying. Would her mouth go thin and sad? And what about her sins? Martin Toohey from number 38 had told Jessica about sins. Martin was eight, and he had made his first Holy Communion a few months earlier. Martin had worn a borrowed suit that was miles too big. He could go to confession if he did anything wrong, but Jessica couldn't, as she was too young to receive the Blessed Sacrament. You had to reach the Age of Reason before you could be absolved. Jessica had no need to worry about the naughty days when she had stolen condensed milk, as she had not reached the Age of Reason. She would go straight to heaven once the breadcrumbs ran out.

Jessica considered heaven. Miss Brown, who was in charge of the infants at St Mary's, seemed very keen on heaven, but Miss Brown was old. Perhaps heaven became a good idea for old people. But Jessica wanted to play shop on the bombsite, wanted to hold Mr Moss's pigeons, throw them into the air and watch them fly away. He was generous with his pigeons, was Mr Moss. He allowed all the local children to handle them.

She wanted to go back to the infants' class. Sheila was in Infant One and so were the twins from Noble Street – Annie and Mary Bowles. Sheila Davies was Jessica's very best friend. Sheila had red hair and freckles, and she could nearly do double-unders with a skipping rope. The twins were Jessica's nearly-best friends, and their mam didn't mind when they played with Theresa Nolan's daughter. Theresa Nolan was upstairs in the front bedroom. She was still and cold, and her mouth was set in a thin, sad line.

Jessica stared fiercely at the coal hole cupboard. No-one would want her. Mam had been cast out in disgrace before Jessica's birth, because Jessica had no dad. Even if she did manage to get out of the house, there would be nowhere to go. She did not understand why not having a dad was disgraceful, because Martin Toohey had no dad. Mr Toohey had been killed in Italy while carrying messages on a motorcycle, but Martin's mother was not in disgrace.

Mam was dead. Jessica stood up, her gaze still welded to the coal hole. Like a sleepwalker, she removed the sock-gloves and walked across the kitchen until she reached the bad place. It was time to go in, time to face whatever lay on the other side. Perhaps Lucy would be in the coal store with the evil ones. In that case, going in was probably the right thing. Or was it? She did not begin to understand her actions, yet she recognized their importance. Slowly, her hand raised itself and touched the handle. It was a latch fastener with a spoon-shaped dent where many thumbs had pressed. She opened the door and walked into hell.

The darkness was terrible. For a split second, the urge to run back into comparative safety was almost overwhelming, but Jessica resisted. The bad things under the stairs were very quiet. She still failed to comprehend why she had entered the coal hole, yet she knew that this act was significant. If the bad things got her, she would die. If she died, she would not be hungry and cold, because nobody was hungry or cold in heaven. There was no threat of limbo, as Jessica had been baptised. Straight to heaven, then. Too early, she supposed, because most people who died were old, like Mr Moss. Still, dead was better than no mam and no dad, better than the orphanage and the sad, grey clothes the mother-and-fatherless children were forced to wear.

She stood very still, her heart thumping against both ear-drums. If she survived this encounter, she might just break a window and get out into the yard. But why should she? Where could she go? Except for Mam, no-one wanted her.

Something moved, scuttered across her feet and scrambled its way into a pile of slack coal. It was either a mouse or a rat, but Jessica remained motionless. Mice and rats would not kill a little girl. 'Are you there?' she asked tremulously. Her voice was thinned by lack of use. She waited, every pore on her body open, every hair on her skin erect.

No reply came. 'You're not here.' Her tone was stronger. A small part of Jessica felt a flicker of disappointment. Fearing things under the stairs had taken her mind off other subjects like the bombed-out people in the next street. 'You've never been here,' she advised her indiscernible enemies. 'You've been in my head like the stories and like Lucy.' Lucy had lived in the roof, had hummed songs while Jessica lay in bed waiting to sleep. Lucy was made up; so were the other beings, Jessica surmised. There were no demons in 34, Emblem Street, Bolton, Lancashire.

Another terrified creature rattled about where the devil should have hid. 'I'm not afraid any more.' Jessica sank to her knees, did not feel the splinters of coal as they cut into her legs. She said an Our Father and a Glory Be, then leaned her weight against the door. Mam was dead. Mam wasn't going to wake up. Mam's heart had been weak ever since she'd been a little girl with fever.

The idea of a world without Mam was not acceptable. There was an orphanage in Lostock where children lived. Some came to St Mary's for lessons, and they all had dull clothes. But the orphanage was not the real worry. It was the thought of a Mam-less existence. Mam played with Jessica, taught her to read and write, helped her with sums and colouring. Mam worked just part-time because of her heart, so Jessica always knew that Mam would be waiting inside number 34 when she came home from school.

She closed her eyes at last. There was nothing to fear, because she had faced the ultimate darkness. Tears squashed their way past tight-closed lids, collected on her face, dripped down onto her hands. Mam had beautiful red hair, a sort of golden red that was lighter in summer. She had large grey-blue eyes, a beautiful smile and a lovely voice. She sang, did Mam. She sang all Irish songs about mothers waiting for their sons and daughters to return from abroad. She sang 'Danny Boy', 'The Rose of Tralee', 'Irish Eyes'.

With sobs shattering the lyrics, Jessica sang 'Irish Eyes', but she never got to the end. Her exhausted little body could take no more, so it closed down and allowed her to dream of happier times. She saw Mam laughing while she threw darts at playing cards, saw her trying to win a coconut and a goldfish at St Mary's School Fair. Then Jessica was in the front room laughing while Mam attempted to paint the walls. There was more distemper in Mam's hair than on the crumbling plaster. Theresa Nolan came to life for a few short moments in her little daughter's subconscious mind. In her sleep, Jessica smiled, though the quiet sobbing continued.

Ernie Moss was an air-raid warden. He lived at 26, Emblem Street with a three-legged dog called Albert and a loft filled with prize-winning pigeons. Although the Germans had practically given up the ghost, Ernie still took his job seriously. Rome and other foreign parts could be as near liberated as they liked; Ernie would carry on making sure that nobody on his patch showed so much as a flicker during the hours of darkness.

He was a bit worried about number 34. She kept herself to herself, did Theresa Nolan. A grand-looking lass, she had been cast out by her father and was making a fair job of bringing up little Jessica on her own. But no milk had been delivered, and the upstairs black-out had been in place for a while. 'What must I do?' Ernie enquired of Albert.

The three-legged Welsh collie gazed adoringly at his master, a black ear fully alert, a white one at half-mast.

'I mean, she often leaves black-outs up, like. She's got a funny heart, needs to rest. But she should have gone to work today, I'm sure.' Theresa worked just three mornings each week, helping to prepare food for munitions workers.

Ernie bent down and scratched the side of Albert

that was unreachable to the dog. Ernie often acted *in loco* missing leg; he seemed to know when Albert needed a bit of relief or grooming. 'Last time I knocked to see if she were all right, I got sent off with a couple of fleas down me lug'ole,' the warden muttered. 'She were in bed with a cold nearing bronchitis, didn't want disturbing. So I don't know what to do.'

Albert shared his master's unease. He stood to attention on his front legs, balanced his weight on the over-burdened third and cocked his head to one side. Albert could hear the silence, was able to sense disquiet behind the green-painted door of number 34. He barked and lolloped towards the house, his tail dragging sadly over the single rear limb.

Ernie had a lot of faith in dogs. If a dog was worried, then the world should follow suit. Unlike felines, who simply tolerated mankind in return for food and shelter, dogs had an affinity with their human companions. There was something wrong in Theresa Nolan's house. Ernie Moss walked to the top of Emblem Street, where he saw the local bobby having a word with Danny Walsh, the fishmonger. The latter stood by his shattered window, while two small boys hung their heads in shame.

'You shouldn't play cricket on the road,' said the policeman. 'It's dangerous.'

Ernie Moss interrupted the proceedings. 'Can you come down Emblem Street, George?' he asked the constable. 'I could be wrong, but there might be summat up inside one of the houses. No sight of nobody for a day or two.'

George Marsden spoke to the pair of lads. 'I'll be round to see your mams later,' he promised ominously. 'That window's going to cost a bob or two. Get home before I lose my temper.'

Ernie knew that George Marsden had no temper to lose. George was a mild-mannered man who should have retired from the police force. Because of the war, many older and experienced men had been required to retain their jobs while younger ones fought for King and country. 'There's the kiddy to think on,' Ernie told the constable. 'Only four, a nice little lass. I've not seen her, neither.'

Halfway down Emblem Street, warden and policeman hammered at Theresa Nolan's door. The sound echoed throughout the small house, as if the place had been emptied of its contents overnight.

'I'll have to break in,' muttered George.

'Do it, then.' The feeling in Ernie Moss's bones was intensifying. He was prepared to accept 'Mrs' Nolan's wrath, would be grateful for it. If she would only open the door, give him that famous cool stare and tell him to mind his own business and be on his way quick smart, Ernie would be a happy man. 'Get on with it,' he urged.

George Marsden removed his helmet, placed a hand inside this item and used the headgear to smash the front window. Molly Kershaw put in an appearance on the step next door. 'What's going on?' she asked.

'Have you seen her?' Ernie nodded in the direction of number 34. 'Or the kiddy?'

Molly Kershaw shook her turbaned head. 'She's on the quiet side, is Theresa, doesn't want no interference, like. Come to think, I've heard nowt for a while.' There had been no rattling of a sweeping brush, no battering of rugs in the back yard. Molly felt a bit guilty. She should have noticed, should have done something about it. 'I never thought,' she muttered softly.

George climbed into the front room of 34, Emblem Street, stepped round a few items of furniture, then let himself into the narrow hall. There was an empty feeling, a sort of aged, almost professional silence that had seeped its way into the building's fabric. In the kitchen, two gas mantles flickered uncertainly, while no fire occupied the neglected black grate. On the mantelpiece, a cheap clock had given up the ghost at ten minutes past six this morning, or yesterday evening, or whenever.

He left the empty room and climbed the stairs. As a veteran of the Bolton police force, George had encountered many situations like this one. A sixth sense had developed over the years, a feeling that went beyond all normal perceptions like sight and hearing. Death was spreading his dark cloak over this place. But when he entered Mrs Nolan's bedroom, George heard a small, shuddering breath, crossed the floor in two strides and found a flickering pulse in a chilled wrist. The soul had not quite left the body, yet Theresa was just a hair's breadth from kingdom come.

George tore off his jacket and threw it over the still form. He wrenched a dressing gown from a hook, a rug from the floor. Frantically, he rubbed at Theresa's hands, then he strode across the bedroom and opened the window. 'Ernie?'

The warden took a backward step and looked up at his old friend. 'What's up?' he asked anxiously.

'Ambulance,' replied George. 'She's had some sort of a turn – out for the count and very cold, she is.'

Doors opened, spilling women and children onto the pavements. Some members of the audience ventured across cobbles to get a better view of the crisis. Cissie Monkton, who had lived through two wars and two husbands, craned her stiff neck. The crusty, unwashed shawl stayed exactly where it was, as if obeying its mistress, as if it dared not budge on pain of death or laundering. 'Where's the kiddy?' These words shot smoothly past a clay pipe from which noxious fumes emerged in staggered puffs.

George re-entered the house and searched. He finally found the chilled and blackened little girl in the coal store beneath Theresa Nolan's stairs.

Jessica rubbed her eyes, felt grit scraping beneath the lids. 'Is Mam dead?' she asked when her senses began to return. She felt weak and giddy, while her eyes perceived the policeman through a fog, as if she were watching a very poor copy of some aged movie.

'No,' murmured George. 'She's not well, like, and she'll be needing a bit of looking after.' If she survives, the man commented inwardly.

'But she had a sad face and a straight-line mouth and she was cold.'

Theresa Nolan was very cold, but George could not tell the little girl about hypothermia. He could not tell Jessica anything which might upset her. Part of George's training had covered shock and bad news. He had to be positive, no matter what his own deductions were. 'She's going to the infirmary. So are you.'

Jessica absorbed the information. Mam, who had not moved all night and all day, was alive. A bubble of hope spilled onto the child's face, allowing a tentative smile to play on the coal-streaked face. 'The devil isn't under the stairs,' she informed her saviour.

'Who said he was?' George perched on the rocker with Jessica on his lap.

She lifted thin shoulders. 'It was all in my . . . imagining,' she managed. 'Lucy, too.'

George sniffed. This kiddy's imaginings were doing her no good at all.

'There's only Mam who wants me, you see,' she said as if reading his thoughts. 'I've got no dad, so Grandad doesn't visit us, not ever.'

'You'll be all right,' replied George, the words seasoned with a decisiveness he did not feel. What sort of a family did Theresa Nolan have? A dad who had turned her out for being pregnant, a sister who, by all accounts, was as unpredictable as a mad dog in a thunderstorm? Theresa wasn't the sort to go mucking about with men. She was a decent body, a girl who had made one mistake. And if such mistakes brought forth children like young Jess, then there should be more of them.

'Mr Marsden?'

'Yes, love?'

'Can I stop with Mr Moss till Mam's better? I'll see to the pigeons.'

George knew that no-one on God's supposedly good earth would place a four-year-old child in the custody of a man with six or seven decades under his belt. What would happen to her, then? Would she finish up in the orphanage until Theresa Nolan got better? Theresa might not get better. He cleared his throat. 'I want you to go in with Mrs Kershaw for now,' he advised. 'She'll give you a good wash and find you something clean to wear and a bite to eat till the ambulance comes. The hospital will want a look at you.' George had, within the last few seconds, decided what must be done. Ernie Moss would have to be the do-er, as George intended to travel to the infirmary with Theresa and

Jessica. They had no-one, so he would be there for them.

After settling the child next door, Ernie Moss and George Marsden had a chat. When everything had been mulled over, Ernie shut Albert in his house, explaining that a three-legged canine was not equipped for the long trek up Derby Street. Albert, who knew a great deal about human nature, curled up for a rest. Ernie would not desert him. Ernie would be back to feed him later.

The warden walked past the Tivoli cinema, caught his breath, then resolutely carried on struggling up the slope. The ambulance would probably have arrived by now, and Theresa Nolan would be in good hands. What about the kiddy, though? There probably wasn't much wrong with her apart from shock, so the hospital might kick her out tomorrow with a clean bill of health. Where to? Lostock? The orphanage up Edgeworth?

He stood outside the door of number 35, View Street. Mike Nolan lived here, Big Michael, the one with a gob like the Grand Canyon and a lot more than enough to say for himself. Big Mike should have been dead years ago, by all accounts, due to pneumonia, pleurisy, liver trouble, leg ulcers. But only the good died young, and this man was far from good. Big Mike Nolan had won the Great War all by himself. He had routed the Kaiser, killed a million Germans, had saved the lives of countless inept men, was worth more than ten regiments.

Ernie raised his hand to knock, but decided to get his breath back first. Big Michael Nolan had fists like lump hammers and was not averse to using them. Even the slightest hint of criticism could cause Big Mike to let fly. He had thrown out poor Theresa in her hour of greatest need, had caused all but one of his other children to escape as soon as they were grown, and lived now in the company of Ruth, the one and only Nolan who could match him for strangeness.

The door opened. Ruth McManus poked out her less than attractive face. At the age of thirty, she was already wrinkled, her face criss-crossed with lines caused by ill-temper. 'What do you want?' she snapped. Her neck, too thin for the largeish head it supported, was stringy, like something that should have poked out of a shell – the front end of a turtle or a tortoise.

Perhaps the orphanage was the best place, thought Ernie. Blood was thicker than water, but this one here seemed to have ice-filled veins. Her husband had buggered off back to Ireland when the clouds of war had gathered, and Ruth's temper had not been improved by Joseph McManus's sudden disappearance. 'I've not got all day,' she snapped. 'I were watching you from the parlour – are you going to stand out there for ever?' She pulled at a lock of her thick, black hair and twisted it about her fingers.

Ernie swallowed. 'It's your sister—'

'Which one? I've five altogether, and three brothers.'

'Theresa.'

Ruth's mouth snapped shut. Beady brown eyes fixed themselves on the unwelcome caller. 'She's no sister to me, no daughter to my dad, either. She refused to budge herself to visit him when he were at death's door, so she's nowt a pound, our Theresa.'

Ernie squashed his temper. The female on the doorstep had chased Joseph McManus three times round Bolton before managing to get herself in the family way. McManus, who had not been able to escape quickly enough at that particular time, had been dragged up the aisle of St Mary's by a very annoyed Big Mike Nolan. 'She's ill,' he muttered at last.

'She were always ill,' replied Ruth. 'Always wanting attention, always needing summat or other.'

'Rheumatic fever leaves kiddies weak,' Ernie said. 'And she grew up weak and all.'

'And who said she had the rheumatic?' asked Ruth scathingly.

'It's common knowledge. Everybody knows about her heart being affected.'

Ruth McManus sniffed disdainfully. She could have just about killed for a Woodbine. 'Have you got a ciggy?' she asked.

'I don't smoke, sorry.'

The woman folded thin arms about her flat chest. 'What's up with her this time?'

'She's in hospital. We had to break in and she was very near death.'

She nodded. 'So what do you want me to do about it?'

Ernie cleared his throat, trying to make a space in which he might think. 'It's Jess,' he said eventually. 'Theresa's little girl.'

'I see.' Ruth opened the door, then opened her mouth. 'Dad?' she screamed.

'What?' Even from the back of the house, Michael Nolan's voice was loud.

'Some feller from down the road. Wants you to do summat about our Theresa.'

Ernie stepped back when Big Mike strode down the hall. He was a bull of a man, red-faced, sweaty and as Irish as the gill of black beer in his hand.

'What about you?' he asked. 'Did you want something from me, Mr . . . er?'

'Moss. Ernie Moss. I live a few doors down from your Theresa—'

'Who?'

'Your daughter.'

Mike Nolan placed his pint glass on a small table just inside the door, then pulled Ruth back into the house before stepping out. 'I have no daughter of that name,' he said coldly. 'Ruth should know that by now.'

'But little Jessica—'

'Jess-i-ca?' There was mockery in the three syllables. 'There's nobody here knows a Jess-i-ca. Or a Theresa. Ruth must have been confused when she called me, because we've had no Theresa here for as long as I can remember. And a name like Jess-i-ca would be a bit sick, for wasn't that the name of my sainted wife? No, I've no memory of either of the people you're talking about. So be on your way, Mr . . . er.'

Mike Nolan's memory was as short as his neck, thought Ernie. He looked at the ugly man, at the ugly woman, then noticed a child peeping round Ruth's skirts. She looked to be about ten or eleven, though thirteen was nearer the actual mark. Starved, she was, deprived of love and decent nourishment, concluded the warden. He eyed Irene. It was a sin to call a child ugly, he told himself. But the flat, colourless face and those glassy eyes were reminiscent of a sad field-beast – a goat, perhaps, or a particularly unlovely and unloved sheep.

'Come away, Irene,' chided Ruth when the girl pushed her way to the door.

Ernie shuddered. The orphanage, then. From

what he had just seen in Big Mike Nolan's lobby, this was a family unfit for little Jessica Nolan.

Theresa groaned, opened her eyes and saw a beautiful man looking down on her. He was not handsome, not rugged or manly, but simply beautiful. Jessica. Where was she?

'Mrs Nolan?'

It was Miss Nolan, though she had not the strength to argue.

'Can you hear me?'

She could hear him, all right, could see his bright blue eyes and his yellow, damped-down shock of curls. He was too young to be a doctor. Perhaps she was dead and in some waiting room outside St Peter's gates. No, no, there was work to be done . . .

'You're going to be all right,' he announced cheerfully. 'You just wore yourself out and got very cold.'

She coughed, was lifted by strong arms into a sitting position. Her tongue accepted gratefully a few drops of water. The room was stifling, and she was swaddled in half a dozen blankets.

'Mrs Nolan?'

She was drifting away again. Somewhere, Jessica was calling out, but the sound was inside the dream, not here, not in this hard bed. It was time to leave Jessica with Eva Harris, wasn't it?

'Mrs Nolan?'

'Leave her.' The female voice was strong, authoritative. 'Let her sleep, Dr Marshall.'

Theresa slept. She walked up those four well-worn steps into her home on View Street. Dad was there, was smoking his pipe and spitting into the fire.

Ruth's husband, drunk as usual, was counting money at the table.

'Who did you rob this time?' screamed Ruth. 'Dad – he's got a gold watch in his pocket. We'll be getting the police round if he doesn't start behaving.'

Big Mike Nolan swivelled slowly in his chair. 'Shut up,' he bellowed. He didn't care how Joseph McManus acquired the money. As long as he got his baccy and his pint, Nolan was not interested in the finer details.

Theresa stood near the door. Her heart was jumping crazily in her chest. She could not tell Dad. There had been trouble enough over Ruth's recent shotgun wedding. She turned away and trudged wearily up the stairs.

'Mrs Nolan?'

She opened her eyes.

'Nice cup of tea?'

The nurse had a pleasant, round face, dark eyes and a starched white cap. Theresa's eyelids, still heavy with sleep, returned to the closed position.

The alley was darkening in the drizzly April dusk. She could hear them breathing, sniggering as they jumped out of a back yard. Her coat was ripped away, then her blouse, her skirt, her undergarments. When her arms were pinned down by two of them, the third tore his way into her. He was rough, but very quick.

The second attacker took longer. Beery breath filled her nostrils as the beast grunted its way towards some kind of seizure. The ogre shuddered, cried out, bit her chest. She knew him. By the time the third monster had performed his vile act, the first deemed himself fit for a repeat performance. Whatever he was doing did not work. The others mocked him. Her eyes adjusted to the dying light and she recognized the criminals.

Carelessly, they spoke to one another, tossed names about. Theresa took those names and scorched them into the forefront of her brain. She would never forget, would never forgive. These filthy articles were privileged, supposedly educated creatures, were from the better end of town. Theresa knew their fathers, their families, their businesses. These articles had sprung from the loins of successful men.

'What a gem,' breathed Theresa Nolan.

'Just a sip.' The nurse supported her, guided the cup to her lips. 'Who's a gem?' she asked.

The patient flopped back into the pillows. 'A rough diamond,' she mumbled. 'Set in fools' gold.' In her delirium, she referred to Roy Chorlton, son of the master jeweller.

She lost count after a while. For at least half an hour, she was left on rain-slicked cobbles while they drank and smoked. Matches and lighters illuminated their faces. They were hideous. She was used and abused repeatedly until the trio lost interest. Laughing and joking, the three revellers staggered away towards their next adventure.

She sat up, leaned herself against a wall, vomited, removed an object from between her thighs. She stared through the gloom at the beer bottle. This was almost more humiliating than the actual rapes had been. Their final act had been to use her as a dustbin, a rubbish heap for their discarded debris.

'Mrs Nolan?'

'Where is my daughter?'

The nurse smiled reassuringly, carried on administering tea. 'She's tucked up in bed on the children's ward.'

Theresa had to stay alive. There were things she had to do, people to be dealt with. Had she waited too long? she wondered. Jessica had come first. Theresa had always wanted Jess to be older before . . . before what? Was she going to kill those men – was that to be the plan? Was blackmail not enough? 'What happened?' she managed to ask the nurse. And the leaving of Jessica was going to be so difficult. 'What happened?' she whispered again.

'Never mind that now. Just get some rest.'

Rest? There was none. She stood on the doorstep of her home, picked up belongings that had been tossed through an upper window. Ruth hadn't said anything. Ruth never said much. But Big Mike Nolan had lived up to his reputation, had unleashed his famous Irish temper. 'Get out of my house! You're no better than any other stinking English whore!'

Theresa gathered her few possessions and moved into number 27. Mrs Eva Harris, midwife and mentor to the troubled, was the only person who knew the full story. Dad had refused to listen, would never have believed it.

Mrs Harris's husband knew somebody who knew somebody else. The somebody else found the Emblem Street house and a job in a small newspaper shop. As the pregnancy progressed, Theresa found herself tired to the point of collapse. Eva had come to the fore yet again, had demanded money from the jeweller and his friends. Fearful for his reputation, the coward coughed up, as did his fellow business associates. And since then, Eva Harris had continued to extract money from the rapists' families.

The blue-eyed doctor returned, listened to her heart, nodded, walked away. A woman across the room screamed for a bedpan. Theresa watched the ward's activities, refused soup, drifted in and out of sleep. She had not looked after herself. There was money in a tin under a bedroom floorboard, but she had never used much of it. The money was for Jessica, because Jessica was the blameless child of rape.

Which one was the father? Was it the jeweller, the tanner or the furniture dealer? Which one of those heroes had planted Jess inside Theresa's body? Strange how those men of substance feared a woman as tiny as Eva Harris. They paid up each time, quickly and almost noiselessly. Why?

Her eyes fixed themselves on a grimy window pane. There had been a fourth man. He had crossed the bottom of the alley – she remembered seeing him outlined against the sky. For a few seconds, he had seemed riveted to the spot. Yes, there had been a witness, a good man who had arrived far too late to intervene. Bernard Walsh had smelled of fish. He had offered comfort, had wept silently into Theresa's hair. Later, the same man had ridden shotgun on Eva's 'blackmail' visits.

Oh, Jessica. Time was running out for Theresa Nolan. Rheumatic fever had left her weak and available to any passing germ. Diminished even further by a harrowing pregnancy and a difficult birthing, she was exhausted. She must use what was left of her life to bring to justice those so-called men who had used her so carelessly. The legal system had nothing to offer, not after this length of time; Theresa must mete out the punishments herself. To do that, Theresa must leave behind the light of her life, her one and only love, her little Jessica.

The child needed to be kept safe, must be protected while Theresa went about her business. But who would minister to a fatherless waif? Who could be trusted to take care of that precious child? Eva. There was no-one but Eva, yet Eva was a busy woman with a job to do and a husband to care for. And nothing could be arranged properly until the end of the war, because all the attackers were abroad fighting for King and country. Perhaps the German army would do the job for her.

Theresa drifted off to sleep and the intensity of the dreams diminished. She returned to the time when Bernard Walsh had talked softly about being a witness should she choose to bring in the law, to the evening when he had held her sobbing against his hard shoulder. That was no coward; Bernard had been a man in shock, a good person who had not believed the horror before his eyes. The Walshes were lovely, kind people. How many times had Bernard said, 'I felt riveted to the spot'? How many times had Theresa been the comforter? 'You arrived when it was all over.'

The patient dozed, her expression more peaceful, the sobs less frequent. They had given her some sweet-tasting medicine in a little cup, something to trim the edges off painful memories. Nevertheless, while Theresa floated on the soft wings of sedation, three faces passed in turn before her mind's eye, and the memory of wet cobbles forced hard against vulnerable flesh caused a sharp intake of breath from time to time.

'She's settling,' the nurse advised the doctor. All the same, whenever she passed Theresa Nolan's bed, the same nurse wiped tears from the face of her charge.

FOUR

While her mother clung uncertainly to the rim of life, Jessica found herself surrounded by a set of people whose components might have been fascinating had the circumstances been different. Doctors poked and prodded at her chest and back, pushed thermometers in her mouth, stared down her throat while making clicking noises with their tongues. One had bad breath; another, a bald man with sad eyes, was quite the nicest of them all. The bald one had told Jessica that her mother, though poorly, would survive.

Nurses fluttered about in white aprons that crackled with starch; then, when a visiting chest specialist took too close an interest, Jessica was wheeled into a little room for photographs to be taken. These were not ordinary likenesses; the pictures taken in the infirmary were all bones and shadows. Jessica was a skeleton. Underneath layers of dermis and flesh, she was a thing encountered only on ghost trains at fairs. She was more frightening than any imagined devil in a coal hole. She was a living monster wearing a borrowed garment of skin. And everyone else was the same, because a man in a white coat had told her so.

After X-rays had been assessed, the little girl was moved from the medical ward and placed in total isolation. Attendants came in with masks on their faces and food on trays. Books were made available, but they smelled funny and were placed inside a bag marked TB before being taken from the room. It was all so boring. Jessica did not feel particularly ill. Hospital food was all right, but the bed was hard and she wanted to play outside in the snow. 'I want my mam,' she advised a masked invader.

'She's still asleep,' came Staff Nurse Joan Bowker's muffled reply. 'She needs rest, love.'

'And I want to play out. Mr Moss says children should play out like pigeons do. He says children need fresh air and—'

'You'll be getting plenty of that at the sanatorium,' replied the overworked angel of mercy.

'What's a san . . . it . . . that word you just said?'

'It's a place for TB.'

'What's TB?'

'A germ that makes you cough.'

The child sighed heavily. 'I haven't got a cough.'

'You will have if you don't shape. Stop in bed and keep warm.'

Warm? The infirmary had three temperatures – hot, boiling and fit to roast the dinner. 'But I'm already warm. When am I going to the sanity place?'

The mask changed shape as the nurse allowed herself a smile. It was a damned shame, a little lass like this having TB and a mother in and out of coma. Places at children's sanatoriums in East Lancashire, Yorkshire and Cheshire were as rare as pigs in flight, so Jessica would be kept with Theresa. 'You're both going soon. You and your mother. It's nice up at

Williamson's San. You get really good food, no rationing there. And there's all trees and flowers.' Like her daughter, Theresa Nolan had tuberculosis, though the child's problem was comparatively mild. Both Nolans would be transferred within days to a place where TB was the norm, where everyone fought daily battles with the same bloodthirsty disease, where new antibiotics were being tested on those human volunteers for whom penicillin was not always the answer.

'No rationing?' The child's eyes were widened by this news. Jessica had never known a world without points and coupons. 'Will I have a lot of meat and stuff?'

'Oh, yes. The patients who are getting better plant vegetables. The sanatorium's even got its own bakery and milking herd. Jelly every Sunday, ice cream with it. I've some friends who work there. They get well fed, too.' Joan Bowker's friends were nourished against the possibility of miliary tuberculosis, the type that spread via veins and arteries throughout the whole body. Bribed during wartime by the certainty of good food, nurses braved lethal bacteria, ignored the future and lived comfortably, dangerously, in the present.

Jessica hugged the nightdress round her knees and rocked herself against stony pillows. 'I thought my mam was dead,' she said. 'She went all cold and quiet.'

'Your mam hasn't been looking after herself.' Theresa Nolan weighed about six stones. A slight woman, she was meant to be a lightweight, but there was a difference between slimness and emaciation. 'She got much too cold.'

Jessica nodded pensively. 'Like the mice, with a

sad smile. I told Lucy about it when she came back, and she thought Mam was dead, too.'

'Lucy?'

It was the child's turn to smile. 'I think Lucy is really a smaller me. When I was little, I saw myself in the mirror and I called the other girl Lucy. I know she's only pretend, but . . . talking out loud to her makes me feel better.' Jessica sensed the heat in her cheeks. 'Am I daft?' She hadn't told many people about Lucy.

'No.' As Joan Bowker closed the door in her wake, she felt a lump in her throat. Poor Jessica Nolan was lonely, while her mother was an outcast because she had given birth out of wedlock. Theresa Nolan had kept her child. She hadn't gone to a so-called mid-wife for help in getting rid of it, hadn't strangled the baby with its cord in order to claim a stillbirth and a fresh start in another town. As far as Nurse Bowker was concerned, Theresa deserved praise, not con-demnation.

The nurse left the ward, removed from her person an all-over muslin wrap and placed it in the con-tamination bin. Soft paper slippers found the same destination before Joan Bowker went forth to tend patients on women's medical. Theresa Nolan, too, had been removed from the ward. Like her daugh-ter, Theresa was in a small room of her own, was lying on sheets and under-blankets that would be fumigated before resurfacing for use. Soon, both Nolans would be due for transfer to Williamson's Sanatorium up on the moors. Ready or not, Theresa would have to be moved.

'Can I have a bedpan?'

Joan Bowker moved towards the sluice, grim de-termination quickening her stride. She loved nursing, had always wanted to care for the sick. But if any daft swine were to write an opera about a hospital, 'Can I Have a Bedpan' would form the chorus for women's medical. Men were easier. They felt so apologetic and stupid about being ill that they often struggled to straighten their beds even on their dying day. She rattled through the steam-sterilizer and came up with what she needed. It wasn't fair. Rheumatic fever, damaged heart, childbirth, malnourishment and TB. The odds were not exactly stacked in Theresa Nolan's favour. And somebody was still screaming for a bedpan.

Danny Walsh surveyed the shop's two-day-old replacement window. It might last five minutes if his luck held. Children had no respect for property these days – and was it any wonder? Dads at war, mams stuck in factories, grandparents expected to mind youngsters during school holidays. The war was winding down a bit – fewer raids, even in the south of the country, fewer sirens screeching at night – but the kiddies had seen too many newsreels, too many smashed houses. A broken window was nothing compared to London, Liverpool, Coventry.

He hated living here. Bernard, Liz and Katherine now occupied Danny's Bromley Cross cottage on a so-called temporary basis. Liz had become hysterical when bombs had fallen, had declared her intention to leave Derby Street with Katherine and with or without her husband. As soon as the war ended, they were supposed to swap back again, and Danny could scarcely wait. The large rear garden he had treasured was a barren, iced-up mess, because Bernard simply wasn't interested in the art of cultivation. But Liz wasn't going to be easy to shift. Liz liked the country, while Katherine was settled happily in the village school. All the same, Danny meant to have his house back, because he, too, was a man with responsibilities.

He sighed resignedly, went into the shop and sorted through an icy jumble of cod's heads. These delicacies were kept on one side for the owners of cats. With water just short of boiling, he swabbed down marble slabs and wooden blocks. After years spent fishmongering, Danny was impervious to both ends of the temperature's spectrum.

The inner door opened. 'Your tea's ready,' snapped a turbaned dragon.

Danny grinned broadly. Edna Greenhalgh was loathed and feared north, south, east and west of Derby Street. She had as many enemies as Judas and she feared nothing on earth. Well, almost nothing. Danny had seen into the heart of his monstrous mother-in-law, had managed to lay bare a small fissure in the iron cladding. Edna doted on her only daughter. The fear of losing Pauline was never expressed, seldom shown, but Danny had cared enough to seek it out. Like Pauline's first husband, he had brought Mother Greenhalgh into his life. The house on Tonge Moor Road remained Pauline's property for the time being. After the war, it would probably be sold.

He ascended the stairs and entered the lion's den. Mother was cooking something delicious in a large cast iron pan. 'All right, Mother?' he asked. She was standing with her feet well apart, the sturdy body encased in a bright-patterned wrap-around apron, grey frazzled hair twisted into curlers and Ladye Jayne wave-grips and wrapped in a scarf. With a wooden spoon, she stirred the soup, tasted, stirred again. Danny smiled to himself. This was no witch from the heath, no product of some bloodied Shakespearian tragedy. She was just an old woman with pride, dignity and a terrible way with words. 'Smells good.'

Edna sniffed. She had perfected the craft of nasal inhalation, had developed a set of sniffs to cover almost any occasion. The recently delivered offering was one of the 'don't talk daft' items in her repertoire. 'I'd be better off with a bit more barley. And a lot better if Longshanks would give up helping on that bloody market. She could lose a finger.' Longshanks was one of Edna's nicknames for her daughter. Nicknames were the nearest she could manage to get towards terms of endearment.

Danny sat in his usual chair. Pauline liked working. She had been more than happy to put a bit of space between herself and Maurice the Mole in the jewellery shop. 'She loves the market, Mother. It doesn't seem to be doing her any harm.'

Nostrils dilated, Edna delivered an 'I know better than you' before dumping a dish of steaming soup on Danny's portion of the table. 'It's nearly all men down yon,' she stated unnecessarily.

'I know.'

'I dare say some of that there backspeak's not ladylike.'

'She's not bothered.' Pauline still didn't fully understand the fishmarket's language.

Edna sat down to supervise her client's sampling of food. 'Too much salt? It looked a bit salty, that ham shank.'

'No, it's lovely.'

'And her hands is going all rough.'

Danny attempted no reply. Edna Greenhalgh,

129

many of whose recent years had been spent in a fireside chair, was alive again. She took stairs, fish and rheumatism in her stride and was a sight more active than many women half her age. She cooked, cleaned, polished, washed and ironed. At every conceivable opportunity, she invaded the shop and plagued the life out of regular customers. Armed with a new pair of spectacles, she read all newspapers within reach, did the crosswords in the twinkling of an eye, educated all within earshot on the state of the war and the stupidity of mankind in general.

Danny mopped out his dish with a lump of home-made bread. 'That was better than good,' he sighed.

Edna eyed him suspiciously. 'Have you lost weight? You're like a pair of coathangers, you and our Pauline.'

He was the same weight as ever. Danny reckoned he could have eaten a U-boat with impunity, while Bernard, his poor brother, could gain several pounds by simply standing within two yards of a raised pork pie. Edna was up to something. Edna was looking for a project, something to occupy her overactive mind. 'There's nothing wrong with either of us,' he answered.

Nostrils stretched themselves, though a sniff was not employed at this juncture. 'She's thirty-five.'

'Aye, and I'm nobbut thirty-four. That daughter of yours is a blinking cradle-snatcher.'

Edna messed about with teacups and milk jug. 'And you've been wed three year. It doesn't last for ever, you know.'

'What doesn't?'

The old lady poured tea. 'Fertility. Women goes . . . well, they goes off, you know.'

'Like fish in summer?'

She bridled. 'You understand me, so don't go piking about as if you don't. If you want a family, you'd best get weaving. And for a start, you both want feeding up. Men needs to be healthy to make babies. It's not all down just to the woman and I—'

'I do know it's a joint effort,' interrupted Danny.

Edna studied the tablecloth. Danny had dropped soup and made a stain. 'I'm interfering, aren't I?'

His jaw dropped slightly. Edna Greenhalgh was not one to question her own undoubted perfection. She was never wrong, never mistaken, never to be interrogated. Danny shrugged lightly. 'Well, you're just taking an interest, I suppose. It's only natural.' Lovemaking was only natural, he told himself. It was wonderful, beautiful and seldom satisfactory, because Edna slept in the next room.

'So I might move back to Tonge Moor,' she said, her voice softer than usual. 'See, I'm not daft. It can't be easy with me here. But I'll still come every day and do the housework. You and our Pauline need to be . . . getting on with your lives.' They had a squeaky bed. Reluctant to go into too much embarrassing detail, Edna was conveying her thoughts as best she could. The headboard banged against the wall sometimes. Her heart bled because she knew they needed privacy and that she was very much in the way.

Danny lowered his head. The number of occasions when he and Pauline had enjoyed privacy could be counted on his fingers. While Edna was out at the Co-op or the butcher's, Walsh's Fish was usually open. Pauline worked with Bernard on the market, Danny ran the shop single-handed unless Mother butted in with her three penn'orth of insults and fish recipes. A rare trip out to the countryside, a hurried fumbling in a barn or behind questionable screens formed by bushes and moors – these had provided backcloths for the only true intimacies between the couple.

'Good job you're a patient man,' said Edna.

Danny found no words.

'I'm not what people think, lad.'

'I had worked that out.'

She took a slurp of tea and grimaced. 'Tell you what, I'll be glad when they start selling proper tea again – I'm sick of these here floor-sweepings. I bet the bloody government's got proper tea. I bet them at the palace gets more nor two ounces of meat.'

Danny, who nurtured a fondness for the King and his family, tut-tutted. 'They're suffering the same as us, Mother. The Queen said she couldn't look the East End in the eye till after Buckingham Palace got bombed.'

Edna sniffed loudly. Her dislike for the royal 'hangers-on' was a legend in her own teatime. She wanted a president like they had in America, wanted the palace turned into a children's home, wanted the royals to live in two-up-two-downs with outside lavs to bring them back to earth. 'Well, they have it too easy,' she concluded, wanting the last word, as ever. 'Anybody'd think they were made different, but they're not.'

The war was going to be won soon – everybody knew that. Danny Walsh nursed the suspicion that his mother-in-law might have done a better job than Hitler, might have kept things on the boil for a bit longer. 'Are you sure you'll be all right on your own up Tonge Moor?'

'Course I will.' She wanted a grandchild, wanted to see Pauline with a baby. 'She'll make a good mother,' Edna pronounced.

'Don't count your chickens.'

'I weren't on about chickens, Danny Walsh.' She settled back and looked at him. He was just about the grandest chap she had ever encountered. He was kind, generous to a fault, and his philosophy was simple. Danny worked to live, did not allow the job to rule his existence. Money was needed, so he earned it. What he earned he spent on his household after saving a bit towards the unknown. Edna loved him.

'Is there something wrong with my face?' he asked.

It wasn't a handsome face, yet it was lovely. 'Your soul shows,' Edna said quietly. 'I never had a son, but, well . . . you'll do.'

This was praise indeed. 'Blooming heck,' laughed Danny. 'Don't start going all nice. You'll only upset everybody. Just imagine what a shock it would be if you went nice, Mother. Me customers'd be keeling over with heart attacks.'

Edna's facial expression remained untouched. 'It's been a hard life, so I've hardened meself against it. When we lost Pauline's dad, then when John Chadwick got himself blew up . . . Well, you've got to find your own way of keeping going, haven't you?'

Danny nodded his agreement.

'So don't go mauling about and playing heroes if there's any more fires. Our Pauline needs you.'

He stirred his tea. Mother Greenhalgh's speech was probably as near as she had ever come to apology or declaration of affection. She was a good woman, a frightened woman. In the house up Tonge Moor, she'd sat still deliberately, as if doing nothing would prevent any further nasty happenings. 'Like Buddha,' he said aloud.

'Eh?'

133

'You were. Waiting, not wanting to touch anything.'

'What the hell's that got to do with foreigners' religions? I'm Church of England, me.'

Danny chortled. There was no point in telling Mother about Buddha's theories. 'Never mind. I was just thinking out loud.'

Edna squared her shoulders. 'Aye, well, think yourself down to that market and fetch your missus home. She'll want thawing out.'

'Our Bernard'll bring her. He's got the van—'

'You bring her. Tell her what I said before about sleeping up Tonge Moor, because I'm not making the same speech twice.'

As he walked down the road towards his wife, Danny Walsh found himself humming. He was content, happier than he'd ever been in his whole existence. Once he got back into his garden, he would have everything. But how strange life was. Dragged by Eva Harris into Chorlton's Jewellery, he had met Pauline. Dragged through an alley by three bad buggers, Theresa Nolan had become the reason behind that first meeting between Mr and Mrs Daniel Walsh.

Life was bloody peculiar, all right. People were always laughing at Danny, especially the men, joking about mothers-in-law, ragging him because he was forced to live with Edna Greenhalgh. He wouldn't have missed getting acquainted with Edna, not for the world. You knew where you were with Mother Greenhalgh. She was straight.

On the market, Pauline and Bernard greeted Danny. 'Have you heard owt?' Bernard asked immediately.

'About what?'

'Theresa Nolan and little Jessica. They've been down the infirmary for a couple of days now. Ernie Moss and George Marsden broke in, found Theresa near pegged out upstairs. Little lass was stuck in the coal hole.'

Danny absorbed the information, remembered Constable Marsden's quick exit from the scene of the crime after the shop window had been broken. 'What happened?' he asked. 'I know Ernie Moss dragged the bobby off quick smart, but why?'

Pauline took over. 'Billy Isherwood from Jubilee Fish and Fruit's got a daughter in nursing. Theresa Nolan was near starved to death.' Pauline, who had been told by Danny about the rapes and the payments, lowered her tone. 'What's she doing not eating? There must be money, love. I mean, is she trying to die?'

Bernard stared hard at his brother. 'If she's saving it, what's she saving it for, Dan?'

'I don't know.' He didn't want to know, not really, didn't want to think. Because when he did allow his mind free rein, a few funny thoughts sometimes chased about in the tortuous canals of grey matter. 'It's her business, Bernard.'

The younger brother went away to finish clearing his stall.

'What's up?' Pauline asked her husband.

Danny shrugged. 'I'm not sure.'

'They say she's got TB – the little girl and all. Going up to the sanatorium soon. Once they're there and on the mend, they can happen have visitors.'

Danny stopped in his tracks and placed a restraining hand on Pauline's sleeve. 'No, love.'

'You what?'

'Stay out of it.'

Pauline peered though the gloom at her husband's troubled face. 'What am I stopping out of?'

'I'm not sure.'

'But—'

'Leave it, love.'

Pauline kept her counsel. She had the best husband in the world, but Danny was a deep thinker. If he was uneasy, then there must be something to be uneasy about. He would tell her in time. And Pauline was going nowhere, as she had found her true place and a love as valuable as breath itself. She could wait.

Eva Harris drew the sheet over the dead man's face. She couldn't manage to cry, because she felt dry all through, right into the marrow of her bones. Sam had been ill for nearly three years. A gentle and unassuming man, Sam Harris had allowed his wife her head, had never complained when she had left him to go out and minister to mothers and babies.

She turned from the bed and picked up a photograph from the dressing table. 'Eeh, Sam, I wish we'd had a kiddy. But it were too late for us.' A loyal and loving daughter, Eva had nursed her parents to the end of their lives and had only married in her early forties. 'You'd have been a smashing dad.' The man in the suit smiled back at her through a sheet of glass that wanted dusting. Who would value this picture once Eva had shuffled off to meet her Maker? No close relatives to speak of, no-one to worry or wonder about the couple in their silver-plated frame.

She walked down the stairs and set a blackened kettle to boil on the range. The doctor would have to be sent for. As far as the doctor was concerned, Eva's

Sam would be just another piece of paper that needed signing.

Then there was this National Health thing. In spite of Churchill's popularity as leader of a war-torn country, a Labour government was a possibility, and Labour would mean a Welfare State. Who would want a paid midwife when qualified doctors and suchlike were going to come free? Eva's mother had been a midwife, had taught Eva all she knew. No Sam, no job, no reasons to get up in a morning. What was Eva going to do with her remaining years? Oh, but she was going to miss him. Even when sick, he had made her laugh with his wry comments and mimicry. 'So you're dead and I'm a relic from the last century,' she mouthed.

Eva gazed around her rented home, the house in which she had been born, where she had nursed aged parents, where Sam had breathed his last not five minutes since. On the dresser, Mam's pot spaniels shared space with two ceramic cottages and a cluster of photographs of Eva's babies. Not everyone could afford photos, but there were at least two dozen framed portraits of features not yet completed, faces still to be visited by the lines of experience. Her babies. 'You are playing God.' Danny Walsh's remembered voice was strident, almost angry. 'Who's the real mother? What if she wants the baby back?'

A sampler made by Eva sat above the fireplace. She remembered stitching away at the thing for months on end, being forced to undo and redo, getting criticized for untidy knots when she finished off a thread on the reverse side of her work. She'd kept going, though. All the other girls had moved on to cookery aprons and cushion covers, but Eva had continued with letters, numbers, lazy-daisy-stitched flowers, cross-stitched border, her name in red at the top, 'EVA MALLINSON 1910'.

Seven years, she'd had with Sam Harris. For the first four, he had worked as a coalman, had brought in a wage to supplement Eva's modest income. Coal had eaten its way into the corner of an eye, had distorted his lower lid. That had been the visible part, the easy side of things. The real war had waged inside Sam's body, had laid him low for months on end. 'You'll suffer no more,' Eva told the ceiling. 'But I don't know how to carry on without you.' Black tar had lined Sam's lungs. For a couple of years, he had coughed up coal, then, too weak to splutter, he had choked on what miners had chosen to term the Black Death, their own particular brand of plague.

Eva brewed tea, set out two mugs, put one away. She didn't need to go running up the stairs with bits of rice pudding and tempting soups. She didn't need to listen from the foot of the stairs, her own breath held while Sam rasped his way towards release. No-one needed her any more. She was surplus to requirements, neither use nor ornament, just another piece of extra dross on the planet's war-scarred face.

Eva could not remember a time when she had not been an absolute necessity. Dad had died relatively quickly; but Mam, already bedridden when widowed, had lingered for years. Nursing was all Eva knew. She could cook a bit, sew a bit, though she hadn't improved greatly since producing the sampler. Babies had been her whole life.

Playing God? Had there been an alternative, had there been a real set of choices? A decision made in the twinkling of an eye, a torn newspaper, a scrap of blanket containing a scrap of life. Why was this so important now, so significant? She should have been running to a neighbour, sending for the doctor, washing Sam's body while it remained easy and warm.

Birth and death, beginnings and endings. Eva felt strangely peaceful, as if there would be few more challenges, certainly none to match the one she had faced this very day. The man she had loved was gone, as was her job. She was going on fifty years of age, and she was finished. The sin she had committed – had it been a sin? – was excusable. She could die now. She could put an end to it, leave the policies next to the pot dog on the dresser so that someone would find them and use the money for a double funeral. There were two at a wedding, so why not have a double burial? But Eva knew that she could never strike herself down, because she possessed no special strength, no particular weakness.

Yet there remained one thing, one task that she must complete before getting much older. That baby. Katherine Walsh, daughter of Bernard and Elizabeth, was not Katherine Walsh at all. Apart from Eva, no-one in the world knew the full story.

She sipped tea, tasted nothing, waited for her brain to kick itself into gear. Ever the practical one, Eva Harris didn't hold with whimsy. The feeling of unreality would pass soon, she reminded herself. After years spent delivering children, seeing them die, watching mothers fade away, she knew all about shock. Trauma often displayed itself as a terrible quietness, a placidity that could even finish off its victim. No, Eva would not kill herself. Eva would simply carry on getting work where she could, living cheaply, spending little. There was no easy way out for people like Eva, folk with consciences and a sense of commitment.

When her cup was emptied, Eva took a small enamel bowl and filled it with water. Strange how the tools of laying-out echoed so perfectly the tools of lying-in. Cotton wool, towels, a bar of soap. The only difference lay in shaving equipment, because Eva's husband would meet his Maker clean-faced and tidy, no shadow of beard, no straggle to his moustache.

As she washed Sam's limp form, she sent up a prayer to the Almighty, begging Him for strength and mercy. Sam wanted burying, so that was the first thing. Afterwards, the other business must be done, the action that Eva had postponed again and again for going on five years. There would be no immediate need to inform Liz, but Bernard must be told. Circumstances might well arise, occasions on which Eva's secret might explode of its own accord. Best to warn him, then. Forewarned was forearmed.

Bernard Walsh raised an arm and lifted a rabbit from the steel bar above his counter. He handed it to his sister-in-law, then turned to greet the next customer. It was poor little Eva Harris, newly widowed, dressed in black. Poor little Eva reached over and pointed to a pair of kippers. They weren't the same with margarine, but she'd have to manage. And anyway, the kippers were just an excuse, because she had far too much on her mind to care about food and suchlike.

'How did it go?' asked Bernard.

The tiny woman raised a shoulder. 'How do they all go? Prayers, a church filled with neighbours – even them I've never got on with turned up. I felt sorry for the gravediggers. It must have been like digging into iron with a teaspoon, the ground were that hard. Still, if the sun had come out, it wouldn't have made any difference. Sam's gone and that's the top and tail of it.'

Bernard wrapped the kippers. 'Sorry I couldn't get there.'

'That's all right. Life has to go on, as they say.'

She hadn't been crying. Bernard scoured the lived-in face, found no tear-tracks, no sign of emotion. But her eyes looked empty. Eva was a very mobile woman, always on the dash, forever talking and waving her arms about. Her eyes were usually all over the place, missing nothing, taking in all that happened around her. But today, she was . . . blank, like a page waiting to be written on. 'Are you all right?' he asked feebly.

Her mouth smiled, though the rest of her face remained sombre. 'I have to talk to you before it's too late.' Sam hadn't reached far past the fifty mark. What if Eva died tonight with a guilty secret to her credit?

Bernard's heart seemed to miss a beat. 'What about?'

Eva stared at him, said nothing.

'Important, is it?'

She nodded just once.

With fingers whose tremblings owed nothing to the weather, the fishmonger removed his apron, pulled on a jacket and a flat cap, then asked Pauline to hold the fort for ten minutes. Something momentous was about to take place – he felt that in his bones. Answers. Did he want them? The questions had been damped down, ignored, yet never completely forgotten.

He followed Eva into Ashburner Street and towards deserted stalls on the open market. He stopped walking when she stopped, placed his back against the corner of a stall, steadied himself and waited. It was a good job that the general market was closed, or this place would have been seething like an ant colony.

'You'll have to get out of Bolton,' she told him baldly. 'And I'm not messing, Bernard.'

'Eh?'

'If you hadn't moved up Bromley Cross way for the duration, there could have been blinking murder before now. The road things have turned out, we've been lucky this far. But we don't want no trouble starting up, lad.'

Bernard scratched his head, dislodging the cap and setting it further back on his large head. 'Trouble?'

'Spitting image,' mused Eva aloud. 'Identical, two for the price of one, both from the same egg. I always hoped they'd be the other kind of twins, them as looks nowt like one another.'

His heart pounded anew.

Eva sighed, raised her head to heaven for a brief second before continuing. 'When Liz had that stillbirth, I cried me eyes out. I knew how desperate she were to have a baby. Thank God she's had no more pregnancies, because the lass isn't built for breeding.' She paused, chewing her lower lip. 'Theresa Nolan passed out after Jessica were born. Right in the middle of a good, strong pain, she went absent without leave on me. I were stood there waiting for the afterbirth, and . . . Oh, God help me.'

Bernard closed his eyes against the truth, though his ears continued to function well enough to get Eva's drift. 'And Katherine came instead?'

Eva inhaled sharply. The emotional dam burst suddenly and poured down her face in twin tracks. 'I knew, you see. I knew she couldn't . . . I mean, one were enough . . . one were too many . . . her heart's not sound.'

Bernard opened his eyes, reached out and dragged the sobbing woman into his arms. He stank of fish, but he couldn't have cared less. His own tears fell into Eva's black felt hat, the one she kept specially for funerals. The smell of mothballs mingled with the tang of raw cod. She'd be needing a good bath tonight, would little Eva Harris.

She snatched herself away from him. 'It were just so quick. I shoved the second kiddy in the front room, wrapped her up in whatever was to hand – paper and a bit of blanket. When Theresa came round, I got a neighbour in and ran up to yours, said Liz were still in labour. Told lies, I did. It seemed so right at the time, so sensible.'

Bernard mopped at his face with a crumpled rag.

'No, that's not true,' said Eva. 'It weren't even a question of right or wrong or sensible – I just did it.'

'Automatic. You never even thought.'

'That's it. Sometimes, there's no chance of thinking and wondering what you're doing and why you're doing it. All I can say is that I must have acted from a place inside me.' She inhaled deeply, shuddering against a rising tide of sobs. 'They're identical, Bernard. Absolutely the same as one another. Like I said afore, I were hoping they'd be separate – you know, there's fraternals, twins as don't favour one another, even if they're both boys or both girls. But Jessica and Katherine are identical. Just imagine if they met in town, or if—'

'They're in the sanatorium, Theresa and Jessica.'

Eva shook her head. 'Not for ever. And don't tell me you'd never noticed. You must have seen it, must have looked at Jessica and wondered.'

Bernard rubbed at his chin. 'It's never registered. But now as you come to mention it, there is a resemblance.'

'Resemblance? Good God, man, are you blind? Do your specs want changing? Theresa keeps Jessica's hair short, but that's the only thing that comes to my mind. Same big blue eyes, just a shade or two difference in their hair colour. Stands to sense they'll meet some time if they're both in Bolton. My heart's been in my mouth whenever your Liz and Katherine have come visiting Pauline and Danny. It only needed for Theresa to walk into your shop . . .' She shook her head in dismay. 'Don't you be stopping on at Derby Street when the war finishes, lad. In fact, you'd be better piking off to Manchester or Bury.'

Manchester? Bury? Bernard was Bolton born and bred. 'But we've always been here. It's not easy, upping sticks and moving like that. Liz won't wear it.' He stared long and hard at Eva. 'I'm not telling her. She really believes Katherine's ours. I can't just march Liz off up Bury Road and tell her we're starting fresh, either. She's not stubborn, but she knows her mind. And I daren't push her near the edge again, Eva. You remember how she was when ours was born not breathing.'

Eva shook her head slowly. 'Aye, it's a bugger. But if you really want to keep Liz in the dark, you'd best put space between you and Theresa Nolan.' She pondered for a moment. 'Isn't she on the bright side, your Katherine?'

'She read at three, if that's what you mean.'

'Is she in front of all the rest at school?'

'Aye, she is.'

'Then she mun get catered for. You're not a poor man, Bernard Walsh. Send her to a gradely school, somewhere special. I reckon Liz'd move to Russia if she thought it were in the kiddy's interests. I don't know much about these public schools and suchlike, but—'

'She's not going boarding, Eva.'

'In that case, you'd best shift near to one of them there preparation schools, them that gets children ready for posh learning – French and all that kind of stuff they might just find a use for. Senior schools are usually nearby, so she wouldn't need to sleep at school if you played your cards right.'

Bernard scratched his head again, then pulled the cap over the chilled forehead. 'Where, though?'

'They've got them in Liverpool, I think,' said Eva.

'Liverpool? Who wants to move to bloody Liverpool?'

'You do,' snapped the small woman. 'For a kick-off, they eat a lot of fish, do Liverpudlians. Then there's Katherine's education and Liz's peace of mind. Not to mention your own, of course. Start sending for them brochures and tell Liz you want the best for that little girl.'

Bernard shuffled about on the spot, his weight shifting from one foot to the other while thoughts skittered about in his mind. Liverpool? Bernard knew Ashburner Street Market like the back of his own hand. He knew every fishmonger in Bolton, every stallholder, every porter down at the sidings. His mates at the market – Bob Hewitt, Ernie Kershaw, Les Pickering with a limp from the Great War and a sense of humour worth bottling. A pasty and a gill in the Wheatsheaf, a florin each way on a horse, bets taken behind the big weighing scales near the New Street end, somebody watching out for the bobbies.

'I know you'll be homesick,' sighed Eva.

'We will that.'

'But what's most important, Bernard? Katherine or stopping in Bolton?'

'Katherine.' He doted on his daughter. And she was his daughter, no matter who had fathered her in the merely physical sense.

'See, I got thinking when my Sam passed on.' Eva dabbed at her face with one of her dead husband's handkerchiefs. 'Life and death – it's all the same, like a circle, all part of whatever we're put here for. I couldn't leave things as they were. The truth's the truth. I had to pass it on before my turn comes.'

Bernard gazed at her. 'Are you ill?'

'No.'

He continued to stare hard at his companion. The small woman's world was falling apart, it seemed. 'All you need now is a Labour government, and that'd be you out on your ear. Would there be work for you?'

Eva raised a shoulder. 'I'll find summat,' she replied. 'Trust you to go worrying over somebody else. Too saintly for your own good, you are. Just you mind yourself and Liz and Katherine.'

Bernard waited until a group of clog-shod mill-workers had dashed homeward through the market. 'If there's anything I can do for you, please ask.'

'I will.' She would, too. Bernard and Danny Walsh were rare folk, because they didn't like to watch others suffering. 'You'll mind what I've said today, Bernard?'

'Yes.'

She turned away and sniffed the air. 'More snow, I shouldn't wonder.'

Bernard reached out and touched her arm. 'Eva? You know our Danny's set against letting Pauline visit Theresa and Jessica?'

She shook her head. 'That's news to me.'

He sighed, sending a plume of cloudy breath into the air. 'I reckon our Danny knows about the two girls being twins. Pauline was saying that he'd told her to stay away from the TB sanatorium. It's not germs he's worried about, is it?'

Eva clicked her tongue. 'Nay, lad, I wouldn't have a clue. Happen you'd best tell him anyway. Because he'll want to know why you're moving – if you do move.'

'There's not much choice, is there?' replied Bernard. 'I mean, we could stop up Bromley Cross, buy another house, but what if the girls met in town a few years from now?'

Eva's thoughts had travelled beyond Bernard's. 'There's more to it than that,' she said. 'A lot more. They're sisters. They were born to the same mam on the same day. When all's said and done, them two lasses have a right to be together.'

Bernard thought that his heart would stop.

'Now calm yourself,' chided Eva. 'I'm not going to start any wars, or I wouldn't have told you to get out of Bolton. What I'm saying is that eventually, when they're grown up, like, there might come a time for them to be told.'

He swallowed painfully.

'They're blood, Bernard. At the end of the day, they're as near to one another as they can be without being Siamese. Shared a womb, they did. Some folk say they hold hands, you know, touch one another's faces, play about and kick before they're even born. It's a God-given gift and—'

'Stop it, Eva.' Bernard found himself trembling again. 'Don't try to make me feel even more guilty, please.'

She pulled herself up to full height. 'I'm guilty, not you. I separated them, because I realized that Theresa Nolan could hardly manage one, let alone twins. Like I said before, I never even thought, not proper, like. You just need to know everything, Bernard. Knowing makes you more . . . It makes you fit for whatever happens.'

'I thought . . . I even hoped that the mother had died. Or that Katherine came from a family with a dozen children and not a pair of boots between them. It was easier to think along them lines, I suppose.'

She inclined her head. 'But it's not so easy now, eh?'

'No.'

Eva wondered why she had told this poor man the truth. Had she been trying to ease her own burden by passing half of it to him? None of this was Bernard Walsh's fault. He had seen his wife keening silently, inwardly, dangerously, for a dead child, had watched Liz crumbling, falling into that dark, formless place halfway between sanity and madness. 'I had to do this,' Eva told him. 'There's the chance of Theresa noticing, of others seeing how alike the kiddies are. The girls themselves might meet one day by accident. I had to tell you,' she repeated, as if underlining her decision would prove its correctness. 'As for the rest of it – them being twins – well, that's just my guilt talking.'

'Go home, love,' he said. 'You must be frozen.'

She touched his arm, then walked away.

Bernard perched on the edge of an empty stall's counter. Katherine had a sister. Little Jessica Nolan was Katherine's twin. This hadn't happened suddenly – the girls were five years old and they had always been related. But fear wrapped its tentacles around Bernard's heart because he had new knowledge. In this particular case, that knowledge decreased its owner's power. This was the famous exception which might prove the rule.

FIVE

The Merchants' Club Inn was an unprepossessing piece of architecture. It was flanked by education offices and a notorious public lavatory around which dark-clad men hovered in the hope of meeting fellow members of their often taunted minority.

Inside the tradesmen's club, members of a more acceptable society enjoyed the privileges accompanying stamped and paid-for membership cards. Travelling businessmen could buy a bed for the night, while Bolton traders were often to be found negotiating deals, entertaining prospective clients, or simply reaching a state of inebriation that allowed them to forget or ignore their various positions in life.

The interior of this exclusive club was not beautiful. Shoddy plasterwork and squeaking floorboards had been garnished in glory – wood panelling, red carpets, shiny-topped tables and maroon curtains. A small bar occupied one corner of the meeting room and, at the opposite end, dartboard and billiard table offered cheap recreation to anyone with a modicum of energy.

Three men hung over a table in the quiet room, each staring into his drink as if searching for a spiritual hand to reach out from within the soul of alcohol to offer guidance. Drooping shoulders and bowed heads made the group an ideal subject for any passing impressionist who might have cared to capture the essence of depression.

'What a bloody mess life is. I can't cope with this any more,' mumbled a pale-skinned, well-spoken man in a very decent suit. He was referring not only to Theresa Nolan, but also to other areas of his life. 'We must continue to pay, and to pay more. After what our sons did, there can be no question of neglecting the woman and her child.'

When the statement bore no fruit, George Hardman settled back and gazed once more into a pint of bitter beer. He had meant what he had just said. More than ever before, he pitied Theresa Nolan, but his own existence was about to alter so radically that he had little energy and little real interest in lives other than his own. Theresa was just one of many last straws heaped on his aching back. 'Things must change,' he added in a whisper.

Maurice Chorlton clicked his tongue. 'Yes, I suppose you have too much to lose by refusing to pay, as have I,' he advised George Hardman. Hardman's Hides, which had been in the family for almost a century, was a thriving business even now, before the cessation of hostilities. 'Once the war's over, you'll be back on your feet properly,' added the jeweller. 'And with young Ged to help you.' Roy, too, would be coming home. Roy Chorlton's interest in the art of jewellery manufacture was practically non-existent.

The third man, Alan Betteridge, chuckled softly. 'You'd think this were the bloody dark ages,' he told his companions. 'Who cares, eh? Our sons had their wicked way with a girl – so what? So bloody what? She can sod off. How would she manage in court, eh? If she sued, she'd be laughed at after all these years.'

'Morality, not legalities,' said George Hardman softly. 'Put up and shut up, that's my advice to you, Alan.'

Maurice sighed, inflating his rounded stomach until the buttons on his waistcoat all but screamed for mercy. He leaned forward, causing further stress to his clothing. 'There is yet another form of proof, Alan.' He still didn't care much for Alan Betteridge, was inclined to dislike a man so crude, so common. 'As well as Bernard Walsh's statement, that is. My son offered to marry the girl, remember? Years back, when the lads were still in training, he went to see her.'

'Daft sod, that one of yours,' spat Betteridge. 'No bloody guts and no sense.'

Maurice glared at the so-called fine furnisher of homes. 'And Eva Harris was a witness to that – well, she says she was. She was the one who told me about the stupid proposal. I felt like killing him, but you have to admit, there's no denying the truth now. Anyway, my business depends on good will. I can't have Bolton running off to Manchester for its wedding rings just because one of our lads fathered a bastard.' Once again, he singled out Alan Betteridge. 'And there's bigger fish than you in the cities, too.'

'Don't talk to me about fish,' snapped Betteridge. 'Them bloody Walshes are at the back of Eva Harris, you know.'

'Nobody's forced to buy their chairs and tables from you,' continued Maurice, 'I reckon there'll be all sorts of changes once the black-outs are over.

Folk'll want new stuff. They'll be chucking out all sorts just to be rid of all the junk they've sat amongst during air raids. You stand to make a fortune when Utility stops sticking its stamp on matchwood. So forget about the Walshes and the Nolans of this world. I say we pay up again. The Harris woman's on the warpath, because the Nolans are both in poor health up at the TB sanatorium.' He glanced now at the tanner. 'Well?'

George Hardman raised his hands in a gesture of hopelessness. 'Please yourselves,' he said. 'Because I won't be here for much longer.' He attempted a light shrug. 'It's nothing to do with the girl, or her child, or our sons. As I said before, everything must change.' He took a deep breath. 'I've had about as much as I can take. I intend to make my exit from the scene at the earliest opportunity.'

The other two stared closely at George Hardman. 'You what?' asked Alan Betteridge.

George let out a deep, heartfelt sigh. 'Look,' he said with exaggerated patience. 'For a start, there's Lily.' He pursed his lips, as if the sound of his wife's name had left a bitter taste in its wake.

'What about her?' asked Alan Betteridge.

'She's been at it again.'

Maurice Chorlton kept his composure, while Alan Betteridge leaned forward like a hungry animal expecting scraps from some medieval banquet.

George Hardman ran long, thin fingers through a thatch that had been grey for over twenty years. A tall, slender man, he carried himself with an elegance that had never visited the other two tradesmen. 'My head went white within twelve months of marrying Lillian,' he stated bluntly. 'I don't even know if Ged is my son.'

'Who's she messed with this time?' persisted Betteridge.

George Hardman cleared his throat. He had nothing to lose, he informed himself firmly. His wife was a tramp and the truth would come out eventually. 'Her *pièce de résistance*,' he announced, the words trimmed with damped-down anger, 'is our vicar.' He shook his head sadly. 'Man of God, shepherd of a parish, bringer of the word and an ugly beggar if ever I saw one.'

It was an unwritten rule at Merchants' that no-one ever laughed at George Hardman. His wife might be a nymphomaniac, while his son wasn't much to write home about, yet George Hardman stood head and shoulders above every man in the club. But Alan Betteridge, the balance of whose chair had slipped during recent moments, fell underneath the table, his laugh almost loud enough to shatter glassware.

Maurice Chorlton, unable to bear public embarrassment, was glad that the club was almost empty. He dragged the man off the floor, righted the chair and thrust the drunken Alan Betteridge back into his seat. 'Shut up,' he muttered.

Betteridge groaned with the pain of suppressed glee, then banged his head on the table rather sharply. Pictures of Lily Hardman and a man of the cloth played naughtily across his small, active mind. 'I'm all right now,' he announced through tears and sobs produced by near-hysteria. He was seeing stars, and Lily Hardman continued to dance behind lights produced by near-concussion. 'I'll have a bloody headache tomorrow,' he grumbled.

George Hardman appeared not to have noticed anything amiss. 'She started going to church a lot.

Good, I thought. Perhaps she's mending her ways, I thought. But she wasn't mending her ways. She was mending hymn books in the vestry while he looked at her.' He paused for a couple of seconds. 'Last summer, it was. Her sister called unexpectedly, so I went to fetch Lily from church.'

Alan Betteridge blinked twice, suspense etched into his features.

Maurice Chorlton slipped a hand into his pocket and brought forth a silver hip flask. Deftly, he poured whisky into a tumbler, then passed the drink to George.

The tanner drank, grimaced against the cheap Scotch, yet claimed a refill. When the second drink had disappeared, he continued. 'She was on a high stool in front of a pile of Books of Common Prayer, blouse undone to the waist. The reverend was behind her, left hand on her bosom and the right one attending to other business.'

'What did you do?' breathed Alan Betteridge.

'I battered the living daylights out of him.' George Hardman's voice remained steady. 'Then I . . . well . . . I suppose I clouted my own wife, gave her a couple of black eyes and a very thick ear. She had to stay in the house for ten days.'

'You hit her in front of the vicar?' asked Maurice Chorlton.

'Oh yes. Even if the bishop had turned up, I would have acted in the same disgusting way. I was so bloody furious.' He paused, nodding. 'You know, I even felt like raping her. I was suddenly a savage. Rape's nothing to do with sex,' he advised his companions. 'It's power. It's devaluing somebody's currency, lessening their worth. That's what our sons did to that young woman. It was a terrible crime, and

I should know, because I could easily have been as guilty as they are.'

'Nay,' said Betteridge. 'That were different. Lily's your wife. You would have been claiming your rights.'

George Hardman shook his head. 'No, that's not the case. I wanted to dirty her, make her less than human, make myself less than human.' He looked down at his hands, as if he expected to see filthy claws rather than well-manicured fingernails. 'She's hardly come out of her bedroom for the last six months. Not when I've been in the house, anyway. I don't like her. I could stay on at home without loving, but not without liking. So I've been shifting money, salting it away. When Ged gets back from the war, he'll be in charge of the tannery.' He smiled grimly. 'What's left of it. They deserve one another, Lily and Ged.'

Maurice swallowed. 'Where will you go?'

For the first time, George Hardman grinned properly. 'I'm running away with Emily Birchall,' he sighed blissfully. 'Her husband died early on in the war, some sort of stomach thing he picked up in barracks.'

'She's your secretary.' Maurice's tone was accusing. 'Yes.'

'And she's only about twenty-five,' continued the jeweller.

'Twenty-seven,' George said. 'A nice, gentle girl. There's been no funny business, mind, just a peck on the cheek now and then. I shall get divorced. My solicitor's holding enough evidence against Lily and the vicar. I don't reckon the reverend's chances of turning out to be Archbishop of Canterbury after this little lot.'

'Well, bugger me,' said Alan Betteridge.

George, in happier mood now that his intentions had been aired, managed a laugh. 'No, thanks.'

Maurice was thoughtful. 'So it'll be down to me and Alan, then. I take it you won't be sending money for the Nolans?'

'I might,' replied George. 'Depends, I suppose. But I will keep in touch.'

Troubled glances passed between Maurice and Alan. George Hardman, richer than the two of them put together, was going to clear off. 'When do you go?' asked Maurice.

'When I've spoken face-to-face with Ged and his mother. There'll still be a tannery for them to run, but they must start from as near to scratch as I dare leave them.'

The jeweller groaned. 'We'll all suffer, man,' he exclaimed. 'You employ a fair number in this town. Who's going to want brooches and beds if they've no jobs?'

George nodded benignly. 'That's your problem, not mine. I don't mean to sound so callous, but my marriage has been hell on earth, so I'm saving my own skin this time instead of worrying about cow-hide.' He nodded. 'There's no need for the captain to go down with the ship.' He blinked rapidly, realized that he was drunk and muttering what almost amounted to gibberish. 'Emily and I will be climbing into a lifeboat,' he concluded, the words colliding with each other as they fell from his lips.

'You're scuttling the bloody ship, you are.' Alan Betteridge, whose wife had cleared off years earlier with the insurance man, quietened after a few seconds, becoming almost pensive. 'Oh, do what you must,' he added softly. 'You wonder where you went wrong, don't you?'

Maurice Chorlton kept his counsel. A widower, he saw himself as clean where marital matters were concerned. George Hardman had married a sex-crazed witch, while Alan Betteridge's wife, tired of being a punchbag for her inebriate partner, had absconded in the company of a nice, quiet, bespectacled chap with bicycle clips and an insurance round.

George cleared his throat. 'I went wrong the minute I bought three diamonds on a twist from you, Maurice. As soon as Lily got that ring on, she started having ideas. I mean, you both remember my dad, solid as a rock, no airs and graces. But the top of Deane Road wasn't good enough for Lily. Oh no, we had to buy The Villa, five bedrooms, conservatory, big gardens, then a couple of servants living in the roof space. I must have stripped the skins off a thousand animals just to pay for the curtains.'

Maurice sighed. 'You've to forgive and forget, George. That's what marriage is all about—'

'Forgive and for-bloody-get?' roared the tanner, the veins across his temples throbbing in the heat of anger and drunkenness. 'I found her with the gardener when she was six months gone with our Ged! She's . . . there's something wrong with her.'

Maurice smiled reassuringly at the bartender and a small clutch of greengrocers three tables away. 'Keep your voice down,' he muttered.

George gripped the edge of the table. 'I'm going,' he said, quieter now. 'Once the troops are home and the ink's dry on Churchill's bits of paper, I'm taking Emily abroad, somewhere nice and warm. There'll be no more work for either of us.' He blinked against a temporary doubt. Life without work could well turn out to be fish without chips, a cart with no horse. 'We might buy a little café or something,' he added lamely. 'Just to keep us out of mischief.'

The jeweller closed his eyes and leaned back against a mahogany panel. Ged Hardman couldn't run a bath, let alone a tannery. Like Maurice Chorlton's own son, the tanner's boy was not particularly interested in his family's business. 'I can't see Roy knowing a Ceylon sapphire from a blue topaz. As for your Ged, the stench at Hardman's will make him fetch up last night's beer.'

The furnisher shrugged. 'Aye, and our Teddy's not what you might call a gift from heaven. The last time I left him in charge, he sold a chest of drawers for next to nothing, got the prices mixed up. And he scratched a good dining table. Inlaid, it was. Octagonal.' Alan was fed up. Utility had marked his card, had shifted him into the second-hand market. 'We've no support from our sons, none of us,' he moaned.

George Hardman stood up. 'I'm off now,' he said. Back to that house, back to a silence punctuated only by the chiming of clocks and the mewing of Lily's Persians. Lily's Persians were flaming nuisances. They dropped hair, shredded upholstery, clawed at clothing. 'No use sitting here,' he told his companions. 'Get up, get out and get a life worth living.'

Maurice Chorlton didn't want any changes. He loved gems and precious metals, could not wait for the war to end. 'We'll miss you,' he told the owner of Hardman's Hides. 'But Alan and I are set in our ways.' Without George, Maurice would be stuck with Alan Betteridge, welded to him by the sins of their sons. George Hardman had a bit of class, but the furniture salesman was crude, vulgar and alarmingly uninhibited.

In a rare moment of empathy, Alan Betteridge rose and shook George Hardman's hand. 'I'll be sorry to see you leave Bolton,' he said. 'You've been a good mate to me and Mo.'

'Mo' shivered. Maurice was not the name he might have chosen for himself, but Mo was dreadful.

'As I said before, I'll keep in touch.' He extracted his fingers from Alan's vice-like grip, then directed a few words at the seated jeweller. 'I'll leave something in an account for the Nolans. Talk to my solicitor when things get hot, let him do the sorting out.'

Left alone with Alan Betteridge, Maurice drew a hand across his forehead as if smoothing the path for a headache borrowed from his companion. 'What on earth will Lily Hardman do with a tannery?' he mused aloud.

Betteridge shrugged. 'There's some big lads working in yon factory. She'll have plenty to keep her busy, I daresay.'

Maurice shuddered. With George Hardman, there had been decent conversation; with Alan, there was little more than utter tomfoolery. 'Do you ever take anything seriously?' asked the jeweller now.

Betteridge considered the question. 'Money, I take that serious, I dare say. And Hilda going off to live in a slum with that stupid bugger was a bit of a sobering experience.'

'Yet you carry on acting the goat.'

Alan stared hard at his companion. 'What's the alternative? Finish up a picture of misery like you? They call you Maurice the Mole, you know, and—'

'Yes, I'm aware of that.'

'Because you're so . . .' Greasy wouldn't do. Oily would be far too unkind. 'Well, the way you treat folk, crawling halfway up their backsides so's they'll buy a dearer watch.'

'That's called salesmanship, Alan.'

'Where I come from, it's called arse-kissing.'

'It works.'

Alan lit a Pasha, coughing as he exhaled the pungent, harsh tobacco. 'Then all that Methodism lark . . . I mean, what do you want to be joining the Holy Joes for? Stood up there every Sunday in your black suit, listening to folk going on about drinking and smoking. I went to school, you know. I were taught about loving thy bloody neighbour. If you're a true Christian, I'll eat my next delivery of bedroom suites. Religion's about more than church, lad. See, I'm no hypocrite. I know I'm in business for the money and not to help worthy causes.'

Maurice felt the heat in his face. 'Are you calling me a hypocrite?'

'Please yourself,' came the swift response. 'Wear the bloody cap if it fits. You've stuff stashed on Deansgate as'd keep a family in food for donkey's years. Can't you be honest? What's wrong with being a clever so-and-so? Only don't go bleating to Jesus on a Sunday, because the rest of the week you're as near a copy to Scrooge as anybody could imagine.'

Maurice suddenly sensed a weakness in his knees, was glad that he was seated. How could a man as low as this one cause Maurice Chorlton to feel . . . confused? Maurice had always managed to keep his mind clear and sure, had been convinced of the correctness of his lifestyle. God was for Sundays and business was what happened for the other six days.

'I'm sorry,' mumbled Alan Betteridge.

The jeweller blinked.

'I mean, I shouldn't be criticizing and . . .' His voice faded to nothing.

'Why are we doing it?' Maurice asked.

'Eh?'

'Working. Saving. For what?'

Alan placed the Turkish cigarette in an ashtray, allowed the tasteless thing to cremate its own remains. 'For our sons?' he pondered. 'For posterity?'

Maurice shook his head. 'Let's be honest for once. Is your Teddy going to make a success of Betteridge's Fine Furnishings? Is my son interested in the manufacture of jewellery?'

The furniture salesman leaned back in his seat. 'Our Teddy wants a bellyful of ale every night and a woman on Fridays, specially one as won't make any trouble, won't want a wedding ring in exchange for favours, like.'

'While Roy thinks he's a cut above the rest of them.'

Alan bit back the opinion that Roy had taken after his father.

'We do the job because it's there,' said Maurice. 'Because we've got into the habit, because we've lived through two wars and a depression.' He looked at his companion. 'Too late to change, Alan. We are formed and we can't alter our ways.'

'Aye, you could be right there.' Alan wished he'd never started this particular conversation. Things were getting a bit philosophical, and he wasn't quite up to putting the world right after three pints and two shorts.

'I can't help it,' continued Maurice Chorlton. 'I see a nice bit of silver and I have to have it. You see a brass bedstead at a clearing-out sale and you grab it, clean it up and sell it.'

'But I don't go mee-mawing in a pew every flaming Sunday.'

'Well, I do,' replied Maurice heatedly. 'And I can't see why that makes me any worse than you. Perhaps I am a hypocrite, but I try to make my peace with God, at least.'

'Waste of time,' declared Alan before standing up. 'Fancy another?'

'No,' answered Maurice. He was tired. He was going home.

The sanatorium was a weird place. Although there were plenty of patients, the Nolans' section felt empty, like a huge cave divided into smaller sections inside which animals nested silently, each scrap of life curled into its proper niche. Corridors were wide, broad enough to take a tram, while the cells flanking these thoroughfares tended to be small, naked and very white.

Perched loftily on a moor and purpose-built for the sufferers of tuberculosis, the main body of Williamson's was a large, single-storeyed structure. It was a plain, no-nonsense piece of architecture, soulless, almost sad in its isolation from places built to house mankind's sounder members.

On arrival, most residents were placed in single rooms while the severity of their ailment was assessed. Jessica had been allowed to stay with her mother, because Jessica had screamed blue murder until permission had been granted. But Mam slept a lot. Jessica, bored almost to tears after a couple of days, took to sneaking along corridors to investigate other occupants of Williamson's, especially those at the other end of the building, lucky people with company, jigsaws and newspapers.

Those in solitary confinement tended to be quite poorly, so they weren't up to much. But others, on the way to recovery, were in larger, four-bedded wards, some with a wireless, some with gramophones and records that could be played from two o'clock until three each afternoon. When music spilled through doorways, it got tangled up like runaway balls of wool in a variety of colours. Vera Lynn competed with Bing Crosby, Richard Tauber tried to fight his tenor-pitched way past Glenn Miller and George Formby.

Jessica liked George Formby. He played something called a ukulele and he seemed to laugh in the middle of his songs. Glenn Miller was just tunes, though the band sometimes shouted out the name of a town and a long number. The men in Room Fourteen of the shared section joined in with the town and the number, and they sounded quite happy and jolly while the music played.

The rest of the time was tedious. Meals were huge. Jessica was expected to put away porridge, bacon, eggs and toast every morning, though she had made an arrangement with some mallards in the grounds. These ducks, gleaming with health and loud of voice, quacked near the Nolans' iron-railed ground-level balcony at seven-thirty every morning, retreating only after Jessica had deposited half her breakfast on the lawn. Similar tactics were employed at lunch, afternoon tea and supper, with the result that Jessica and the birds became reasonably content with regard to mealtimes.

Theresa was not always forced to eat. She managed a few crumbs from time to time, a mere forkful of mash and a bit of gravy, but no-one pressed her. Jessica, alert, young and not as ill as most, had to show clean plates after every meal, so her gratitude to the visiting waterfowl knew no bounds.

The room occupied by the Nolans was very tiny, made smaller by Jessica's bed. Really, Theresa Nolan should have been the sole occupant of Room Two (Single), but Jessica needed to keep a weather eye on Mam. Mam could not be trusted to look after herself, and Jessica placed little faith in nurses. They popped in occasionally, sometimes with food, sometimes in the wake of a doctor with a flapping white coat, red cheeks and a rather jolly Father Christmas-like nose. The men in Room Fourteen (Shared) were always joking about Dr Blake and his fondness for drink, so Jessica decided not to place a lot of faith in him. According to Mam, alcohol was the cause of most of the world's crimes.

While Theresa slept her way towards a hoped-for recovery, the child found herself wandering further afield with each passing day, even daring to venture into some of the wards at the opposite side of the building. Everyone was always glad to see her. As the only child in the sanatorium, she was thoroughly spoilt with fruit, chocolate and sticky sweets, most of which she ate, some of which she saved for Mam. Mam would get better soon. Mam would take Jessica home and they could start all over again in 34, Emblem Street, all cosy and warm in their own little house.

Warmth was becoming a distant memory. Jessica remembered how she had objected to the heat in the hospital, how she had declared time after time that she intended to emigrate and live with penguins. Was there no happy medium? Couldn't a person be just right, neither too warm nor too cold?

It was the windows that caused the trouble. Each room had three walls, then sliding windows in the fourth. These were locked in the open position before breakfast and left wide all day so that the TB germs could be blown away over the railings of the wrap-around porch and up into the hills where they could do no harm.

After a week or so of duck-feeding and sneaking round in corridors, Jessica noticed smoke rising from behind a clump of trees. Where there was smoke, there was fire and, where there was fire, there was probably a house. She stared for ages at the rising plume, watching as it climbed upward into an icy blue sky. She looked at Mam, made sure that her breathing was even and quiet, then slipped along deserted passageways towards the Shared section. Sneaking was getting easier, even though footsteps often echoed. According to those in Room Fourteen, nurses kept as far away from patients as was possible. They were scared of TB and were working here simply because the food was good and plentiful.

Mr Coates was in a good mood, as usual. 'Me little ray of sunshine,' he declared.

'Sunshine?' laughed Jessica. She was entombed in clothes, dressing gown buttoned to the throat, woollen bonnet, gloves, boots. 'I'm freezing.' She placed herself in a visitors' chair. Mr Coates looked very comical, scarf tied round his head, flat cap on top of the scarf, gloved hands struggling to turn the pages of a book. 'Is there a house in the trees?' she asked.

'Oh aye,' he replied. 'That's the farmhouse. That's where we all live for a while when we're nearly ready to go home. There's cows and hens, even a few pigs. We get our strength back working the land. Farmer Williamson left the house and the land, you see. His wife died of consumption.'

Jessica stared hard at the old man. 'Consumption?'

'TB,' he explained.

Panic hit the little girl's chest like a hammer. 'Will Mam die?' she asked, her voice squeaky and high.

'Nay, lass.' He laid down his book and pointed to the other three men. 'We've all been like your mam, love. Old Humphries there stopped breathing three times and he's still with us.'

Old Humphries awarded the visitor a gummy smile. 'You'd not be here if there were no hope, sweetheart,' he wheezed. 'They don't put you in Willy's unless you've got a good chance. The no-hopers go to Manchester. So stop fretting.'

Jessica wanted to go to the farmhouse. Inside, there would be a roaring fire with cats spread out on the hearthrug. Bread would be rising in rows of enamel bowls, and shelves would be covered in preserves bottled in syrup. 'Will me and Mam go in the house?' she asked.

Mr Coates scratched his chin, making a sound like sandpaper as the woollen glove caught against stubbly whiskers. 'In time,' he replied eventually. 'They have to be sure that her sputum's negative and that the X-rays look all right. From what I've heard, you're not too bad, love.'

'Oh.' Sputum. It was horrible, really nasty. Twice a day, she was required to clear her throat and spit into a lidded mug. Often, she didn't have any spit, so there would be nothing for the nurses to analyse. Mam got her throat poked into every morning, which unwelcome intrusion sometimes caused retching. No wonder, thought Jessica. If some daft woman had to go rooting around with metal prongs and cotton wool, a person had the right to be sick. 'It'll be a long time before Mam gets well enough for the farm,' she said sadly. 'She's always asleep.'

'Come on, Jess,' chided Mr Coates. 'I was like that for a while. With TB, there's no way of knowing. Folk have come in here at death's door, then, six months later, they've been back at work and back with their families.'

'Six months?' Jessica knew that her eyes were rounded in surprise. She was just turning five. In six months, she'd be nearly five and a half. She could not hang around in this terrible place for . . . 'How many weeks is six months?' she asked.

'Twenty-six,' came the shocking reply.

Jessica gulped. 'Days?'

Mr Coates did a bit of mental arithmetic. 'A hundred and eighty-odd,' he said.

'I can't stop here all that long,' she cried. 'It's been ages already. I'm sick of creeping about in case anybody catches me. And Dr Blake says I've not got bad TB.'

'Then you'll go home soon.'

The child bit her lower lip. 'Mam's my home,' she whispered.

'No dad?' asked Mr Coates.

She shook her head. 'Not even at the war. I never had one.'

'Grandma?'

'No.' Jessica inhaled deeply. 'She's dead and my grandad doesn't want me. There's an Auntie Ruth in Grandad's house, and she doesn't want me, too.' She let the air out slowly, noticed that it made a little cloud in the ice-cold ward.

Jimmy Coates lowered his head. What was the world coming to? Lovely kiddy like this, no father, nobody to step in while her mother was ill.

'Are you all right?' asked Jessica. He looked ready to cry. She couldn't remember seeing a man in tears.

'Aye,' he replied gruffly. He lifted his face and made it smile. 'Who were that woman you were going on about?'

'Auntie Eva? She's not my real auntie, Mr Coates. She . . . she borned me in our house. She visits us sometimes when we're at home, about once a week, I think.'

'Do you know where she lives? The street and the number?'

Jessica nodded.

Jimmy Coates swung his legs over the side of the bed. He was wearing proper trousers, socks and a massive grey cardigan. 'Kill us with bloody double pneumonia, they will.' He walked across the room. 'Give us an envelope,' he demanded of Mr Humphries. 'And a sheet of paper.' If nobody else cared a toss about the future of Jessica Nolan, he, James Edward Coates, most certainly did.

Eva's eyes limped over the address, worked their troubled way across the spidery, uneducated hand. She hadn't been able to visit Theresa and Jessica because they were in isolation. If they could be moved into a recovery ward, visitors would be allowed. This letter was from a patient in recovery.

It was no use. Eva rattled about in a dresser drawer until she found Sam's reading specs. Even dead, the man remained useful, since Eva's sight was not as good as it might have been. 'Dear Mrs Harris,' she read.

My name is James Edward Coates and I have been stuck up here at Willie's for going on eight month. A little lass called Jessica is here with her mam. Jess is the only kiddy in the san, so she is right fed up what with having no visitors and not much to keep her amused.

Her mother is still not taking much notice of anything because one of her lungs is very weak. There's some treatment now that can shut down a lung to make it rest, so happen the doctors are thinking about that. We don't know what goes on really, because nobody ever says much. They just come in with food and they do bed baths if you're not well enough to get yourself clean, but they always wear masks except for Doc Blake. Doc Blake is often as not three parts cut, so he's the only one who comes in bare-faced. There's no point talking to him. He goes on about us all getting better and not worrying about anybody else, so we keep our gobs shut.

Anyroad, little Jess is a right gem and she visits us nearly every day. She's not supposed to, so don't go telling on her. The thing is, we can have visitors. Visiting is every afternoon from one till five for us that's on the mend. I don't get anybody coming to see me because my wife is dead and my son is still abroad. He's missing believed dead.

Eva suspected that there had been a pause after that last sentence, as if the man had done a bit of grieving before continuing his letter in a different colour of ink.

The next paragraph had been written more carefully, slightly more clearly, probably a day or so later than the rest.

> I hope you don't take offence, but I'm sure young Jess would like to see you. If you would kindly visit me in Room Fourteen (Shared), I'm sure that Jess would be delighted.
>
> Yours faithful,
> Jimmy Coates

She would go to visit Mr Coates. He sounded a nice man, seemed to care about what happened to poor little Jessica Nolan. The other child, Jessica's twin, was still ensconced in Bromley Cross with Bernard and Liz Walsh. Bernard had been looking at North Liverpool, was hoping to put Katherine into a prep school in Crosby once the war had ended. Liz wasn't taken with the idea of moving, but Eva had pleaded with Bernard to stick to his guns. Those two girls needed separating or putting together immediately; there could be no half-measures. For Liz Walsh's sake, for everyone's sake, a move seemed by far the best solution.

She drained her cup and fixed her eyes on Sam's image. 'You're best out of it, lad,' she advised him. 'This world isn't really fit for decent folk.' But, all the same, decent folk remained and, in a day or so, Eva would be visiting a couple of that number.

'Eeh, you do look bonny.' Eva clung to the sobbing child and gazed over Jessica's head into the sad eyes of Jimmy Coates. 'Doesn't she look well?' she asked the man.

'Aye, she gets nearly as much dinner as the ducks,' he chuckled. 'She gives more nor half her food to the birds. She'll stop scriking in a minute – she never creates for long.'

Jessica buried her face in the visitor's coat. This was the first human contact she had experienced for weeks, because pokings and proddings didn't count. Mam had started to talk at last, but she still wasn't well enough for playing or story-telling. Mrs Harris seemed to smell of home, too, her clothing a bit smoky, as if the scents of Bolton had soaked into the fibres.

'Come on, lass,' pleaded Eva. 'If I'm upsetting you, I might just as well have stopped at home.'

Jessica raised her face. 'Take me with you,' she begged.

'What? And leave your mam all on her own?'

The child dried her tears. Things had changed; she was confused and weary. Mam hadn't been the same since she'd fallen asleep in the bedroom. It could be ages and ages before Mam got right. Jessica knew that Mam was ill, much iller than Jessica herself. Although the idea seemed treacherous, even traitorous, Jessica wanted to get out of the sanatorium, even if that meant leaving Mam behind. 'I can't stop here till Mam gets well,' she said.

'You've got TB and all,' Jimmy Coates reminded the child. He heard a distant footfall. 'Quick, Jess,' he whispered.

Like the professional trickster she had become, the little girl dived into a cupboard. When Jimmy Coates whistled the all-clear, she opened the door and ran back to Eva. 'Take me to your house,' she begged.

Eva struggled with her own emotions. Determinedly, she inhaled before speaking. 'I'll talk to that doctor,' she promised.

'If he's sober,' muttered another occupant of the room.

'I'll ask if he has any idea when you'll be better. Then, when I find a few things out, I'll get the doctor to talk to your mam. See, we have to get you right first, love. And, like you say, you'll happen be on the mend before Theresa is. We might be able to get you out then, when your TB's cleared up.'

Jessica calmed down and released her hold on the visitor. Eva pulled a chair over to Jimmy's bedside and gave him the once-over. He was a bit on the thin side, but he had roses in his cheeks. 'You must get cold living like this.' She jerked a thumb at the missing wall. 'What happens if it rains?'

Jimmy grinned. 'We put sou'westers on and borrow brollies if the wind's in our direction. Good job old Humphries did his life-saving badge at the swimming baths. He's had to swim us out of here a couple of times, no lifeboats, no Mae Wests.'

He was a character, Eva decided. 'Where do you live?'

Jimmy shrugged. 'This bed's me only address. The house got rented out to somebody else. One of the neighbours grabbed me bits and pieces, sold the furniture for me and kept . . . well, papers, photos and all that. Brandon Street, it was.'

'So what happens when you get out?'

He shrugged.

'What's your job?'

She asked a lot of questions, he thought. 'I'm a time-served carpenter. I can easy get work, but not till these buggers let me out. Mind, I'm definitely on the mend.'

Eva pondered. She wasn't one for quick decisions, but she recognized a sad man when she saw one.

Jimmy Coates made people laugh on purpose, because he was crying inside. He was a decent man with nothing to aim for, no reason to get better. 'I've a spare room,' she said casually. 'Me husband died not long since and the house seems empty, you know.'

Jimmy swallowed painfully. 'I know, all right.' He couldn't believe his ears or his luck. 'I'm fully house-trained, clean in me habits,' he said.

'Get well first. While you're getting better, think about my offer, Mr Coates.' Had she finally gone mad? He could be a murderer or a thief. But no. Nobody with those gentle grey eyes could be bad. 'You know my name and address.'

'Aye.' He nodded vigorously. 'And I shan't forget, neither, Mrs Harris.'

'Eva'll do.'

'Right, Eva.' He felt a million times better, was sure that he could take on the world at that moment. There was hope. There was a name, an address, a future.

Jessica's goodbye to Mrs Harris was restrained. If she carried on weeping, nobody would want her. She had to be good, had to look cheerful and sensible.

Eva wandered the corridors of Williamson's, redirecting herself only when a notice informed her to go no further. 'CONTAMINATED AREA, STAFF ONLY,' screamed the message in capitals over a door.

Eva knew in her bones that Jessica was not ill enough to warrant solitary confinement. She should not be cooped up, should not be bored stiff while sitting and waiting for Theresa to improve. The staff probably allowed the child to stay with her mam because she had already been exposed to Theresa's germs for long enough.

Impatient now, Eva swivelled on her heels and searched anew, finally locating a staffroom where two nurses sat reading, one smoking a cigarette, the other gnawing at an apple. 'Excuse me.' Eva entered the room. 'I wanted to ask somebody about little Jessica Nolan.'

The younger nurse leapt to her feet. 'Is she on the prowl again? We keep telling her, but she—'

'No, she's not on the prowl,' replied Eva smartly. She closed the door and placed herself squarely in front of it, eyeing the nurses up and down for a second or two. 'It just so happens that I brought Jessica Nolan into this world. I also just happen to know a Mr James Coates – I came to offer him lodgings when he gets out of here. Killing two birds with one stone, you might say, though I hope they stay alive, both of them. All three, if you count Theresa.'

The older nurse crushed her cigarette end in a saucer. 'Mrs Nolan's not well,' she began.

'I know. She had rheumatic fever as a kiddy and she's never caught up with herself. Is it both lungs?'

'She needs a lot of rest,' continued the nurse. 'She'll still be here in twelve months, I dare say.'

'And the child?' asked Eva.

'Six months at the outside. She's in good general health, so we might move her to a shared ward once she gets used to leaving her mother at night. We've not been able to persuade her yet.'

Eva kept her counsel. If these two were anything to go by, the place might well go up in flames. She bit back a few words about how they should have tried to get to know Jessica, how they ought to have been looking after folk and cheering them up. There was more to nursing than just the medical side – a lot more. 'She's a grand little lass,' she said eventually. 'And her mother will let her come and stay with me once she's better.'

'Right.' The older woman looked at the upside-down watch on her apron. 'Time to do our rounds,' she said.

Eva, having satisfied herself with regard to Jessica's longer-term prospects, left the staffroom and stood for a while in the deserted corridor. What a devil of a place this was. Jessica must leave here as soon as possible, because even the walls seemed to be soaked in misery, a shade of palest sepia that looked like an onset of jaundice.

'Hello?'

She swivelled to find an open-faced man standing just behind her. He must have been creeping about on soft-soled shoes, since Eva's hearing was almost perfect. 'Who are you?' She knew he was a doctor, because he was wearing a coffee- or gravy-splashed white coat, while the statutory stethoscope dangled round his neck.

'Blake,' he said.

'Dr Blake?'

'That's right. I'm in charge here, for my sins.'

He wasn't young, wasn't old, wasn't up to much in the looks department. A good scrubbing would have done no harm, in Eva's opinion, and a new razor blade was called for, too. 'How long will you be keeping young Jessica Nolan in this God-forsaken place?' she asked.

The doctor smiled, displaying a collection of white, slightly uneven teeth.

'Well?' asked Eva. He seemed a genuine enough bloke, though a tracery of veins betrayed a fondness for the bottle.

'She's clear, more or less,' replied Dr Blake. 'In fact, the exposure to her mother has probably given her an excellent level of immunity against TB. We're just making sure, playing on the safe side. After all, we don't want her going home ill, do we?'

Eva decided that she liked him in spite of his appearance. If his skin was anything to go by, there'd be little of his liver left in ten years. But he cared about the kiddy, she could hear that in his voice. 'Tell her mam that Eva Harris visited, will you? Tell her I'll have Jessica whenever the time comes. All right?'

He smiled again. 'Splendid,' he said before dashing off towards the wards.

Eva shook her head slowly, thoughtfully. He shouldn't be drinking, not after all that education. Ah well. Life was a bugger, and no mistake.

SIX

Katherine Walsh was ready for school. Her dad had gone to work, while Mam was fussing and messing about with Katherine's plaits. Mam always did a little braid at each side of the central parting, working these smaller sections in with the rest of the darkish blonde mass and making two thick, beribboned ropes which hung down the child's maroon jumper.

'We don't want you having nits,' declared Liz. 'And remember, they moved you up early from nursery to infants because you're clever. Clever people work hard and do well for themselves. There's more than a dozen lady doctors in town now. In my day, you'd have had a hard time finding a woman doing anything important.' She spun her daughter round and fixed a couple of hair slides at the beginning of the smaller plaits. 'Don't let yourself down and don't sit next to any dirty children.'

Katherine sighed. There were no dirty children in Bromley Cross. Some wore poor clothing, but noone came to school filthy. 'Mam?'

'Yes, love?'

'Can I have a sister?'

Liz gulped hard. Her insides were wrong. She had been into hospital for a big operation, a procedure which invariably made pregnancy an absolute impossibility. Bernard had stayed off work for three whole weeks, had been heartbroken by his wife's pain and disappointment and by his own distress. 'I don't know,' she answered at last.

'Other girls have sisters.'

'Yes, yes. Now, you mustn't be late and—'

'Jean Morris has four sisters.'

'Did you find a clean hanky?'

'Yes. I just feel as if I should have a sister. There's other children at St Aiden's with no brothers or sisters, and they don't seem bothered. But I'm different and I know I should have a sister.' Had it come out right? How could Katherine persuade – no, convince her mother that she felt like . . . like half of something, as if she had been left unfinished.

Liz crammed a woollen bonnet onto her daughter's head. She would have given anything for another baby, anything except Katherine herself. 'We don't always get what we want in this life,' she muttered. 'Put your gloves on.'

'It's nice out,' moaned Katherine. 'It's springtime.'

'Do as you're told.'

'Yes, Mam.' She pulled on the red mittens. 'Where do they come from? Babies, I mean. Jean Morris says her mother grows her own in her belly.' The idea of a sister had always been there. Katherine could not remember a time when she had not needed, even expected a female sibling. 'How do we get a baby?' she persisted. 'What do we have to do?'

Liz didn't hold with this sort of talk, not for a child of Katherine's tender years. Yet something wanted saying, something that would stop the mithering. 'Jean Wotsername's right,' she conceded. 'Babies grow inside their mothers.' She knew the next question, was waiting for it.

'Can't you make a sister for me?'

Liz looked at herself in the overmantel mirror, saw a face thinner than the one she remembered. The brown hair remained vital, but dark smudges had appeared beneath eyes described by Bernard as milk chocolate. The lips were narrower, as if life had disappointed them and caused them to draw inward. 'I can't, love,' she whispered.

'Why? You growed me.'

'Grew, Katherine. I grew you.'

'So why can't we have a sister?'

Liz sighed, remembered how she had fought against the doctors' decision. The general practitioner had referred her to a specialist, then the specialist had decided to remove Liz's womb because there was a growth in it. She had been bleeding profusely and irregularly, had suffered great discomfort until the operation had removed all symptoms and all hope.

'Mam?'

She had screamed and shouted all the way down to theatre, had become silent only when anaesthetized.

'Can you grow a brother, then?' At a pinch, a boy might have done. Lads were terrible pests, but a brother might have been better than . . . than this emptiness. 'Mam?' Katherine's voice raised itself. 'Can you hear me?'

'Yes, sweetheart.' She was useless now. Bernard should have married someone else, a woman who might have provided him with an heir. He was a strong man, a man capable of fathering many children. Yet he seemed so happy, so content with just

Katherine. No. It wasn't a case of 'just Katherine'. Katherine was everything to her daddy, but . . . but oh, he must have had some regrets, must have wondered about a son. All men wanted sons. 'It's quarter to nine, love. Come on, let's be getting you along the road.' Determined to endure no further upsetting nonsense, Liz dragged her daughter out of the cottage and along Darwen Road.

As she watched her only child dashing off towards the infants' cloakroom, Liz wiped a tear from her eye. She stood uncertainly outside the railings, a few drops of rain wetting her cheeks. March was going out like a lamb, was drifting prettily towards April, just a gentle breeze, a tiny shower, daffodil buds shaking themselves into wakefulness. Even the tulips, slower than their golden-trumpeted fellows, were starting to pierce the soil like rows of soldiers carrying green bayonets.

She stepped back from the school wall and continued up the moor to Brook Farm. Brook Farm would offer no real sister-substitute for Katherine, but perhaps an alternative might be found, a scrap of warmth for the little girl to nurture and love. Anyway, every child should have a pet, Liz reminded herself as she reached the wooden gateway. The notice was still there, dampened by rain, but readable, 'GOLDEN RETRIEVER PUPPIES FOR SALE'. Liz Walsh rubbed a mixture of spring rain and raw emotion from her face. A dog would help, she told herself.

Jessica had not been allowed to go into the house. Williamson's Farmhouse was for adults who needed what Dr Blake termed minimal supervision. Jessica glared at him across his desk. His hair was all over the place again, and he had spilled two dribbles of brownish liquid down the white coat. Dr Blake had no-one to look after him. He lived in a small room near the main entrance of Williamson's, and he ate his dinners here, in the office. Well, he ate most of his dinners. Quite a lot of food finished up on his clothes, bits of gravy, spots of yolk, streaks of tea and coffee. 'Why haven't you got your own house to live in?' she surprised herself by asking. He should wear a bib when eating, she decided. Or one of those cloth napkins tucked into the shirt collar.

'I'm from London.'

That explained nothing. 'But you live up here now.'

'For a while. I might go back.'

'What for?'

'I don't know, Jessica.' He needed a drink. Really, he needed several, but he tried not to overindulge while on duty. 'But I haven't bought a house here because . . . well, I may move on after the war.'

'Why?'

To get away from inquisitive little madams like you, the doctor thought. 'It depends where I get a job.' Patience was engraved deeply into his words.

'A TB job?'

'Possibly.'

Jessica folded her arms. 'Why can't I go in the house, doctor? I can look after myself. I can get washed and dressed, I can even help with things like making beds. Mam says I'm a very good helper.'

He sighed inwardly. 'There aren't any children over there. As I explained before, you would be on your own, bored. You would miss your mother and—'

'I'm not with my mother any more.'

Stephen Blake tapped blunt fingernails against his

desk. He couldn't help liking Jessica. Everybody liked Jessica.

'I'm fed up,' she wailed. 'And I've been good. And I'm nearly better.'

He shook his head. Jessica had consented to the move from her mother's room, had even managed to be quite pleased about it at first. Truthfully, she required stimuli, education, other children. Like all young ones, she was in need of activity.

The child continued to stare hard at her adversary. He was a very sad man, she concluded after a short period of study. 'I'm really, really fed up,' she insisted.

'I know.'

She folded her arms and waited. Mam was a lot better. She was still forbidden to mix, but she didn't cough pink froth any more and she could walk about, read, knit. In spite of the embargo on visitors, Mam had made a friend, a man from Liverpool who talked funny and got Woodbines smuggled in every Friday. Yes, Mam was fine and Jessica wanted to get on with life.

'I can't work out which is worse,' she said airily. 'Being squashed in with Mam, or getting stuck with Mrs Knowles and Mrs Crabtree.' Sadie Knowles snored, she sounded like a train pulling into Trinity Street, while Ellen Crabtree knew everything about everything. Both women kept their teeth grinning in tumblers, and Mrs Knowles drank tea very loudly, as if trying to suck it up from a great distance. 'They even eat without them,' remarked Jessica. 'They only put them in for visitors and Mrs Crabtree won't wear the bottom ones at all, wouldn't put them in even for the King.'

The doctor stopped drumming on the table. 'I beg your pardon?'

'Teeth,' she said.

'Oh.'

'And I should be at school. I'm going to be behind everybody and I've always been best at reading and sums and singing and—'

'Jessica?'

'Yes?' She pasted a smile across her face. Was he weakening?'

'Hush a moment.'

The child froze. Whatever it took, she was going to break out of this prison – even on a part-time basis. It was awful. No matter what Jessica did, Mrs Crabtree criticized, complained, moaned. And older people smelled funny, as if they had gone stale or something.

Dr Stephen Blake felt like a man encountering his Waterloo. He couldn't send Jessica Nolan into the house. What if one of the men turned out to be a molester of children? What if the little girl got out and got lost? He tut-tutted. 'What will I do with you?'

Invited to break the brief silence, she spoke up brightly. 'I could stay with the housekeeper. She'd look after me, so nothing would happen.'

Did the child read minds, too?

'And I'd be good. Very, very good.'

Good? There was far too much merriment in those cornflower eyes, too much bounce in the ash-blond curls. 'Shall we compromise?' he asked.

She didn't know the word, but it sounded encouraging, as if she might get some of her own way. She nodded quickly.

'You go to the farm after lunch each day, help with jobs in the kitchen, then come back into your ward when you've had a play in the farmyard.'

Jessica considered this option. She would still have

to sleep in the same room as Mrs Knowles, Mrs Crabtree and all those terrible teeth. 'So I told the dentist, if my teeth wants to make trouble, take them out, let them fight among themselves in a jar,' Mrs Knowles was always saying. As for Mrs Crabtree . . . 'All right,' said Jessica.

'Splendid.' With any luck, she would disappear now and leave him to his nip of whisky.

'It's just that I'm not getting enough sleep.' Was she pushing her luck now? She took a deep breath. 'Mrs Knowles sounds like German bombers. That's what Mrs Crabtree says, anyroad.'

She was as old as the hills. 'What is your exact age, Jessica?' he asked.

'Five and nearly two months, doctor.'

'Would you like to live to be six?'

Jessica's cheeks dimpled; she knew what was coming next. 'If I want to live to be six, I have to make myself scarce,' she told him. 'You've said that to me before.'

'Exactly.' When she ran round the desk and kissed him, he felt the heat of embarrassment in his cheeks. Within seconds, the little charmer had disappeared, leaving in her wake a feeling of warmth and promise. If he could only stop drinking, he could perhaps meet a nice woman, have young ones of his own. If he could only stop drinking, or cut down, or . . .

'No. No, not now.' The nightmare was returning, was paying an unwelcome visit in the middle of the day. He closed his eyes, gripped the arms of his chair, felt his teeth grinding harshly. Dr Stephen Blake had cleaned up many messes. But that particular mess, that lump of bloody flesh . . .

He dragged the bottle from a drawer, drank deeply.

'No!' The nights were bad enough, but daymares? Were there such things? Should he see another psychiatrist? For the thousandth time, he peeled back the khaki jacket, watched arterial bleeding, knew that the lad was done for. All around him people were crying, dying, puffing desperately on a last smoke, clinging to whatever remained in the few moments between here and eternity. There wasn't much morphine, but this boy was past needing it.

The tag in his hand, bloodied metal, a name, a rank, a number. Falling down into black silence, waking up in a Portsmouth hospital. How had they got him home? Some garbled story about a fishing boat, a destroyer, a lifeboat, a miracle. A long rest, a stay in a convalescent home, a couple of brain bods asking questions to which only a god might have stood a chance of compiling the answers.

And here he was, drinking himself to death in a TB hospital, nothing left, nobody in London, nobody anywhere. 'Goodnight, Jack,' he murmured, lifting the bottle to his lips once more. What had they done with Jack's body? After the war, there would be a place to visit, no doubt, rows and rows of white gravestones, trees growing as if nothing had ever happened, as if Jack and the others had not existed.

'Just like last time,' he murmured. 'Just like the so-called Great War. The only people who made a profit were stonemasons.'

Dr Stephen Blake's eyes opened. He stared through the office window, watched clouds scuttering across a promising sky. Life went on. It had to go on, because the living had needs.

But oh, dear God. Was there a God? If there was, could not a supreme being help to bandage a broken mind?

Losing a member of one's family was a dreadful thing. Losing a twin brother had proved devastating.

May was spreading her polka-dotted skirts across Danny Walsh's unkempt lawn, almond, apple and cherry blossoms scattered over dandelion and dock leaves. Danny looked to the moors, noticed how green they were becoming. A busy April had wept for days on end, removing the grey scum of winter from pasture, leaving acres of lush grasses in her wake. 'Soon,' mumbled Danny. 'The war has to finish any minute now.' He could scarcely wait to get the teeth of his forks and rakes into this lot.

He swivelled once more and surveyed his own neglected portion of England, battered lawn, untidy flower-beds, three panes missing from the greenhouse. It would take a lot of work, but Danny was raring to go. If only Pauline could be happy, his life would be complete. But Pauline was having difficulty conceiving.

Danny thrust his hands deep into pockets, as if to stop them itching in their need to pick up the tools of cultivation. Pauline would have no truck with the idea of adoption. Inside the house, Danny's wife was playing with Katherine, who was a stolen child. Should he tell Pauline about Katherine's true origin? She knew about the rape of Theresa Nolan, but as for the rest of the tale . . . Katherine was sort of adopted. No, no, he must keep quiet for now.

'Are you coming in, or what?' screamed Pauline from the back door.

'Later,' he replied.

It was almost over. Benito Mussolini had been strung up like a dead chicken, his remains left on show for Italians to gloat or wonder over. Hitler was dead, had blown out his disturbed brain just a couple of days earlier. Berlin was becoming a flattened wreck, its surviving civilians waiting for Russian flak to finish them off.

Danny tried to feel some joy, but he couldn't. Belsen. The pictures had arrived, soldiers crying their eyes out, living skulls staring into a camera lens, their dead brothers and sisters piled up behind them. Measured against that, Pauline's infertility was a mere comma, a pause among several million full stops.

Like many whose occupations had kept them at home, the Walsh brothers felt a degree of guilt. They could have managed as long as their spectacles had remained intact. Lately, they had even achieved some decent scores in darts, so a full-grown German would have been no problem. Pauline and Liz were forever berating them, reminding Danny and Bernard that myopia and war were poor bedfellows, but it didn't make any difference. In Bolton, fatherless children, widows and grieving mothers made the stay-at-homes culpable, inadequate.

Katherine came out, a daft dog at her heels. Chaplin, who had been named after the cinema's greatest clown, was a badly co-ordinated puppy, all feet, floppy ears and lolling tongue. He ate most things in his path, including underwear from the washing basket and slippers from the fireside, the latter items being his favourite pudding after the evening meal. Liz had threatened to drown him, to return him to the farm, to have him 'seen to' at Vernon Street, the destination of many unwanted pets. But Liz loved the rascal, as did everyone else who came across him.

'Uncle Danny!' yelled the child. 'He's had the

pillow off my bed. There's feathers everywhere and Mam's looking for him.'

The dog sat down, scratched an ear, fell over.

'He can't do anything right,' laughed Katherine.

'Aye, he's a nutcase, that dog of yours.'

Katherine decided to ask a very important question. 'Uncle Danny?'

'Yes, love?'

'If Auntie Pauline has a baby, can it live with us?'

He closed his eyes in case the pain showed. 'Katherine, go in and tidy up Chaplin's mess, there's a good girl.'

Sensing her uncle's sombre mood, the little girl turned to leave.

Danny watched child and dog as they scampered off, then he kicked a few stones down the flagged path.

Bernard appeared. 'Danny?'

'Hello, our kid.'

'Katherine says you're sad.'

Danny pushed his hands deep into pockets, shrugged. 'Pauline would love a baby. So would I. Why does life have to be so hard?' Greedily, his eyes scoured the moors. Only here would he find a modicum of peace.

Bernard sighed. Their Danny was an extra-sensitive soul. He took things in and nursed them, worried about all kinds of events, couldn't seem to come to terms with what was happening around him. 'You've to stop this and get back to normal,' said Bernard. 'There's no good'll come of your fretting.'

There was only one way for Danny to distract himself. He needed to be creative, longed to clean up his own garden. 'I want the house back, Bernard,' he said baldly. 'We're selling Tonge Moor, so Edna will be living here, too, in time. I can't carry on down yonder, you see. I need to be up here where it's fresher. Tell Liz there won't be any more bombs. It's safe to go back now.' He thought about that statement. 'Well, safe from attacks. But as for the rest . . .' His words died. There was no need for him to embroider the fact that Bernard's daughter was half of a set of identical twins.

Bernard breathed in deeply. He had become fond of Danny's little cottage, but fair was fair and he had been looking into the situation. 'Give us a few weeks,' he begged. After glancing over his shoulder, the younger brother lowered his voice. 'They're still in the sanatorium.' There was no need for names. 'But we don't know for how long. Eva Harris says the kiddy's well on the way to recovering, but Theresa's going to be inside for a while. We can't risk it, Danny. You'll have to put Pauline and her mam to run the shop while you see to the market – or vice versa, whatever suits. Like we said before, the rooms over the shop can be rented out.'

Danny nodded. This was no shock, no news to him. 'You're going, then? Leaving Bolton?'

'Aye.'

'What's Liz said?'

Bernard attempted a careless shrug. 'I've not told her yet.'

'You what?'

'You heard me, our kid.'

Danny Walsh scratched his head. 'I'm not saying that Liz is the boss, Bernard, but she can be a bit on the determined side.'

'Aye, we know all about that.'

'What are you . . . I mean, how are you going to break it to her?'

Bernard grinned sheepishly. 'A bit at a time,

Danny. First, I've got to get her interested in fancy schools for Katherine. Liz is keen on the lass getting a proper education.'

'There's preparatories here. Then there's Bolton School—'

'We're supposed to be Catholics.'

Danny stared at his brother. 'You what? You've not seen the inside of a church since Adam was a lad in a very small figleaf.'

'I've started going again, sometimes. And Liz attends mass every Sunday. She takes Katherine.'

'There's Mount St Joseph's—'

'Liverpool schools are better.'

'Rubbish,' replied Danny.

Bernard rubbed a hand across his brow with the air of a man struggling to impart information to a deaf foreigner. 'I know that and you know that. Let's just hope Liz doesn't. It would kill her, Danny. If she found out about where our girl really came from, she'd go straight out of her mind. We have to leave Bolton. We'll be living in Crosby.'

Danny studied his shoes. 'Aye, you're not wrong, I suppose. But you'll have to be getting on with it in case young Jessica gets the all-clear. Eva Harris is going to have her till Theresa comes home. I mean, I suppose you could stop here a bit longer, but if you go back to Derby Street, even for a few weeks . . .' He shook his head. 'Something'll have to be done.'

'I have been getting on with it. I've found a place with a nice big garden and a park down the road. There's good shops, decent houses, then there's sand. It's only a few miles from Southport. You know how Liz has always liked Southport.'

'Bloody hell, Bernard. You've not gone and bought a bloody house, have you?'

'No.' It was an empty house where a chemist had lived. The old man had died, and his son, also a pharmacist, had moved on to a different part of Liverpool, had left his inherited home in the safe-keeping of solicitors. 'I'm not that daft. You should know me better than that. There's quite a few properties on the market. The population hasn't been on the move while the war's been on. So it's mine if I want it.' He cleared his throat. 'And if Liz wants it, too.'

Danny chuckled. 'Will she need much persuading?'

Bernard thought not. 'Four bedrooms, nice bathroom, downstairs toilet as well. We'll be going up in the world, I suppose. She's got to like the house. So I thought we might run out to Southport this weekend, me, Liz and Katherine.'

'And happen to pass through Crosby on your way home.'

'That's it.'

Danny placed an arm across his brother's shoulders. 'Well, good luck with it.' Knowing Liz, Danny felt that Bernard would need some luck. 'And make sure you've no heavy objects in the car. We don't want her clattering you round the ear with a starting handle.'

As if he already felt the blow, Bernard rubbed his ear. 'Leave her to me,' he said. 'I can manage her.'

Danny bit back the line about famous last words and followed his brother into the house. Liz, a large brown paper bag in her arms, bumped into her husband. Her hair was spotted with feathers, while several clumps of fine down clung to her clothes. She blew a ticklish item from the end of her nose before speaking. 'Don't say a word, either of you,' she said.

Obediently, Daniel and Bernard Walsh entered the cottage. When Liz was riled, silence was the preferred option.

The dog ran and ran as if he would never tire. Bernard, who had given up the chase, leaned on a stile next to his wife and watched their daughter running behind a dafter-even-than-usual Chaplin.

'She might get lost,' fretted Liz.

'Nay, she won't. She's got radar, our Katherine. Remember when she was two and we lost her in Moss Bank? She was back in a few minutes with a paper bag full of conkers.' He was proud of his daughter. She was pretty, cheerful and clever. She loved life, her parents, her schoolfriends and her dog. 'I can't remember when she last cried,' he said.

'I can.' Liz strained her eyes, caught no sight of Katherine. 'She said her chest hurt. I took her to see the doctor, but there's nothing wrong with her.'

Bernard's heart seemed to skip a couple of beats. He remembered reading about identical twins who had been separated as children. Sometimes, when one twin was ill, the other displayed similar symptoms. But no. According to Eva Harris, little Jessica's TB was so mild that the child had felt little discomfort. The mother was quite ill, though. He shook his head to chase away unwelcome thoughts. They had to get away from here, had to move to Liverpool quick smart as soon as the war ended – before, if possible.

'You'd best go and look for her,' said Liz.

Bernard nodded. He had just a few hours during which he would have to tell Liz that Southport was on tomorrow's itinerary. 'All right, lass,' he sighed as he gazed into her worried face. 'Let's see how far

that bloody mad dog has gone. I'll find them, don't
fret.'

Jessica Nolan, pink, breathless and wonderfully
naughty, sat on a tree stump. She was being so
disobedient that she could scarcely believe herself.
The potatoes were peeled and washed, the floor was
clean, the cutlery drawer had been tidied. Encour-
aged to play alone in the fresh air after her chores,
Jessica had seen a couple of hares leaping about in a
field. March was long over, as was April, but the
madness endured and, fascinated by the animals'
antics, Jessica had sped across meadows, laughing
each time those ridiculously long ears popped out of
a clump of foliage.

She looked up into the trees, saw the sun sparkling
through newborn leaves, heard music created by
birds and by a gentle breeze that rocked overhead
branches. This was the country, then. This was where
lucky people lived, people who kept sheep, cows and
chickens. Men who stayed at the farm strode about
all day in rubber boots, farm smells clinging to their
clothing, faces shining as a result of toiling out of
doors.

Of course, Jessica had seen the country for several
months, had viewed it from the peeled-back windows
of Williamson's Sanatorium. But this was her first
real experience, her first bodily contact with Nature's true wildness. She bent over, lifted a clump of
moist earth and held it to her nose. It had a beautiful
smell, clean, exciting. Opening her fingers, she
allowed the crumbs to trickle back to their home,
amazed to see that her hand remained clean. Dirt
and soil were not even related, she decided.

There were no clocks here in the woods. The

seasons dictated time, short days in the winter, longer days in summer. She could have lived here quite happily, she thought, imagining herself as a Robinson Crusoe, a human forced by circumstance to create from natural materials a shelter, a place all her own.

But she had to go back. If she did not return to the house soon, Dr Blake might well change his mind and force her to stay within the confines of the main building. Retracing the route back to the farmhouse would be no problem, because Jessica seemed incapable of getting lost. Always, she found her way home in the end, depending on instinct or, perhaps, on exterior forces of which she was not fully aware, like the position of the sun or the general drift of wind and rain.

Emblem Street. Until recently, a weary little house, set with others against a backdrop of factories, had been her home. Up here on the moors, air was plentiful and sweet. Jessica and her mother would be forced to go back, she supposed, back to pinched, cobbled streets and dark alleyways, back to foul air, a pub on every corner, back to monotony.

She had expected the countryside to be quiet, but it wasn't. Birds fought their territorial wars, built nests, fed young, called out to one another when separated. Sometimes, in the night, foxes barked, often travelling miles to search the sanatorium's bins for food scraps. Unwanted food was saved for the pigs, but wily foxes learned quickly how to up-end a container and remove its lid. One night, Jessica promised herself, she would meet a fox.

As if summoned by her thoughts, an animal yelped. She sat up straight, only to be bowled over by a large puppy, all big feet, long legs and vigorous tail. 'Where did you come from?' she asked.

Chaplin grinned at this Katherine-type creature. Her smell was not quite right, but it was familiar. 'Woof,' he said by way of introduction.

Jessica frowned. Was this poor little dog lost? And, if he was, would Dr Blake allow her to keep him? Perhaps he could live at the farm or in Mam's room. Somehow, Jessica knew that there was no possibility of either option being viable. Grown-ups made so many complicated rules across which children stumbled blindly every day. Older folk altered regulations to suit themselves, never bothering to consult children, the particular group which was affected by constantly moving goalposts. Life would have been so much easier for everyone, adults included, if simpler ideas could only get a look-in. Dog needed man, man needed dog, so the answer was easy: take the dog in, feed it, treat it well, make a friend. 'Whose are you?' she asked.

Chaplin sniffed the girl's hair, then cocked his head to one side. The nearly-Katherine was definitely a friend, but he still wanted the real Katherine. Where was she? Why wasn't she here, with this other one? They belonged together, he decided.

The child's heart was beating faster and she didn't know why. She was hovering on the brink of . . . of a happening. Tiny hairs on her arms stood to attention when pores opened expectantly. Somebody or something was coming towards her. Far from feeling threatened, she found herself hoping, wishing, wanting.

Jessica patted the dog's neck, sniffed his warm fur, held him close. The excitement had settled slightly, was becoming a warm, inexplicable emotion deep down in her stomach. She studied the animal, gave him a huge smile, wished that she could have a dog of her very own. There was probably no chance, because there was no dad. After the war, a dad would have gone to work, leaving Mam at home to look after the puppy. Puppies wanted company, wanted feeding. There was not enough money to buy food for an animal and, once well, Mam would return to a job and Jessica would be at school, so a pet would be lonely.

She lifted her head, saw a figure moving through the small copse. Here came the dog's true owner, then. Jessica rose to her feet and whipped a few bits of moss off the skirt of her blue coat.

'Hello.'

Jessica looked at the girl, knew that her jaw had dropped. It was Lucy. Lucy, who had kept Jessica company for years, had virtually disappeared after that night in the coal hole, only to materialize here, in the middle of nowhere. 'Who are you?' she asked, her voice almost a whisper.

Katherine stood as still as stone for several seconds. She felt drawn to this girl, as if she had known her for ages. She wanted to touch her, hold her hand, talk to her at length. 'Katherine,' she replied eventually.

'Oh.' It wasn't Lucy, yet it was. 'I'm Jessica.'

The dog charged about, fussing each girl in turn, pushing them closer together. He felt happy inside, a silly, bubbling kind of happy that burst from his mouth in a series of excited barks.

'He's called Chaplin,' said Katherine.

'Oh.'

'Because he's so funny and his feet are too big.'

'Yes.'

Katherine bit her lip. 'You're . . . like me,' she mumbled. The longed-for sister seemed to have turned up. But that was silly, because a sister would have been born young, would have been a baby, not a girl as big as this one.

'You look like me, you mean.' Jessica was determined to be at least as important as this dog owner. Her heart was a bit loud, as if the volume knob on a wireless had been turned up. It was almost like looking in a mirror, except that the girl was the right way round. Both had blond/brown hair, Jessica's slightly fairer than Katherine's. Each pair of eyes was wide-set and cornflower-blue, while noses and mouths were exactly the same.

'Like in a mirror,' announced Katherine.

'But the proper way round. Things always finish up backwards when you look in a mirror.'

'Yes.' Katherine leaned against a tree. 'Do you live near here?'

Jessica looked at the girl's beautiful clothes, the satin hair ribbons, the patent-leather ankle-strap shoes. 'I live on a farm,' she answered, wondering why she was lying. Well, was it really a lie? She spent each afternoon at the farmhouse, though she still slept in the sanatorium.

'How exciting. I love animals,' said Katherine.

'We've got cows, hens and pigs. And we grow all our own vegetables. We've got a great big house with loads of rooms and a proper bath with taps. We make our own butter and cream. And I can play out whenever I want to. Foxes come at night. I was just chasing some big rabbits called hares.'

'How lucky you are,' smiled Katherine.

It was too late for the truth now. 'This is where I look for the foxes. They come to our house at night, but they're hard to find in the daytime. They're forever pinching all the leavings from the pigswill buckets.'

Katherine hooked a lead through Chaplin's collar. 'I'd better go,' she said. 'Mam and Dad are waiting for me.'

'Oh.' People who had dads were so lucky. 'Will you come again?' asked Jessica wistfully.

'I expect so.'

'Katherine?' boomed a man's voice.

'Here, Dad.' Katherine waved at her father. 'Come here. I've met a girl who looks just like me.' She turned to grab Jessica, reached out and snatched at a handful of air. 'She's gone.' Katherine's voice raised itself. 'Jessica? Jessica, where are you? Come and meet my dad.'

Three or four trees away, Jessica crouched and peeped through a drooping branch. The girl was not Lucy. She belonged to a different place, a different life. Chaplin, straining on his leash, was doing his best to bring Katherine back to Jessica, but the man, who was strangely familiar and red in the face from running, took charge. He looked a bit like one of the fishmen, Jessica thought, though she was far from convinced with regard to his identity, as she had never seen the Walshes wearing ordinary clothes.

'It's getting late,' said Bernard quietly. 'Your mam's just at the edge of the wood looking for you.' The unthinkable had happened; the twins had found one another. He had caught a glimpse of Katherine's sister, just a split-second's view, had heard Katherine calling out the dreaded name. Why hadn't he realized that he had brought his family so close to Belmont? And what the hell was Jessica Nolan doing wandering about through fields and woods? She was supposed to be locked away with TB.

199

He stumbled on blindly, dragging the dog with one hand and the backward-looking Katherine with the other.

Liz stared at her husband when he reached her side. 'What's the matter?' she asked. 'You look as if you've seen a ghost.'

A ghost would have been preferable.

'I met a girl who looks just like me,' repeated Katherine. 'Mam, you have to come. I want you to meet her. She's called Jessica.'

Bernard held his daughter's hand tightly, prayed that Liz would not put two and two together – or one and one, come to that. Jessica Nolan wasn't the only Jessica in the Bolton area, he reminded himself. 'We're going home,' he announced now. 'I feel a bit tired after all that chasing about.'

Jessica, who had crept to the edge of the wood, watched as the family walked away, the mother, the father, the girl and her dog. She wanted to follow them, to beg to be taken to their home: a cosy fire, toast, a dog basket in the corner. But she had told lies. And anyway, nobody would want a TB girl to visit a proper house, because TB girls belonged in hospitals.

Sadly, she trudged her way back to the farm. If her absence had been noticed, she would be in trouble. But she had not been missed. Katherine had been missed, though. Her parents had come dashing across fields to find her. They had bought her a dog and shiny shoes and ribbons for her hair.

The housekeeper pushed a mug of cocoa into Jessica's hands. 'Have you had a nice play, love?'

Jessica nodded.

'Do you want a scone with that?'

'No, thank you.' Jessica's appetite had disappeared.

All she could see was a girl with a dog, a girl who looked uncannily like herself. She felt cold inside, as if something important had been taken away from her. 'I wish I had a sister,' she said mournfully.

Alice Sharples laughed. 'Nay, love. I think your mam has enough to worry about. Off you go now, back to your ward.' The child looked so sad. 'Are you all right?'

Jessica drained her cup. 'Yes, thank you.' She wasn't all right, but who cared?

It was a long, long corridor with cream-painted walls, rows of doors punctuating the monotony. Jessica floated along, hands held out before her, feet trailing just above ground level. Dr Blake stood outside the X-ray room with a fox. The fox, who was remarkably well behaved, sat decorously at the end of a lead. Dr Blake's white coat was spotted with custard, gravy and what looked like beetroot juice.

Mam was well again. She wore a pretty blue suit and a hat with an open-weave veil. Next to Mam, the girl called Katherine was bedecked in satin ribbons, black shoes with T-bar straps, a red coat and white stockings. Jessica arrived at Mam's side.

'Who are you?' asked Theresa Nolan.

'I'm Jessica.'

Katherine beamed upon her lookalike. 'We're better,' she said. 'We're both going home.'

Jessica wept. She was Mam's daughter. Mam had got mixed up. Or had she decided to take the other girl because she was prettier and better dressed? 'You can't go home with my mam,' announced Jessica crossly.

'Of course I can. I can do anything I like, because I have a dad.'

'She can do anything she likes,' repeated Theresa Nolan. 'She has a dad, so I'm taking her home with me.'

This wasn't right. Jessica watched the two figures as they moved away from her. They burst through a doorway and into a meadow full of dancing hares. When the door closed in Jessica's face, she wept uncontrollably.

'Jessica! Jessica, wake up!'

The little girl opened her eyes and reached for Ellen Crabtree. 'She's taken my mam,' she wailed.

'Who has?'

'Katherine. The one who looks like . . .' Jessica inhaled, tried to control her sobs.

'It were nobbut a dream, lass,' said Ellen Crabtree. 'I reckon they're giving you too much cheese. Cheese never sits easy in a young stomach. Makes you have nightmares. That's all it is, love. That were all down to a bit of undigested Cheddar.'

For once, Jessica was pleased that the toothless Mrs Crabtree knew everything. The night nurse came in, made tutting noises and soothed Jessica's brow.

'This is no life for a kiddy,' snapped Mrs Crabtree. 'Is there not a place for children with TB? She shouldn't be shut in here with old women like me and Sadie Knowles.' As if agreeing with her companion, Sadie let out an extra-loud snore. 'There's nowt'll wake her,' grumbled Ellen. 'But she keeps the bloody rest of us red-eyed, I'm telling you.'

The nurse gave Jessica a sip of water. 'There's no hospital round here for kiddies,' she replied. 'And them in Yorkshire and Cheshire are all full up. Anyway, Jessica won't be here for much longer. She only had a bit of a spot on one lung, and that's on the mend.' She grinned at Jessica. 'You'll be living with Mrs Harris, or so I'm told. Just have a bit of patience, sweetheart. We have to make sure you're all right, or the TB'll be spreading like wildfire all over the place.'

'I bet she won't get TB,' muttered the child.

'Who?' asked the nurse and Ellen Crabtree simultaneously.

Jessica dared not tell them. If the powers found out that she had travelled beyond the farm's boundaries, she could well be grounded. 'Somebody in the dream,' she replied at last.

'Dreams aren't real,' said the nurse by way of comfort.

Jessica lay back on her pillows. Katherine was real. Katherine's dad and her dog were real. Surely she hadn't fallen asleep in the woods? No, no, it had all happened.

'All right now?' asked the nurse.

'Yes,' replied Jessica. But she wasn't.

'What's the matter with you, Bernard?' Liz tugged at a sleeve of her husband's pyjama jacket. 'What are you doing stuck down here in the middle of the night?'

Bernard turned from the window. Somewhere, up on the moors, a child slept. The child belonged to Theresa Nolan, as did Katherine, the little girl who slumbered peacefully in the back bedroom of her 'Uncle Danny's' cottage. 'I can't settle,' he replied.

Liz scratched her head. She was thoroughly perplexed, because her husband had never had trouble sleeping. In fact, had sleeping been an Olympic sport, he might have qualified to enter once the games resumed. 'There must be something keeping you awake. Will I make a brew?'

He shook his head.

'Not tea – what about a mug of cocoa? We've still got a bit left. And I could make a sandwich—'

'No, Liz, I don't want anything.' He wanted Katherine to be his own, to be Liz's own. He wanted Katherine to be safe, to live in a place where no-one knew her, where the resemblance between her and Theresa Nolan's daughter could pass unremarked.

'Bernard?'

'What?'

'You've got to tell me what's on your mind.'

He sat down and waited until Liz was seated opposite him. 'I've been thinking,' he began tentatively.

'I can see that. You've thought your way well past two o'clock in the morning. Now, I know it's Saturday – well, Sunday now – but you need your rest.'

He nodded. 'I want a fresh start,' he said.

'What?'

'Somewhere else. Somewhere with good schools for our Katherine.'

Liz stared at him. 'Leave Bolton?' she asked. 'Leave the business and Danny and Pauline? Everything you've worked for is here,' she reminded him.

'It still will be,' he replied. 'It'll be fifty-fifty no matter what. You see, Liz, they eat a lot of fish in Liverpool.'

'Liverpool? Who's talking about Liverpool?'

'I am. We want to expand, me and our Danny, broaden our scope. I thought I'd take a lock-up near the city and buy us a nice house, a semi with a back garden. It's got a garage, too. We could have a car as well as a van—'

'What's got a garage?'

Bernard swallowed. 'It just so happens that I've

204

seen this house. It belonged to a chemist, one of them old-fashioned ones who make their own medicines. He's selling it, or his son's selling it. Four bedrooms, it's got.'

Liz closed her mouth with an audible snap. 'What do we want with four bedrooms? I can't have any more kiddies, so why such a big house?'

Bernard sagged wearily against the arm of his chair. In his mind's eye, he saw Katherine's sister running away, turning back, running towards . . . 'We're going up in the world, Liz.' He didn't want to leave Bolton, the fishmarket, his friends, his customers. 'We could end up with a chain of shops, love. Danny wants his cottage back. Do you fancy living on Derby Street again? Do you want to go back to the smell of fish?'

'We could buy a house round here,' answered Liz.

Was Bromley Cross far enough? No. People from Bromley Cross shopped in Bolton, as would Theresa Nolan, as would all who knew Theresa, Jessica, Katherine and Liz. 'Just come and look at the house,' he begged. 'That's all I ask.'

Liz felt uneasy. It wasn't like Bernard to have life-altering ideas such as this one. 'Have you and Danny been planning this?' she asked.

'Yes,' he replied. That, at least, was the truth.

'All right.' Liz stood up. 'Come on, back to bed this minute. I promise I'll look at the house. But I shan't promise to like it.'

And that, thought Bernard, would have to be enough for now. Once Liz saw Crosby with its quaint shops, thatched cottages and decent, middle-class houses, she would surely make the desired decision.

SEVEN

Maurice Chorlton could not quite manage to meet Lily Hardman's eyes. Looking at human perfection was never easy, even when such excellence was merely skin deep. Lillian Hardman had the sort of looks that should have been sent off to Hollywood: perfect legs, wavy, jet-black hair grown to shoulder length, huge blue eyes, a tiny waist and very clearly defined breasts. The latter items were so remarkable that Maurice had his work cut out to fix his attention on Lily's face. Lily's top half was slightly out of proportion to the rest of her chassis, as if two women had been welded together by an artist in order to exaggerate the full potential of female beauty. Maurice was rather less than comfortable, but Mrs Hardman simply stood and gazed at the bag in her hands.

He coughed, cleared his throat, waited for her to speak. This was a dangerous woman. She had been doing things with a vicar and, as a God-fearing man, Maurice felt uneasy in the presence of such a sinner. Unclean thoughts sat at the edge of the jeweller's consciousness, causing him to cough again in order to relieve his own tension. Was she going to start on him? Was he an item on Lillian's list of future projects? Perhaps he might try a toupee or—

'Maurice,' she began. 'I came because . . . well
. . .' Her voice tailed away on a drawn-out shuddering sigh.

He tidied a pile of tissue paper which didn't need
tidying. The woman had power, the sort of tacit
energy that hung in the air, its invisible tentacles
poised to consume all mere males who ventured
within striking distance. She had put herself into
weeping mode, too, was mopping up a sudden out-
burst of saline with a scrap of lace-edged linen, too
tiny to do the job properly. 'Here,' he said gruffly,
pushing his handkerchief into her perfectly white
fingers with their almond-shaped, manicured and
rose-stained tips.

'Thank you,' she murmured pitiably.

'You're welcome.'

'I can't believe it,' she wailed. 'Ged isn't home yet.
The war might be finished, but God knows when
he'll get demobbed. Couldn't George have waited?
He's taken everything, even some money from the
wages account.'

This news came as something of a shock, because
George had always stated his intention to remain at
home until Ged's return. Hardman's Hides must be
in trouble now, mused the jeweller. So George had
finally done it, had even upped and offed before
Ged's demobilization. George, a decent chap, had
meant to stay until able to speak to his son, but things
had got too much for him, it seemed. Maurice
shuffled about uncomfortably, grateful that a glass-
topped counter separated him from this woman. He
was no good with females. His own wife had been a
gentle soul, one not inclined to visit the various
zeniths and nadirs of human emotions. 'I don't
know what to say,' he muttered truthfully.

Lily blew her perfect little nose. 'He's left me the house and seven thousand pounds. I understand that the tannery is now in my name and Ged's. What a homecoming poor Ged will have.'

Ged would have a wonderful homecoming, Maurice thought. He'd grab his half of the money, do a bunk, spend the lot and to hell with Hardman's Hides. 'What will you do?' Maurice asked.

Lily slammed a large bag onto the counter, causing glass to shiver and the shopkeeper to flinch. 'First of all, I'm selling my jewellery to you.' She eyed him with a look of pure steel, her flood of tears suddenly dammed. 'And don't you dare try to fob me off with any nonsense, Maurice Chorlton. After what George did to me, I deserve fair play for a change.'

Maurice nodded, then lifted several boxes out of the bag. Fair play? What did Lillian Hardman know about that particular commodity? As Betteridge always said, somewhat crudely, this woman's knickers had suffered more ups and downs than a whore's undergarments.

'It's worth a small fortune,' she snapped. 'There's stuff in there that belonged to my grandmother – and to *his* family.' The 'his' emerged as a hiss. 'If he's planning on asking for any of this back, he can go to hell with his secretary bird.' Lily was deeply insulted. Her husband had made off with a bespectacled child, plain of face, unimaginative in the dress department, a boring, decent, down-to-earth and definitely ordinary woman.

'There are some beautiful pieces here,' squeaked Maurice, the tone altered by a sudden lack of moisture in his throat. 'Could well be out of my league.' Not for years had he glimpsed such treasure. He felt weak at the knees in the presence of this woman and her trappings.

Lily stuffed both waterlogged pieces of linen into her handbag and altered her facial expression yet again. This time, she portrayed herself as angry and fit to burst. 'They're not going to Manchester.' She jabbed an index finger at the row of jewellery boxes. 'You will give me two thousand pounds and we shall exchange receipts. When I can afford to buy back my possessions, you will accept from me the sum of two thousand five hundred pounds, not a penny more or less. This, too, will be documented and signed by each of us.'

Maurice, who could not lay his tongue across a single syllable, said nothing.

'You knew he was going,' continued Lily. 'You and Betteridge must have talked about this at your precious Merchants' Club. So you owe me. It will be an easy five hundred pounds, though it could take some time to acquire, of course. After all, I have a factory to keep up and running.'

Maurice pulled himself together. She was going to run Hardman's? How? How could a woman of this calibre run a business, a factory that stank like hell itself, a place populated by big, brawny men whose fodder was ale and filthy jokes? 'I see,' he managed eventually. 'Two thousand pounds. That will be cash, I take it?'

'Nail on the head,' replied Lily smartly.

'I'll bring the money to you tonight, then.'

She almost laughed. 'Oh, no, Maurice. We'll go for it now. It's a lovely afternoon, so the walk will do us good. Your bank's nearby, isn't it?'

He nodded mutely.

'And I have the paperwork prepared.' She tapped

her handbag. 'I shall trust you for the moment, I think. Take my stuff away and put it under lock and key. Then we shall continue with our business after visiting the bank.'

There was no question of disobedience, no room for discussion or negotiation. It was as if she held a whip with which she would beat him if he refused to co-operate. He excused himself, dashed downstairs and placed Lillian Hardman's jewels in the walk-in strongroom. As he handled some of the items, a long-forgotten thrill visited his spine, a feeling he had experienced many times when in the presence of such classic, rare pieces.

He sighed, allowing a diamond-set gold bracelet to trickle through his fingers, the leaf-shaped stations flowing like molten lava onto a background of blue velvet. The perfect clear stones flashed across his eyes, while a mixed-cut and cushioned ruby winked solemnly from within its blood-red soul. Forty more diamonds, graded carefully and set with loving attention to detail, nestled in a crescent-shaped brooch. Kashmir sapphires, his favourite among all corundums, stared at him from within cool, cornflower-blue depths. No navy or nearly black sapphires for Lily Hardman, then. Oh no, she had wanted the best, had accepted nothing less. More sapphires, probably Ceylonese, some emeralds, diamonds, diamonds, more diamonds, opals, watches—

'Maurice?'

'Coming.' With reluctance, he closed the safe door. Two thousand pounds? This haul was worth twice, three, maybe four times that price. She was being reasonable, he supposed. The war was over, but jewellery would not feature on many shopping lists just now. Luxury items were worth only what people would pay, and no-one wanted precious stones and metals, not yet. Still, parting with two thousand pounds was hardly cause for celebration. But Lillian Hardman was one of those women who always – well, usually got their own way. Even George hadn't been able to face her, had chosen to clear off without a word.

Maurice patted his various pockets, accounted for cheque book, wallet and keys. He would co-operate one hundred per cent with Lily Hardman. After all, her situation cried out for pity and understanding. And there was nothing to lose, not while he held such magnificent collateral.

Katherine Walsh, her heart troubled almost to the point of tears, watched her life being packed away into suitcases and wooden chests. Mam and Dad were buying a partly furnished home, because an old chemist had died and his son had sold the house, together with some of its contents, to the Walshes. It was a nice, spacious semi-detached in Crosby, near Liverpool, or, as Mam was wont to put it, 'halfway between Liverpool and Southport'. Southport was all right, Katherine supposed, though the sea seemed rather coy. On all the occasions when she had visited the seaside town, the water had been a mere grey ribbon stretched across the horizon. But the shops were nice, Mam thought.

There was the Mersey, too, a large river into whose mouth ships drifted every day when there wasn't a war on, so the docks promised to be interesting once bomb damage had been righted. Dad had become quite excited, had started reading books about the cotton exchange and the wholesale fishmarket. But

Katherine was not fooled. Both senior Walshes were unsure about this move, and they compensated by being over-bright and rather too cheerful when discussing the future.

Chaplin huddled by his young mistress's side. Something terrible was happening. His basket, which bore the marks of several weeks' labour necessitated by teething, had been removed and shoved into the bowels of a large black vehicle. Ball, bone and blanket had suffered the same fate, so he was sticking by Katherine, who seemed the sanest of all the humans. The other two were running daft, shouting out to one another and wrapping pots in newspapers.

Katherine sat herself down in Uncle Danny's rocker and stared at the moors. There would be no chance now, she told herself. Even when visiting Danny, she would never rediscover that special place, the little copse inside which she had met her double. Dad had refused to take her again, had ranted on about farmers shooting dogs, something to do with sheep-worrying.

Absently, she patted the nervous dog's head. She had argued ceaselessly, had suggested that Chaplin could be taken to the copse on a lead, or that he should be left at home. And anyway, there hadn't been any sheep near that spot. But Dad had become quite cross, not at all like his real self. The child shivered and hugged herself, though the day was far from chilly. All she wanted was a chance to meet the girl again, to talk, to get to know Jessica. Why were grown-ups so silly and childish? Dad's final answer had been, 'We're not going because I said we're not going.' Daft reason. No reason at all, just a stupid decision based on nonsense.

Liz stopped rushing about for a few moments. 'Have you been crying, Katherine?'

'No.'

'Yes, you have.' The child was clinging fiercely to her roots, was even talking about a girl she had met, someone who bore a resemblance to herself.

Katherine sighed deeply. She couldn't go back to that thicket because Dad had said no, and she would never be able to find it by herself, as Dad had driven the family to the Belmont area on that day. Now, she must have been crying because Mam said she had been crying. After all, adults were always, always right. She hadn't cried, not quite. 'I'm sad, but I'm not crying,' she replied. 'I don't want to move to Liverpool. I want to stay here in this house and carry on at my own school. But I'm only five, so I don't count. What I want doesn't matter.'

Liz inhaled. 'This is Uncle Danny's house. We borrowed it to keep you safe from bombs. Now, Uncle Danny wants to come back here with Auntie Pauline and Pauline's mother. He misses his garden, you see.'

'Yes, but we could buy another house just the same. There's hundreds.'

These had been Liz's thoughts, but, after discussions with Bernard, Danny and Pauline, a decision had been reached with regard to the fish business and expansion to Liverpool. Prices at Liverpool's wholesale fishmarket were competitive. Once the dross of war had been removed, the Walsh brothers could take advantage of broader purchasing bases, allowing Bernard to bargain for bigger and better deals. With a decent van, Danny could easily fetch fish from Liverpool a couple of times a week.

'I'm all right, Mam,' insisted the child.

Liz gulped back her own uncertainties, squashing all doubts so firmly that her stomach almost ached. 'Please, Katherine,' she began.

'I've told you, Mam, don't worry, 'cos I'm all right.'

Liz squatted down until she was at her daughter's level. 'It's time to move on, pet. The war's over and done with at long last. Your dad's got a special job to do, because so many people in Liverpool got killed. Remember? We explained to you about bombs, didn't we?'

Katherine nodded.

'Thousands died in Liverpool. Bernard's going to help the ones who're left to get things back together. Three of the fishmongers aren't there any more, so your dad and a few other men are going to help with mending some shops and getting them open as soon as possible. It's important work.'

Katherine bit her lower lip. 'Is the shop in Crosby?'

'No. It's in a place called Scotland Road, just a little lock-up. Every afternoon, when the shop shuts, your dad'll come home. He won't have to go fire-watching three nights a week any more.'

'What about my school?'

'Ainsley House, it's called. It'll get you ready for the grammar school. Nuns are very good teachers – the best – and you'll—'

'I don't like nuns.'

Neither did Liz. But, by fair means or foul, nuns forced children to learn. They used moral blackmail, prayer, detention and any other weapon they could lay hands and tongues across. Nuns never accepted second best. In their book, a day of idleness was a day of sin thrown into the face of God Himself. And, in Liz's opinion, every bride of Christ had endured a

214

sense-of-humourectomy, a total removal of mankind's most endearing grace, so they stuck to teaching with grim-faced tenacity and left little room for diversion. 'I think they're good women inside,' Liz managed.

Katherine shrugged. She couldn't seem to care any more. The adults had taken over again and, as always, they were hot in pursuit of trouble and complications. Jessica would have understood, no doubt. Jessica was another wise child, a girl whose vision probably spread itself far beyond the blinkered view of myopic, silly grown-ups. Yet how did Katherine know all that about the girl in the woods? How could she?

'Katherine?'

She looked at her mother. 'I'm not happy, Mam, but I know I have to go where you go. If I ask to stay here, with Uncle Danny and Auntie Pauline, you won't let me.' No, that solution would have been too easy, too sensible. And really, Katherine did not want to lose Mam and Dad, as they were more important than houses and schools and beloved places.

Liz stood up, bit back words of wisdom. Katherine was grieving and should be left alone with this particular sadness.

In the doorway, Bernard watched the scene, his daughter's words seeming to echo round the room. This move was for Katherine's sake, though neither child nor woman realized that truth and its implications. Even if she had to be dragged kicking and screaming, Katherine's address had to change now, today, for her own safety's sake. Pauline and Danny were remaining in Bolton because they had nothing to hide. Bernard's whole life revolved round a lie, and the embodiment of that untruth was railing against change. If Katherine stayed here with her uncle and aunt, the move would be completely unnecessary.

Katherine studied her father, found uncertainty in his expression. He, too, was afraid. She looked up at Liz, noticed misgivings there, a slight frown, a narrowing of the eyes. 'If it doesn't work, can we come home?' Katherine asked her father.

'Yes,' he lied. He couldn't lose her, couldn't lose either of them. What might have happened had he not followed Katherine into the trees that day? Would the girls have compared birth dates, eye colour, other similarities? If Liz were to lose her daughter, she could well give up and die. 'Let's just see how it goes, Katherine,' he said. 'You'll take a while to settle – we all will.'

Liz bent down to stroke Chaplin's silky head. 'Look at him – you'd think he was going to prison.'

Katherine, who shared the dog's feelings, held her tongue. Forces above and beyond child and dog had planned the move. Liz and Bernard were the makers of decisions, while she and Chaplin didn't even get to vote.

She picked up a pile of comics, grabbed Chaplin's lead and made for the door. Without a single backward glance, Katherine Walsh walked away from the only home she remembered and towards a future in whose choice she had played no part.

Jessica Nolan, who still had to visit her doctor once a week and the sanatorium's clinic on the last Thursday of each month, was living quite comfortably in the home of Eva Harris. Eva, directed by Theresa Nolan, had visited the Emblem Street house to retrieve a box of money from beneath a floorboard in Theresa's bedroom. After opening this container, Eva had shaken her head angrily, had rambled endlessly about folk with no sense who didn't eat while there was money in the house, who ended up in Williamson's because they didn't care about living or dying, who had no thought for anyone who cared about them, who were as daft as brushes, selfish, stupid . . . She went on about things a fair bit, did Eva.

Jessica was allowed to visit Mam during her own trips to the clinic. Theresa, who was eating and sleeping well, had roses in her cheeks and a lovely sheen on that famous strawberry-blonde hair. Mam was beautiful once more. Dr Blake kept saying that Theresa needed at least a year in the sanatorium, since she continued poorly in spite of looking so well. Still, Jessica's mam was safe, and safe would have to be good enough for now.

For the first time in months, Jessica was relatively content. Sometimes, when she remembered that strange, brief meeting with Katherine, she felt a bit lonely, but she didn't really need a Lucy figure any more, because there were so many children in the View Street area, real children who lived in the here and now, who played hopscotch, skipping rope and ball games.

Occasionally, Jessica came into contact with Auntie Ruth or Cousin Irene. They lived nearby, just a few doors away from Eva, with a grandfather who kept nearly dying and who didn't want to know Jessica. Other aunts and uncles visited the grandfather, often staring at Jessica as they passed by. But the child instructed herself not to care. They didn't want Mam, either, so they didn't matter at all.

On a Friday afternoon in July, Jessica meandered

homeward, stopping to look in shop windows, passing the time of day with a couple of Magee's dray horses, watching trolley buses as they hummed and clicked their way up Derby Street.

A hand clamped itself onto her shoulder. Startled, Jessica swung round to find herself face to chest with Cousin Irene, who was thirteen and rather tall. Irene had eyes which were hard to describe, rather flat in her face, glassy, greenish, yellowish, devoid of expression. Like a pot doll's eyes, thought Jessica. When Irene spoke, her lips scarcely parted. 'Grandad's dying,' the girl said. 'He's been dying a few times, like, only I think he's doing it proper this time.'

Jessica had never seen anyone quite as plain as Irene. Pasty-faced and marble-eyed, the girl bore no resemblance to Ruth, her mother. Ruth's ugliness was born of bitterness – lines too deep for a woman of her years, a downturned mouth, shifty eyes, one with a slight tendency to squint inward towards an upturned and freckled nose. But Irene had been born unfortunate and, denounced loudly and frequently by her own mother, had resigned herself to being hideous and to acting hideously. 'Dying,' she repeated, a strange, damped-down pleasure in the muted tone.

'Oh,' squeaked Jessica.

'Do you want to come and see him? His mouth's open and he makes right funny noises. He had a fly in his gob this morning. Come on, I'll show you.'

'He doesn't want me there,' managed Jessica.

'He won't bloody know – he's three parts dead already, me mam said so. I could sneak you in the back road while nobody's looking.' The older girl took a threepenny bit from a pocket and pressed it into Jessica's trembling hand. 'Here,' she said. 'That's for you.'

The metal felt hot enough to burn its way right through Jessica's palm. She didn't want the money, didn't want to be bought or to stand here shivering and shaking, but she was almost immobilized by the presence of this strange, unwholesome creature.

'You can be me friend now,' Irene was saying. 'I've give you money, so you've got fer t' be me friend.'

Irene's Bolton accent was the most pronounced that Jessica had ever heard in a person so young. She sounded like a very old woman, one of those black-shawled Victorian remnants who stood on street corners taking snuff and puffing on clay pipes. 'All right,' breathed Jessica, who nursed the suspicion that to refuse Irene's friendship would be to court disaster.

'If you don't be me friend, I'll hit you,' added Irene, her voice still monotonous. 'Right hard and all. I know how to hit. I learned it off me mam.'

For the first time in her short life, Jessica experienced real dislike. She also caught an uncomfortable echo of the terror she had felt that night in the coal hole. Cousin Irene was horrible, even bad. There were some people whom Jessica thought were not particularly lovable, but actual antipathy was a new emotion for her.

'Did you hear me?'

Jessica nodded.

'Is your mam going fer t' die?'

'No. But she has to stay at the sanatorium.'

Irene nodded jerkily, as if the movement caused a degree of discomfort. 'Do they all spit blood? Me mam says they choke to death on it, blue and purple in t' face, blood shooting out all over the floor and that.'

It occurred to Jessica that Irene took pleasure from the concept of others' sufferings. She was creepy, far more dangerous than any of the coal hole's imagined inhabitants. Yet there remained something pathetic in Irene's demeanour, as if the girl's shoulders bore an invisible burden of immense proportions. 'I've got to go home now,' said Jessica.

'Home?'

'Well, Mrs Harris's house. I'm stopping there until my mam gets well enough to come out of hospital.'

Irene bit a thumbnail, chewing absently. 'See, I've got a dad,' she pronounced. 'He's no good, like, 'cos he ran off and left us. And he were always beating folk up for their money and their watches. He did a bunk years ago, 'cos police was after him. So we're a bit the same, you and me, just a mam.'

Jessica gulped quietly. She didn't want to be like Irene, didn't even want to talk to her. For a split second, a picture of Katherine flashed across her inner mind. Being like Katherine would have been all right: chasing about with a dog, racing through trees and meadows, those activities would have suited Jessica. But this older girl with her terrible stillness, her fixations with illness and death – she was absolutely terrifying.

'Are you coming to see Grandad, then?'

'No, thank you.'

Irene understood the concept of rejection. 'I don't blame you, 'cos he never wanted you while he were alive, so why should you visit him when he's nearly dead? Mam reckons he'll be well gone by tomorrow, then there'll be a funeral. Have you ever been to a funeral?'

'No.'

'They go in a coffin, then they get buried in a big, wet hole full of beetles and stuff. Coffins fall to bits, so worms get in and eat dead bodies.'

Jessica noticed that Irene's eyes were completely closed, as if the girl had immersed herself in a dream that would have fallen far short of palatable for a normal person, but which absorbed the dreamer totally.

The eyes opened slowly. 'I can show him to you once he's dead. He'll be in the front room in his best suit, me mam says.'

Death in the sanatorium had been a quiet, respectful affair, a few closed curtains, men in black suits, the wheels of a trolley caressing a tiled floor with their soft, rubber surfaces. 'I don't want to see anybody dead, Irene.'

'Why not?'

'I don't know.'

Irene pondered for a second. 'You don't know owt, you. Never mind, I'll look after you.'

The prospect of being looked after by Irene was disconcerting. The unprepossessing girl was grim, almost macabre, knowledgeable in a nasty and unnatural way. Katherine Walsh was clever, but Katherine Walsh was just another bright, ordinary child, a girl who appreciated the pleasanter sides of life. 'You're a lot older than me,' offered Jessica after a pause. 'I don't need looking after. I've got Mrs Harris and loads of friends the same age as me.'

Irene had few friends. Occasionally, she bought a couple of satellites, persuading them with money from her mother's slim purse or with bits snatched from a counter in the local sweets-and-tobacco shop. No-one liked her. She expected not to be loved, because even her own mother had no time for her. 'Ooh, Dad, isn't she ugly?' How many times had Irene heard that piece of rhetoric? The words were scored into the front of her consciousness, as was Ruth's other accusation. 'Your dad left home when he saw you. He couldn't believe his eyes, so he went back to his pigs and cows, because they're better looking.'

Jessica shuffled on the spot, needing to go, too afraid to take the first step.

Irene looked at her pretty young cousin. Unable to sustain actual affection for anyone, Irene found herself drawn magnetically towards beautiful people. They fascinated her. Their appearance endowed them with a power about which she was destined merely to speculate.

However, most young people, plain or pretty, were purchasable. Adults, on the other hand, had always insulted her, derided her, or, worse still, had ignored her. The only grown-ups she trusted not to judge her ugliness were those in silk-lined boxes in the back parlour of McRae's Funeral Home. She liked them. She could curse them, laugh at them, even poke them with a pencil or a ruler. There were other possibilities, too, but they wanted thinking about first. If she stole wedding rings, would the under-takers notice?

Jessica bit her lip. When could she get away? What was this girl thinking about?

Children responded to Irene when she produced sherbet dabs, halfpenny spanishes or, at a push, cocoa and sugar. For sixpence, she could get a crowd, while a full shilling had the ability to invite a congregation. It seemed doubtful, however, that Jessica Nolan would be willing to join an audience with Irene. 'I've give you threepence,' she accused, little anger in the words.

Irene always sounded the same, pondered Jessica. There was no anger, no laughter – did she ever cry? Probably not.

The older girl, inexplicably keen to captivate the attention of her younger cousin, peeled a thread-bare coat from her thin body before turning around. 'Look,' she commanded. 'Look at me neck.'

Jessica looked. A huge purple bruise sat beneath the basin-cut, mouse-coloured hair. 'How did that happen?'

Expressionless as before, Irene swivelled on the spot. 'Me mam did it. She knocked me head against a drawer, kept hitting me, she did, shouted as she wanted to kill me. The room went all dark and I nearly died. Grandad saved me. Then he fell down and now he's dying with the pneumonia. But I'm not, I'm all right now.'

Jessica nursed the strong suspicion that death would have been welcomed.

'I went to sleep for three days,' continued Irene. 'When I woke up, I was thirsty and Grandad was dying.'

Jessica shook as she dropped the unwelcome threepenny piece into its owner's frayed pocket. She wanted to run, needed to escape from this weird child. But Jessica's feet felt as if they had been welded to the pavement.

'Do you not want t' money, then?'

'No.'

The lifeless eyes scanned Jessica's face. 'I haven't got no sisters. Neither have you.'

Jessica swallowed.

'So we should pal up, like.'

It was like being in the presence of a reptile, a beast whose unpredictable temperament never showed through the thick outer skin. What had happened to make Irene so awful? Why didn't she muck about with hoops and sticks like other children?

'What do you think, Jessica?'

Jessica thought she felt sorry for her mother's sister's daughter, but sorrier for herself. She struggled to find an answer, because Irene was one of those people who commanded answers. It wasn't fair, Jessica thought. She was only five years old, still unable to work things out properly, and her mother was in the TB place. Irene was thirteen years of age, and her mother had tried to kill her. The idea of a mother trying to kill her own daughter was terrifying. And was it the real truth? Was Auntie Ruth capable of hurting Irene, or had Irene invented the whole terrible story? 'I don't know,' she said again.

'Like I said before, you know nowt.' Irene walked away at a leisurely pace, no sign of resentment in her demeanour.

Jessica found herself scratching her own neck, her scalp, the backs of her hands. Had she caught fleas, or some terrible skin disease? When her cousin had disappeared round the View Street corner, Jessica crawled homeward. Although technically clean, the child felt a sudden and overwhelming need for an all-over wash.

She fell in at Mrs Harris's door.

'What's up with you?' asked Eva. 'Have you seen a ghost or summat?'

Jessica sat down at the table. 'I met my cousin Irene,' she answered eventually. 'On Derby Street on my way home from school. She kept . . . talking to me.'

Eva studied the face of her young charge. 'Ah, so you have seen the dark side. Stop away from her – she's got some funny habits.' Like messing about in the funeral parlour, stealing money, pinching fruit from outside the greengrocery. The midwife decided not to enlighten Jessica any further on this particular occasion.

But Jessica already knew about the funny habits. 'She's not like other people,' she said.

Eva carried on peeling potatoes. 'You can say that again, love.' She inhaled deeply. 'Wash your hands, then set the table, Jessica. Mr Coates'll be here soon. He's going to lodge with us.'

Excited now, Jessica ran into the scullery and washed her hands. Mr Coates was nice. There were good people in the world. Irene just wasn't one of them.

Maurice Chorlton lifted the last tray of cheap and cheerful jewellery from the window display, flicked a desultory duster over diamond chips in illusion settings, closed and locked the casement's inner safety barrier. Another Saturday over, another session of mending watch straps and straightening fastenings on brooches. Soon, he reminded himself yet again. The war's end had been celebrated, street parties, bonfires, bunting, singing. Once the economy stabilized, Maurice Chorlton could become a prosperous businessman once more. Patience, patience, he urged himself grimly.

He had never replaced Pauline Chadwick, now Pauline Walsh. Because of that, all business had to be transacted within the body of the shop, as Maurice could not leave his counter and be in attendance downstairs at one and the same time. People selling to him had learned to come at lunchtime, knocking at a door which bore the legend 'CLOSED' in order to do business with the jeweller.

Pickings had been slim of late. Most family valuables had been off-loaded in the war's earlier years, while thieves seemed to have gone on strike. Not that Maurice had ever knowingly purchased items from criminals, though he had to admit to a degree of uncertainty with regard to the sources of some goods. Still, the sins had never been his. As a Christian, he had merely helped customers through some appalling times.

Twelve to eighteen months, he reckoned, before the country could learn to walk again. That wasn't long; Maurice had enough put by to see him through the rest of the decade. Reunion babies would begin to appear, necessitating a decent level of stock in expanding silver bracelets and christening mugs. Marriage would be reinstated as a national sport, so engagement and wedding rings would need to become readily available.

He placed velvet-lined trays on a counter in readiness for transfer to the cellar. From the cash till, he reaped a few miserable pounds, writing the sum in a ledger, sighing heavily as he totted up the week's takings. While he added two pounds, eleven shillings and ninepence to the larger sum, the shop door opened. 'A moment, please,' he murmured.

'Put the pen down now, Mr Chorlton.'

Maurice raised his head. 'I beg your pardon?' He saw that the customer was dressed as if for winter, woollen hat pulled over the eyes, a scarf stretched across the mouth. 'Is this a robbery?' The words emerged with difficulty as Maurice's dry tongue appeared to cleave to an even drier palate.

'That's right.'

Stunned, Maurice dropped the pen.

'We'll be going downstairs,' said the masked man.

Maurice was riveted to the spot. Here was the nightmare scenario he had envisaged for so many years. Here was a clear demonstration of the fact that all jewellers needed an assistant, even if the back-up was female. After all, a mere woman could have been a witness, might have managed to stamp on the button beneath a counter, a system designed to ring a huge alarm bell outside in the yard. But Maurice was alone except for this uninvited and frightening guest.

'Move.'

Maurice moved.

'One foot wrong and you get this.' The intruder waved a crowbar. 'Now, down the stairs and get that safe open.' The man stepped back, locked and bolted the shop's front door, and drew down the blind so that the glazed section would be covered.

'There's not much worth taking.' The jeweller's voice trembled.

'Tell that to the taxman,' suggested the stranger. 'Everyone for miles around knows what goes on in your cellar, Mr Chorlton.' He laughed drily. 'Maurice the Mole, I believe they call you. Fat, greasy little bastard, always with your snout halfway up somebody's arse.' He paused for a split second. 'Losing your hair? You've done one of them wind-around jobs, haven't you? Aye, I can see it now. I reckon you could drive a horse and cart down your parting.'

Maurice tried to clear a sandpaper throat.

'Enough small talk, eh, Mr Chorlton? Go on. Get yourself down them stairs.'

The jeweller stumbled down the first few steps,

heart clanging in his ears. No-one would come, not at this time. No face would appear at the back-yard window, no customer anxious to liquidate an asset. This was terrible, unbelievable.

The cellar was stuffy, workbench piled up with the neglected tools of Maurice Chorlton's noble trade, dust hanging in the air, a few shards of light from a window piercing the gloom.

'Open it.' The crowbar was waved in the direction of the large, walk-in safe.

'I can't.'

'Can't? Or is it won't?'

Maurice flinched, but tried not to let his fear show too clearly. 'It's a two-key job,' he lied.

'And where's the other key?'

'Er . . . next door, in the shoe shop.'

'Lying bugger.' The man crossed the room in two strides, raising the metal bar as he moved. 'Open it or die,' he mumbled through his scarf.

'I can't. There has to be a second key.'

By way of reply, the man in black dragged Maurice across the cellar and pinned down one of his hands on the workbench. 'Fingers important in your line of work?'

Maurice's lips failed to frame a reply.

'Can you set stones with just the one hand?'

The jeweller shook his head.

'Because I'll break every finger on your right hand if you don't shape up, Chorlton. There is no bloody second key. Everybody for miles knows you work on your own, too much of a Scrooge to pay a minder. Well?'

Maurice groaned. 'Don't hurt me.' The words were forced through stiff lips.

'I don't want to hurt you.' The tone was soft,

almost gentle. 'The last thing I want to do is break your fingers, Mr Chorlton. On the other hand – the hand I won't be breaking at the moment – I have to point out . . .' A smile entered the man's voice as he acknowledged his own feeble pun. '. . . I have to tell you that I'll stop at nothing to get into yon safe.'

'Why me?' the shopkeeper moaned.

'Just because you're here and because I need the stuff. You were handy – now, there's another joke for you – so I picked you out. You were on my way from here to there, so you got chosen. Hand-picked.' He raised the crowbar.

'I'll open it,' whispered Maurice.

'Good. I knew you'd see sense.'

Released, Maurice shoved the hand into his pocket. 'Can I ask why you're doing this?' It was a Bolton man – Maurice could discern that much from the accent.

'You're rich,' came the swift reply. 'And there's folk out there with nowt to their name, not a penny in the purse, kiddies to feed, old grannies to care for.'

'And you're Robin Hood?'

The man nodded. 'I drew the line at green tights and I'm useless with a bow and arrow. All right? Anything else you'd like to know? Like name, address, what I had for my breakfast and do I vote Labour?'

Maurice took the keys from his pocket and walked slowly to the safe. The number combination was etched deep into his consciousness, though that particular secret was no use, not now. If he refused to comply with the intruder's wishes, he could end up with no fingers and, possibly, with a fractured skull. Here he stood, a few feet from riches galore. In his mind's eye, he pictured valuable prints, some priceless china, gems of almost matchless quality. He could not lose all that, surely?

'Open it.'

Even now, Maurice played for time. 'The key's no use without the numbers,' he said. 'And I'd have a better chance of remembering the combination if you'd put that thing down.' He glared at the crowbar. Nothing would save him. All the tea in China, all the diamonds in Africa were useless now. For a split second, Maurice recognized his own foolishness. Bodily integrity was worth far more than priceless artefacts. He paused mid-thought. Did he really want to live without his treasures? And how could he claim on insurance for items that were not strictly kosher? 'I'm thinking,' he mumbled. 'Trying to get the numbers in order.'

'I'm not daft,' said the unwelcome guest.

'Aren't you?' Maurice looked down at his own flabby body. 'Do you think I could win if we came to blows? You need no crowbar, son.'

The man shrugged impatiently.

'Look, the numbers are in my brain and my brain's gone numb. The combination got changed just days ago,' he lied. 'I've a job to think of it without all this carry-on.'

The thief placed his weapon on a work table, folded his arms and waited.

Maurice swallowed a lump of pain. For decades, he had run this shop. To the outside world, Maurice Chorlton was a funny little man, short, unattractive, going bald. But here, in his own tiny cavern, Maurice was a king. He could polish gold to perfection, could shape gems, string beads, manufacture jewellery to virtually any set of specifications. He loved his work, could not imagine life without it. 'What would you say to five hundred pounds?' he asked.

'Cash?'

Maurice inclined his head in compliance.

'Today?'

'Tomorrow. The bank's closed and—'

'And, by tomorrow, you'll have this place crawling with police.'

Maurice pondered. 'A thousand. Come home with me, spend the weekend at my house. I live alone. You can rip out the phone, then travel with me on Monday morning, come to the bank for the money and—'

'What's in that bloody safe, then?'

'Stuff you couldn't fence up here, stuff that'll need to go to London – Birmingham at least. Have you ever fenced?'

The man failed to answer.

'It's not easy. Some of the things inside my safe are here just for the duration – monogrammed family silver, original paintings. You'll not get rid of that kind of loot from a barrow on Bolton Market. This is all good merchandise – you'd need experts.'

'Happen I know some.'

'Really?'

'Really,' mimicked the man. 'Now, get on with it.'

Maurice spun the wheel, thirty-five left, back to centre, twenty-seven right . . . 'One second,' he begged. 'Thirty-five, twenty-seven, centre . . . it'll come to me in a minute.' He leaned against the bench, his body turned slightly sideways to the robber. Deft fingers picked up a hammer. Could he?

'What are you playing at?'

The jeweller blundered forward, saw the enemy reaching for his crowbar. Nothing mattered now.

Maurice Chorlton felt a blow across his shoulder, ignored the pain and smashed the hammer's head between the young man's eyes. The thief folded himself into a neat heap on the floor, blood seeping from his forehead, cries of anger emerging from his throat.

Swiftly, Maurice found nineteen on the dial, spun the wheel, turned the key and entered the safe. His shoulder throbbed and the door was heavy, but he managed to shift it home. This was foolproof. No-one else could enter the safe now, as it locked itself automatically once closed.

It was pitch dark inside. Maurice reached for a cord and switched on the single bulb. He breathed deeply, rubbed his injured shoulder and perched on a stool. The thief would go soon, he told himself firmly. Once the man had left the shop, Maurice could let himself out and . . .

Panic flooded his veins, causing his head to pound. What had he done? There was no way out. The mechanism could not be employed from the inside. He should have allowed the burglar into the safe, should have locked him in.

Silence burned his ears. The concrete and steel storeroom allowed no sound to permeate its fabric. This was Saturday. By Monday morning, he would be dead. There was no water, no food and the air supply was limited. The only man who knew of Maurice's whereabouts was a thief with his own skin to save.

'I'll be missed at chapel,' he whispered. But no-one would look for him on Sunday, he supposed. The shop would remain closed on Monday, but who was going to care about that?

He looked at his collection, but found no joy in the exercise. For the sake of these precious possessions, he was going to die. If and when the police broke in, Maurice would be long departed. He thought about his son, realized anew that he had little affection for the lad.

While hours passed and the air thinned, Maurice climbed down from his stool and laid himself on the hard floor. His thoughts became disjointed as he drifted towards his final sleep. For a breath of oxygen, he would have given away every piece in the safe. His chest tightened as if it meant to burst wide open. For the sake of a few ornaments, Maurice Chorlton had given up his hold on life.

EIGHT

Christmas loomed large, its advent proclaimed by crêpe paper streamers and a large tree placed between the staffroom and a women's toilet. Cotton wool caused branches to hang low, while a few baubles added further weight to the matter, giving the fir a slightly depressed appearance, as if some of Earth's worries rested in its frail, spiky arms.

Theresa Nolan, who felt as if she had been in Williamson's for ever, closed her eyes and leaned the back of her head against the corridor wall. She was waiting, had been waiting for months on end for the all-clear, the ticket that would set her free. Now, more than ever before, she needed to get out of this dressed-up fortress. Christmas made everything worse, since Christmas was a time for families. She swallowed her sadness, because she had to continue now without Jessica. It was time to move on, as Williamson's was becoming a dangerous place for Theresa Nolan. And she had to get out into the world, needed to earn so that her daughter might have a bit put by for the future.

'Hello.'

Theresa glanced upward and smiled. Monty Sexton, an older man and a patient in Room Fifteen

(Shared), had been visiting Theresa for some weeks, had brought her extra magazines, a few old books, some scented soap. Although Theresa could have moved into a ward, she had begged to remain alone until her room was needed. Her plans, her schemes for the immediate hereafter, required silence and a lot of thought. She sighed, shook her head at her companion. It was all right for him – he had an official clean bill of health on a signed sheet, every 't' crossed, every 'i' dotted. Monty was due to leave in a matter of weeks.

He looked around furtively. 'What are you up to?' he asked, his accent announcing a close relationship with the city of Liverpool. Monty was not a great talker. He was the sort of man with whom Theresa could sit for half an hour without the need for senseless prattle and gossip. As always, he dived straight into the heart of the matter. 'You're stewing on something.'

She shrugged lightly. 'What on earth gives you that idea?'

Monty Sexton scratched his head. 'You've a suitcase under your bed for a start.'

'It might be empty,' she replied.

'Well, it's not. I picked it up and it was heavy.'

Theresa sighed. 'I'm getting out.'

'Really? Are you signed clear?'

'No.'

'Then what are you playing at?'

Theresa raised her shoulders again. 'Well, it's not a game of marbles, I can tell you that. In fact, it's not a game at all.' She sighed. 'I am going to put my winter coat on and go through that front door, then I'll walk and walk until something happens.'

'Up here? What's going to happen on these

bloody moors?' An ex-seaman from the largest port in England, Monty was not keen on miles and miles of grass.

'I'll find a pub or a big house where help's needed. I'm going, Monty.' She looked him up and down. 'Or, if you like, I'll come with you. There must be work to be had in Liverpool.'

He opened his mouth, closed it, turned away and walked down the corridor.

'Coward,' Theresa hissed in his wake. She closed her eyes again and picked up the frayed edges of her thoughts. Jessica was Theresa Nolan's only family, and the poor, sweet child could no longer figure in Theresa's plans. Although Jessica must, of necessity, become a no-go area, Theresa felt the loss deeply. The woman's existence was emptier and sadder since her daughter's departure. 'Work from your head, not from your heart,' she told herself softly.

A complication had arisen, the sort of complexity that could not have been envisaged. Theresa Nolan, victim of rheumatic fever, rape and tuberculosis, was balanced on a precipice she had never intended to visit. She could not, must not fall in love. Love between a man and a woman was a precious, fragile thing, a vulnerable flower that needed nurturing, attention and time. She had no space in her agenda for that sort of commitment; she was impervious to it, had been denied the chance of ever countenancing it. And yet her heart was warm because a certain man existed, a man who seemed to care for her. And no, she was not daydreaming.

The chair was uncomfortable, but she remained where she was, considering the concept that a viable opening might just be about to present itself, a chance to get out of the sanatorium, to begin again.

She would have to work on Monty, but he had a soft spot for Theresa, had become something of a father figure in recent weeks. Liverpool would be ideal. Near enough, far enough, absolutely suitable. Later, she would start to persuade him.

The opportunity to be helped to escape from Williamson's might not occur again for months. Theresa guessed that her life would be short; therefore, she could not afford to linger here while three newly demobilized menaces were allowed to continue their lives as normal, decent people. With a frail constitution, Theresa needed luck and as much time as she could grab before her erratic heart gave up the ghost. Time. Time to plan her revenge, time to work out how to obtain her sorry three pounds of flesh, time to save up for the orphan Jessica was destined to become. And space, she needed that commodity, too, because—

'Theresa?'

This was not Monty. This was the wrong man in more ways than one, because Dr Stephen Blake represented no sensible chance at all. He was, in fact, the embodiment of Theresa's recently discovered danger within the walls of the hospital. 'Yes?'

He smiled, sat next to her. 'Your results are very encouraging again. In fact, they're absolutely marvellous.'

He sounded like a child who had just won a bag of toffees in a game of musical chairs. 'Oh,' she breathed.

'The photographs are wonderful.'

Theresa sighed inwardly. It was like humouring a little boy, she reminded herself. No matter how long she lived, she would never understand how a grown man could wax lyrical over a cage of ribs and some greyish shadows. He had begun to clean up his act, was slightly neater, less red in the face, was probably nudging his slow way towards sobriety. 'Can I go home soon?' she asked.

She knew the answer; she didn't want to hear it all over again. And she had no home. Number 34, Emblem Street had been given to another family. Maurice Chorlton, who had owned the house, was dead, so his executors had sorted out his son's various holdings. An air of mystery still surrounded Maurice Chorlton's death, as he had suffocated in a safe, while a young man had perished in the shop's cellar from a single, well-aimed blow to his skull. It had been a robbery, everyone had assumed, a crime which had gone horribly wrong.

'Theresa?'

Roy Chorlton. She remembered his proposal and shuddered inwardly. Roy, Teddy Betteridge and Ged Hardman were three of the reasons for Theresa's need to escape soon – yesterday, if possible – from the sanatorium. 'Oh, sorry,' she said to the doctor. 'Did you say something?' He was too close. Whatever was happening between them became stronger each day, harder to deny when physical proximity strengthened the curse. She could not allow herself to experience . . . need, desire for a man. The rapists had wrenched all feeling from her body, yet she craved to touch this untidy fellow, this doctor who drank too much, smoked too much, cared too much for the human flotsam among which he slaved for eighteen hours of each God-given day.

To distract herself again, she thought about George Hardman, who, before leaving his wife, had sent a one-off payment of five hundred pounds to Theresa. The nest egg had been laid and set to incubate in the bank, but she needed to add to it, to nourish and care for Jessica's small inheritance.

'I said no, you can't go home yet. You must learn to walk before trying to run. TB takes its own time.'

Theresa opened her ears to the present and sighed her exasperation. She had never felt better in her adult life. She was rested, well fed and was the recipient of more fresh air than the average privet hedge. 'When?' she persisted.

'Some time next year. Probably towards the end.'

Another year? Here she sat, teetering on the brink of 1946 – could she wait until 1947? Another twelve months stuck in jail for a crime she had not committed? But Stephen Blake would be here . . . yes, he would be here, and the magnetism was intensifying with every passing hour. She was inexplicably angry with him, even more furious with herself. In her mind, she was pacing about like a distracted Victorian maiden with her virtue at stake.

'Theresa?'

His voice was like warm honey, his hands were kind, his eyes soft and gentle. She was falling . . . Theresa amputated the thought, warned it not to regenerate. If she could bear to live in a world without Jessica, she could surely manage without this masculine hiccup. 'I can't stand this place,' she said. 'It's like jail.' There was business to do, business that needed thinking about. Until now, until her health had bucked up, she had felt thoroughly stuck inside a dimension that differed so keenly from normal life. But she needed to get moving while she felt well, she wanted work, money, a roof, some freedom. She had to go, had to start making preparation for . . . for whatever. 'My life is on a back burner,' she muttered. Then, raising her voice, she asked, 'What happens if I just walk out of here?'

The doctor raised a shoulder.

She closed her eyes again in case the quickness of her thoughts might show in her expression. There had to be positions in Liverpool. The place had been bombed, flattened, especially near the docks. Yes, there must be work there, cleaning, tidying up, serving those who slaved to rebuild their city. Anything would do, anything at all. Once settled in a job, she would not leave it, would not risk returning to Bolton. She had TB. Just like a criminal, she would need to keep a low profile. She would do anything, anything at all for a wage packet and somewhere safe to live until . . . until some unspecifiable time in the future.

He cleared his throat as if to remind her of his presence.

'What would happen if I walked out?' she asked again.

'We would try to bring you back, because your saliva is still registering positive. You might reinfect your daughter, for example. Though she is probably fairly immune by now.'

Jessica would play no role in Theresa's half-formed plan, because Theresa's life was about to change radically if and when she made her break for freedom. Jessica was better off with Eva, Theresa said inwardly for the umpteenth time. 'So I'd be arrested?'

'Not quite.'

Theresa tried to glare at him, but discovered that the action was impossible. 'Have you any idea of what it's like for us in here?'

Stephen Blake raised an eyebrow. 'I live here myself,' he said.

'From choice, though.'

He had never said the words, had never told anyone except the headshrinkers, and headshrinkers scarcely qualified as human. Now, for the first time ever, he framed the words voluntarily. 'I'm not here from choice, Theresa. I'm here because . . .' He was here because he was crazy, afraid of life on the outside, of crowds, of empty spaces, of the weighty loneliness in his chest, of free-floating panics, of too-dark nights and over-bright days. Afraid of decision-making, terrified of existence itself.

'Are you all right, doctor?'

Was he? 'I'm here because I found my absolute double blown to bits on the edge of a battlefield.' He paused, inhaled. 'My twin brother was in several pieces, most of which I managed to collect in various containers. It was an awful experience.' *Awful* did not begin to touch the hem.

Theresa gasped. 'Oh, God. Dr Blake, I'm so sorry.' She looked at him, feeling pity and something far deeper than simple empathy in her heart. He was a lovely man with a good, solid heart and, God help her, she loved him.

At first, she hadn't really noticed him. He had been another jailor, another bloody nuisance who kept coming up with all the wrong answers. But oh, he was so sad, so frail around the eyes. 'I had no idea,' she murmured. He was hiding here, just as she intended to conceal herself in a city that bordered the Mersey. The poor man had found a place that was an island in itself, a community set aside deliberately so that the rest of society would be safe from disease. Perversely, Stephen Blake had grabbed his own special sanctuary in this grey, miserable commune where a plague named tuberculosis was reigning monarch.

He attempted a grin, but managed a pale imitation. 'The world outside is just too large for me at the moment. I'm useful here, clearing up a small corner of mankind's miseries.'

She waited for him to continue, saw the terrible apprehension in his face. The silence continued. 'You're a lovely man,' she said eventually. There, it was said. No matter what she did, no matter where she went, Dr Blake would always know that she had cared about him. 'And losing someone so close – that must have been unbearable.' No wonder the pain showed. No wonder he had spent time walking about looking like an over-large and much-used tablecloth.

'And you're a beautiful woman.' The first. The first real person who had been allowed to share Stephen's misery was Theresa Nolan. She had tuberculosis of the lungs and a face as sweet as a spring morning. When had it happened? he wondered. When, exactly, had he fallen in love?

She shifted in her chair, suddenly aware of her attire. Up and about, she was allowed to wear a skirt and blouse. Was the neck buttoned properly? Did any cleavage show? She pulled tight the open cardigan and folded her arms across her chest. And why was she worrying so much these days? This man had seen her almost naked, had been present every time her bared chest had made contact with a cold contraption that penetrated flesh to photograph distressed innards. He was blushing. She was a woman and he was a man and he was . . . interested.

'Did I embarrass you?' he asked.

Theresa shook her head, knowing that the gesture

was a mimed untruth, because she was embarrassed by his tentative attentions – but flattered too.

'You are a special woman, Theresa. Give yourself time and—'

'And what?' Her face glowed. 'And I'll get out of here fit and well?'

'Better,' he amended.

'Better. Not well, never completely well, not after rheumatic fever.'

He waited for her to continue.

'During my life, I've spent months in bed. I had to learn to walk all over again when I was a child. And now, this.'

Stephen's hands were tight fists. He pressed one against his mouth for a second, as if he could not bear the idea of her distress. 'Is Jessica well?' He spoke as if his main aim was to fill the gap with some sort of inanity, anything to help the moment on its way.

She nodded. 'She's with Eva. Jimmy Coates is renting a room at Eva's, too. They're very good people. Between them, they'll keep an eye on my daughter.'

Stephen Blake used a fingernail to scrape a bit of rice pudding from his stethoscope.

'You're still a bit of a sight at times,' she advised him. 'Better than you used to be,' she added hastily.

'Always was. I jump into things, you see.'

'Yes. Like custard and gravy, usually head first, I'd say.' They had both jumped. They had leapt like a pair of lemmings into territory as yet uncharted. She loved him. The thought of living in a world that contained him yet set him apart from her was so horribly miserable. Touch him, ordered an inner voice. Tell him, make the words, find the language.

Oh, how she would miss him, how she would grieve for him and for another innocent soul, her precious, beautiful little Jessica.

He sighed. Her pain was his pain; her lack of hope was communicating itself to him. Without even turning his head, he knew her facial expression. She was right, of course. He could not manage to remain tidy, was forever covered in drops of ink, spots of food, drips of tea and coffee. Now, he was experiencing a love which must, of necessity, become messy or remain unfulfilled and unconsummated. Had his heart chosen Theresa deliberately? A doctor was supposed to be immune to the charms of his patients. Had he picked on this woman, however unconsciously, so that he would be forced to maintain a distance?

Theresa, sensing his discomfort, kept her mouth closed. The atmosphere was tense, as if a message tried to write itself in the heavily disinfected air that divided them.

Stephen Blake knew that she had stiffened. Theresa was aware of him, then. Theresa was slender, perfectly built. Theresa's strawberry-blonde hair was the result of an impossible alliance between ripe corn and the sweeter, softer fruits of summer. Theresa. That was a lovely name. Her eyes, wide-set and large, were framed by thick, brown lashes. She was so terribly, so dreadfully lovely. 'I wish I could help you,' he murmured. 'I'd do anything.'

'Yes.'

Yes, what? he wondered.

'But you can't,' she said quietly. 'You're forced to keep me here.'

A house on the moors, he speculated stupidly. They could live together, sleep in separate rooms until the bacterium had died its death. Theresa's windows would need enlarging to let in the air, but nothing was absolutely impossible. He could bring her into the clinic, could treat her, take her home—

'What are you thinking about?' Afraid beyond measure of the answer, Theresa felt strangely compelled to pose the question. Something was happening to her – to him, as well.

'I'm fond of you.' He cleared a throat clogged by emotion.

'I like you, too,' she replied.

He turned and saw the heightened colour in her cheeks. 'You're so pretty,' he whispered.

Stephen Blake was not pretty, but he had a wonderful voice and a kind face. She wanted to soothe his brow, to clean his clothes, to protect a heartbroken man whose brother had died, whose life had been cruelly altered by violence. 'A bad thing happened to me, too,' she ventured. Could she? An impatient voice in her head told her sharply, Yes, of course you can. So she did. 'I was hurt by three men. Jessica came along nine months later.'

Stephen froze.

'So my world got turned upside down, too.'

'I'm sorry,' he managed, his tongue stiffened by shock.

'Wasn't your fault.'

He didn't understand rape, certainly was not prepared for the deep fury he felt now. 'Do you know . . . them?'

'Yes.'

Theresa had few visitors, so her parents must have died, he supposed. 'Have you any family?'

'I've brothers and sisters. But my father cast me out as a Jezebel. He's dead at last. My sisters and brothers didn't bother to defy him, so they can keep their distance for ever as far as I'm concerned. There's just me and Jessica.'

He waited, but received no further information. 'How do you manage?' he asked at last.

'Their fathers have paid for my silence,' she answered. 'It's called blackmail.' Theresa swivelled in her chair, waited until he turned and looked into her eyes. 'I'll get over TB,' she promised. 'I have to. You see, doctor, the money isn't enough. It doesn't even take the edge off my fury. I hate those men.'

A thrill of unease crept up Stephen's spine.

'They altered my life. My daughter is a little creature who was put into this world by one of the three criminals who attacked me. You know, I think I've stayed alive just to have my day with them.' Theresa blinked slowly, realizing what she had just done. No-one knew of her plans. She had not perfected them, was still unsure of the details. How could she trust this man? How could she fail to trust him? Her instincts were strong; this was a good person, a lovable human.

'Revenge starts wars,' he advised her.

'I know.' She was fully conversant with her own will, her own state of mind.

'You might destroy yourself while seeking to destroy others. The good gets damaged along with the bad.'

She nodded. 'Yes, some nasty things have to happen. And my life is already ruined, I suppose.'

He took her hand. 'There can be a new beginning,' he said.

The words were not lost on her. His caress, no more than a cradling of her fingers, made molten lava of her blood, sent it rushing crazily through her veins. One word from her lips, and she could have this doctor, could cherish him, and the task would not be arduous. He was lonely, hurt, charitable. He was what Eva Harris might have termed 'a gradely chap'. 'There are things I've got to do,' she muttered. 'There's no choice.'

'Free will,' he answered. 'Always, always, there are options.'

Options? Where had her choices been that night? Theresa heard the drunken laughter echoing down the years, felt clammy, rough fingers on her body, took in the nauseating stench of breath tainted by vomit and ale. The agony was still with her, was stored, filed away for future reference, written in a clear and certain hand. Nothing would distract her. No flirting for Theresa Nolan, no marriage, no lover. 'I have made my decision,' she said.

'You could change your mind.'

'No.' That monosyllable seemed to seal her fate, because she saw the disappointment in her companion's eyes. He released his hold on her, allowing her hand to join its partner in her lap. Dr Stephen Blake could never want a woman who lived for vengeance.

'I must get on,' he mumbled, stethoscope swinging as he rose to his feet.

Theresa smiled vaguely, nodded, bit back tears as he walked away. That had been just another silly moment, anyway, she informed herself. No-one fell in love in a series of split seconds while discussing sputum and X-rays. No-one could possibly want a man in a soup-stained shirt, or a woman who manufactured germs inside her chest. So. She had to go, had to get out now.

Stephen Blake turned and looked at the woman

he desired so much. As still as a painted Madonna, she sat, hands folded, face serene, feet angled to one side, slender ankles crossed. She was waiting for life to start up again, waiting to get out and avenge herself. Although he shivered, he could not bring himself to blame her. It occurred to him that he might have offered help if she had asked. But no. A doctor did not destroy. He had put himself through rigorous training in order to maintain life, not to make others suffer.

As he walked on, the picture of a bloodied field entered his mind. If he had found his brother's killer, what might he have perpetrated? He shook his head, went to a cabinet and picked out a file. In Room Eleven (Single) a man lay dying, lungs hacked to pieces, throat cut to accommodate a breathing tube, wife and children weeping at home. There was work to be done.

'There are two choices, Monty. Either you take me with you, or I walk out of here and grab my own chances.'

'That's bloody blackmail.'

'Yes.' She was good at blackmail . . . 'Look, I don't care what I have to do. I'll sweep floors, clean windows . . . Why are you laughing?'

'You're not fit.' But he knew of a job, one that would be less than arduous, a cash-in-hand and no-questions-asked position that might just suit the determined little madam.

Sensing that he was weakening, Theresa maintained a difficult silence. She was desperate enough to know when to shut up.

'You want to get away from Bolton,' he stated slowly. 'But to stay near enough to your daughter so that you can see her from time to time.' He walked to the window. 'I help to run a place for retired sailors,' he told her. 'Even though I've been stuck in here for months, the job's still there for me. It's in Waterloo, the north end of Liverpool.'

She held her breath, held her tongue.

'They need a housekeeper.' He swivelled and faced her. 'Somebody discreet and sensible. It's a charity, run by business folk, lawyers, doctors, the police force.'

It sounded ideal. Housekeepers were elevated people, folk who were often strangers to dusters, mops and scouring powders.

Monty sat down. 'I'm staying here through Christmas,' he said. 'I might as well. So, while there's a bit of time, I want you to think about this job before you snatch at it. It's not as straightforward as it sounds.'

'Oh?' The syllable emerged as an excited squeak.

He nodded, his eyes fixed on her. 'There are a couple of . . . a few girls upstairs.' He pulled at his collar. 'They entertain gentlemen.'

Theresa swallowed. Girls? What sort of girls?

'You'll need time to think,' said Monty.

'No.' Beggars could not be choosers. Hadn't she decided already that any kind of work would do? 'The pay?' she managed to ask.

'It's good,' he told her. 'Eight pounds a week with all found.'

All found? Eight pounds, no bills to pay, no food to buy? If Theresa survived for a couple of years . . . She calculated. Three hundred pounds a year might be saved, even if she allowed herself a modest income from the spoils. 'I'll take it,' she said. Prostitutes were no problem, she insisted inwardly. They probably saved other women from all kinds of attacks.

'Unless it has already gone to someone else.'

She jumped up. 'Ask Dr Blake if you can use the phone privately, Monty. That job is mine.'

He was as sober as a judge, as wise as Solomon before offering to cleave that baby into two halves in order to discover its true mother. Along the corridor, Bing Crosby sang of children listening for bells on Santa's sleigh. 'Come here,' ordered Dr Stephen Blake. He wore a new suit and a shirt white enough to hurt the eye even in this darkened room.

Mesmerized, limb and nerve loosened after one tot of Navy rum, Theresa obeyed her master. Christmas was happening somewhere else, not here, not in this spartan cubicle with its narrow bed, hard chairs and chipped, paper-strewn desk. Yet she would not have lost this moment for anything, least of all for the privilege of taking part in Williamson's festive cheer.

The nearer she came to him, the more slowly her heart seemed to beat. Surely the opposite should be happening?

'I love you, Theresa,' he said. 'And if you want me to bite back those words, I can't, because they're said, they've floated off to wherever words go when they're done with.'

The man was a piece of pure magic. 'I think I love you, too,' said Theresa Nolan. She thought she loved him? Thought? She knew, understood, though emotion had little to do with understanding. Love simply happened, came along at the least convenient of times. With the exception of her daughter, Theresa had felt little for anyone.

Beyond help, they entered a world created exclusively for them, a timeless zone where nothing mattered save the pleasing of each other. He buried his face in her hair while she breathed in the scent of his throat, her fingertips seeking the pulse in his neck before allowing her lips to capture his life-beat. Remembering nothing, expecting everything, she lay down with him and gave herself up to a joy she had not expected to experience.

'Marry me,' he begged afterwards.

Wrapped in a rough blanket and a layer of passion that threatened to return, Theresa smiled into darkness. She was capable of love. She was able to relate to this one, precious man, yet she must leave him. 'Not yet,' she replied. 'Not just yet.'

He touched her hair. 'When?'

'That depends on how much "when" I have left.'

'I want us both to live for ever.'

In that moment, Theresa came to terms with the true identity of love, its symptoms, its side-effects. Love meant that she did not want to live for ever. Love meant that she needed to die before he did.

She could not, dared not bid him goodbye. Dejected beyond measure, Theresa sat on her lonely bed and watched the heavy sky as it darkened to envelop completely a clump of trees. She had made an arrangement with herself, had decided that she would remain here only if pregnant. Pressing her hands against a firm belly, she felt the warning signs, the dull ache that preceded menstruation. There was no baby, then. Disappointment dashed through her heart, while her brain insisted on rejoicing. Deserting her man was almost as confusing as leaving Jessica behind.

She sighed, leaning back against a pillow harder than concrete. Theresa Nolan, mother, ex-mill worker, ex-maker of meals in a munitions factory, was about to become a not-quite-madam.

She remained on her bed, watching the corridor lights dimming as night approached. After dark, alternate sets of lamps extinguished themselves, leaving sufficient illumination for the patients to walk to and from the bathrooms, not enough for reading or playing cards outside the wards.

Williamson's was as silent as a graveyard. Her transport to Liverpool was to be parked at the other side of a small wood, the copse she had stared into for almost a whole year. At first light, she would slip out through her window and make for that country road. She could do it; she could run a seaman's retreat. There was a full staff of domestics to do the heavy work, and the . . . the other business, the less savoury side of the post would be manageable, she felt sure. Monty, who had left a few days earlier, would be driving the van, would be taking her away from Jessica, from Stephen, from Bolton.

She turned her head to look at the single room which had been her home for such a long time. How she would miss Stephen. She could see him now in her mind's eye, tousled hair, his never-quite-white coat, a stethoscope that went missing several times a day, his smile, that square, strong jawline. He was her heartbeat, her strength, and she could not stay.

The fingers attached to her handbag stiffened. She could not remain with Stephen, could not risk being dragged back to Williamson's. But oh, how badly she needed his love, his touch, his scent, the sight of him. It was like being split in two, one half trying to remain with her lover and her daughter, the other half screaming for vengeance. But oh, how she needed to have her day with those three men. She was going; she was going to prepare.

In Liverpool, she would be near enough and distant enough, ideally placed for the fulfilment of her requirements, the culmination of all those years of thinking, wondering and plotting. Betteridge, Chorlton and Hardman would become lulled into a false sense of security, would believe that their luck had changed, that Theresa Nolan had lost interest, disappeared or died. But before she could punish them she had to make sure her daughter's future was secure. That must be her first concern.

Jessica must be all right. Eva had taken the savings from Emblem Street, and Theresa would continue to send money for the child's upkeep. The little girl needed to be safe, must play no part in her mother's intended actions. 'I'm a madam,' whispered Theresa into the thick pall of a winter night. 'And those three men had better watch out, because I'm coming for them. Madams are tough. I am tough.' Who on earth was she trying to convince?

The time dragged. Anxious to be alert before breakfast-bearing trolleys began their rattling, Theresa paced the floor, visited the bathroom a dozen times, allowed various scenarios to play their pictures across her mind's eye. In each drama, she had the upper hand, while three men grovelled across cobbles, clothing torn from their bodies, mouths widened by fear, eyes fixed on the woman whose life they had virtually destroyed.

It was almost morning, surely? On a whim, she pulled a page from a crumpled pad, rooted around for a pencil, then repaired once more to the ladies' in search of ample light. After chewing absently on wood for several seconds, she wrote her message.

Dearest Stephen,
    Please believe that I love you. But I couldn't stay. When you said another year, it nearly killed me on the spot. It's hell here, especially for somebody like me, because I don't know how much time I have left to live.
    I want to thank you for all your help, for your care and understanding. I have become [she chewed the pencil again] very fond of you and I know you like me. Stephen, I cannot stay in the same place as you, because I need you and would never leave your side. You might lose your job because of me. But I will miss you so very much. There aren't enough words to say how I feel, but life without you is going to be far from easy. I've got things to do, things I can't write down. I could die in here, you see. I could die without seeing to certain matters first.
    Please look after yourself and don't send anybody to look for me. I'm going a long way away from Bolton. Jessica will be staying with Eva. I'd be grateful if you would keep in touch with Eva, just to make sure that my daughter is all right.
                            With love, Theresa Nolan

She folded the paper and addressed it to Dr Stephen Blake before pinning it to a staff noticeboard. It was time. With a heart labouring beneath the onus of mixed emotions, Theresa Nolan walked out of prison and into a silent, frost-crisped dawn. Sliding across icy grasses, the escapee made for the woods and the road, stopping only when an owl swooped down into the blackened fingers of a skeletal tree. She was as free as a bird. Or was she?

It was a massive house, three-storeyed and built of sandstone, big enough to be a school, thought Theresa as Monty, taciturn as ever, swept his vehicle along a pebbled, semi-circular path. Neat gardens fronted the hostel, clean lawns punctuated by beds filled with dormant rose bushes. Across the road, gilt-tipped iron railings, proud survivors of the wartime purloining of metals, edged a public lawn which, in turn, ran parallel with a beach and the rather choppy estuary.

'Some of them fell into the sea.'

Startled by the driver's voice, Theresa awarded him a nervous smile. After forty-odd miles of virtual silence, she had not expected him to be forthcoming once their destination had been achieved. Monty was famous for his silences. His accent was strange, while the particular damage he inflicted on the King's English was of a sort she had not encountered before meeting Monty. His breed of slang came from Liverpool. But she was used to him and he could be her touchstone. 'What fell into the sea?' she asked.

'Houses, like. Rich Blundellsands buggers kept finding bits of their back kitchens under water, so they had to move away. Sea's eating land here.'

'Oh.'

'They're holding it back, but King Canute never managed it, did he? I can't see Liverpool doing what nobody's never done before. River Alt, you see.'

'Oh.'

He was warming to his subject. 'River Alt started rubbing up and down the front, so the houses were all collapsing in big heaps. You've got your Mersey, your Alt and your Irish Sea, three waterways battering away and trying to be boss.' He grinned. 'How are the mighty fallen, eh? Into the bloody drink, too, loads of big businessmen and doctors.'

She smiled again.

Monty Sexton studied his companion as if assessing her for the first time. She wasn't one of the so-called educated, but she had dignity, a kind of classiness, a suspicion of innocence in those large eyes. He suddenly wished he had not brought her. 'Hey, love, do you know what you're taking on?'

She nodded. 'You told me often enough.'

'It might not be as easy as I made out. This seamen's shelter is all right. Thirty-two years I was a merchant man, and I've lived in one of the attics for a lot of years now. I've got a funny neck, so I retired early and I do odd jobs. Downstairs is dead straight, like, reading rooms, billiards, bar, dining room and all that. Now, the upstairs is a different pot of porridge altogether. Everybody knows it's there, but no bugger talks about it. Right?'

She nodded again.

He pointed. 'Ground floor's where the lads come, but they're not really lads as such – some of them's in their nineties. They have a nosh and a natter, game of cards, go home, you know the score.' His finger moved upwards. 'Them three attics in the roof is mine and storage. Top floor under me's a couple of big rooms for parties and meetings on one side, then the business is on the other side. Six little rooms, but there's never been more than four or five girls. Some of them are all right, but there's a couple of them could scald the lugs off a docker with their language. You have to shut your ears.'

Theresa swallowed.

'First floor's bedrooms for old sailors with no-where to live. They come and go and they pay a bit of rent – I collect that. Your apartment's there, too, on that floor.'

Theresa nodded. 'Ground floor for day visitors, first floor for old sailors, second floor is . . . the girls. Right, I've heard and understood, Mr Sexton.' She gave 'Mr Sexton' an encouraging smile. 'I'll be all right.'

Out here, in the real world, she looked too nice, too genteel. The so-called board of directors would approve of Theresa. She was a looker, she was the picture of righteousness and she had no family in the area. 'The police are in on it,' he reminded her. 'They know the score and take their cut for staying blind. So, if there's trouble, they'll keep you nice and clean as long as you do as your bosses tell you. Not that you'll be meeting them very often.'

A question hovered and Theresa forced it out. 'What happened to the housekeeper before me?'

Monty paused. 'She went off, like. Disappeared. According to the chap who did my job while I was in hospital, she upped sticks and cleared off without saying a word.'

Theresa was dumbstruck for a few moments. 'Did they search for her?'

Monty shrugged, placed his hands on the steering wheel. 'What I'm saying, love, is that you have to play the game. It's no use running to the police if any-thing happens. Fair weather or foul, the busies turn a blind eye.'

'If anything happens? What's going to happen?'

Slowly, Monty Sexton turned and looked his pas-senger full in the face. 'The last housekeeper was a good-looking girl from somewhere outside Dublin. A police chief took a shine to her, wouldn't have one of the pros instead. He had her beat up, but there was no proof as such. She went moaning to anybody and everybody, threatened to have the chief prosecuted, then she was never seen again, and her belongings went AWOL. The police called round, had a few drinks and a laugh, and that was the end of it. Since her, they've had to manage without a housekeeper, because local folk won't do – they know too much and they have friends and families.'

Theresa felt her heart beating erratically. 'What about her family?'

'She was Irish and she never mentioned home.' This one, too, was disposable, he said inwardly. 'Can I give you some advice, Theresa?'

'Please.'

He sniffed. 'Don't take offence, queen. Dye your hair brown and wear dark clothes, flat shoes, a big cardigan. Flatten your bust and don't smile. No rouge, no powder, no lipstick. Just do the job, collect your money and say nothing.'

Theresa sighed shakily. 'You know I have to stay,' she told her companion. 'There's no way I can walk out. I can't go back to Bolton and I need to earn money.' She stiffened her spine deliberately. 'But I'm not changing how I look. I'll manage them, no matter what. There'll be new rules printed, I shall make sure of that.'

Monty closed his eyes. The select few who presided over the seamen's haven were not beyond taking a fancy to this newcomer. Councillors, accountants, doctors, police officers and high-flying tradesmen were backers of this so-called charity, and they were not averse to pleasuring themselves by enjoying fringe benefits, as they called the seamy side of their benevolent works. 'Just wait till they see what you look like,' he said softly.

Theresa sat and stared at the house. She had been raped and terrified, but she was wiser now. She would oil this machine till it ran like Swiss clockwork, no hiccups, no windings-down. 'I'll be safe enough,' she replied. 'You said I'd have a free hand within the household. So I'll make sure they keep their hands off me, don't you worry.' If she couldn't cope, she would have to do her own disappearing act.

'Right, let's get you inside, then.' He stepped out of the car, his feet crunching on gravel as he went to open the boot.

Theresa alighted from the vehicle and stood poised on the brink of an uncertain future. At a push, she could go back, she supposed, back to the safety of the sanatorium, back to imprisonment, back to a doctor whose facial features haunted her now, while she felt lonely and vulnerable. She noticed the name of the place. 'JUTLAND HOUSE' was etched on a plaque next to large double doors.

'Are you fit, then?' asked Monty.

She noticed yet again how kind his face was and was glad to have a friend in this strange city. 'I'm fit,' she replied, though the rhythm of her heartbeat told a different story.

Monty hesitated for a split second. He had just caught sight of something in the girl's eyes, a hardness, a flash of iron. She wouldn't take much without a fight, this one. If she offered that expression to anybody round here, there'd be no danger for her, none at all.

*   *   *

Bernard Walsh dozed in a fireside chair. He was a contented man, a man who had done everything possible to keep his family safe and comfortable. The house in which he and his family had lived for the best part of a year was all he had promised to his beloved Liz.

Smiling through a thousand happy memories, he chose his favourite and relived his first day in Crosby, watched it like a film, remembering the script perfectly. As he nodded off, his wife's voice spoke the opening lines.

'I like it.' Liz Walsh fluttered like a bird as she investigated her new front parlour. 'God, you could fit the Coldstream Guards in here, horses and all.'

Bernard smiled benignly upon his wife. To please her, to keep the secret of Katherine safe, he would have crossed Niagara Falls in a colander, but all Liz had needed was a change of house. She would have preferred Bolton, he supposed, but she had got used to Crosby after a dozen visits. It was a good enough place, with a working flour mill, thatched cottages, homely shops and pleasant people. Outside, Katherine and the dog leapt about on ice-crisped grass, dashing from apple to pear trees, from greenhouse to gate. Yes, Crosby would do quite nicely.

Liz marched into the dining room, then round a small morning room and into the kitchen, Bernard hot on her heels. Next to the sink, a boiler of uncertain temperament spat water into radiators, while a tall fridge hummed its intention to care for leftovers whatever the weather. Laughing inwardly, the fishmonger enjoyed the pleasure in Liz's face.

Bernard left his wife to her little celebration, walked through the hall and joined John Povey outside. John Povey was a chemist and a character. His father, also a pharmacist, had lived and died in number 1, and John had just sold the large semi-detached house to the Walshes. The man ran a hand through greying hair. 'If the boiler starts acting up, kick it,' he advised the new owner. 'If that doesn't do it, contact me. I know a few good plumbers, you see.'

Bernard studied the man. He looked for all the world like something that had been shut away in a cellar with test tubes and potions, a mad scientist whose mission in life was to harness lightning or turn water to petrol, sand to sugar. 'Are you married?' asked Bernard.

The chemist looked at him vaguely. 'No. I think I'll send Harry Foster to look at your downstairs toilet – I don't like the sound of that flush.'

It was Bernard's turn to be confused for a split second. '*Caveat emptor,*' he pronounced eventually. 'You've already been very good to us, John. The caveat's in the contract because I've bought this house as seen and I'm happy with it. My house now, lad. My house, my problems.'

'Scotland Road,' came the reply.

'What?'

'Your fish shop.'

'Aye, that's right.'

'Bloody mess the Germans made of that.' John fiddled with the gate, trying to make the hinges line up. 'A lot dead, a lot alive and cursing. Decent people; they'll look after you.'

'They already do. I've been down there a few times and they can't do enough for me.'

'Salt of the earth, God bless them.' The gate was a hopeless case, so John started on the fence. 'I know a man who'll replace this rotted section for you.'

Bernard sighed and gave up. It was like talking to the fireback, he decided.

'The previous owner used to deliver,' continued the chemist.

The fishmonger was beginning to follow the meandering path of his companion's probably brilliant mind. 'The owner of the fish shop?' he offered.

'I'll call into your place of work,' said John. 'There's a list of nursing homes, hospitals and so on – places where I'm responsible for medicines and herbal infusions. You'll get the fish contracts if I put in the odd word.'

'Thank you.'

'Not at all.' The pharmacist turned his back on the fence and looked at Father's house. John Povey Senior had been a grand man, the sort of person who would have done anything for anyone. 'I miss him,' he mumbled.

'Aye, we know that, lad.'

'Chess. Every Thursday evening, we played. He died winning, of course. I'd just set up a supposedly undefeatable stratagem, and he died before I could move a single piece. Now, I'll never know how that game would have worked out.'

Bernard stared into the road, pretending not to see a tear being dashed from John Junior's eye.

'We never know how anything ends, do we?' mused John Povey. 'We play the game with the pieces we have and we never guess the outcome. The proof of everyone's dispensability lies with the grim reaper. People force themselves to work while ill, convinced that no-one else can fill their shoes. But there's always a pair of size nines ready to jump into our footwear.'

Bernard felt the chemist's grief, wanted to reach

out and touch his arm. Being a man was sometimes a burden, because only women were allowed to offer a shoulder at times like this. 'Would visiting us do any good?' he asked.

John looked into Bernard's round, open face. The man who had bought Father's house was already on John's list. Occasionally, one met a person who had always been an old friend, a new man or woman whose goodness precluded all need for introduction or potted histories. 'I'd be delighted to come,' he replied.

'And we'll be glad to have you.'

Knowing that Bernard spoke the truth, John Povey clapped a battered trilby onto his shaggy head and set off for home. Home was in Walton. He lived a solitary life, just a very tolerant cleaning lady and several stray felines, most of which had moved in while he wasn't looking.

Bernard leaned on the wonky gate and stared across the road.

'Nice, that house over there.'

He turned, found Liz at his side. 'Aye, that's the Corner House. John said it was built by a sea-captain in 1926.'

'Worth a few bob,' commented Liz.

'Aye, it might be.' In reality, the Corner House was no larger than number 1, but its detached status probably added to its value. The house's 'eyes' were bright and studded with sections of stained glass. 'Proper leading,' said Bernard. 'Every little pane separate – look how the light bounces off all over the place. There's not another house exactly like that one anywhere in the world. It's a one-off, is that.'

'I'd love to get inside,' commented Liz. 'Just to be nosy, see what's what.'

'Yes.' Bernard knew that it was silly to fall in love with another house, especially so soon after buying number 1. But the Corner House looked so happy, so welcoming with its open-arched porch and its setting of laurel and holly. One day, Bernard promised himself. One day, he and Liz would see the interior.

The pair waved as John Povey departed in a cloud of blue smoke. 'He wants his exhaust seeing to,' commented Bernard.

'And his shirt collar turning,' said Liz. 'And a square meal now and again wouldn't do any harm.'

'We'll feed him up,' answered Bernard. 'Come on, lass, let's get the rest of our worldly goods inside before it goes completely dark.'

Inside the house, a grandfather clock, a camphor wood chest and a lovely old bureau spoke volumes for John Povey's generosity. 'Use them in good health,' he had told the new owners. Liz sighed. The Walshes' own belongings looked lost in a place of this size. They needed a proper dining table with carvers, some easy chairs, sofas, bookcases, display cabinets. 'Like trying to furnish the Albert Hall,' she told the parlour fireplace. The house wanted brass candelabra, some Staffordshire dogs, a couple of nice vases.

Bernard slid a tea chest across the parquet. 'There's a good second-hand furniture shop on Scotland Road,' he informed her. 'One of the few places still intact. Some pretty bits and pieces in there, love. We'll get your house filled, never worry.'

Liz gave him a huge smile. 'You couldn't have picked a nicer place for us, Bernard. You were right enough – it was time for a change. And Katherine's bedroom is marvellous.' The little girl's room had a door in one corner, a low opening which led into the roof space above the attached garage. With electric light and a proper sprung floor, it promised to be an excellent playroom.

Bernard experienced a feeling of near-perfect contentment as he and his wife carried the last of their belongings up the pathway of number 1. The chances of Katherine coming face to face with Jessica Nolan were now negligible. Here, in North Liverpool, the Walsh family was almost forty miles away from poor Theresa Nolan and her problems.

'Bernard?'

He swung round. 'What?'

'Thanks.' Liz looked up and down the road, watched a coalman delivering a hundredweight, saw people scurrying home from work or from shops that were ready to close.

'What for?' he asked.

'For all this.' Liz swept a hand across the pebble-dashed frontage of her new home. 'And most of all, for our Katherine. I couldn't have made her on my own, could I?'

The fishmonger embraced his wife, glanced upwards and caught sight of his daughter's face at an upstairs window—

'Bernard?' Liz shook her husband's arm. 'You've fallen asleep again.'

He abandoned his dream, looked around his fully furnished home, saw Liz's Staffordshire dogs, her vases, the new dining suite. 'We did right coming here,' he said.

Liz laughed. 'Been dreaming again, have you?'

Bernard scratched his balding head and smiled. They were safe. Theresa Nolan was miles away and all was well.

*   *   *

There was certainly plenty of work to be done. Theresa rose at six o'clock, prepared a hasty breakfast, tidied her living quarters, then set forth to tackle the day's business.

The day's business was a strange mixture, to say the least of it. There was what Monty Sexton termed the 'kosher' side, which involved the cleaning of rooms where retired sailors slept and the daily turning out of communal facilities on the ground floor. Theresa did no manual work, but she was responsible for the supervision of a score of women who cooked, scrubbed and polished for several hours each day, including Sundays.

The 'girls' did not rise until well past noon. They had their own attendants, a pair of withered women who kept the younger prostitutes' garish settings as clean as possible. Theresa found all the women daunting. The working girls bartered their bodies to make a living, while the older pair were raddled, their wrinkled faces seeming to express all that they had been through, as if life had left its map across cheeks, foreheads and necks.

There was no boss. Theresa collected money from the two old dears and passed it on to Monty Sexton. Monty added to this amount rent collected from the old sailors, then placed it in a poste restante box at Liverpool's main post office.

The job description was rather vague. The invisible bosses had listed Theresa's duties on a card fastened to the inside of her own door. She was instructed to take charge of staff, to check the wellbeing of resident seamen, and to 'ensure that all business carried out in Jutland House was handled efficiently and discreetly'. Monty had informed Theresa that she must keep a weather eye on the ladies of the night and their customers, so Theresa found herself occupied from dawn until well past midnight, though she did manage to grab a few hours in the afternoons. Her day off was Sunday, and she could also take time 'whenever necessary and suitable' for her own rest and recreation.

After a fortnight, she was beginning to know the score. The battalion of cleaners, cooks and bottle-washers was made up of decent, hard-working people, so Theresa was able to leave them more or less to get on with things. Two or three times a day, she visited the retired sailors, listened to their tales, made sure that they were comfortable and that a doctor was sent for whenever necessary.

Gradually, she began to push herself into the lives of the girls upstairs. She wrote down their moans, negotiated a truce when an argument erupted and, surprisingly, found herself enjoying their company. Although the admission came as a shock, Theresa was forced to take on board the knowledge that most of the women were decent, that they had morals of a sort, that they saw their work as necessary and vitally important.

Maggie Courtney was Theresa's favourite. She was much older than the rest, a jolly, large-breasted Irishwoman with bright blue eyes and impossibly red hair whose shade varied in accordance with the amount of henna used. 'I haven't got nothing catching,' she told Theresa one Thursday afternoon after they collided in a doorway.

'Sorry,' muttered the new housekeeper.

'It's all right. I'm used to it. Here, have a seat.' She opened her door wide, swept some nonsensical underwear from a chair and beamed upon her visitor. 'Give us your hand,' she commanded.

After a short pause, Theresa complied with the order.

Maggie studied the right hand, grabbed the left, turned both over. 'I see you've had an interesting life up to now. Been sick, have you?'

Theresa nodded.

'You've had a few illnesses.' She stared into Theresa's eyes. 'Your mam dead?'

'Yes.'

'Your dad?'

Theresa raised her shoulders. 'Dead.'

'I think he's still around. In the spirit world, but not at ease. Probably a bad bugger.' She sat opposite Theresa and shuffled a pack of cards. 'Cut,' she said. 'Into four piles.'

'I've work to do, Maggie—'

'Just cut. It won't take long.'

Theresa cut.

'Now, I've to do the heart of the matter, your present, your past and your future. These are tarot cards. A sailor friend of mine brought them back from America. They've been blessed by an American holy man, a proper one.' She nodded swiftly. 'They call them Indians, but they're not. They're the real American people and they've been treated like shit.'

Theresa flinched at the language, then ordered herself to get used to it. It was just as well that she hadn't brought Jessica anywhere near this den of iniquity, she told herself yet again.

'Thinking about her again?'

Theresa's pores opened. 'What?'

'She's all right for now, that child.'

Theresa did not believe in fortune-tellers. No-one but God could read minds. All the crystal balls, tarot cards and palmistry in the world would never convince Theresa that a sixth sense really did exist.

'She's been ill, too. Never mind, queen, let's see what the cards have got to say today.'

Theresa's uneasiness grew until her skin crawled. The heart-of-the-matter set produced cards showing a search for truth and justice, while the pile representing the past found fertility, pregnancy and ill-health. It was all nonsense, of course.

'Three bad men.' The woman shook her head. 'You're looking for vengeance,' announced Maggie stridently after a pause. 'There's victory of a sort, then the death card.' She looked hard at Theresa. 'Death cards don't always mean physical death. This can also be a change of some sort.'

Theresa, unable to meet the woman's penetrating stare, allowed her eyes to take in the room. Purple rugs, purple curtains, a mauve scarf draped over a small table. On the table sat a square wooden box. Maggie was reaching for it. 'I'll go now,' said Theresa.

'No.'

'But—'

'Humour me. Just a few seconds more, that's all.' She took from the box a small sphere of crystal, tiny enough to be held inside a closed fist. 'I'll warm it up,' declared Maggie.

Theresa remembered a wireless like that, an old thing that had taken ages to find a station. She felt oppressed, as if the air in the room had gathered weight before coming to rest on top of her head. That wireless had often found the wrong station and—

'Two children here,' murmured Maggie.

'They must be very small to fit in there.'

Unimpressed by the quip, the woman carried on. 'I'm of Irish gypsy stock,' she warned her visitor. 'So take heed. Three men, two children, same size, same age. They could be cousins, I suppose, but they're more like sisters.'

Theresa felt herself squirming in the chair. 'I've just one child.'

'Two,' Maggie insisted. 'And they're sisters, definitely.'

'No.'

The raddled face peered deeply into the ball. 'These are not children of the future. They are already among us.'

Theresa raised a shoulder.

'Ah well, if you won't co-operate.' Maggie returned the globe to its box. 'That's a shame, because you'd be quite receptive to the gift if you'd open your heart. Never mind.'

Theresa rose and walked to the door.

'There's a man who loves you. He's looking for you.'

Theresa froze for an instant.

'Take care.'

Back in her own room, Theresa Nolan found herself shaking. Three men, revenge, death. But two children? It was all a great heap of rubbish. And it was time to check the table linen.

NINE

The men who frequented the second floor of Jutland House learned, over the years, to treat Theresa Nolan with something rather stronger than respect, though no man feared her absolutely. She was a gently spoken woman from inner Lancashire, a female who would allow few breaches of the rules, yet one who never berated anybody unduly. This small, pretty and eminently desirable young woman had eyes cold enough, stern enough, to stop any man within a twenty-yard radius. It was as if the often steely irises had the power to shape themselves into well-honed weaponry of a similar colour, so piercing and angry were their depths. After a couple of skirmishes early on in her career, Theresa found herself ignored and almost avoided by the girls' clientele.

With a determination that would have been remarkable in a whole-bodied, agile human, Theresa stuck fiercely to her original brief. She was here to earn, to save, to provide for her child and to bide time until vengeance could be served up coldly and completely. Let the three of them breathe easily, let them live without anxiety. Theresa was simply preparing herself.

It would soon be 1952. For the past six years, Theresa had worked and lived in the Waterloo area of Liverpool. She had registered with no doctor, as she was terrified of being diagnosed once more as a sufferer from tuberculosis. When ill, she took herself off to a Liverpool pharmacy for cough medicines and other potions. She shopped mainly in Waterloo, venturing into the city only when meeting Jessica or visiting Povey's chemist shop.

Eva brought the child to Liverpool three times each year and, after these brief reunions, Theresa always sank into a depression that lifted only when the weeping was forced to make way for routine. The supervision of staff, the checking of laundry, bedrooms, cutlery and menus was Theresa's mind-balm. But, behind a façade of capability, she missed Jessica as if she had abandoned a five-year-old child just a matter of days earlier.

No-one in Bolton knew where Theresa worked. Even Jessica's guardian was kept in the dark, because Theresa was afraid of being traced, even by Eva. But what if Jessica became ill? Theresa's shame with regard to her work proved more powerful than such worries. Also, Dr Stephen Blake, who still worked at Williamson's, had a habit of turning up at Eva Harris's house to ask about Jessica's health and Theresa's whereabouts. So far, Eva had managed to stop the child from mentioning Liverpool. The less the now eleven-year-old Jessica knew about her mother's address and profession, the safer Theresa felt.

Theresa had missed Stephen acutely at first, though time made of him a happy memory, one of the good men who wore white hats and rode grey horses as they overcame the baddies at Saturday cinema matinées. Well, that was the situation during hours of wakefulness, when Theresa could file her ex-lover in a small section marked 'heroes'. Nights were a different matter, because dreams took on an uncontrollable identity of their own, a life that sometimes left the waking woman lonely and bereft. He was gone; she could never have him, would not meet his like again. Often, on waking, she could scarcely tolerate the certainty that, although her man was in the world, she could not be with him. The flame of hatred burned brighter than the flame of love, it seemed. Not for one moment did Theresa allow herself to forget her one, true aim. Soon, she would be picking off her rapists one by one.

With the exception of Maggie Courtney, the working girls kept as great a distance as possible between themselves and the housekeeper. Theresa Nolan was, in the streetwomen's books, a Woollyback, a creature from inland Lancashire, the place where stupid accents were bred. Yet this bold little person was far from stupid. She had no patience with a bit of tomfoolery, was forever leaping onto those whose clients caused a rumpus. The big, faceless bosses kept away, leaving Theresa in sole charge, so her ultimate power was beyond measure. Although she had never sacked a girl, she made it quite plain that such action lay well within her reach.

Theresa entered her living room and tore off a pair of knitted gloves, her face still glowing after the latest altercation. For a madam, she was prudish, to say the least. Occasionally, the carryings-on got out of hand, and she had just lost her temper. Three people in one bed? Theresa had never heard of such a notion. On her way back from the shops, she had met and tackled the ringleader, had made her feelings more than plain.

The door crept inward and a small voice presented itself through the resulting crack. 'Mrs Nolan?'

'Come in.'

A childlike figure entered the room. Maria Martin looked about twelve, although she was in fact much older, and the men loved her. Flat-chested and angular, this waif attracted far more business than the fuller-figured variety of prostitute. The small, streetwise face was white, the eyes wide with a mock-innocence that never fooled the housekeeper.

Theresa sighed, wondering yet again what made mankind tick. 'Well?' she asked, sounding for all the world like some prim, virgin schoolteacher in her fifties.

'Sorry, like,' mumbled the visitor.

Theresa had understood the women's predicament for some time. They saw no other way of making money. Many had escaped from households containing ten or more children, homes where education was judged to be a privilege rather than a right. Maria could scarcely read. She had spent most of her life rearing siblings before running off into the open maw of some pimp. 'One man at a time, Maria,' Theresa advised softly. 'Sometimes, there is danger in numbers, and we don't want the powers that be to be displeased, do we? I mean, if the big boys ever found out . . .' She left the rest of this sentence to the imagination of her companion.

'All right.'

'I make the rules – please remember that.' Sometimes, the committee sent letters to Theresa, usually filled with words of praise, sometimes containing suggestions, never signed. She was probably the most efficient housekeeper the home had ever employed.

274

'I won't do it again.' Maria crept back to her boudoir, a room scented by attar of roses, which sickly fragrance failed completely to disguise the lingering odours of constant sexual activity.

Theresa stood and watched until her door was closed. She ran a tight ship and could not be faulted for her decision-making or her efficiency. Nevertheless, she, too, would disappear soon. Unlike the previous incumbent, Theresa intended to vanish of her own accord.

Newly returned from Povey's pharmacy, Theresa emptied her spoils onto a small table. The pharmacist was a genius of the old school, while his shop was an Aladdin's cave, all tiny wooden drawers from which a pot pourri of odours spilled with every opening. He made his own pills, dropping measured ingredients into an ancient press which crushed and compressed its contents before spitting out little spheres of pure magic.

Recently, John Povey had begun to look quizzically at Theresa. 'Have you ever had TB?' the chemist had asked on several occasions. Theresa's cough was legendary. Often, during the night, she hacked away until she vomited. 'Who's your doctor?' John Povey had asked today. Theresa had snatched up her purchases, had left the shop in double-quick time. She must begin immediately to think her way out of Liverpool. Yes, her moment was about to arrive.

She tut-tutted under her breath, casting an eye round the room. She had spent a lot of time in here, reading, sewing, knitting jumpers for Jessica. Crime novels were piled high next to the fireplace, pages dog-eared where she had marked a murder. It was all down to orchestration, really. She didn't want Jessica to go through life knowing that her mother was a killer. In the stories, detectives were clever. In reality, police were nowt a pound. In the here and now, Theresa planned to become a homicidal genius. Her hatred for Chorlton, Betteridge and Hardman had not abated over the years. She would get them, would pick them off cold-bloodedly, one by one, taking her time, making sure that—

Someone tapped at the door, pushed it inward. 'Mrs Nolan?'

It was Maria Martin again. 'What is it?' Theresa asked.

Maria burst into tears. Maria could burst into tears at the drop of a headscarf. 'It's come back,' she wailed. 'I've just noticed when I went to the lav.'

Theresa walked towards the girl. 'Are you sure?'

Through a flood of crocodile tears, Maria managed a strangled, 'Yes.'

'You know the rules,' sighed Theresa. 'Did Maggie write down the names of all your clients and put the list in the safe?' Maggie was in charge of gentleman callers, keeping lists of names, preferences, dislikes. The pair of old ladies who had 'minded' the girls when Theresa had arrived at Jutland House were now retired, leaving Maggie Courtney to shoulder all responsibility. 'Do you remember the names of your clients, Maria?'

A nod conveyed the answer.

'Right.' Maggie would now have to give the list to Monty, who would arrange, with Theresa's help, treatment for little Maria's venereal illness. Clients, too, must be advised of the situation so that they could seek medical help. What about their wives? Theresa asked herself for the umpteenth time.

'Shall I pack me stuff?' wailed the supposedly hysterical girl.

Theresa sighed thoughtfully.

'When am I going into the clinic?'

'Soon.' Theresa's mind began to tick, slowly at first, gaining pace as the thoughts blossomed and took root. Oh, yes, yes. How sweet this particular revenge might prove to be. According to Eva Harris, Ged Hardman was still unable to get himself a girlfriend, though the tannery was a thriving concern in spite of George Hardman Senior's prolonged absence abroad with his secretary. Ged, whose prime loyalty was to beer, was a well-off hooligan with a desperate need for female company. The other two—

'Mrs Nolan?'

Could she? Of course she could. The housekeeper's breathing quickened. Elation shot through veins like red hot lava, while goosebumps advertised a cooling, shivery skin. Maria needed money. Here was a chance to help Maria, to help herself, to damage and weaken the foe before the final strike.

'Only I don't feel well, see. It's horrible.'

Gonorrhoea was nasty. It spread like wildfire and thrived with the least encouragement, running through anyone it encountered, leaving grown men shamefaced and their wives in need of penicillin and nerve tablets. 'I might need you to do something for me,' said Theresa carefully.

The tears dried magically. 'You what?'

Theresa's heart threw one of its quick tantrums. 'There's fifty pounds in it, plus expenses. When you get back, you can go into the clinic. I'll cover for you, say that you're in bed having your time of the month.'

'Oh.' Maria scratched her head, grinned broadly through crocodile tears. 'Fifty quid? Just for me?'

'It's a very delicate matter.'

'Right.' Astonishment was leaving its mark on the young-old face.

'Just a night or two, you'll be away. That's all the time we can spare without drawing attention to you being missing.' She would tell Maggie. It was a strange thing to admit, but the person Theresa trusted most was a haggard old whore.

'What have I to do, like?' Maria glowed. In her mind, she was already spending her spoils on clothes, perhaps a fur jacket, some elegant evening shoes in silver. Fifty whole pounds was a tremendous amount of money.

'I'll tell you tomorrow. But it will be a secret – do you understand?'

Maria's brown curls bounced in agreement.

'Go now. I have some thinking to do.'

Alone again, the housekeeper sat down and stared at the wall. It had taken a long time to collect the money. Living frugally and taking most of her own food from downstairs, Theresa had struggled to provide for her daughter's future. But Theresa's post called for decent clothing, while Jessica, who had won a place at a girls' grammar school, required several pounds each month for food, books, uniform and other clothing. Still, the several hundred stashed in the Co-operative bank should suffice as deposit on a decent property once Jessica came of age.

Theresa would not live to see her daughter's twenty-first birthday. Although no doctor had been consulted in recent years, Theresa recognized her own deterioration. Her heart was getting worse. The missed beats and near black-outs were now an everyday occurrence. 'There has to be enough saved,' she murmured. 'There's hardly any time left.' Strangely, she did not fear death. Jessica would scarcely mourn her, as the child had been raised for six years by another woman. Dying might well be a release, a way out of a life that had been hard. But there were things to be done, and they must be done soon. Dying before dealing with the three creatures was unthinkable. 'Live,' she commanded herself. 'Live long enough to destroy them.'

She closed her eyes, leaned back and dozed. Maurice Chorlton was dead, had finished up suffocating in his own safe. The police had had a field day with the contents of the strongroom, while many Bolton families had eventually been able to reclaim stolen valuables from the shop's cellar. Roy, left comfortably off but unloved and unmarried, had closed the business and started out on his own venture.

Alan Betteridge had been taken to a hospital for drying out, had returned to Bolton, had been re-moved again rather smartly during a fit of delirium tremens. The furniture shop had fizzled out due to neglect, so Teddy Betteridge now ran an ironmongery stall on Bolton Market. The jeweller's son was well set up in a double-fronted clothing shop, his business just a cockstride away from Teddy Betteridge's stall near the centre of Bolton.

Theresa opened her eyes. Two eggs in adjacent baskets, though Chorlton would be the easier, as he worked inside a building. Her heart raced, fluttered, faltered, so she took in air, blew it out slowly, filling and emptying her lungs until the breathing eased and her heart settled to a grudging steadiness.

Ged Hardman, still clinging to his mother's skirts,

was the only supposed success among the three rapists. Lily, a remarkable woman, had given up men completely in order to take on the world. According to Eva Harris, the recycled virgin had turned very prim and proper, a credit to the leather business and to Bolton as a whole. Mrs Hardman now led a decent, God-fearing life. She ran her tannery for six days a week, attended church twice every Sunday. She kept her distance from the minister, mended no hymn books and entertained no callers. All her energies were directed into the business, which she had turned round for her doltish son. Ged Hardman, whose face had never been pretty, was pock-marked to the point of hideousness. Following years spent indulging a morbid need to pick at eruptions, the man had reaped a bitter, nasty harvest on his face. He was reputed to snarl angrily at his workforce, treating only his mother with a grudging respect.

Only one of the rapists had married. Teddy Betteridge had hitched himself to a blowsy woman, a fat piece who, in Eva Harris's book, was no better than she ought to have been. Driven by pregnancy into marriage, Elsie Marsh had produced two children, one of each kind. She spent her days gossiping on the market, standing in for her husband on the ironmongery stall, then going home to drink more gin than was good for her.

The other two, in their early thirties, remained stacked on the shelf, ugly, selfish and unwanted. A corner of Theresa's mouth flickered. Two would die lonely young men; the third would die married and harassed.

'Theresa?'

The eyes flew open. 'Hello?'

Maggie Courtney entered. The years had not treated Maggie well, but she bore her wrinkles with an air of gratified acceptance, referring to them often as her scars of battle. Her preference for purples remained apparent, as did her love for long, dangly earrings with blobs of glass depending from silver wires. She placed her hands on her hips and gazed at Theresa. 'Well? Have I to get it or not?'

'I suppose so.'

Maggie eased herself into the second armchair. She glared hard at her companion, causing forehead lines to turn downward between heavy eyebrows. 'I tried, but I can't get none no cheaper, queen. Captain Tom knows more about . . .' As if expecting to find an audience, she glanced over her shoulder, then lowered her tone. 'About guns and ammo and all that than anybody else I've met. And he says you've to remember to lose it afterwards, like. He doesn't want nothing tracing back to him.'

Theresa sighed heavily.

'Is there no other way?' Maggie asked.

'Not that I can think of, no,' answered Theresa.

The visitor adjusted a frill of violet lace on her blouse. 'Well, I can't for the life of me see the need to kill nobody – there's no sense in bringing trouble on yourself. Better off to leave the buggers alive, because there's more suffering in this world than the next. Shoot some daft sod and he's getting off easy. And I mean – how long ago did all that business happen?'

'Thirteen years, all but a few months.'

'Then put a stop to this – let it go.'

'I can't.'

Maggie shook her head, causing much-dyed magenta curls to bounce free of hairclipped moorings.

'Rape's terrible. I know, because I've had it done to me more than once and never got paid for it.' It was plain from her tone that Maggie considered non-payment to be a crime far worse than molestation. 'But you're not well,' Maggie continued. 'You're not well enough to be gallivanting about with guns all over Bolton and—'

'I'm dying, Maggie.'

The older woman, who had developed a soft spot for Theresa, bit hard on her lower lip before speaking again. 'If you must go, love, do it peaceful. No point in taking them bastards with you.' Maggie, a dedicated Catholic, had remained fastened to her faith throughout a long, arduous career in prostitution. In spite of her advancing years, Maggie retained a solid core of regular clients who needed her 'special' abilities. She concentrated on what she called penance, enslaving her 'boys' and forcing them to sweep, scrub and polish while she waved a leather whip. Despite that, a simple soul, she placed her faith in God's willingness to forgive most kinds of sin. 'You have to go in a state of grace, Theresa,' she insisted.

Theresa, smiling grimly, managed not to laugh. Firstly, there was her accent, a very interesting mix of soft Southern Irish and harsh Scouse. Then, there were the homilies, the lessons in morals. Maggie's lectures were always long, very serious and well intentioned. The woman could see no wrong in her own attitude – she could lay down the whip and pick up her rosary in one movement.

'You want heaven, not hell,' concluded the older woman.

Theresa could not remember being in a state of grace. Since 1939, her prime concern in life had been revenge; her strongest emotion, repugnance. She loved Jessica with all her heart, yet her most powerful feeling was often a terrible, passionate hatred for the attackers. Sustained by the need for justice, Theresa staggered on through life, hanging on by the skin of her teeth at times.

Now, while clock and calendar marked the passing of each day, Theresa had to make herself ready for her last terrible stand. And here was Maggie Courtney, a whore, saying all the things Stephen would have said, a woman to be trusted alongside that educated, wise and good man.

'How ill are you?' asked Maggie.

'Bad enough.'

'Near the end?'

Theresa lifted a shoulder. 'I've felt better.'

'See a doctor, queen, and—'

'No.' Often, while Maggie preached, Theresa thought about Stephen Blake, about his wonderful nature, about his suffering, about how he had lost his twin brother during the war. But Dr Blake, the man she loved, was an enemy. He and others of his kind might well lock Theresa away again because of the cough, because of her lungs.

'Why not? Even if you can't be cured, you could get some medicine.'

Theresa had told no-one of her time in the sanatorium. After all, tubercular people were not exactly welcomed with open arms. 'I don't like doctors.'

'Neither do I, but I'd have been dead with the clap if I'd taken your bloody attitude.'

Theresa shook her head. 'Maggie, I'm on borrowed time. I don't need to hear somebody say there's nothing to be done. I've heard it all before, you see. Rheumatic fever left its mark.'

'And you're going to kill three men?'

'I hope so.'

Maggie played with some imitation pearls at her throat. 'What happens when you get caught?'

'I won't get caught.'

'How do you know? What makes you so clever?'

'Years of planning.' She stood up. 'I'm sending Maria to Bolton,' she said softly. 'To do a bit of business. Don't tell Monty. I know Monty's on our side, but he has to answer to his masters.'

Maggie closed her mouth with a snap. 'To Bolton? Maria couldn't find her way to the corner shop without a map and a bloody guide dog. What's she going for?'

'To spread a little happiness,' replied Theresa.

Maggie pondered, then sent her eyebrows up to meet a shock of dry, treatment-battered curls. 'She's not dripping with it again, is she? I've told her to make sure they're clean—'

'They look clean, Maggie. You know yourself that it's hard to tell who's got it and who hasn't.'

'But what . . . ? I mean why are you . . . ?' Maggie jumped to her feet. 'Are you expecting her to pass it on to anybody in particular? Like three people in particular?'

Theresa nodded.

'But how will she do that? How will she know who they are and how to find them?'

'King's Head, once a week at least,' replied Theresa smartly. According to Eva, the three leopards had never changed their spots. 'I'll make sure she knows what she's doing. After all, young Maria seems to enjoy entertaining groups.' She inhaled deeply. 'I'm booking her a room. They can do what they like with her, then they can pay for it.' Her spine tingled as she spoke. Years ago, when those three had snatched away Theresa's virginity, she had been able to do little beyond taking money for Jessica. Now, this idea was so sweet, so wonderful. This was justice, because they, too, would suffer as a result of sexual activity. 'Oh yes, they'll pay,' she murmured.

'In more ways than one, eh?'

'Exactly.'

Maggie was painfully aware that she was sharing space with a woman who was more than furious. This was the cart driving the horse all right, because the anger was keeping Theresa going, was fuelling the frail body. 'You can't die till you've punished them – am I right?'

'Yes.'

'The only thing that's keeping you alive is hatred.' Maggie's voice was sad. 'You know, love, I've been a very sinful woman. I've sold my body hundreds of times and I've been driven by hunger to steal more than once. But I've never felt what you feel. People do bad things, Theresa. You've had bad things done to you, but you have to make your peace with God. Murder's a mortal sin. You'll go straight to hell.'

'I'm already there.'

Maggie rooted in the canals of her mind for some idea that might alter her friend's intended course. 'What about Jessica?' she asked.

'She's got Eva.'

'Not for ever. What if anything happens to Eva? Who'll have Jessica then? That crazy sister of yours? That Ruth, the one who keeps trying to bribe your child with toffees? The one who beat her own daughter until the girl went mad? The one who'd love to get her hands on Jessica?'

Theresa suppressed a shudder. Thus far, Ruth had

failed in her attempts to charm Jessica. She was always turning up on Eva's doorstep for a chat, a bag of sweets in her hand for Jessica. Irene, Ruth's ill-treated and unstable daughter, had escaped, had married herself off at nineteen to a daft lad who did exactly as he was told. 'Ruth won't get my daughter,' she replied.

'How do you know? You won't be there. You'll be dead, or you'll be waiting in a cell for the hangman's noose.'

Theresa ran a hand over her hair. 'Look, I'm dying anyway. Jessica's going to be without a mother no matter what happens. I can't start what-iffing over Eva and our Ruth. But I can make damned sure that Chorlton, Betteridge and Hardman are out of the way. God, they sound like a firm of solicitors, don't they?'

'Theresa—'

'No, my mind's made up, Maggie. Get me that gun and say no more about this, please.'

But Maggie persisted. 'Hell is for ever,' she intoned. 'Hell's the torment of eternity away from God.'

The jaded conversation was beginning to rattle Theresa's nerves. Time after time, Theresa's past had been mulled over in this very room. Maggie would keep Theresa's secrets, but she would never come to terms with her friend's attitude.

'What if you die when you're in the middle of battering a policeman or a bank manager? There'd be no time for confession if you passed on with the whip in your hand.'

Maggie lifted a shoulder. 'God forgives me. You should know that, anyway, because you're supposed to be a bloody Catholic yourself.'

'A priest forgives you.' False patience was etched deeply in the words.

'On God's behalf.'

Theresa let out a long-drawn breath of impatience. 'You'd die in sin unless a priest was at the receiving end of the whip. An ordinary man can't give you the last rites. So unless you get a priest on your menu, there'll be no chance of confession.'

'But you are deliberately planning to take lives, Theresa. You are deliberately setting out to kill. And don't be talking about Catholic priests like that. They don't need what I have to offer.'

'Oh, shut up, will you?' Theresa picked up a small framed photograph of Jessica at Eva and Jimmy's wedding. Homeless, wifeless and once tubercular, Jimmy was now Eva's second husband and Jessica's adopted uncle.

'You're thinking about her,' said Maggie. 'And rightly so. Poor child will have a murderer for a mother.'

'You've already said that.' Theresa replaced the photograph.

'Shame,' continued Maggie. 'No dad, then a killer for a mam. Prison's horrible. I should know, I've been inside twice.'

'I will not go to prison.' The words arrived squashed, forced past gritted teeth.

'Course you will. You can't blow three men's heads off without putting your own in a noose.'

Theresa made no reply.

Maggie dropped back into her chair, a hand at her throat. 'Sweet Jesus,' she whispered. 'You're going to kill yourself as well. Aren't you?'

The housekeeper maintained her silence.

'You can't do that.'

'Why not?' snapped Theresa. 'Will I go to hell four times, once for each of them, once for myself? Might as well get punished for the full-grown sheep, Maggie.'

Maggie leapt up, paced about, ground to a halt in front of the window. The Welsh hills were invisible today, shrouded in low cloud. The Mersey and the sea fought along the eroded shore, saline and mucky river water battling for dominance, waves threatening to gush inland to swamp the coast where Vikings had landed centuries earlier. 'You're like that water, a desperate mess,' she commented. 'All seething and angry and not knowing which way to turn.'

'I know what I'm doing.' Theresa's head was beginning to throb. 'Leave me alone, Maggie.'

'No, I won't.' She stayed where she was, her back turned against Theresa. 'Look, I know I might be a bit soft in the head, like, but I really believed you when you said the gun was just to frighten them into giving more money for your daughter. Then I started thinking—'

'Don't wear your brain out, love.'

The sarcasm was lost on Maggie. 'Then I started thinking.' There was a hard edge to these repeated words. 'You can see your own end coming, and you've no intention of shuffling off on your own. Am I right?'

'Probably.'

Maggie swivelled on the spot. 'Sorry, queen, but you'll have to find your own gun.'

Smiling grimly, Theresa walked to the fireplace and opened a door in the ornate overmantel. She drew out a piece of blue cloth and unfolded it to reveal a small handgun. 'I found it,' she said. 'With bullets, too. I wanted you to get me the second one in case this doesn't work.' She stroked the mother-of-pearl handle. 'I've had no chance to practise yet.'

'Where did you find it?'

'In a dead man's chest.'

Maggie blinked rapidly, processing the words. 'One of ours?' Many of the old sailors kept belongings in metal trunks. 'The stuff's supposed to go to relatives or friends, or towards the cost of a burial at sea or whatever—'

'So I'm a thief,' said Theresa, no emotion in the words.

'You just took it after the bloke died?'

'That's right.'

'Yankee Jack,' pronounced Maggie. 'It's his lady's gun, the one he bought in Chicago years since. It was his lucky charm.'

'And now it's mine, bullets included.' There were twelve pieces of ammunition in a small cardboard box. A dozen should be plenty, she thought.

It was plain that Maggie could not lay her tongue across one more sensible syllable. She tapped an impatient toe on the floor, raised both hands in a gesture of despair, then left the room.

Theresa wrapped the small weapon and locked the package in the casing of a wall clock. The home was full of timepieces, each one ticking away vital seconds while three men thrived, drank beer, laughed.

Teddy Betteridge was married. Theresa thought about Maria, balking slightly at the idea of deliberately passing on a venereal illness to Teddy's wife. Whether or not the woman was worthless, she did not deserve the clap. Should Maria confine her favours to Chorlton and Hardman, who both remained single? No, no. It was every man and woman for him- or herself, no room for exceptions.

Theresa set the kettle to boil in her neat little kitchen. Today, in an hour or so, she would set forth to meet the Manchester train. Eva would be full of gossip, Jessica full of bounce. She was doing very well in her first term at the grammar. If the child carried on working so assiduously, she might even end up with a decent career.

A clock chimed, marked another quarter. 'Will this be the last time?' Theresa asked the empty room. 'Will I ever see Jessica again?' It was becoming so hard. Walking tired her, breathing was sometimes difficult, headaches were frequent. But oh, no. Not yet. She had no intention of dying now, of giving up while there remained so much to do.

With cup and saucer on a low table, Theresa sat in her living room and gazed across the water. She had not been unhappy here. The flat was well furnished and decently carpeted. She had a bathroom, a bedroom, a kitchen and a living room. She had chosen wallpaper and paint, was given permission and money to decorate every alternate year.

The bosses remained invisible up to a point. Every summer since 1947, a Strawberry Fayre had been held in the grounds, stalls supervised by the wives of eminent citizens, entertainment laid on by the board of governors. At these affairs, councillors patted one another on well-padded backs, policemen paced about with their feet in the ten minutes to two position, while doctors and lawyers huddled in their sombre, dark-suited fraternal groups. At the Strawberry Fayres, there were no upstairs girls, though their clients and clients' wives were very much in evidence. The wives had fur coats, double chins and smiles that spoke volumes of their patronizing attitude towards their husbands' favourite charity. If only they knew what went on just yards away . . .

Theresa watched a tanker floating across the horizon. Although the water near the coast was choppy, the big ship seemed to glide along on glass. 'I got used to this,' she told the estuary. 'I got used to running a brothel. They say you can get used to anything.' She didn't really manage the upstairs, she reminded herself yet again. She was housekeeper to men who had served their country, some in the Royal Navy, others with the Merchant Fleet. Many had been injured and most were grand men. The other side of the business was nothing to do with her except for the occasional keeping of order during cat fights, and the provision of bed linen and towels. Even those items were laundered by someone else.

She had learned, over the years, to cope with all kinds of people, could even look without flinching into the eyes of the clientele of Maria, Brigitte and Adele. Some males she had seen in a state of accidental undress as they rushed towards a forgotten meeting. Others were wont to acknowledge Theresa even while they sneaked towards their bodily pleasures with collars turned up and scarves wound high to disguise delicate, important identities. She was trusted, was trustworthy. How little they knew of human nature, these men. Theresa despised them, laughed inwardly at the stupid creatures who kept their brains in their trousers. Still, at least they paid for their sins, didn't hover in back alleyways waiting to commit rape.

Theresa closed her eyes again, heard her attackers, allowed herself to feel the pain, to breathe in their stench. In order to strengthen her resolve, she replayed the scene over and over like a cinema advertisement. She could not, must not weaken.

But her eyelids flew open of their own accord, and her heart jumped about, causing her to catch her breath. Could she? Could she? Yes, yes! First, Maria would go in and leave a gift for Betteridge, Chorlton and Hardman. Then . . . then Theresa herself had to finish the job, leaving enough time for the ugly illness to show itself in full glory.

'Stand firm,' she begged herself. 'Remember, remember.' Some animals toyed with their prey. The three Jutland House cats were beggars for messing about with mice, patting, biting, plucking up the poor little rodents and tossing them in the air before the kill. Winston, Viscount and Ike lived for cruelty, often not bothering to finish off their wounded victims, never eating the spoils. Theresa was not a particular lover of cats, because she saw evil in the slanted eyes and murder in those vicious claws. They were walking, stalking killers – and so was she. Sending in Maria would be a cat-like thing, an interesting exercise in the art of torture. VD just before death – what an excellent last meal for those condemned creatures.

It was one o'clock. Theresa went into her bath-room, closed the door, took an aspirin, washed her face. Sometimes, when she gazed in the mirror, she shuddered inwardly at the echo of herself in the glass. She was thinner and paler than ever. Dark shadows beneath the eyes demanded cream and powder, and she had to fight to keep the corners of her mouth upturned. Once made up, she looked all right; passable, though not quite healthy.

She brushed her hair savagely, as if trying to

unravel a tangle of knotted thoughts. It was time to go, time to meet her daughter.

Jessica and Eva stepped off the train and into noise that made Bolton's Trinity Street seem like a poorly attended church. People darted about with luggage, children, boxes and bags. A man propped on crutches yelled as he sold newspapers, an upturned orange box waiting to act as seating when the job became too tiring. A couple of painted ladies leaned against the waiting-room wall, one filing her nails, the other rouging cheeks that were already over-bright, both pairs of eyes assessing every man who passed by.

Eva marched out into the city street, almost falling over a flower-seller's cart. As ever, Liverpool heaved with life. Jessica, who had grown fond of the place, strained her ears in preparation for tuning into the dialect. Folk here had 'never dun nuttin', didn't 'ave a lorra money', waited for 'are kid', promised to be 'bach in a mini'. The end of 'back' seemed to prompt the speaker to clear his throat of some heavy congestion. It was great, almost like being in a different country. Here, Jessica was 'queen' or 'gairl' and it wasn't 'fur' that she had such lovely 'fur hur', better than a 'fair' coat any day. They were a friendly people, generous, noisy and mischievous. One day, Jessica would live here.

Eva and Jessica strode towards the little café in which they always drank tea or coffee with Theresa. It was a comfortable place with circular tables covered in floor-length linen cloths. They took their usual place by the window, ordered tea for Eva, cocoa for Jessica. People rushed by in winter clothing, small clouds of breath preceding them, shoes and boots sliding occasionally on thin skids of ice.

Eva took a sip of hot, sweet tea and dabbed at her lips with a starched napkin. In spite of the passage of time, Eva had not managed to get used to this situation. She didn't know where Theresa worked, because Theresa refused to tell her. There was a poste restante number to which Eva and the child could write, but Theresa withheld any further information.

Jessica, who had laboured long under the delusion that her mother's work involved a lot of travel, meant business this time. In a few weeks, it would be Christmas. No matter what the nature of Theresa's work, she could surely come home this one time. 'We could hide her if anyone came,' she said.

'What?' Eva placed her cup in the centre of its saucer.

'Mam. If she comes for Christmas, we'll pretend she's not there. Dr Blake will have to give up looking for her soon. They wouldn't put her back in the sanatorium, anyway.'

'They might,' replied Eva. She didn't like the state of Theresa's health. The girl was going down, was on her way out if Eva wasn't very much mistaken. As for Stephen Blake – well, his whole reason for living seemed rooted in the pursuit of Theresa Nolan. Like a man obsessed, like Emily Brontë's Heathcliff, Dr Blake never gave up, was always questioning. One day, he would probably follow Jessica to Liverpool, Eva mused.

Jessica studied Eva closely. Mam could not stay away for ever, surely? 'What if you die?' the girl asked.

'Oh, thank you very much, I'm sure,' came the taut reply. 'That should go down very nice with my afternoon cuppa.'

Jessica grinned impishly. 'You know what I mean.

We should have a telephone number, at least. Even if she travels, her bosses probably know where to find her. How would you send for Mam in a hurry if I had an accident?'

Eva shrugged. 'I'd have to write,' she replied lamely. This was none of her own fault, Eva told her troublesome conscience. Theresa's desperate need for secrecy had caused this problem, but Eva was the one who had to listen to the child and answer all her questions.

'Writing's no good if you're in a hurry.' Jessica reached across the table and patted 'Auntie' Eva's hand. 'You know I love you,' she said. 'Uncle Jimmy, too. But she's my mother.'

Eva nodded. She agreed completely with the child – young woman was a nearer description of her wise companion. In spite of being a clever clogs, Jessica was commonsensical, down to earth. At eleven-going-on-twelve years of age, she was easily as adult as many whose majority was expressed on yellowing birth certificates. And the fact remained that Jessica had a right to know where her mother lived. Eva's hands closed tightly round the napkin. Bernard Walsh was in Liverpool, too.

'Mam'll be here soon,' muttered Jessica.

Eva did not reply. Fortunately, Liverpool was a large city, big enough to make space between Theresa and Bernard. What if . . . ? Eva shuddered inwardly. To think that she had practically forced the Walshes to move to Liverpool . . . Oh, it didn't bear thinking about, not on a day as cold as this one. How short-lived Eva's sigh of relief had been, because Theresa had run off to Liverpool without so much as a by-your-leave after escaping from Williamson's sanatorium.

'Are you cold, Auntie?'

She was very cold. 'I'm all right.'

Jessica pursed her lips in the manner of a much older person. She had decided some years earlier that grown-ups didn't know whether they were coming or going. The simplest question could give rise to the most complicated thought processes, many of which brought forth either no response at all, or a stumbling, monosyllabic reply. Auntie Eva was thinking. Thinking never did much good, so Jessica decided to shut up.

Eva stared through the window, watching a man helping an old woman whose apples had tumbled from her basket. Here, somewhere on the outskirts, Katherine Walsh lived with her supposed parents. Danny, who still ran the stall in the Bolton fishmarket, had said that Katherine's family lived in Crosby. Where the hell was Crosby – and where did Theresa live and work? Why did she have to be so secretive? Surely Theresa knew by now that Eva would never betray her? And God forbid that Theresa should ever come across Katherine Walsh. Perhaps similarities between the girls had diminished with the passing of time. Perhaps pigs would grow wings and—

'Hello.'

Eva brought herself back into the present, saw Theresa dropping a kiss onto Jessica's head. 'Eeh, you made me jump,' the older woman declared.

Theresa sat down next to her daughter. Jessica was so, so beautiful, with good, strong bones, lovely colouring, gorgeous hair. She would grow up soon. The idea of men taking an interest in Jessica made Theresa catch her breath. She covered the gasp by prattling on. 'I've bought you some clothes. A skirt and two blouses. They're behind the counter being looked after till we leave.'

Jessica managed a grim smile. 'Thank you,' she mumbled.

Eva watched them. The girl was very much alive, healthy, glowing. The mother remained structurally pretty, but make-up did not cover the greyish pallor, the small pockets of skin where flesh had melted away. Panic fluttered its wings in Eva's breast. When Theresa died, who would take care of Jessica? Would blood relatives claim her, take her away from Eva and Jimmy?

Theresa felt the atmosphere acutely. She glanced from Eva to Jessica, back to Eva. Hoping that the situation would improve in her absence, Theresa went up to the counter to order biscuits and more drinks.

'She's got to come for Christmas,' said Jessica, her voice loud enough to reach every ear in the shop.

Eva sniffed wisely. 'Your mam has to work.'

'All year? All three hundred and sixty-five days? No holidays, no time off?'

Eva understood. Jessica was standing on the outer rim of childhood, preparing to leap into life. She knew too much, understood too little. 'Don't go upsetting your mam,' she warned.

The girl shrugged carelessly. She was fed up with having no mother. Most of the girls at school had two parents, but Jessica was stuck with a foster family and no real roots. Strangely, she never mentioned a father. Sensing a great hurt in Theresa, Jessica had decided not to ask questions about her sire just yet. To have a full-time mother would have sufficed.

Jessica watched her mother. She was small and frail, she appeared to have shrunk more rapidly than

297

usual. Had she been able to read minds, Jessica would have realized that she and Auntie Eva were entertaining very similar thoughts. If Mam died, would Jessica remain with Eva, or would she finish up with Auntie Ruth? God forbid.

'All right, pet?' asked Eva.

Jessica shifted in her chair. Everyone knew that Auntie Ruth had made Irene bad. Irene was like a witch, an evil person who preyed on the weak and the hurt.

'Jess?'

The girl swallowed painfully. Mam looked so weary. 'Yes,' she told Eva softly. 'Yes, I'm all right.'

Theresa returned. 'The waitress is bringing tea and cakes,' she said. 'And we are going to have two Christmases this year.'

Jessica, suddenly happier, grinned broadly. 'Two?'

Theresa nodded. 'When it's really Christmas, I shall have to be in Liverpool. You see, Jess, I look after people who were in the war. Sailors from the navy, other sailors who brought food into the docks.' She patted her daughter's arm. 'Some of them were hurt. Many can't look after themselves.'

Jessica frowned. 'Why didn't you tell us about your job before?'

Theresa rooted round for an answer. 'I'm all over the place, love. I even live in a sort of hotel filled with poor old men. You see, I was afraid that you'd want to visit me or live with me, and you can't. There's too much illness.'

Eva listened hard and decided that Theresa was speaking some of the truth. 'Two Christmases?' she enquired.

Theresa nodded. 'I'll come over for a few days. I'll buy a big chicken and some crackers. We'll have a 'grand time.' The thought of visiting Bolton made her heart beat erratically. But she would go. She would go with Maria Martin, if necessary, would make sure that Maria carried out her unsavoury mission.

'When?' asked Jessica.

'Next week, I think. Just expect me when you see me.' She had taken very little time off; even when ill, Theresa had struggled and gasped her way through endless hours and days. The committee owed her something, she judged. And Maggie was easily capable of keeping the place ticking over. 'There you are, Jessica.' She passed a chocolate biscuit to her daughter.

Jessica laughed. What more could she ask? Two digestives, a new skirt and Mam coming home? Jessica's cup was suddenly filled to the brim. The vessel was not running over, not yet. But this was the first step. Perhaps Mam would return to Bolton for ever in the near future. Tasting a mixture of hope and chocolate, Jessica was content. Almost.

TEN

Teddy Betteridge stared gloomily into his pint of ale. He was fed up to the back teeth, wisdoms included. It was all right for his two companions. They weren't married and stuck with a couple of kids. And the kids were a bloody picnic compared to the flaming wife. Bugger Elsie, he cursed inwardly. He took a swig, then slammed the glass down.

'How's your dad?' asked Roy Chorlton. He had resigned himself to spending Saturday nights in the company of these two cretins. With his pale skin, bulbous eyes and thinning hair, Roy was not popular with members of either sex. Nobody gave a tuppenny damn about him. Ged and Teddy tolerated him because he bought his share of drinks and, anyway, they had got used to his appearance over the years.

'Still as daft as a brush,' Teddy replied. 'He was a strait-jacket job up to last Tuesday, thought he had a plague of giant red ants crawling all over him. That's what drink's done to him, I suppose.' He downed half a pint in one swallow.

Ged Hardman shook his head gravely. 'You want to watch yourself,' he advised Betteridge. 'Or you'll be joining him in the next padded cell.'

Teddy bridled slightly. Who the hell did Ged

Hardman think he was? 'I know what I'm doing,' he replied smartly, swallowing a remark about clever folk who picked their spots and ended up full of holes. He knew what he was doing, all right. He was drinking himself into oblivion so that he wouldn't notice his pathetic little life. What did he have? A load of responsibility, that was all. An ironmongery stall, a wife who looked like a brewer's nag, and two kids with voices loud enough to strip paint off the doors.

Ged, who was easily as unhappy as Teddy, drummed his fingertips on the table. His legendary mother, Lily Hardman, was a demanding, selfish harridan. Although she still doted on her son, Lily kept him dangling, made him wait for every few bob, rendered him childlike and dependent. 'I feel like . . .' Ged's words trailed away.

'Like what?' asked Roy.

'Like hell.'

Roy understood. Roy had a theory, an idea that he had entertained for some years. Having come to suspect the existence of God, the man both feared and accepted the concept of retribution. His soul was tortured, mostly during the hours of darkness, because dreams were beyond his control, while wakefulness was scarcely bearable. Almost every night, he saw her, heard her whimpering, felt her soft flesh beneath his hands. He swallowed painfully. 'We're probably getting what we deserve.'

Ged Hardman threw up his hands. 'Don't start all that again, Roy,' he warned. 'Or I'll take you outside and change your appearance.'

Roy shrugged. 'Please yourself,' he invited.

Teddy Betteridge looked from one to the other. 'You can shut up and all,' he advised Ged Hardman.

Glaring at Roy, he lowered his tone. 'If you want to carry on being some kind of a martyr, bugger off and do it somewhere else.'

Roy raised a shoulder. 'Don't you ever wonder what happened to her?'

'Only when you start whining,' snapped Teddy. 'I wouldn't care – you were the one who moaned when me and Ged talked about her just before the war.'

'She could be dead,' murmured Roy.

'We could all be bloody dead,' replied Teddy, impatience narrowing the syllables. 'We fought for King and country, didn't we? So be a hero and leave the past where it belongs.'

'And the child . . .' Roy took a sip of bitter.

'Look.' Ged leaned forward, allowing his companions a closer view of facial skin textured like crumpets before toasting, sickly-white and covered in craters. 'I'm not saying we did the right thing. What we did that night was wrong. But life has to go on.'

'There's not one of us happy,' stated Roy flatly.

'That's nowt to do with owt,' barked Teddy. 'And we agreed about forty-seven times to stop talking about this.'

Roy sighed inwardly. He sometimes drew a strange comfort from Betteridge and Hardman, because they were the only humans on God's earth who might just understand the nature of his mental torture. Yet they were little help, he acknowledged. Ged laboured under his mother's thumb, while Teddy drank himself into a stupor just so that he could face his wife. 'I've no-one else to talk to,' Roy said now.

Ged and Teddy rose simultaneously from the table. Roy was in one of his moods again. They were sick of telling him to let go, to get on with his life, but the man seemed bent on his own peculiar brand of self-destruction. Without speaking another word, they left to take their custom across the road to the Hen and Chickens.

Roy watched his two so-called friends as they sauntered out onto the pavement. Although Teddy Betteridge and Ged Hardman seemed not to care, Roy knew that both had changed after the rape. Life had provided few distractions for Roy Chorlton. While Ged and his mother had fought to preserve Hardman's Hides, while Teddy had struggled with an alcoholic father and an unhappy wife, Roy had 'fallen on his feet'. After all, hadn't Maurice Chorlton left a small fortune for his son? Even after the disgrace of dealing with police and stolen property, Roy had emerged with a fair packet of money. If only he hadn't been born with a silver spoon in his mouth and several precious gems in the safe, he might have found something to do, some activity that might have taken his mind off Theresa Nolan and her child.

Yes, it had all been too easy. With one hand, Roy had closed a jewellery shop; with the other hand, he had opened a tailoring business catering to the better end of the clothing market, a small empire from which he took little real pleasure. Behind the selling area, men and women laboured with scissors, chalk, machines and half-clothed dummies, while Roy, alone in his shop, courted customers with an air of benevolence that might have suited a Uriah Heep. He disgusted himself.

He had never expected to develop a conscience of such gigantic proportions. Surely, these thoughts and memories should have diminished after all the intervening years? She was always inside his head, usually slightly hidden behind other thoughts, often gliding noiselessly through the mist to accuse him, curse him.

Suddenly, he was aware of eyes boring into his skull from the outside rather than from within his brain. As if feeling pain, he brushed a hand across his forehead before looking up. It was Eva Harris, now Mrs Coates. Her husband accompanied her, and he, too, was staring at Roy.

They walked to his table as few seats were available now, most having been occupied by the newly released patrons of several town cinemas.

Eva sat down while her husband went to the bar.

Roy's breath quickened and thickened. A tightness at his throat caused a short bout of coughing.

Eva took a compact from her bag and powdered her nose. 'Nice to see you, Mr Chorlton,' she said, though her tone belied the message. She replaced the compact in the depths of her capacious bag. 'Jimmy knows who you are, I think,' she continued, her eyes straying to the crowded bar. 'We've been to the pictures. Some daft cowboy thing with John Wayne in a big hat.'

He gulped, mopped his brow with a handkerchief. 'How is she?' he managed eventually.

'Theresa?'

He nodded.

'Oh, fair to middling, I suppose.'

Roy Chorlton gripped the edge of the table. 'Where is she?'

Eva shrugged. 'No idea,' she lied easily.

'The child?'

'Still with me.'

He shifted in his chair. 'Will . . . er . . . Theresa be coming back?'

Eva turned down the corners of her mouth, shrugged. 'How would I know the answer to that?'

'Surely she keeps in touch with you,' he answered. 'After all, there's the little girl to consider.'

Eva leaned her head to one side. 'You talking about duty?' she asked. 'About folk owing stuff to other folk?' Her teeth bared themselves in a mockery of a grin. 'Listen, sunshine,' she spat. 'Wherever she is, she's got a good job and she sends money for Jess— for her daughter. Apart from that bit left by George Hardman before he scarpered, there's been nowt from any of you. Not that she wants anything, mind. She says she needs no help and you've to stop away from the kiddy.' She paused for a couple of seconds. 'You're likely the father – is that it? Is that why you've took an interest all of a sudden? Do you want to groom the lass to make buttonholes for you?'

'No.'

'Then what's the matter with you?'

He didn't know the complete answer, though he had his theories.

'Conscience let itself out for an airing, has it?'

He held her gaze before nodding just once. 'It's always troubled me,' he admitted.

She laughed mirthlessly. 'You've got no blinking conscience, you and them other two buggers. If you'd any decency, what happened wouldn't have happened and Theresa would have been all right. You make me sick.'

'I make myself sick,' he replied softly.

Eva studied him. Like his dad, he was greasy, soft and plump. Like his dad, he was going to be bald on top. His eyes were convex and heavy-lidded, while the hands were smooth enough to belong to a female member of the aristocracy. 'You're . . . sorry?' she asked, astonishment lifting her tone.

He lowered his head. 'I've always been sorry.' He licked drying lips, wished for more beer to slake a fierce thirst. 'When I asked her to marry me, I suppose I was being a bit arrogant, as if she should have been grateful.' He let out a long, hopeless sigh. 'But who would look at me? I know I'm ugly. I know what you see when you look at me. She was so beautiful, so frail—'

'She's still frail.' Eva didn't feel sorry for the man, even though he plainly regretted his actions.

'So you do know where she is?'

Eva paused before answering. 'Aye, I've a fair idea, only I'm bound to secrecy.' She leaned across the table. 'She's told nobody where she works – even her daughter.'

Roy looked hard at his companion. 'I want to help her.'

Eva nodded curtly, then shook her head. 'Best help for her's if you stop away. Them other two, and all.' Theresa was working her way up to something. Was that something going to be murder? 'She's not forgot, neither,' continued Eva. 'There's a lot of anger in her, a lot of hatred. She might not be strong, but I'd watch my back if I were you. Theresa's . . . she's clever, if you take my meaning. She stews on things, thinks them through.'

'So do I,' he said.

Jimmy returned, a glass of brown ale in each hand. 'It's like a bloody cup final crowd near that bar,' he grumbled. He placed the dripping containers on the table. 'Half the beer's gone on yon floor.'

'This is Mr Chorlton,' Eva informed her husband.

Jimmy, whose sight was less than perfect, peered at

306

his wife's companion. 'What? Him as . . . him as did the ra—'

'Aye,' snapped his wife. She spotted two vacant chairs at another table, jumped up and dragged her husband across the room. Although Chorlton had become a rather pathetic figure, Eva distanced herself determinedly. She would stand firm for Theresa and for Jessica.

Roy got to his feet and grabbed at his cigarette case and lighter. It was time to go home. He lit a cigarette, flinching when hot smoke scalded an eye. Eva Coates was staring hard at him. Nothing would ever be right, he told his inner self. The pain would go with him to his death, and there was little he could do to change that fact.

With a heavy heart, he left the pub, turned right and wandered in the direction of Chorley New Road. A cold, lonely bed waited to receive him and his brief, tortured dreams.

Pauline Walsh was the happiest woman alive. She sat in her living room with Danny and Edna, both in their Sunday best, both grinning from ear to ear. The impossible had happened; the impossible lay cradled in Pauline's arms, a boy-child clothed in an old Greenhalgh christening gown, over which was wrapped a white shawl. 'I still can't believe it,' sighed the new mother. At the age of forty-two, almost old enough to be a granny, she had finally produced a healthy baby.

Edna cackled, allowing her companions a full view of newly acquired and ill-fitting dentures. Their Pauline had done herself proud in marrying Danny Walsh. Not only had Danny bought two houses, he had also been through all kinds of mental torture before the creation of little Jonathan William Walsh. Pauline's insides weren't up to much, but Danny had insisted that the 'fault' could well have been his. 'I'm that proud, I could burst,' announced Edna.

Danny grinned. 'Please don't explode,' he begged his mother-in-law. 'This house conversion cost me an arm, a leg and fourteen tons of cod.'

Edna chuckled happily. Two weavers' cottages had been made into one, resulting in a big parlour, a decent kitchen, a downstairs washroom and a nice little morning room where Edna spent most of her time. Upstairs, a gleaming new bathroom had been installed, and there were four bedrooms, two large and two small. It was heaven. Edna was a grand-mother, the child was beautiful and all was well with the world.

Danny glanced at the clock. Jonathan had been baptised at Sts Peter and Paul in Bolton, the church in which Danny and Bernard had been named. 'Where have they got to?' he asked of no-one in particular. 'I hope they've not broken down.' He was referring to the other Walsh family, the contingent from Crosby, Liverpool.

Pauline continued to croon softly into her baby's hair.

'They'll be all right,' said Edna. 'They'll be having a look round Bolton – it's ages since they visited.'

'I hope you're right,' said Danny. He and Pauline exchanged glances. Edna knew nothing of Katherine Walsh's true parentage. Edna was ageing and garrulous, could not be trusted with a secret of such immensity.

Danny moved and stared through the front window. For years, Bernard had managed to avoid bringing his family to Bolton or to Bromley Cross.

Danny and Pauline understood Bernard's reasons, because Liz and Katherine must be protected at all costs. But Edna was often annoyed at what she chose to diagnose as an affront. 'It's me they don't like,' she would grumble, volunteering to visit an old crony or a relative. 'If you tell them I'll be out, they'll come,' she was wont to say.

'They came to the baptism,' Pauline told her mother. 'I told you they'd come, Mam. Like you said, they're probably having a drive round.'

Edna employed one of her sniffs. 'Happen we're not good enough for Liz. When Bernard comes to see his mates on the market, she stops at home in her posh house, doesn't she?'

'There's Katherine to see to,' answered Pauline.

'Not in the school holidays.' Once these words had been spoken, Edna smiled at her sleeping grandson and stalked off into the morning room.

'She always has to speak last,' grumbled Pauline. 'Even if it means leaving the room.'

'She's old.' Danny turned from the window. 'And they're here. Let's hope your mam doesn't start, love. Bernard feels bad about stopping away from us, but what can he do? Even though Theresa Nolan's moved out of Bolton, Jessica's still here and they're like peas in a pod, her and our Katherine.' He went to open the front door.

Pauline shook her head. Mam had refused to visit Crosby in recent years. She owned the opinion that she didn't need to go out of her way for folk who never came to see her. Poor Bernard had seemed to be on a knife's edge in church, was probably worrying himself sick about Katherine's natural twin being at or near the church or along the route from town to Bromley Cross. If Mam started upsetting him . . .

It didn't bear thinking about, so Pauline placed her baby in his Silver Cross carriage and went to put the kettle on for a brew to serve up with the already prepared baptismal feast.

It was a lovely farmhouse-sized kitchen with an open fire, a big dining table, an electric cooker. She set the kettle to boil, then stood for a moment, gazing across frost-topped moors. Liz must never find out. Liz's humour and toughness were outer garments. Inside, Liz was as vulnerable as a small child, still raw, still wounded by life. She had wanted at least two children, was sad that Katherine must grow up alone.

Alone? Pauline gripped the edge of her white porcelain sink. Katherine was not alone. She was half of a brace, fifty per cent of a perfectly matched pair. 'Oh, God,' whispered Pauline Walsh. New to motherhood, her senses were acute, painfully alive. 'What would I do if someone knocked on my door in ten years' time? If Jonathan turned out to be some-body else's . . .' She shivered, pulled herself up, warmed the pot. With a smile plastered across her worries, Pauline went forth to make small talk with a precious sister-in-law and a treasured niece.

He didn't know why he had come. The weather was on the cold side and, while the actual chill meant little to a fishmonger, driving conditions were less than perfect. He was supposed to be visiting Charlie Hill, a newly retired chap who had spent the best part of fifty years working in Ashburner Street Market. But for some reason best known to his deep unconscious, Bernard Walsh was sitting at the bottom of View Street with his engine turned off and his eyes glued to a group of playing children. While he lingered here, Liz was helping Pauline to clear away after the christening tea.

Liz was also trying to get round Edna Greenhalgh, while Katherine, completely wrapped up in her baby cousin, was playing happily with child and pram, wheeling Jonathan back and forth in front of Danny's new sofa.

The girl who lived with Eva was so like Katherine. Little Jessica Nolan was no longer little. Both children had shot up like weeds in hot, wet weather: long-limbed, knees a bit knobbly in developing legs, shoulders firm and well formed. Since discovering Katherine's true origin, Bernard had been plagued by worry. Now, he feared family visits to Bolton, dreaded the thought of Liz ever finding out that her baby had died and that Katherine was a replacement. Against all odds, Katherine and Jessica had already met. What if they met again? And what if Theresa ever came across Katherine in Liverpool?

All that house-moving had been a wonderful mess, too. The day when he had found out about Theresa Nolan's relocation to Liverpool, Bernard had feared a heart attack. He stared hard at Jessica as she played. The likeness was terrifying. There was no safety, here or there. There was no certainty anywhere.

The children in the street were honing a slide to glass-like perfection, slithering about, pouring water from a tin pail, stumbling, smoothing the flags with somebody's long-handled mop. By tonight, the area on which the players concentrated might well become a death trap for some unsuspecting adult.

Jessica stopped playing and looked directly at Bernard's car. With his heart beating far too wildly for comfort, Bernard studied a map while his cheeks glowed. When he raised his head, Jessica Nolan was nowhere to be seen. Feeling a disappointment for which he was unable to account, Bernard threw down the map and waited for a few moments. They should have been together all along. Katherine needed a sibling, a companion with whom she could play, eat, sleep, discuss the many problems of puberty.

He folded his hands on the steering wheel, placed his forehead on the 'pillow' formed by leather-coated fingers. His mind was all over the place, was asking unanswerable questions about the basic rights of man, about fairness, about Liz's peace of mind.

Someone tapped on the windscreen. He looked up, saw Eva, watched as she walked to the passenger door and climbed in beside him. 'Drive,' she snapped.

He drove, turning right down Maybank Street, right again onto Derby Street. 'What the hell—?' he began.

'Don't you "what the hell" me, Bernard Walsh. What the hell are you doing? That's more to the point.'

He slewed to a halt on a stretch of ice. 'I don't know, so don't ask,' he begged. 'I just had to see that she was all right.'

'Of course she's all right. She's living with me, isn't she?'

Bernard raised his shoulders. 'They should be together, Eva. They're not just sisters – they're twins.'

'I know that. Wasn't I there when they were born and when your Liz lost her little one?'

'Oh aye, you were there, Eva.'

She bridled. 'And what do you mean by that tone

of voice, Bernard Walsh? I had a young woman who'd been raped and made pregnant at the same time. I never expected her to survive the birth. And we got two for the price of one, though Theresa doesn't know that, thank God. Looking after two would have finished her within months. They'd have ended up in an orphanage, because none of the family would have took them.' She paused. 'No, that daft Ruth might have wanted a couple of pretty dolls to play with. Imagine what would have become of them – look what she's done to her own daughter.'

'Aye, she's a bad lot, is Ruth,' agreed Bernard.

Eva continued. 'Irene works at the undertaker's now, says it's been her life's ambition. What sort of a job is yon for a young married woman, eh? She can't cope with life proper. She rules her husband with a rod of iron, makes her neighbours miserable, gossips like a vicious old crone. Who made her like that? Bloody Ruth, that's who. So don't go criticizing me, lad. I saved them twins a lot of bother.'

He removed his hat and scratched the spreading bald patch. 'Did Jessica . . . did she know me?'

'No,' answered Eva smartly. 'She seems to have forgotten you. And I've brought her up to tell me about strangers. Ever since little Sheila Fox disappeared, kiddies has to be on their guard. Then, when I came out and saw you . . . Are you going to try and make something of this? Are you after getting custody of Jessica Nolan?'

'No,' he whispered.

'Because you could, I suppose. You could stand up and say that you knew nothing about my famous swap, that you've always thought Katherine was your own. And let's face it, Theresa's in no position to look after twins. Aye, possession's nine-tenths of the law and you already have Katherine and enough money to get your own road.'

'I won't—'

'You could cod on about noticing the likeness and guessing what had happened, and put the blame on me, where it belongs. You could even pretend that I'd pinched a twin from you and given her to Theresa.'

He turned and faced her. 'That's not why I'm here. Like you, I didn't think. Remember? Remember how you never thought that night?'

Eva nodded.

'Just instinct, Eva. See, I've got this stupid dream about the two of them being there for one another. I know it's daft . . .'

Eva let out a long sigh of relief. 'It's not daft, son. Oh, I know what you mean. When we're dead, who's to tell them the truth? They might never meet.'

Bernard swallowed. 'They've already met, Eva. When your little lass was in Williamson's and our Katherine was chasing the dog.' He paused. 'I could tell from her face that the meeting was important to her. Then we moved to Liverpool. And so did Theresa Nolan.'

Eva sat perfectly still for several seconds. 'Has Katherine been off-colour lately?'

'Tonsils,' he replied. 'They need taking out.'

Eva lowered her chin and addressed the dashboard. 'Jessica's been having sore throats. Only when we took her to the doctor's, there was nowt wrong with her. Same with her wrist last . . . about August, it would be.'

'A bad sprain,' replied Bernard. 'Mind, I've always thought it was rubbish, that stuff about twins having the same things happening to them, the same pains.'

'Makes you wonder, though, eh?'

He tapped the steering wheel with a gloved hand. 'Katherine had itchy skin last New Year . . .'

'When Jess had chicken pox.' Eva raised her head. 'What have I done?' she whispered. 'I feel like one person's been cut in half.'

'I've been reading,' said Bernard. 'That's how they kicked off – as one creature. Then they split in two. Twins who don't look alike were always separate people. Katherine and Jessica are special.' He continued to stare at his companion. 'I'm putting it in my will,' he said. 'That they must be told when they're old enough – in their twenties. If I live till then, I'll tell them myself.'

'What about Theresa?' Eva asked. She left unspoken the belief that Theresa would not last much longer.

Bernard had already considered the matter. 'The girls have to come first. There's too many lonely people in this world, Eva. They'll need one another sooner or later.' He leaned back in the seat, closed his eyes. 'Whether Theresa Nolan likes it or not, whether Liz likes it or not, it'll have to be done.'

'Have you been to the christening?' Eva had seen the announcement in the local paper.

He nodded. 'That's what got me thinking again. A new baby, a new life. See, with Pauline's trouble, I doubt they'll manage any more babies. Liz – well, she had to have the operation, so we'll not be blessed again. And I keep mithering inside about Jessica and Katherine, so I just drifted up here today, wanted to see the other little lass with my own eyes. Eva, the likeness is amazing.'

'Aye, well, I'll have to get back.' Eva drew a hand across tired eyes. 'Drive me to the bottom of our

315

street, lad. I'll tell Jess who you are and that you were looking for an old friend.' She placed a hand on his arm. 'Don't worry, Bernard. It'll all come out in the dolly tub, you'll see.'

Theresa smiled to herself as she walked with Maggie Courtney along Liverpool's Bold Street. Little Maria Martin, armed with a multiplicity of sketched instructions and a map, had done her job very well indeed. Maria, better off to the tune of fifty pounds, was enjoying her rest in the clinic, her mind occupied by plans connected with the sudden windfall. Theresa, having decided against visiting Bolton at this juncture, had made much of Maria on her return. For the remaining weeks of their lives, the terrible trio would endure the misery of a nasty illness.

Theresa had begun to avoid John Povey's pharmacy. The good man had continued to ask questions about her cough, about its chronic nature, was wanting to know whether any blood had appeared. But John Povey was a magician with medicines. He made his own formulae, liquid and solid, was forever consulting yellowing books and papers from a drawer beneath one of his counters.

So Theresa got into the habit of taking Maggie with her whenever she visited Liverpool. Maggie went into the chemist's shop, consulted Theresa's list, insisting that the order was for seamen who resided at the retirement home. Theresa got her medicines without the third degree, while Maggie enjoyed her outings to what the locals called 'town'.

On a crisp December afternoon, Theresa popped into the bacon shop for some lean back and a quarter of thin-sliced ham. Sometimes, she treated herself to these small luxuries, though she took most meals from the home's kitchen as part of her salary. While Maggie was in the pharmacy's queue, Theresa grabbed the chance to do some window shopping across the road. As she studied a jersey suit in the window of Modern Modes, some instinct made her turn round to face the road.

Jessica was on the opposite pavement. Theresa opened her mouth to shout, closed it with a sharp snap. Jessica was in Bolton with Eva. Jessica did not have a navy blue princess-line coat with a fur collar. Jessica had a different hairstyle altogether. And yet . . .

Maggie skirted her way round a bus, arrived at Theresa's side. 'The bloody queue in there,' she moaned. 'About fourteen in front of me, and one old feller going on so much about his piles that the rest of us were itching.' She stopped. 'What's up with your gob?' she asked. 'You look as if your last farthing's just fell down a drain hole.'

Theresa leaned on the window of Modern Modes. 'Oh, my God,' she managed.

'You what?'

'That's Liz Walsh. And there's her husband.'

Bold Street was moderately busy. 'Who?' asked Maggie. 'Where?'

Theresa felt faint, but she clung to her companion and breathed deeply. 'The girl in the navy coat,' she answered. 'Man with the trilby, woman in grey.'

Maggie found the targets. 'Yes?'

'The girl. It's . . . my daughter. But it's not – it can't be.'

The older woman frowned. 'Are you all right?' she asked.

'No.'

'It's your Jessica, only it's not your Jessica?'

Theresa's knees were decidedly wobbly. Liz Walsh's baby had been born on the same day as Jessica. 'I had a bad time,' she whispered.

'Eh?'

'The birth. I passed out at least twice. My heart's never been good.' An enormous thought was growing in her head, in her chest. The thought was bigger than Theresa, bigger than the world. 'She wouldn't do that,' she whispered. 'Not Eva. Eva's too straight. But . . . but that girl's my Jessica. Maggie . . .' Theresa swallowed audibly. 'Do you think you could have twins without knowing?'

Maggie scratched her head thoughtfully. 'Well, if you kept passing out . . .' Two children. Maggie had seen them in the cards, in the crystal, on Theresa's palm. Yes, two babies already born.

'And if Liz had a stillbirth . . .' This was too terrible. Yet she had to know, had to follow the Walshes. 'Stay here,' she ordered Maggie.

'But you're not fit, love.'

Theresa nodded her agreement. 'I know that, Maggie. But this is something I have to do by myself.' She took a step towards the pavement's edge. Liz Walsh and the girl were laughing. Bernard Walsh was looking at his watch.

'Theresa?' Maggie clutched frantically at her friend's sleeve. 'Look, queen. That girl over there what looks like yours – well, what if she isn't Jessica's twin?'

'She is.' The certainty was plain in Theresa's voice.

'What if she is, then?' persisted Maggie. 'Do you want to go upsetting her? Whatever the rights and the wrongs, she's the innocent one. I bet she's grew up all these years thinking she belonged to them.'

She waved a hand in the direction of the group. 'Think before you do anything, Theresa.'

The younger woman paused. 'I might never see them again.'

Maggie thought about that. 'Get back home,' she ordered, pushing a bagful of medicines into Theresa's hands. 'I'll follow them, see what I can find out. I'll talk to anybody, me. By hook or by crook, I'll sort this out for you.' Theresa looked so shocked, so drained. 'Go on,' Maggie urged. 'No use making a mess of it. Get back and sort the laundry or something.'

Theresa looked at Maggie, looked at the three people across the road. A cold hand seemed to have closed itself around her stomach. Bernard Walsh was guffawing at some joke or other. Liz was smiling fit to burst. They looked so happy. The child was grinning, too, was looking at her mother, then at her father. 'Eva knows I'm in Liverpool,' muttered Theresa. 'And I'll bet she knows they're here, too. They ran away – for obvious reasons – never thinking I'd be living in these parts. They ran away, Maggie, I'm sure they must have. I wonder why they've stayed, though? Oh, I have to get to the bottom of this.'

'If you say so.'

Theresa inhaled steadily. 'I am not talking daft, you know. If I'd seen just the girl, I'd have thought I'd found Jessica's double. We're all supposed to have a double. But Bernard Walsh and his wife are here, as well. That's too much of a coincidence. Follow them. Find out where they live.'

'I will.' Maggie tried to deliver a reassuring smile. 'Stop here a minute,' she said. 'I might get the answer straightaway. If I make no progress, you just get yourself home and put the kettle on.' She dashed across the road.

Theresa held her breath, watched while Maggie staged a fall in front of the Walshes. Bernard picked her up, drew her towards the wall. They talked for a minute or two, then Bernard took Maggie back into the pharmacy.

For what seemed like an age, Theresa watched the child and the mother. There was a great deal of love between them. They fussed one another, touched one another. Liz straightened the child's fur collar, rubbed at her cheek with a handkerchief. Theresa gulped down a knot of pain. She had missed so much, had given up so much. For what? For revenge? 'Your choice,' she mumbled to herself. 'You let Jessica go.' She hadn't wanted Jessica to be a part of her plans, still didn't want the child to get too close. Working on the theory that Jessica would never miss what she had never had, Theresa had distanced herself. She was going to die young and in a state of mortal sin, and she didn't want Jessica to grieve. Even so, the anger bubbled very near the surface. Theresa's choices had been removed by Eva in a high-handed and despicable fashion.

A bus rattled along, stopped, deprived the watcher of her view. People alighted from the vehicle, others jumped aboard. When the road was clear again, Theresa watched the older, plumper Bernard guiding Maggie out of Povey's Pharmacy. Liz, slim and smartly dressed, talked to Maggie, patted the supposedly injured woman's shoulder. Maggie might have made a good actress, Theresa mused.

The Walshes had named their daughter Kathleen or Katherine. According to Eva, Katherine had been very tiny. The family had swapped places with Danny

Walsh, had moved up to Bromley Cross for the duration. Of course, they had had a great deal to hide. Theirs was a stolen child. Eva, though. How on earth had Eva concealed this for so long? What had prompted her to act in such a manner?

Liz and the girl were walking away. Bernard stood and waved until they disappeared into a shop, then he crossed the road with Maggie.

Theresa flattened herself against the wall.

'Mrs Nolan?' His voice was thick with tension.

Maggie looked from one to the other. 'I told him in the chemist's, told him all you'd said to me,' she explained. 'It seemed the quickest way.'

Theresa nodded curtly at Bernard.

'How are you?' he managed.

Theresa didn't know how she was. 'Katherine,' she stated. 'I remember asking your Danny about his niece when you were living up on the moors. She's mine. You stole my child.' Perhaps she would have given Katherine away, but that was not the point. Jessica could have had a companion, someone in whom she might have confided. 'You took my child,' repeated Theresa.

Desperate now, Bernard clung to the remnants of hope. 'I beg your pardon?'

Maggie cleared her throat. 'He knows what you're talking about, all right. So does that Mr Povey.' She jerked a thumb towards the shop across the road. 'Bloody chemist knows all about it, too. He came round the back, did Mr Povey, let us use the room behind the shop.' She turned her full attention on Bernard. 'Is he a mate of yours, that Povey?'

Bernard nodded.

'All in it together,' judged Maggie aloud.

Theresa took a small step forward and touched

Maggie's arm. 'Go home, love,' she begged. 'I won't be long.'

Maggie deflated visibly. She prided herself on her verbal abilities, on the God-given talents which enabled her to win almost any fight. She looked Bernard up and down. He was only a Woollyback, a slow-talking Lancastrian. Woollyback men had no chance when in the presence of a full-blown female Irish Scouser. 'What if you need me?' she asked Theresa.

'I won't. I'll be all right – I've known Bernard all my life.' The Walshes had been so kind, had sent fish when Theresa had been pregnant. Bernard had been there on that fateful night, had plagued the Hardmans, the Chorltons and the Betteridges, forcing them to part with money for Jessica. 'Maggie, I'll be fine,' she said again.

Maggie gave Bernard a look that was meant to be withering. 'Don't go upsetting her,' she snapped. 'Or I'll bring a few of my friends down Scotland Road, see how you like fish paste after we've flattened your stock.'

Theresa sighed. Bernard Walsh was a gentleman, one of the best. 'Oh, shut up, Maggie,' she pleaded.

'I know where you work,' said Maggie, the words forcing their way through clenched dentures. 'And I'll find out where you live, too. Bloody child-thief.' She turned and addressed Theresa. 'White as a sheet, he was, in that room behind the shop. And the other feller was all worried about him, did he want a glass of water and some calming herbs. Guilty as sin,' she pronounced before stalking off.

An awkward silence hovered above the heads of the two remaining people. A sudden feeling that she might be wrong after all caused Theresa's speech to seize up. Bernard, fearing that Liz and Katherine might reappear at any moment, was riveted to the spot. For the first time in ages, he actually felt cold.

'So,' began Theresa, the short word emerging rusty and dry.

Bernard coughed. 'I can't stop here,' he said. 'Liz might see me.'

'Might see me, you mean.'

'That, too,' he agreed.

Did Liz know the truth, then? 'How did you and Eva manage this, Bernard?' She wanted to hit him hard across his face, but she managed to maintain her dignity and his, just about. 'I might have given her to you anyway if you'd asked,' she added. The Walshes could have had both girls, could have kept them together.

Bernard sighed. 'Ours died,' he said bluntly. 'Liz couldn't take in what had happened. She was . . . strange for hours. Then Eva turned up and . . . well, it was just . . .' The words died.

'Just Eva's decision. You didn't send her out to steal a baby for you. She took one look at me and decided that I'd never cope.' No-one had the right to make such judgements. 'Does your wife believe that Katherine is hers?' she asked.

'Yes. She knows nothing about what happened that night. We just got this newspaper parcel with a baby in it. Liz was screaming, telling us to warm her baby near the fire. It all seemed to happen without any of us taking part. Before we knew where we were, Liz got a grip on . . . on your child.'

Theresa thought about that and found the ability to forgive Liz Walsh immediately. Women who had just given birth were vulnerable, unsteady. 'This is not your wife's fault,' she said.

'We came to Crosby after the war. Eva thought

323

we'd be best out of Bolton. Then I found out that you had come to Waterloo.'

Waterloo was a mere stride from Crosby. 'So we've been right on top of one another for years,' said Theresa.

He nodded vigorously, almost unseating his trilby. 'I tried to get Liz to move back to Blackburn or Bury, but she'd had enough of flitting.' He looked over his shoulder. 'I'll have to be going. Can we meet again?'

Theresa was lost in thought. 'Eva was clever, then.'

Bernard lowered his head and pondered. 'It happened to her, and all,' he said. 'She didn't even think. One minute, you had a baby, then, the next minute, you had two. She'd delivered our stillborn and she acted without thinking.'

'She could have told me afterwards.'

Bernard was gazing up the street, his eyes darting frantically from shop to shop. 'Could she?'

'I made it plain that I couldn't mind Jessica. I had to get away from Bolton.' She paused for a second. 'God, she must have nearly had a heart attack when she realized we were all in the same city.'

Bernard could scarcely stand still. He was waiting for Liz on Bold Street in Liverpool, yet he was back in 1939, was standing in an alley watching three drunks as they lurched away from their victim. One of those objects was Katherine's father. 'I've got to go,' he muttered. He gripped Theresa's arm. 'Don't be thinking I've got no conscience, please. It's in my will that the two girls have to be brought together. If I live, I'll introduce them to one another myself. In their early twenties, I thought.' He paused for a second. 'Liz will have to be told, too, when the time comes.'

Theresa nodded her agreement. 'Bring my daughter to the Mustard Pot in South Road on Saturday. I want to meet her.'

He gulped. 'But—'

'It's all right. You and I know one another from Bolton. We can act surprised, have a cup of tea together.'

'But what about Liz?' he asked.

Theresa raised a shoulder. 'Please yourself. Only I'd leave her at home if I were you.'

He swallowed again. He could pretend to be Christmas shopping. But what if Theresa came over all emotional? He looked at her. She didn't seem to be experiencing anything. A door had closed over her face, leaving the expression frigid and empty. There was a definite look of Theresa in Katherine. Would the child recognize her own birth mother? There were instincts, finer feelings for which the female of the species was eminently famous. What could he do? 'I'll bring her,' he said. He owed Theresa Nolan that much, he supposed. The rest would have to take care of itself.

Bernard had felt numb for days. His wife's questions had been answered vaguely – he thought he might have a cold coming on, fish prices were in danger of rising, the shop needed doing up. Now, seated with his borrowed daughter in the window of the Mustard Pot, he simply waited for life to take its course. Liz and Katherine were his life. Deprived of either, he might well cease to exist altogether.

'Dad?'

'Yes, love?' He saw that her eyes were round and sad.

'Will we find another dog just like Chaplin?'

Bernard bit his lip before answering. The dog had

been a charmer, a clown. 'Very similar,' he answered.

Katherine, heartbroken by the premature death of her canine friend, could not imagine an animal as clever as Chaplin. 'He was special,' she sighed, a tear threatening to spill from one china-blue eye.

Bernard patted her hand. 'All dogs are special. They all have their different ways. You just eat your cake,' he said.

Katherine shook her head. 'I can't.' She knew that Dad had done his best, that Chaplin had been in pain. But she missed him so badly that her insides felt empty. The space within could not be satisfied by food.

'We've told you that there'll be one ready in a few weeks. Puppies mustn't leave their mothers too soon.' Katherine had been taken from her mother within minutes of birth . . .

'Will he be ready by Christmas?'

The tired man drew a hand across his eyes. 'No, but I've arranged for you to visit him on Christmas Eve. You'll be able to see him with his brothers and sisters, then you just have to wait until he's six or seven weeks old.'

Katherine forced herself to smile. Dad looked exhausted. Poor Dad had taken Chaplin to the vet, had sat with the dog until the injection had done its work. 'Thank you,' she whispered.

'What for?'

'For Chaplin. For my school. Most of all, for being a good dad.'

Bernard inhaled, felt the breath catching the back of his throat. Katherine deserved the best. She was an unassuming, undemanding child. If she had a fault, it was that she loved too much and too easily.

She raved about her teachers, her schoolfriends, her dog. Katherine's fault was that she saw no faults in others. What was her sister like? he wondered.

'Dad?'

'Yes, love?'

'Are you all right?'

'Yes.' Of course he was all right. His little girl's real mother was about to walk into the café at any moment. His little girl's other mother, her actual mother and nurturer, was sorting out Christmas decorations and polishing her brasses. His little girl's real sister was living in Bolton with Eva Harris, now Coates, who had started all this damned mess in the first place.

'What shall we get Mam for Christmas?'

He produced a shadowy smile. 'I thought we'd get her a bit of jewellery.' Theresa Nolan was standing across the road. 'Pearls. She's always liked pearls.' Theresa was crossing the road. 'Necklace from you, earrings from me.' She was almost at the shop door. 'All wrapped in nice paper and ribbon.'

Katherine clapped her hands. 'Can I do the wrapping?'

'Course you can, love. I'm fit to wrap nothing unless it's come in on a trawler.'

Theresa entered the shop, went to the counter to order a cup of tea. With her fingertips clutching the edge of her handbag, she waited for her order to be filled. Behind her, framed by a slightly steamy window with green check curtains, Katherine Walsh was discussing Christmas with her excellent father.

Bernard stood. 'Is that Mrs Nolan?' he asked.

Theresa picked up her tea and the cue. She turned and faced a piece of a past she had never known, stared head on into a limited future over which, if she chose, she might take full control. Even from this distance, she could see beads of sweat on the worried man's brow. 'Mr Walsh?'

'Come and sit with us,' he said, his voice rather unsteady.

Theresa looked at the child. Like Jessica, she was beautiful. This one's clothes were better than Jessica's, but, apart from this outer layer, there were few differences. The faces were the same, the eyes, the set of the chin. Katherine's hair was a mere shade away from Jessica's. Even the hands, long-fingered and with deep, well-shaped nails, were the same, right down to a slight double-jointedness in the thumbs.

Theresa sat, the cup rattling nervously in its saucer until she placed these items down on the table.

'This is my daughter,' said Bernard. 'Katherine, meet Mrs Nolan. She used to live near Uncle Danny's shop on Derby Street.'

'Hello, Mrs Nolan,' said Katherine.

Theresa smiled nervously. The child's speech was almost perfect, with just a hint of Liverpool trimming its edges. 'Hello,' she replied.

'Are you Christmas shopping?' Katherine glanced at her father. 'We are. We're going to buy pearls for my mam.'

Theresa sipped hot tea, then set the cup down with both hands in an attempt to attain some steadiness. 'I've done my shopping,' she answered. 'Just a few bits and pieces to buy.'

Bernard held his breath. This must be so hard for Theresa. She had abandoned the other child, had reputedly run away from a sanatorium, but she still had rights. Over Katherine, Theresa had been permitted to make no choices. Even now, the woman had every right to scream from the rooftops, to claim her child.

'You remind me of somebody,' Katherine was saying now.

Theresa attempted a laugh. 'You know, people are always saying that to me. I must have one of those faces.'

A hint of relief entered Bernard's bones. Grasping at hope, he pretended to study Theresa's face. 'Well, I know who you are anyway,' he said. 'And you don't look like anybody else except yourself.'

For a split second, Katherine was in a wood with a puppy called Chaplin and a girl called Jessica. But when she thought about her dog, she was back in the here and now. 'My dog died,' she told Theresa. 'He was a golden retriever. We're going to get another one in January.'

'Nice dogs, retrievers,' commented Theresa.

Katherine smiled. 'He was very funny when he was a pup. Mam says we'll have all that trouble again.'

Mam. The pain scalded Theresa's chest, made her reach for another sip of tea. 'Would you go next door and get me an *Echo*?' she asked the child. She fought for composure as she reached into her bag to snatch up some money.

Katherine took the proffered coin and left the shop.

Theresa, as if burned by the touch of the girl's hand, nursed her fingers. 'She's lovely,' she told Bernard when they were alone.

'They both are,' he replied. 'I saw Jessica last week.' He turned and grasped his companion's hand. 'They'll both be all right, I promise. Even if Liz has to be told, I'll make sure the twins come to no harm. And if I'm not around to tell the tale, John

329

Povey will do it. He sold us our house, and we've been friends ever since.'

Theresa shook her head wearily. 'I don't blame you or your wife, not for one minute. There's no way I could have looked after two. I even left the other one.' She paused, chewing her lip. 'I'm no good as a mother,' she muttered.

'Rubbish. You were injured, you were hurt and . . . Don't carry on like this, love,' he begged. 'Look, if it'll make you feel any better, I'll think about telling Liz what happened—'

'No.' The ferocity of her response amazed both of them. 'You've done a good job. It's no use telling the truth now, because I've not got long. And don't start trying to talk me out of dying, because that's something we can't alter. If you go upsetting Liz and telling Katherine who I am – well, it'll be for nothing, because I'll not live to be a mother to anybody.'

'I'm sorry, lass.' And he was sorry. Her skin was thin to the point of transparency, pale, unhealthy. 'She'll catch no harm with us.'

Katherine dashed in with Theresa's newspaper, her face aglow from exposure to an icy breeze that skittered from the water and up South Road. 'Can I go and look at the pearls, Dad?' she asked.

Bernard gauged Theresa's mood, decided that Katherine's presence was upsetting the woman. 'Say goodbye to Mrs Nolan,' he instructed.

Katherine looked at the frail lady, then, following an instinct whose origins she did not question, planted a kiss on a pallid cheek. 'Have a lovely Christmas,' she said before dashing off to the jeweller's.

'Oh, Bernard.' The use of surnames seemed silly on an occasion such as this. 'She's a wonderful girl.'

330

'Aye, she is that.' He tried a change of subject. 'Are you working?'

She nodded. 'I'm housekeeper at Jutland House.'

Bernard's jaw dropped. 'There's talk about that place,' he said, almost without thinking.

She made no reply.

'It's a bit more than a seamen's rest, or so I'm told.'

'Oh.'

Bernard rearranged salt, pepper and mustard, just to give his hands an occupation while he sought the right words. 'There's nowt goes on in Liverpool without John Povey knowing the details. There's going to be a raid. Soon, too.'

Theresa stiffened. 'A raid? Half the police force visit the place.'

'Aye, well, perhaps it'll be a different force that does the questioning, police from another town.' He pondered for a while. 'You'd best get the hell out of there, love. John Povey – the chemist – reckons that the Liverpool police are sick of themselves. It's been a very corrupt force.'

'There are others as well as police.'

'Yes. Only the police are supposed to guard the law, not break it. There'll be heads rolling any day. What'll you do?'

She couldn't manage to care. She was the mother of two beautiful girls whose welfare would be secured by this lovely man. She had scores to settle. Even now, she knew that she would not give up the search for justice. For so long, it had been her sole reason for surviving.

'What are you going to do?' repeated Bernard.

She was going to get out right away and she was going to take Maggie with her. 'Go home to Bolton, I suppose,' she replied. 'I'm going for a visit, anyway, in a day or two. Might as well stay. I'm going to see Jessica, anyway. So I might just buy a house in her name and you can see to the paperwork.' She paused. 'Can I do all that through your Danny?'

'Of course.'

Theresa rose from her seat. 'In case Katherine comes back – I want to be gone.' She shook his hand. 'Thanks for letting me meet her. Give my regards to Liz and tell her I'm going back to Bolton – that should stop her inviting me for tea.'

Bernard understood. 'I'm sorry,' he muttered.

'Don't be.' She awarded him the widest smile she could manage. 'You've done nothing but good,' she advised him. Which was more than could be said for some people – including Eva Harris-as-was.

ELEVEN

Theresa, having confided in Maggie, found that she dared not say a word to anyone else about the imminent raid, because such information could result in a mass exodus from the house. Monty Sexton, who had been better than good to Theresa, would have to take his chances with the rest of them. As go-between, Monty could not be relied upon completely, because he sometimes consorted with the enemy. So Theresa and Maggie were the only two who knew that a raid was on the cards.

'Maggie,' said Theresa, a layer of patience etched into the name. 'You can't take everything. We're supposed to be getting out without being noticed.'

Maggie grimaced. She had enough bits and pieces to fill a seaman's trunk, and she was very attached to all her possessions. The bed was covered in a river of purple imitation silks and satins, nightgowns, peignoirs, scarves, blouses. 'I don't know what to choose,' she moaned.

'Take just enough,' chided Theresa. 'Wear as much as you can, then pack one bag.'

Maggie sulked. She sat in a wicker chair and stared gloomily at her friend. 'I've been here a long time,' she moaned. 'I've never been to Bolton. Who wants to go to bloody Bolton? It's all cotton mills, isn't it? And the people talk funny.'

Theresa laughed. 'You'll be the odd one out. You'll be the one who talks funny.'

Maggie picked up a mauve garter. 'I've had some fun in that. There was a pair, but somebody pinched one in 1944. I can't remember whether it was an alderman or a detective inspector. We had a load in that night from one of the lodges.'

Theresa shook her head in mock despair. 'Look, leave the Bolton men alone,' she said. 'There's trouble enough without you starting lessons in obedience.' She pointed to a leather whip. 'So you can leave that behind for a start.'

'Yes, Mother.'

Theresa could not manage to analyse her reasons, but her faith in Maggie was implicit. Maggie was going to take charge of Jessica. Eva, that nice little body, the one who would help anyone in a crisis, had turned out to be a liar. This street-woman, who had performed with and for hundreds of men, would be a great guardian for Jessica. Maggie was as straight as a die. In a strange way, Maggie was a lady, because she could alter herself to fit the requirements of almost any situation.

As if reading Theresa's thoughts, the older woman spoke up. 'I've never had much to do with kids.'

'I know that.'

Maggie sighed sadly. 'Am I fit after the life I've led?'

The life Maggie had led was part of her value. Theresa saw Maggie as an honest, God-fearing woman whose choices had been diminished by overcrowding and a severe lack of education. 'You are a very decent woman,' said Theresa. 'You'd have made a good mother, but I'm telling you now, love, that you can't be hanging about in purple for the rest of your days. There are other colours, you know, like green and blue. And no, you will not have a bad effect on my daughter.' Theresa realized that the conversation was deliberately light, as if neither woman could face up to the gravity of their situation. Theresa was feeling like death warmed up, while Maggie was preparing to dash off into the unknown just for the sake of security.

'Does young Jessica like purple?'

Theresa dropped into a chair. 'We'd best stop messing about,' she said. 'This raid could happen any minute.' Maggie would live in Jessica's house. Maggie would be safe. Theresa Nolan had begun to accept the fact that she loved Maggie like an older sister. 'We've no time to hang about,' she added grimly.

Maggie agreed. 'It's poor old Monty I feel sorry for. He's been at the beck and bloody call of his so-called masters ever since he stopped seafaring. I mean, he could end up in the flaming bridewell. Can't we tell him on our way out?'

Theresa was adamant. 'People have disappeared from this house, Maggie. Who's going to be doing the raiding when half the police force use the place as a recreation ground? Have the police turned on themselves all of a sudden? It's all a mystery to me. Perhaps they'll bring in the Cheshire force.'

Maggie threw the garter across the room. 'Bull's-eye,' she yelled when it circled a figure of the Blessed Virgin. 'Shall I go down and pussyfoot round Monty, see if he knows anything?' She didn't want to leave him in a mess. 'He's a nice feller,' she concluded.

Theresa shook her head in despair. Monty and

Maggie fought like cat and dog – their feelings for each other were powerful. 'It's too dangerous, Maggie,' she said. Both women were aware that their bosses were quick-minded, two-faced men with good jobs, well-dressed wives and an eye for a quick return on investments. Nor were they immune to the so-called delights on offer upstairs. 'How can the police investigate themselves?' she asked again.

Maggie shrugged. 'Somebody must have squealed. Or the boys in blue could be doing the dirty on the rest of the committee, damning everybody except themselves. But I wouldn't be surprised what you think is true and another force comes in to do the deed. It's time for a shake-up.' She drew a hand across her forehead. 'Did little Maria get back from Bolton?'

Theresa nodded.

'What happened?'

'Don't ask.' Maria was in a clinic on Parliament Street, a place that was treated by many working women as a holiday resort. They got a good rest, three square meals and plenty of company of their own kind.

'I wonder what'll happen to the girls?' Maggie was fond of her protégées. 'Still, we can't do nothing, can we? They'll be loaded in a cattle van and—'

'Don't,' said Theresa.

'Ah.' Maggie hugged a lilac cushion. 'Conscience troubling you? Does this mean I might not get charged with accessory to murder? Will you throw that bloody gun away and behave?'

Theresa smiled to herself. The incubation period of gonorrhoea was notoriously short. By now, all three would be noticing discomfort when passing water. Other symptoms did not bear thinking about, but they were nasty enough to make the most patient of men curse and swear. Left untreated, the disease had massive potential, including nasty sores, arthritis and even meningitis.

'Theresa?'

'What?'

'I'd sooner face a raid than watch you go down for murder.'

Exasperated, Theresa jumped to her feet. 'Listen, Maggie. I've not got long to live. My heart's all over the place – it keeps missing beats, then it rattles along like a fifty-year-old steam engine with indigestion. I've saved nearly every penny of my wages for years. You are going to have the use of a house for the rest of your life, plus a bit of a wage for food and bills. You can get a little cleaning job, look after my daughter and—'

'And where will you be?'

'Heaton Cemetery.' Theresa raised a hand. 'Don't start on about how I might get better. Come to Bolton and be safe, or stay here – it's all the same to me.' It wasn't all the same to her. She didn't want Jessica to stay with Eva. What Eva had perpetrated was not forgivable. And the thought of Ruth getting her claws into Jessica didn't bear consideration.

'I'm coming with you,' muttered Maggie.

The door opened a crack. 'Are you decent?'

Maggie jumped up and threw a blanket over her packing. 'Come in, Monty.'

He entered, looking over his shoulder as he closed the door.

'What's happened?' asked Maggie. 'You look like you've lost a shilling and found a bottle top.'

The man shambled to the centre of Maggie's gaudy boudoir. 'The raid's tomorrow night,' he said.

Maggie and Theresa exchanged glances.

'Have you finished packing?' he asked.

'Bloody hell,' cursed the older woman. 'He always knows everything, this bugger,' she informed Theresa. 'If a mouse in the cellar farts, Monty can hear it from the attic.'

Monty's sombre face twitched, threatened to burst into a grin, though the promised smile failed to arrive.

'I hope you won't use language like that in front of Jessica,' Theresa told Maggie sternly. 'I don't want her growing up with a mouth like a sewer outlet.'

'Can I come with you?' Monty asked. 'I need a safe place, see, because anything could happen round here, like.'

Maggie closed her eyes in despair. She was taking off with a potential murderess and a man who would be on the run from some very dangerous people. 'You think I've had a life so far?' she asked, the question directed towards the ceiling. 'Well, St Jude, it's only just beginning – you've seen nothing yet.' She opened her eyes. 'Jude's the saint for hopeless cases and you two are the most hopeless I've come across.'

Monty shrugged. 'I might be hopeless, Maggie, but at least I've got a van with a full tank and I can be ready to take off by two o'clock in the morning. So you've four hours to pack your belongings.'

Theresa considered the situation. She had planned to go to Eva's, get through Christmas without mentioning anything to Eva, then, after the festivities, she would buy a house outright with the money she'd saved for Jessica's future. 'Three of us?' she asked. 'Three? There's only one spare room at Eva's.'

'I'll sleep on a floor,' volunteered Monty.

Theresa considered that. 'If you can put up with somebody strange, you can stop at our Ruth's. She's only a few doors away from Eva's and she's got the space since Irene left home.' What was she saying? There could be a manhunt organized by tomorrow. 'They'll know we've cleared off on purpose,' she announced.

'Which "they"?' Maggie asked. 'The goodies or the baddies? There'll be the committee, which is full of police, then there'll be the good police looking for the bad police and—'

'And the good police and the bad police will all be looking for us,' interspersed Monty.

'We can't win,' moaned Maggie.

'Yes we can.' At last, Monty smiled. 'We're immune.'

'I'm very glad to hear it,' answered Maggie. 'Who or what are we immune to?'

'We're goodies,' he replied. 'The new Chief Constable himself has given his word. And he's a goody.'

Theresa coughed in order to get some attention and the chance to put in a word or two. 'How do you know the CC is a goody?'

'Because he's my nephew.' Monty's backbone was suddenly straight. 'And it's not just the brothel side of things. There'll be fraud as well. I've waited years for this, begging and scraping, yes, sir, no, sir. When my sister's lad joined the Liverpool force, I joined as well.' He tucked his thumbs into his braces. 'Not official, as you might say, but I have been working undercover, finding out about the accounts, expenses and all that. You'd be surprised how little money goes to the old sailors.'

Theresa, who had paid food bills for years, was not

at all surprised. She was used to making a pound do the work of a fiver. 'So, we have to get out in the middle of tonight.'

'That's right.' Monty eyed Maggie. He and she had been arguing for years, sounding off about religion, politics, the qualities of brown and white vinegars, the best way to clean dentures.

Maggie stared back at him. 'Bolton won't be big enough for both of us.'

'Biggest town in England,' Theresa informed the pair. 'And it's in a beautiful setting, moors and farms.'

Monty worried about Theresa. He had picked her up from a hospital, and she had seldom seemed well. Would she go back for treatment? Would she get that terrible cough dealt with? 'I'll have to phone my nephew,' he said importantly. 'To tell him where I'll be. Heads are going to roll.' He swept an eye about Maggie's room. 'You'll be glad to leave all this purple behind, I suppose.' He ducked as a violet cushion spun past his head. 'Missed,' he said smartly as he left the room.

Maggie collapsed in an untidy heap on the already disordered bed. 'I'm sorry, Theresa,' she said flatly. 'But I can't do it.'

Theresa was depending on Maggie. 'Stay, then,' she replied with a coolness she did not feel.

'I'm not staying. I'm not finishing up in prison, not for nobody. But I can't leave without giving my girls a chance. I'm going to put notes under the doors. It's all right – I won't sign my name. I'll just put "raid Friday night". That way, they'll be able to make their minds up about stopping or going.'

'Please yourself.' Theresa felt the exhaustion

creeping into her bones like a form of paralysis. 'I'm packed,' she informed her friend. 'And I need to put my head on a pillow for an hour or two. Will you wake me?'

'Course I will.' Maggie stood up, smoothed her wayward hair. 'Hey – don't go dying tonight, will you? Only you're the navigator, so we need you.'

Theresa allowed a pale imitation of a smile to visit her lips. 'No, Maggie. You and Bernard Walsh'll be steering my daughters through life, I hope. As for me – I've other fish to fry.'

'Theresa, I'm warning you—'

'Well, don't. I'll do what wants doing, so save your breath.'

Maggie stared out into the Mersey's darkness for at least half an hour after Theresa's departure. The river glinted occasionally when cloud allowed a quarter-moon to shed a little light on its still, glassy subject. Maggie remembered war and storm, high days and holidays, children playing on sand, crippled sailors gazing across to the horizon where river became salt. The Mersey was in Maggie Courtney's veins. Liverpool was her home, her home by choice, the city in which she had intended to live out her days. Ireland was a mere memory: a crowded house, a series of unhappy shadows.

She shortened her sight, watched Monty as he placed boxes in the van. Soon, it would be time to go. Maggie, as tough as old boots, as wilful as an overworked Blackpool donkey, sobbed and moaned until she felt empty and chilled. She remembered her mam, her sisters and brothers, remembered a drunken sot of a father who used his daughters when his wife wore out. Mam's funeral, her older sister's suicide, three brothers running off to sea. 'I do understand, Theresa,' she mouthed. 'But oh, God, I wish I didn't.'

Jessica's excitement was at fever pitch. Mam was coming home for ever. There was going to be a real Christmas, not just an early pretend one. Then, once Christmas was over, Mam and Jessica would be buying a house where they could live together as a proper family.

'Jessica?'

'Yes, Auntie Eva?'

'Will you run down to the butcher's for some pork sausage? Then call in at the chemist's for Jimmy's medicine.'

Humming with excitement, Jessica set off for the shops.

Eva Coates dropped into a chair. She took the letter from her apron pocket and read it yet again. Theresa's job in Liverpool had reached its terminus. She would be coming back, probably with a woman called Maggie and with the definite intention of buying a house for Jessica. Theresa, Jessica and this Maggie person would be living together. Jessica would continue at the grammar school, so the house would have to be in Bolton.

Eva folded the single sheet and placed it on the table. She was scared, frightened almost to death of losing Jessica. For more than half a decade, Jessica had been a full-time part of Eva's life. Eva's home would become quieter, older, without the presence of Theresa Nolan's daughter. An unhappy victim of circumstance, Eva stared into the fire and tried to count her blessings. She had Jimmy, who worked hard and made a decent living. She had a roof over her head, ample food in her stomach, new table and chairs handmade by her husband. But none of this mattered, because the child she had loved, the girl who had almost become her own, was about to be stolen from her.

An unease slid its cool fingers along the length of Eva's spine. Her girl was being stolen. No, no, this was not theft, because Theresa was Jessica's true parent. But it felt like theft, stung like theft. Eva's hackles were rising. She wanted to deny Theresa, wanted to accuse her of being tubercular and too unhealthy to take Jessica. She wanted . . . she wanted to hang on to the girl, to deprive the mother, to carry on being Jessica's guardian. Perhaps God was getting His own back by punishing Eva for separating twins. She had taken a child; now, a child was to be taken from her.

Eva calmed herself, allowing the pain to flow over her. The letter. There was something missing, something unsaid. She snatched it up, raked her eyes over it once again. There was no thank you. Theresa always thanked Eva for taking such good care of Jessica. But this note was a set of bare bones, a statement of intent, no more. Perhaps it had been written in a hurry. But no, at the bottom, Theresa had simply written her name. In the past, it had been 'love, Theresa'. On this occasion, the love had been kept out of it.

The woman in the chair closed her eyes. It had happened, then. Bernard Walsh and Theresa Nolan lived in the same city, probably used the same shops. They must have bumped into each other at last. So, had Theresa found out about Katherine? Was that the reason for the sudden decision to come home and grab Jessica? No matter how hard she tried, Eva could not relax the muscles of her neck and shoulders. She was tense to the point of rigidity.

Jimmy came in and wondered where his dinner was. 'It's half past twelve,' he complained jovially. At half past twelve on a Friday, the table usually boasted a steaming plateful of finny haddy with a poached egg on top. 'Where's me yellow fish, love?'

Eva shrugged. 'In the Yellow River, go and catch it.'

He sat down at the bare table. 'What's up?'

Eva shrugged. 'Go and get a fish dinner from the chip shop.'

Jimmy wasn't budging. 'I'll not shift till you tell me what's going on,' he insisted.

The shoulders raised themselves again. 'We've lost Jess.'

'Lost her? She's in the butcher's.'

'I know. We've lost her for ever.'

'Oh.' He scratched his head. Jessica was a grand lass. He'd never forgotten how she'd cheered him in the sanatorium. 'She's a big girl now,' he said. 'She'll not forget who her friends are. Anyroad, how could that Ruth touch her? Even if Theresa died . . . Is she dead?'

Eva shook her head.

'Then how can Ruth go for custody when Theresa placed Jessica with you?'

Eva turned and faced him. 'I've said nowt about Ruth, so stop jumping to conclusions. Theresa's given up her job. I got a letter this morning. She's buying a house in Bolton, then somebody called Maggie is going to mind Jessica when Theresa's not well.' She swallowed audibly. 'I reckon Theresa's found out about the other child.' Theresa was about to remove Jessica. At last, Eva Coates was at the receiving end. It was no more than she deserved, an inner voice told her.

344

'Ah. Bernard Walsh's lass?'

'That's the one.'

The carpenter glanced down at his work-scarred hands. He was a lucky man. He'd lost everything, then gained everything all over again. He had a good wife, a nice home, a job. And Jessica. Jessica had always been a large factor in the equation that added up to everything. 'Well, we'll miss her,' he said.

Eva rounded on him, jumping up from her chair and balling her fists. 'It were all done for the best,' she yelled. Jimmy didn't deserve an ear-battering, but Jimmy was the only person available. 'She'd never have managed. Both them babies would have ended up in an orphanage except for me. Two would have overwhelmed her. One were bad enough, 'cos it took Theresa weeks to get back on her feet proper.'

'Calm down, love—'

'Katherine's been doted on. She'd never have had such a good life if I hadn't—'

'Shut up,' said Jimmy.

Unused to being chided, Eva stopped talking.

'Eva,' said Jimmy softly. 'Eva, love. For a kick-off, you could be wrong. You only think Theresa's found out about Katherine. Now, even if she does know the truth, you'll have to hang fire. Don't go crashing about like a bull at a gate, because that'll get you nowhere. Be patient. Wait for Theresa to talk to you. If she knows owt, she'll speak out. If she knows nowt, she'll say nowt.'

Eva sat down again. 'Thanks,' she breathed.

'That's all right.' He got up and gave her a hug. 'Eva?'

'What?'

'Where's me finny haddy?'

She wiped a tear from the corner of her eye. 'It's cod and it's in Foster's chippy.'

Jimmy shook his head. 'Service round here's gone bloody terrible,' he grumbled.

'Jimmy?'

'What?'

'Shut up and get gone.'

He shut up and went.

Ruth was almost surprised, though she did her best to hide the fact. Three people on her doorstep and she hadn't donkey-stoned it for months. Still, they might have brought cigarettes or beer, so she would make an effort to be pleasant. 'What do you want?' she asked her sister. And who were these other characters? There was an older woman draped from head to foot in three shades of purple, then a bloke who seemed to be bowed down by the cares of the world, almost hunchbacked, trying to double in two.

'We stayed at a bed and breakfast last night,' explained Theresa. 'These are my friends from Liverpool.' She turned first to Maggie, then to Monty, speaking their names. 'This is my sister, Ruth,' she told them.

Ruth, still taken aback, tried to keep pace with the thoughts in her head. Irene would be so jealous if Ruth had company. 'Do you want to come in?' Irene had already caused so much trouble up Bury Road that she and her poor, gentle husband had been forced to move. Ruth held the door wide. 'Excuse the mess,' she said. Visitors. Irene would be green with envy.

Theresa hesitated before stepping into the lobby. She had not entered this house since her father had thrown her out. It was a dark, sombre place with

346

brown paintwork and green walls. Nothing had changed. Dad's coat and trilby hung in the hall, while his walking stick remained in a corner. Theresa shivered. 'Go through,' snapped Ruth with her habitual lack of patience.

In the rear living room, Dad's rosary hung on a nail next to the black-leaded grate. His pipes, a set of six stinking black holes, sat in a rack on the mantel. Above the fireplace, a wax version of the Last Supper overlooked the whole area. Theresa shuddered again. 'He's watching you,' Dad had used to say, a nicotined finger pointing at the soon-to-be-betrayed Christ.

Ruth looked hopefully at Maggie. 'Have you got a spare ciggy?'

Maggie obliged and won a smile from the recipient of one Senior Service for now, plus one for later.

Ruth set light to her cigarette, using a spill held to the meagre fire. 'I've not much coal left,' she said.

Monty and Maggie exchanged looks. The house promised to be as warm as Ruth's so-called welcome.

'We need somewhere to stay,' explained Theresa. 'I'll stop at Eva's, but can you find room for Monty and Maggie?'

'Separate rooms,' interjected Maggie, her tone prim.

'What about Christmas?' asked Ruth between frantic puffs.

'Have you got plans?' Theresa asked.

Ruth laughed mirthlessly. 'Plans? With that bloody rat of mine? Depends which road out she is, I suppose. She might invite me if she's got something to show off, same as a new carpet or a couch. Or she might bring me summat on a plate, or she might just leave me to stew. Not that I've got owt to put in a stew, like. She doesn't give a damn about me, our Irene.'

Theresa nodded thoughtfully. The monster created by Ruth would probably seek vengeance for the rest of her life. With her breath suddenly shortened, Theresa dropped into her father's scratchy horsehair rocker. She was like Irene. She had become a monster, had been invented by three drunken men, and she was acting just like Ruth's horrible daughter.

'Are you all right?' Maggie asked.

Ruth blew out a stream of grey smoke. 'She'll never be all right. She'd a bad fever when she were little, then she got herself—'

'That's enough,' gasped Theresa. 'I'll be fine in a minute.'

Maggie perched on a dining chair while Monty, plainly ill at ease, fiddled with his hat near the dresser.

'So all I'm saying is there won't be much of a Christmas in this house.'

Maggie tut-tutted. 'Of course there'll be Christmas. Monty and I will buy food – won't we, Monty? And we can all go to Eva's, share the expense. Monty?'

Monty nodded.

Theresa stood and walked to the door. 'I'm going down to Eva's to see Jessica. Ruth will make you a cup of tea.' She let herself out of the house, hoping against hope that her sister would have the makings of a brew.

Outside on View Street, Theresa surveyed the town for the first time in years. Chimneys of solid brick poked their nostrils into a sky that seemed permanently stained. The Town Hall clock oversaw the area of civic business, while rabbit runs of small houses sloped their blue-slated roofs down Daubhill. A film of ice caused Theresa to slither and slide her way along to Eva's house. She intended to do nothing, to say nothing until after Christmas. Jessica's holiday must not be spoilt.

She was greeted by an enraptured daughter and a very quiet Eva.

'Let your mother sit down, Jessica,' instructed the older woman, her soft tone betraying uncertainty. Theresa didn't look at all well. Her face was pasty-white, while the lips had a decidedly blue tinge.

Jessica detached herself. 'Are you home for ever?' she asked.

Nothing was for ever, and Theresa's time would not stretch far. 'We'll get a place. The house will be in your name,' she advised Jessica. 'That way, you'll get a better start in life than most. And no, I'll not be going back to Liverpool.'

Eva felt her hands shaking, so she busied herself with teapot and cups. 'Where's your friend?' she asked.

'She's stopping at our Ruth's.'

Eva dropped a spoon. 'You what? You've left her with that bad bu—' She pulled herself up in the presence of the child. Jessica was a young lady, a grammar school girl, and she shouldn't hear words like 'bugger'. 'You've left her there? All the kids are feared to death of yon place, specially since Ruth put it about that it's haunted. And by your dad, of all people.' Eva had no time for Michael Nolan, dead or alive. She retrieved the spoon and shoved it into a pocket of her apron.

'Maggie isn't on her own,' said Theresa. 'Monty's with her. He wanted a break from Liverpool and—'

'Your gentleman friend?' asked Eva.

Theresa held on to her patience. It was clear that Eva felt threatened, afraid of losing Jessica. 'He's a friend and a gentleman, but he's not special to me.'

'Oh, I see.' Eva lifted a batch of scones from the oven. 'So.' She tipped the scones deftly onto a cooling rack. 'You'll be taking young Jess away from me and Jimmy. Who'll see to her if you're . . .' She glanced at Jessica, decided that she didn't want the girl worrying about her mother's health. 'If you're busy working or not up to scratch?'

Theresa looked hard at the woman who had helped her for so many years, the woman who had stolen a baby and placed her with a good, hard-working fishmonger.

Jessica sensed the tension in the room. 'I'll go and get my school books,' she told her mother. 'Then you can see how hard the work is.'

Alone, Eva and Theresa stared awkwardly at one another. 'Are you feeling really ill?' Eva asked. Did Theresa know? Did she?

'I'm tired. My heart's a bit wonky again.' Really, Eva had played a large part in the lives of both twins, because she'd looked after Jessica for ages.

Eva arranged the scones in rows. 'Dr Blake still comes round asking about you.' She lifted a circle of marzipan and stuck it on top of her Christmas cake. 'Once Jessica leaves this house, he only needs to follow her from school and he'll find you.'

Theresa watched while the woman who had delivered her twins spread thick, uneven icing on top of the marzipan. 'I'm not bothered any more,' she replied at last.

When a Father Christmas and a snowman sat among miniature peaks of sugary snow, Eva laid down her palette knife. 'Are you still going after them three?' she asked.

Theresa shrugged.

'Because if your mind's set on punishment, you could end up in jail. Then what happens to Jess?'

'Maggie will see to her.'

Eva picked up a red ribbon. 'I'll put that round it when the icing's set. Very nicely decorated, even if I say it myself.' She prodded a couple of puddings with a skewer, withdrew the implement and checked that it was clean. 'Done and dusted,' she declared. 'Full of sixpences and milk stout.' She looked straight into Theresa's eyes. 'Would you pour the tea?' she asked.

Theresa poured.

'Am I not good enough any more?'

The visitor's hand stumbled, bled milk onto the tablecloth. 'I've saved for Jessica, Eva. I don't know how long I've got, and I want her secure. I'm giving her the deeds to a house. Maggie . . . well, she's nowhere to go and nobody to care for her. You've got Jimmy.'

'I'm not bothered about me.' Eva clattered a spoon in a dish of home-made mincemeat. 'It's Jessica that matters. Hasn't she had enough changes?'

Theresa agreed, though she said nothing. But how could she leave Jessica to the mercies of a woman who had stolen a baby?

'Theresa?'

Eva's guest sipped tea. 'If anything happens to me – when it happens – Jessica can live with Maggie and visit you if she wants.'

'When she wants. Whatever I've done and whatever I am, yon lass loves me.' Eva caught sight of pain in Theresa's eyes, a look that advertised hurt tinged with anger. Theresa knew about the other child. Then Theresa smiled and Eva wasn't sure. 'Will your friends want to spend Christmas here?' she asked.

'Possibly. They've offered to chip in with some money or food.'

Jessica ran in with a pile of books. She babbled on about French and history, complained about geometry, declared that algebra made no sense at all.

'You say they're sleeping at Ruth's?' Eva asked when Jessica slowed down.

Theresa nodded absently, her eye fixed to a page filled with foreign words. 'Jessica?'

'Yes, Mam?'

'Do you understand all this?'

Jessica nodded.

'You'll have it all, love,' said Theresa, contentment and pride softening her speech. Jessica was beautiful. She was getting an education, too, and she would soon own a modest house. 'Use it well,' she advised.

'I'd not send me worst enemy to sleep there,' continued Eva.

Theresa settled down to drink a second cup of tea. Perhaps she hadn't done such a bad job after all. She had earned a living, had kept this precious girl at a safe distance, had saved enough to give Jessica a toe-hold on the future. The other one – Katherine – the child who lived a lie, was also gaining an education. Liz and Bernard Walsh had sent Jessica's double to private schools, so she, too, had promising prospects.

'And if that Irene turns up, they'll be wanting the bishop round to bless the house. Who in their right mind wants to spend a lifetime messing about with dead folk?'

Jessica turned to Eva. 'But she isn't in her right mind. Can I have a scone, please?'

Theresa found herself smiling. Even in the midst of the strangest conversation, Jessica's appetite remained unaffected.

Hardman's Hides was set back from the road, though the stench it produced reached its tentacles across several streets. Depending on the wind's direction, windows in areas surrounding the factory would be closed in the finest weather, whole blocks of half-suffocated people enduring heat until the wind turned.

Christmas was finished, and Theresa thanked God that the celebrations were over and done with. It hadn't been easy, but Theresa had managed to say nothing contentious to Eva. Having escaped for the day from View Street, Theresa stood on Doffcocker Lane and congratulated herself on her performance during the festive season. She had been pleasant to Eva, had played charades, Ludo and Monopoly with good grace, had washed dishes, sung carols, had sat through midnight mass at Sts Peter and Paul.

Now, she was supposed to be house-hunting. She stood opposite the factory where Ged Hardman and his famous mother had supposedly performed miracles after the departure of George Senior and his secretary. A feeling that she was being watched made Theresa look around, but she was alone on the lane. Directly across from the tannery, there were no houses. The land near which she stood was scrubby and covered in discarded prams, mattresses and car tyres.

She crossed over and walked along the perimeter fence, realizing with a shudder why she had experienced the sensation of being observed. Into knot-holes of the wooden fence, the eyes of dead animals had been wedged, probably by apprentices in need of distraction. From almost every aperture, the sad, brown eye of a departed cow accused all who passed this way.

She stepped through the gateway, her mind strangely calm, her heartbeat steady and sure. Hardman's, attached to an abattoir owned by a wholesale butcher, had its own skinners' yard. Some small attempt had been made to conceal the area, which lay to the right of the works' entrance, but a low brick wall did little to shield the eye or soothe the soul of any visitor. A river of blood, made thicker by icy air, made its dark, sticky way towards the main courtyard.

Mesmerized by horror, Theresa stepped towards the gore. On this sad, barren lane, abattoir and tannery, separate businesses, had enjoyed a mutually dependent relationship for many years. Huge barrels of entrails spilled their contents onto paving slabs. Butchers' vans, their rear doors open, received the skinned carcasses of animals, raucous shouts and ribald comments accompanying the recently killed beasts on their final journey. Theresa could smell the blood, the discarded guts, the putrefaction. In summer, she could not have stood here.

'Can I help you?'

She swivelled and found herself face to face with a middle-aged woman in a fur coat. This was the notorious Lily Hardman, all subdued make-up, mink and good shoes. 'Good morning,' Theresa replied. 'I'm looking for somewhere to live, but it won't be round here, near all this.'

Lily Hardman's eyes narrowed. 'It has to be done,' she snapped. 'People want leather, therefore we produce it.'

354

'So I see.' Theresa, who enjoyed a beef dinner, decided there and then that she could not eat dead cow ever again.

'Well, unless you've business here, you'd better go. I can see you've no stomach for tanning.'

Theresa ran an eye over Ged Hardman's mother. 'I remember you,' she said softly. 'Your husband ran off. I was very upset for you at the time. Then I went to Liverpool to make my own fortune. I had two or three shops,' she said. Lying was strangely easy in the presence of Mrs Hardman. 'And now, I'm looking to invest my capital in business, as well as in property.'

Lillian Hardman, a pillar of the community, had more than atoned for the lapses of morality which had resulted in George Hardman's departure from these parts. She did not want this pale young woman's sympathy. 'We are always interested in expansion,' she replied carefully. 'Our bank manager is always willing to back us, since we have such an excellent record.'

Theresa gazed around the large premises. 'Well,' she said, a forced smile lightening the tone. 'I suppose you won't be needing my bit of money, will you?'

Lily shrugged. 'That depends what you want. I'm not looking for shareholders. My son and I own the works outright, and the bank is there if and when we need to borrow. However, if your required rate of interest was reasonable, we could use another shed for chroming.'

'Chroming?'

'It's a quick way of tanning.' Lily hesitated. Why was this young woman here? What did she really want? 'You must have a reason for choosing Hardman's,' she added.

Theresa inclined her head as if deep in thought. 'I'm here by accident,' she explained. 'I was seeing a house a few streets away, then, as I passed, I saw Ged's works.'

'Ah. So you know my son?'

'I used to. We were friends long ago.'

Lily bit into her lower lip. Ged was a great source of disappointment to his mother. Now in his early thirties, he showed no sign of settling down, seeming to prefer the company of his friends in public houses. This girl appeared rather frail, but was she going to be the one who could forgive Ged's facial scars, his drinking, his stupidity? 'Are you married?' she asked.

Theresa shook her head. 'My fiancé died,' she said sweetly.

'Oh, I'm sorry to hear that.'

'So I threw myself into my work. Now I'm home and I'm visiting old friends.'

'And your name?'

'Mary. Mary Palmer.'

Lily was on her way out to the hairdresser's. A position like hers called for perfect grooming at all times. 'Go in,' she said. 'Find Ged – he'll be in his office. I'll be back in an hour or so.'

When the woman had left the yard, Theresa made her way into a place in which a variety of stenches battled to claim the contents of her stomach. Bravely, she fought nausea as she walked past a fleshing station where men with double-handed knives shaved reddened tissue from the underside of hides. The stink of lime mingled with odours given off by gallons of brine in which skins soaked themselves towards cleanliness. Dripping bundles of half-tanned leathers sat on the edges of lime pits. It was, Theresa judged, one of the most disgusting places in the civilized world.

She followed a series of signs until she reached the offices. The second door bore the legend: 'GEORGE HARDMAN, MANAGING DIRECTOR'. The first and larger office was labelled: 'LILLIAN HARDMAN, CHAIRMAN'. The masculinity of the title suited Lily, Theresa decided. Lillian Hardman was probably the best man here. She knocked on Ged Hardman's door.

'Come,' boomed the incumbent.

Theresa inhaled deeply before opening the door. With her hair rinsed towards auburn and thick make-up covering her face, Theresa knew that she looked nothing like her old self.

'Yes?' he asked.

He was so ugly. His deeply scored face bore a resemblance to magnified pigskin, though its colour was paler than the lightest hue of any natural leather. He sat behind a mahogany desk, its surface clear except for a square blotter and a couple of pens. 'Mr Hardman?' she asked. If she acted as if she didn't know him, her visit would be far more effective.

'Yes?' The face was familiar, though he could not put a name to it.

'Your mother suggested that I should talk to you.'

'Oh, I see.' The woman was thin, but quite a good looker.

'About investment. I used to live in Bolton, but I've been away for some time. I understand that cotton's future is uncertain, so I'm looking for an alternative. Just short-term, you understand, until I find my feet again.' She sat down and crossed ankles she knew to be perfect. 'My experience has been in

357

retail. We could, perhaps, discuss outlets for leather goods.'

He lit a cigarette, continuing to look her over. She had good legs, a neat figure and a face that was almost heart-shaped. 'Go on,' he invited.

'Well, I haven't thought it through, not really. Mrs Hardman was talking about expanding here, something about chroming sheds. We could discuss several possibilities, I suppose.' She was so grateful for her Liverpool years. In the city, she had learned to talk with all kinds of people, had negotiated prices, had dealt with old sailors, prostitutes, tradespeople. She was, finally, a woman of the world.

He smiled at her. 'How about a cup of tea?'

'That would be lovely.'

He pressed a bell-push on his desk and barked his order when a young lad appeared. 'Tea for both of us and don't spill any.'

Theresa waited for the door to close. 'My name is Mary. Mary Palmer.'

He searched the recesses of his mind, but found no purchase on the name. 'Where are you living?' he asked.

'With a friend. It's a temporary arrangement.'

Ged took a deep draught of Capstan Full Strength, coughed, wondered whether to go for the kill. 'I could . . . show you round the town, take you for a drink.'

Theresa awarded him a broad smile. 'That would be lovely,' she told him. 'If you have a friend, I can bring my friend, make an evening of it. I seem to remember a couple of nice little pubs on Deansgate – the Hen and Chickens? The King's Head?'

Ged considered this suggestion. The friend would have to put up with Roy Chorlton, but Roy was better than nobody. 'Where shall I pick you up?' he asked.

'I'll meet you in the King's Head. Shall we say eight o'clock on Saturday night?'

Ged agreed, telling himself that Teddy Betteridge could play gooseberry or go home. Teddy's wife never came out, preferring to drink stout from the outdoor licence with her cronies and neighbours.

The tea arrived and Ged poured, making sure that Mary Palmer's did not spill into the saucer. She was the best thing that had happened for some considerable time. He straightened his tie, sipped tea and made small talk. With any luck, he'd be the toast of the King's Head come Saturday.

TWELVE

The King's Head was packed, temporarily, more tightly than a sardine tin. There would have been no room for oil or tomato sauce, mused Ged Hardman as he wedged himself into a chair at the usual table near the window. Roy was late, as was Mary Palmer. Ged almost ground his teeth with impatience; the woman was probably all my eye and Betty Martin, somebody who got a lift out of leading men on, too much talk and no delivery date.

Above all things, Ged wanted to be married. A nice young woman on his arm would boost his confidence, give him a reason to stop boozing and to start living. It wasn't fair. He knew other blokes who had suffered with acne, but none had a face like his. If he could only find somebody – anybody – Mother could get in her Bentley and drive to hell on her own.

The solid mass of people began to disperse. They would be going to the Lido or the Odeon to see some war film or other. On Saturday nights, most folk didn't bother with the B movies. They had a few drinks and a laugh before dashing off to munch popcorn and butterscotch through the main feature. It was almost ten minutes past eight, and there was still no sign of Mary Palmer or her friend. And where the hell was Chorlton? It wasn't as if the tailor got many chances to spend an evening with a couple of young women. Like Ged, Roy was a reject, something that should have gone in the entrails bucket with all the other mess.

'What will you have?'

Ged looked up. 'Hello, Roy. A pint of mild and a small Scotch, please.'

'No sign of the ladies?'

Ged shrugged. 'They might have had a better offer,' he answered gloomily.

Roy, who thought this only too likely, drifted off towards the bar. He hoped with all his heart that the women would keep their distance. Rejection terrified him beyond measure. He knew well enough that he was no oil painting, so why invite more pain into his narrow, humdrum life?

Ged drummed his fingers on the table, then indulged in a little deft juggling with cardboard beer mats. Mother had laughed, of course. 'She wants to talk about leather, dear, about getting a foothold in Bolton. So please don't get your hopes up . . .' She was an evil bitch, one who kept a tight rein on money. Mother never told him much, seldom inviting him to partake in any real business. Managing Director? He signed a few orders, did a sum or two, then spent the rest of the day playing with paperclips and appeasing his bookmaker.

Roy returned and placed the drinks on the table. He cleared his throat. 'Have you been feeling all right?' he asked, the tone falsely nonchalant.

'So-so,' replied Ged after a draught of ale.

Roy looked over his shoulder. Having delved into a medical encyclopedia, he was uncomfortable in more ways than one. 'I'm having a bit of trouble down below,' he whispered.

Ged studied his companion, then drank some more. 'Do you mean a sort of burning?'

Roy nodded.

'Bloody hell,' exclaimed the tanner. 'I've been a bit like that, a bit sore.'

Each man stared blankly into the other's eyes. They had the clap. Betteridge, too, had been with them when a bright-faced Liverpool girl had walked into their lives, into this very same inn. 'Bloody hell,' repeated Ged. 'What the flaming Nora do we do now?'

Roy wiped his lips with a handkerchief. A meticulous man, he could not bear the idea of any kind of dirt. The knowledge that he had been with a whore sat uncomfortably in a compartment of his well-disciplined brain. 'There's a VD clinic at the back of the Town Hall,' he said. 'But I wouldn't like to be seen walking through that door. We shall have to visit our doctors.'

Ged pondered. 'Won't it go away on its own?'

'With our luck, probably not.' Using the same square of cotton, Roy mopped his brow. Here he sat in the middle of winter, a draught blowing under the door, yet he was sweating like a pig. 'I think I have a temperature,' he grumbled.

'Dirty little cow,' snapped Ged Hardman. 'No wonder she left Liverpool. She's decided to spread a little happiness round here for a change.'

Roy bowed his head, ashamed of himself. He could scarcely bear to remember what had happened. Like men in a bus queue, he and Betteridge had waited their turn in the bathroom of this seedy old pub, had used the girl, had paid their money.

They had got a little more than they'd bargained for, it seemed. 'What about Teddy's wife?' he asked.

Ged, who was concentrating on his own problem, offered no immediate answer.

'She could catch it,' continued Roy.

Ged nudged himself to life. 'Serve her right,' he declared. 'She looks as if she only has a wash at Christmas and a bath every Preston Guild.'

As far as Roy was concerned, Mrs Betteridge's habits were not the point. The poor woman probably had a venereal disease simply because her husband was an alcoholic philanderer. Roy shifted in his chair, knew that he would need to visit the lavatory yet again at any moment. Was he any better than Teddy or Ged? Sexual frustration was no excuse for using prostitutes. 'It's our own fault,' he opined softly.

'Is it hell as like. They're supposed to keep themselves clean, aren't they? It's part of the job, part of what we pay them for. Four quid for a quicky and a dose of this? It's out and out barefaced robbery.'

Roy knew that his cheeks were burning.

'She'd no right,' muttered Ged angrily. 'Wait till I get my hands on her – she'll soon know which side her head's been clouted.'

The tailor closed his eyes, tried to ignore the discomfort in his bladder. It was as if that part of his anatomy had been peppered with a thousand shards of hot, needle-thin glass.

'Can you imagine talking about this to your doctor? He might tell my flaming mother,' said Ged.

'He won't. They pledge secrecy.'

'Aye, so do the bloody masons, but we all know about their tomfoolery.' He had forgotten about Mary Palmer and her slender, shapely legs. He had given up on the idea of snatching a kiss and a cuddle later on. Let his mother deal with it. Let Lily borrow and pay low interest, because he had had enough.

From the doorway, Theresa Nolan, alias Mary Palmer, surveyed her prey. Again, she was calm and detached, as if this whole scenario had been imagined, as if it were a dream. She walked to the table, smiled when Roy Chorlton, that fat slug of a so-called gentleman, almost choked on a mouthful of beer. Ged Hardman, too, had a puzzled look on his face. 'Good evening,' she said, sitting down next to Roy Chorlton.

Ged smiled hesitantly. Was this Mary Palmer? Mary Palmer had reddish-brownish hair pulled back behind her ears, while this woman was a strawberry blonde, her hair falling forward in soft waves. 'You look different,' he said eventually.

'I am different,' she replied.

'Where's your friend?' Ged asked.

'In my mind,' she answered, gloved hands folded on the table. 'She's all in my mind, Mr Hardman.'

Roy felt as if a hand had reached into his chest to squeeze his heart to death. Theresa Nolan. She looked older, very drawn, yet extremely beautiful.

'Did the cat get your tongue?' she asked Roy. 'Or has your seedy past returned to catch up with you?'

His bladder was close to bursting.

'Are you in pain?'

Roy studied her. He got the message. She had sent Maria Martin to Bolton.

Theresa turned to Ged Hardman. 'I hoped you wouldn't recognize me the other day,' she told him, her tone conversational. 'I rinsed my hair with a wash-out colour.'

'Who the hell are you?' Ged knew her, yet he didn't.

'Just a piece of rubbish you picked up in an alleyway a long time ago. Three of you, there were. You, this poor excuse of a man and an alcoholic called Betteridge. Will he be in this evening?'

Ged's jaw hung like a broken gate. 'You're not her,' he stammered. 'She disappeared years ago, went off without so much as a by-your-leave, by all accounts, and—'

'I went to Liverpool,' she said. 'To work with war-victims and other retired sailors.' She smiled. 'A young woman lived upstairs. She was supposed to be a kitchen maid, but I think she added to her income by working in the evenings, too.' She paused, savouring the moment before the kill. No way would she tell these people that she had lived in a place that housed a brothel. 'The maid's name was Maria. I understand that she visited Bolton a while ago.'

Ged Hardman leapt to his feet, almost upsetting the table in his haste. 'You bloody bitch,' he roared.

The landlord shouted across the room. 'Hey! If you want to carry on that road, do it outside.'

Ged sat down. She was staring straight at him, would not deflect her gaze. Something in her expression threatened him far more effectively than the landlord's words. He looked down, picked up his glass and took a swig.

Roy was shaking. He remembered her, her fear, her pain and her fury. In his mind's eye, he stood once more in a shabby little room, a pink-faced infant in a padded drawer at his feet. The woman was screaming at him. She clutched the edge of a washed-out quilt and begged him to leave. He was her monster, her nightmare. No, she would not marry him. No, this baby would be hers and only hers. He was not fit to be a father, not fit to be alive.

'Bugger off,' spat Ged Hardman. 'We've paid for that mistake, paid through the nose. And now you've given us a bloody dose, you cow.'

Roy jumped up and ran to the men's lavatory.

Unflinching, Theresa held her ground.

'What do you want?' asked Ged.

She shook her head slowly. 'Let's wait till the other hero comes back, shall we?'

'Who? Chorlton? You'll get nothing out of him, either.'

'Pity,' she remarked quietly. 'Because I have a letter from Maria.' How smoothly the untruths flowed after a while. Maria could scarcely write her own name. 'She sent it to my friend's house and says she's sorry about . . . her illness, but she didn't find out about it until she got back to Liverpool.'

'Balls,' he spat.

'And she thought you should be informed.' Theresa gazed around the bar. 'Your mother would be very interested to read Maria's letter.'

He blinked rapidly. 'You can't do that,' he spluttered.

'Oh, but I can. I might even paint a message on the factory fence: "George Hardman Junior picked up a nasty illness in the line of duty".'

Roy dashed back to the table, looked at Ged, then at Theresa. Without saying a word to either, he plucked his trilby from a chair and ran outside.

'Coward,' said Theresa, no expression colouring the words. 'I'll see you soon,' she told the terrified Ged Hardman. 'And don't follow me. I happen to be armed.'

The most worrying thing was that Ged found himself believing her. She wasn't tall, wasn't strong. But she had the sort of demeanour that was decidedly disturbing. 'I'll not follow you. I couldn't be bothered.'

'Good.' She rose gracefully from her seat, every inch the lady. Several men gave her the once-over as she leaned forward and whispered to Ged Hardman. 'Fifteen hundred pounds,' she said. 'I've nothing to lose but face, so save your breath. I'll tell every man and woman in this town about your illness – about the other two sufferers, as well. Five hundred pounds each, please. Give it to Chorlton. Of the three of you, he's probably the most honest.'

'You what?'

'For my daughter. For her security.' She turned to leave, then back-tracked. 'Oh, by the way, Maria would be quite happy to charge you all with rape. That would be a scream, wouldn't it? When you really did it, you got off scot free. Now, when you're innocent, you stand to lose a hell of a lot. See you soon, George.'

She left the pub, rested outside for a few minutes. Only now, in the relatively fresh air, did she realize how smelly and claustrophobic the bar had been. Her clothes reeked of tobacco and ale, no doubt. She shivered, pulled the scarf tightly across her throat, turned up her collar. It was cold enough for snow, though the cloud was thin. Perhaps the fall would come tomorrow.

She began the walk back to Daubhill, wondering what the hell she had been playing at tonight. What did she want? Money for Jessica, money for herself, three men in newly dug graves? Chorlton was pathetic, Betteridge was absent, Hardman was another sad creature, all bad skin and anger. No, no, she would hang on to her resolve; there was no space for doubt, not now, so late in the day and so near to her goal.

'Theresa?'

She swung round. 'Maggie. Where have you been?'

'To London to look at the Queen.' Maggie caught her breath. 'Tell you what, Theresa, you can't half shift. How fast would you go if you had your health?'

'Have you been following me?' asked Theresa.

'Yes. Yes, I have.'

Taken somewhat aback by Maggie's honesty, Theresa was temporarily lost for words.

'You're still looking for those men, aren't you? Well, aren't you?'

'Yes.'

Maggie leaned against a wall. 'What for?' she asked.

'I was thinking of getting a darts team together,' she replied with heavy sarcasm.

'Oh really? You don't go wandering about on a cold night unless you have a very good reason. I don't see why anyone in their right mind—'

'Maggie, shut up. We're not all like you. Some of us aren't perfect. If you'd been through what I've been through . . .' Theresa watched Maggie's face. In the lamplight, the older woman was beautiful, unlined, youthful once more. 'I'm sorry,' Theresa mumbled. 'I shouldn't have said that.' Maggie, a victim of incest, did not deserve harsh words.

'That's all right.'

'No, no. At least none of them was my father.'

Maggie shook her head. 'It took a lot of years and a lot of men to get rid of the smell of him. But you're right, it's the being used that counts most. No matter who the attacker is, you hate him for the rest of your life. He made you less than you were, certainly less than you might have become. But that's no excuse for hunting these men to the ends of the earth.'

'Deansgate is hardly the ends of the earth, Maggie.'

Maggie bridled. 'Don't you go getting clever with me, miss. Was that one of the men – going bald, on the short side, ran out of the place a few minutes ago?'

Theresa nodded.

'What had you done to him?'

Theresa raised her shoulders. 'Nothing yet. Maria's responsible for his condition, I think. She came over some weeks ago and infected them all. Such a shame. I was going to come with her just for the fun of it, only I changed my mind.'

Maggie's anger spilled over. 'Theresa, for God's sake – didn't you say one of those men is married? What about his wife? Have you given no thought to her?'

Theresa had a ready answer. 'Yes, I thought about her. I intend to tell her as soon as possible that she must leave him and take her children with her. After all, she shouldn't be living with a man who uses prostitutes.'

Maggie closed her mouth with a sharp snap. There was little she could do about this stubborn young woman. Theresa's energy burned in one direction only, and nothing would deflect her, it seemed. 'And when do you plan to deal with Eva?' Maggie asked. 'After all, she took away the second baby and gave her to a lovely, caring couple. I suppose she must suffer, too.'

Theresa gazed levelly at her companion. 'I may seem cold and cruel to you, but this is my way of dealing with the cruelty of others. My mother died and my father hated me. I have brothers and sisters who won't talk to me, let alone help with Jessica. I have another daughter, one I wasn't allowed to see. Three men raped me. One of them is the father of those twins. When I die, my sister Ruth will try to claim Jessica as some sort of bauble. Her own daughter was not good enough, too ugly. I've a heart that won't heal, Maggie. There are things I must do—'

'Where's the gun?'

Theresa shook her head. 'Things to do, Maggie. You guard my daughter with your life – promise?'

Maggie sighed. 'I promise.'

A heavy hand clamped itself on each woman's shoulder. They spun round simultaneously. 'Monty!' shrieked Maggie. 'My God, you could have given us both heart attacks.'

The man panted for breath. 'I've been following you,' he told Maggie crossly.

Theresa started to giggle. Laughter poured from her mouth until several passers-by stopped in their tracks. 'You've been following Maggie,' she hooted, 'while Maggie was following me, while I was following the Three Stooges. Where will it all end?'

Maggie was not amused. 'Exactly,' she said ominously. 'Where will it all end? Anyway, you two can please yourselves. I'm off to enjoy another evening of Ruth's hospitality.'

This statement made Theresa double over with mirth. She laughed until the tears came, then she wept on Maggie's shoulder. She didn't know why she had laughed, or why she was crying. But she sobbed all the way back to View Street.

She watched the woman juggling pots and pans, listened as coarse language tumbled from thick lips in a grey, blubbery face. The market hummed with activity, forming a suitable backdrop for Teddy Betteridge's other half. Mrs Elsie Betteridge wore a thick winter coat, a red scarf and a woollen hat that looked like a tea-cosy with the holes sewn up. 'Genuine Crown Derby,' she yelled. 'Only one previous owner, the Hearl of Hipswich.' The mouth spread itself into a broad grin. 'Only kidding, missus. This here dinner set's fresh from the kiln, hot enough to warm your necessaries all the way home.'

Theresa crossed the street to examine some tawdry articles on a clothing stall. She remembered coming here as a young girl to buy cheap stockings, arriving home only to find that the carefully folded and packaged items had included darned holes, no feet or several ladders.

Dobson's was still here, the stall covered in pillowcases, sheets and towels. An Antiquities Corner boasted some silver-plated condiment pots, a few fire irons, the odd antimacassar and a bust of Lord Nelson.

She walked into the covered area, almost raising her hands to protect her ears against the noise of stallholders competing for business. 'Cheapest in town, love', 'Come and get your cups, missus – saucers thrown in free', 'Two for a shilling, five for a florin'. Theresa realized how much she had missed her home town. She felt at home with the accent, the skyline – even the smells.

It was a smell that drew her further, past the

chandlers, the flower-sellers, the loose covers and second-hand books. The fishmarket had never been one of Theresa's favourite places, but there was someone she wanted to see, a man who, like his brother, had always been kind and generous to neighbours and customers alike.

Danny Walsh was still there, at the same stall, in the same uniform of blue-and-white striped apron over a white coat. On his head he wore a white hat with a brim and a chequered band. Into the band he had inserted a small flag which bore the words: 'NO FLIES ON WALSH'S FISH'. He hadn't changed at all. Still as thin as a rake, he presided over his kingdom with a beaming smile and a joke for everyone.

Theresa stood in front of him. His smile wavered, returned, then was switched off like a redundant electric lamp.

'It's all right,' said Theresa. She looked around, made sure that nobody was listening. 'I know about Katherine. I met her.'

'Our Bernard told me.' Danny wrapped some kippers for a woman who was in a hurry.

'I'm not well,' Theresa continued.

'I know,' Danny replied.

'When I'm gone, will you help Bernard to keep an eye on both my children?'

The fishmonger held up a hand to Theresa, indicated that she should wait. He called an assistant to take over, then followed Theresa out to Ashburner Street. 'I didn't know what to do that night,' he began. 'When Liz's little girl died. Neither did our Bernard.' He leaned against a wall. 'That was when we got your baby. I know you met him and Katherine in Liverpool.'

'They're doing a good job on her,' said Theresa. 'She's a nice child, well mannered.'

'She's an angel.' He removed his hat, pulled the silly flag from the band, then replaced the trilby-shaped item on his head. 'Liz knows nothing about it. She thinks Katherine's her own.'

'Yes, so I was told.'

Danny stared at Theresa, but seemed to be looking through her towards the junior library across the road. 'The little one was in a shoe box. Liz kept telling us to warm her near the fire, but she was past warming. Then Eva came, took the box away and left us a bundle.'

'One of my twins.'

'Aye, that's right.' He cleared his throat. 'A few years later, Liz had to have an operation. She can't have any more children.'

Theresa experienced mixed emotions about Liz's predicament. It was a shame that such a good mother could not have a larger family, but, at the same time, Katherine, an only child, could get all the attention and affection she needed. Although she had met her only once, Theresa remained struck by the similarities between Jessica and Katherine. The likeness went beyond the merely physical. Yes, the Walsh family would do very well for Katherine.

'What brings you back to these parts?' Danny was asking.

'Loose ends.'

Something in her tone prompted him to ask no further questions.

'Like I said before, my health isn't up to much. I want as many people as possible to keep a watch over Jessica when I'm gone. I've a feeling our Ruth might try to claim her.'

'Not while there's breath in Eva's body.'

Theresa tutted impatiently. 'I'm not sure that I

trust her any more. She never told me. Even later on, she didn't say a word. I don't want her to have Jessica. I've found someone else to take care of her.'

'But Eva's always done a good job.'

'Has she?' Theresa's anger was inexplicable because it came from instinct only. She did not understand it, could not justify it, could never have described it. 'Time she had a rest, then.' She glanced up and down the street, decided that it was time to face the sizeable Mrs Betteridge. 'I'm buying a house,' she told Danny. 'On Tonge Moor Road.'

'My mother-in-law lived up there.'

Theresa nodded in the manner of someone who wasn't really listening. 'It'll be in Jessica's name. I'll let you and Bernard have the address. Just a weather eye, that's all I ask.'

He reached out and touched her shoulder. 'On my life, I promise you,' he said.

Theresa, who was adept at hiding emotion, found herself close to tears. 'I don't blame you or your brother,' she said. 'And I certainly don't blame Liz. You're good people, all of you.' Sometimes, she felt as if the gun had started to bore a hole through her handbag and into her body. This was one of those times. The bad people needed stopping, deserved punishment, merited no mercy. Good folk should not be standing so close to deadly weaponry.

'Look after yourself, love,' Danny said. 'I'll have to get back to the stall. And don't worry about anything. I'm so sorry. None of this should have happened.'

'It wasn't your fault,' she said yet again.

She looked so thin, so fragile that a wintry blast might well push her out of existence. 'Don't hang about in this weather,' Danny advised. 'You might catch your death.'

A corner of Theresa's mouth twitched. 'It's death that's catching up with me. I reckon I'll take my chances.'

Ruth McManus was, without question, the most irritating person Maggie Courtney had ever met. For a start, Ruth had to be the centre of attention at all times and at any cost. When she wasn't out at work, she sat for endless hours in front of the fire, handing out her opinion on every subject, smoking continuously, pulling at her hair, condemning mankind with her whiplash tongue.

Maggie, who was baking in the kitchen, listened while Ruth went on about nuns and the Catholic Church.

'They're bloody evil, the lot of them,' yelled Ruth.

Maggie, who recognized evil only too well, blessed herself with a floury hand. Evil was in the next room, was burning coal paid for by Monty and tobacco donated by Maggie in the interests of world peace. When she had her smokes, Ruth was simply nasty. Without cigarettes, she was a devil incarnate. After counting to ten, Maggie made her reply. 'I've known some nice nuns.'

'Well, I've not. We got the cane for holes in our stockings, for missing mass, for talking.'

She never stopped talking, thought Maggie. The only chance of a bit of quiet was when the woman was eating.

'What are you making?'

'Steak and kidney pudding.'

'I don't like it.'

'Good,' mouthed Maggie. 'There's bacon,' she called.

'I had that yesterday.'

Maggie walked to the door, poked her head into the living room. 'Hanson's is still open. Would you like to walk down and find yourself something?'

'I've been on my feet all day. You've no idea what it's like in that mill. Hot as hell, it is.'

Maggie returned to her pastry. Ruth McManus belonged in a fiery furnace, so the mill would be good practice for her.

'I'll have a bit of that pudding,' shouted Ruth, as if she were doing Maggie a great favour.

Maggie thought fleetingly of rat poison. In all her years as a professional woman, Maggie had never met anything quite like Theresa's sister. Ruth's daughter, Irene, was another queer one. She used people: scrutinized them, activated them, tossed them away once their purpose had been served. She was ugly, and had been made uglier by her own mother's hatred. 'How's Irene?' shouted Maggie as she shredded suet.

'A rat. She'll always be a rat. Did you know she beats her husband? Such a nice lad, he is. I warned him, you know. I told him she were no good. But once she's got her claws in, she'll not let go till she's good and done. I reckon she'll stick with him, get him insured and then work him to death. I hope she never has a daughter. Girls take after their mothers.'

The ridiculous thing was that Ruth never heard herself, did not realize that she was admitting her own guilt, that she was allowing the world to know that she had created a monster. Who had created Ruth, then? Her bigoted father?

'Our Theresa'll not last long,' Ruth was saying now. 'She were at death's door as a kiddy. Every time she had a cold, there were a song and dance, bloody doctor never away from the door, pills and potions.

376

You can tell how bad – she had Extreme Unction twice. Anyroad, when she pops her clogs, I'll look after Jessica.'

Maggie's hands stilled themselves.

'It'll be nice to have a good-looking kiddy in the house,' continued Ruth. 'Grammar school and all. Jessica'll get a proper job when she's grown. She'll not be washing corpses and ironing shrouds.'

It was little wonder, thought Maggie, that Irene had chosen to work with the dead. The dead didn't answer back, didn't sit there twiddling their hair and shouting the odds through a dense cloud of Kensitas fumes. A corpse couldn't call Irene ugly or accuse her of being a rat.

'I'll be her nearest when Theresa dies. So Jess will come to me.'

Maggie's fingers curled round the rolling pin. She suddenly understood Theresa's need to kill. If she could have been sure of remaining free, Maggie Courtney might well have smashed Ruth McManus's skull there and then. Panic rose, causing the Irishwoman to gag. How? How would she, a retired prostitute, keep hold of Jessica Nolan after Theresa's death?

'That'll be why our Theresa's come home, you know. She's not well and she wanted to be near me. Eva won't be able to hang on to Jessica once our Theresa's dead. Blood's thicker than water.'

Maggie left her pastry and went out to the yard. She locked herself in the lavatory shed and sat down. What on earth could be done to stop Ruth getting her hands on Theresa's daughter? Maggie knew that Theresa, who was feeling particularly depressed, was investing all her limited energy in her stupid search for justice.

'Are you there? Only I'm waiting.'

Even in the outhouses, there was no hiding from Ruth. The wash-house, next door to the lavatory, had provided no sanctuary at the weekend. Ruth had stood, cigarette hanging from her lip, telling Maggie how to poss and washboard properly.

'Maggie?'

'I won't be a minute.'

From what Maggie had heard, Irene had, in her time, been battered halfway to death. She had been locked in cupboards, in the outdoor coal shed, in the space beneath the stairs. She had grown up in a house that was supposedly haunted, had been left to fend for herself in a place without food, warmth or distraction. With no-one to mind her unloved child, Ruth McManus had gone out to work leaving Irene to her own devices. On her own, lonely and furious, the girl had amused herself by inflicting discomfort on others. The inhabitants of the undertaker's premises had fascinated Irene. Frozen into eternal silence, the bodies had not uttered a sound. Maggie shivered as she wondered what on earth Ruth McManus's daughter had done to those dead people.

'I'm plaiting me legs here,' shouted Ruth.

Maggie emerged, stormed past her hostess and shot into the kitchen. As she scrubbed her hands, a terrible anger entered her body, causing her to inflict on her skin what almost amounted to grievous bodily harm. She threw the bar of carbolic back into its dish and picked up a towel.

'You all right, girl?'

Monty was a welcome sight. He was straighter today, happier. 'She's driving me mad,' replied Maggie

'Me, too.' He paused for a few seconds. 'I can go back now,' he told her. 'The job's done.'

'Have they made arrests?'

He nodded. 'But somebody's got to look after all the old boys. Are you coming with me?' He already knew the answer.

'No. That one out there . . .' She jerked a finger towards the yard. 'She thinks she's going to get a grip on Jessica once poor Theresa's gone. Can you imagine that?'

Monty, who had met Irene, didn't want to imagine anything.

'There's something missing in Irene and Ruth, isn't there?' asked Maggie. 'Something normal's missing, and—'

'And something abnormal's in them. My nephew's talked to me about people like Ruth. They don't feel anything for other folk. Well, if they do feel something, it's soon over. It's number one all the way, take, take, take. Stamping on a worm or stabbing a human being – it's all the same to them.'

Maggie's flesh crawled. 'There's a bit of this in Theresa. She wants . . . Oh, never mind.' She could not tell Monty the truth. Theresa had a gun and a stubborn streak.

'No, she's all right,' said Monty. 'Theresa Nolan's a sick girl, but it's her body, not her mind that's letting her down. She's said nothing definite about moving Jessica away from Eva just yet, and Ruth won't be in the picture even then. When Theresa buys the house, the three of you can get away from here.'

'And when Theresa gets too ill? If she dies?'

'Cross that one when you get there, girl.'

Ruth entered the house. 'And another thing,' she

began. 'I don't want anybody touching anything of me dad's. His walking stick's been moved out of the—'

'I knocked it over,' explained Monty. 'When I was getting my cap off the hook.'

Ruth squared her shoulders. 'He'll not be pleased.'

'He haunts the house,' Maggie informed Monty. 'You can hear him climbing the stairs sometimes. You can tell it's him because he walks with a limp. Isn't that the case, Ruth?' Maggie, who knew about such things, was absolutely sure that no spectre existed in this unhappy house.

'Shrapnel.'

Monty blessed himself. 'Holy Mother,' he blasphemed softly. 'Oh, Lord, he's materialized. I've seen him, I think.'

Both women looked around, but saw nothing.

'Not now – the other night. I thought I was dreaming,' continued Monty. 'There I was, lying in bed and—'

'And what?' Ruth, scared halfway to death, was hanging on to every syllable.

'A man with a stick and whiskers. Shouting and bawling, he was. It was an Irish accent and he kept telling me to get out of his room. "Where's Ruth?" he asked me. Then there was the sound of chains rattling and people moaning.'

'Go on.' Ruth's face was a picture of concentration.

Monty, who had seen a photograph of Michael Nolan, was enjoying himself. According to Eva a few doors down, Mr Nolan had been rather less than likeable. 'He calmed down. I still thought I was dreaming, though. After a few minutes, he said something really queer.'

'What?' gasped Ruth, a hand to her throat.

'He said he forgave Theresa. Then he said he wanted Jessica to be brought up by Maggie here.' He jerked a finger towards his friend. 'He disappeared and I must have fallen asleep.' Monty stared at Ruth. 'You're right,' he said. 'This house is haunted, because I saw your father with my own eyes.'

Maggie, fully aware of Monty's deliberate tomfoolery, was fascinated. A very mixed bag of emotions flickered across Ruth McManus's lined face. There was incredulity, shock, fear and determination.

'Well,' Ruth said carefully. 'I've been telling everybody for years that me dad's still here.' She glanced around the room and gulped. Her lies had risen up to face her. Even if this Liverpudlian were telling untruths, there was not a thing she could do about it without betraying herself.

'He didn't seem too happy to me,' said Monty. 'Kept on and on about Theresa and he wanted the quarrel mended. Still, we have to abide by the wishes of the dead, I suppose.' He turned to Maggie. 'So that's you stuck with the little girl if anything happens to Theresa.'

Ruth's lip curled. She had no intention of allowing this loud Irish Liverpudlian woman to deprive her of her niece. Even if Monty Sexton had heard Dad talking, Ruth wanted that child. Irene would never look after her mother. In spite of all Ruth's sacrifices, Irene would neglect the one who had borne and raised her. Jessica was a nice child. Jessica would look after Auntie Ruth in her old age. 'You must have heard him wrong,' Ruth barked at Monty. 'If owt happens to our Theresa, that kiddy comes to me.'

'No,' replied Monty. 'Not if you want to keep your father happy.'

Ruth had enjoyed having visitors and was dreading the day when they would leave. But this bloke was pulling her leg something merciless and she was unable to fight back. The ghost, invented by Ruth to amuse herself, was brought to life now by a know-it-all, a man who was giving her a very funny look. 'If you see my dad again,' she said, 'ask him where he put my scissors. He was always pinching them to cut his toenails.' She marched past the two visitors and stamped her way upstairs.

'Well, that wiped her eye,' commented Maggie.

'It's a kick up the backside she needs,' answered Monty.

Maggie touched her old friend's arm. 'I'll miss you, lad. I'll be stuck here with all these foreigners.'

He laughed. 'You're the foreigner,' he reminded her. 'You're Irish, from another country.'

She punched him. 'You know what I mean. I'm used to the Scouse.'

'And you know where I am, queen.'

'Aye, that I do, Monty. That I do.'

After a bite to eat in a café on Great Moor Street, Theresa felt almost fit enough to confront the next demon. She wandered around Gregory and Porritt's for a while, looking at lampshades and very uninteresting counters packed with nails, screws, nuts and bolts. From there, she sauntered past the Wheatsheaf, glancing across at 'him outside o' Bowies', a plaster figure of a man in overalls. How long had he stood there? How many mothers had goaded a child into action by asking, 'How long are you going to stand there gormless like him outside o' Bowies?'

Theresa was well and truly home. Apart from the job on hand and the worries about her health, she was as happy as a pig in a muckyard. The need to deal with her rapists was an old feeling, as was her tendency to illness, so little had changed. She was on familiar territory, yet, like many a Londoner who had never bothered to visit St Paul's or the museums, Theresa was suddenly aware of how little she knew about her home town.

Within a couple of weeks, she had visited the site of the Bolton Massacre, the place where an Earl of Derby had been executed, the very spot on which John Wesley had tried to preach to a riotous, stone-throwing crowd. She had stood and watched the golden globe above Preston's jewellers, a time-ball which responded and moved in accordance with telegraphed signals from Greenwich. This was a town with a history, a past in which Theresa had shown no interest until recently.

She stood now opposite glorious civic buildings, her eyes glued to the war memorial. Why had she never noticed it before? All those young men killed, wounded, battered in mind and body to the point of suicidal uselessness. A deep unease kept creeping its way through her bones, along vertebrae and into her skull. In war or in peacetime, could there ever be an excuse for killing? Was rape an excuse, a reason?

She sat on a bench and watched the world passing by, doing its shopping, its visiting, its work. Everyone who walked by was a part of something bigger, yet each was trapped inside a body, a mind, a separate essence. Which of these could legitimately judge another? She must not punish Eva. The little woman had probably suffered enough. What, then, must she do about Chorlton, Betteridge and Hardman?

At this point, Theresa's heart and mind hardened.

Sometimes, a crime was too bad to be tried by a jury of passers-by. No-one could know the pain of rape without having been on the receiving end. She might have married, might have become stronger, might have led a decent, ordinary life. All choices and chances had been stolen from her. They had no right to live, no right to remain intact after a crime of such magnitude.

Theresa rose, shivered, pulled the scarf closer to her throat. Extremes of cold and heat were never bearable, never easy for a woman whose heart was scarred. With a renewed sense of purpose, Theresa Nolan went forth to seek her prey.

When she reached the stall, Teddy Betteridge was reeling about and laughing at some joke which appealed to him, but to no-one else. Potential customers hung back while Elsie Betteridge dealt with the bane of her life. 'Get gone and sober up,' said the large woman, her voice loud enough to travel several yards. 'You're no bloody use at all, you, least of all near breakables.'

Theresa comforted herself with the near-knowledge that Elsie had already learned to dislike Teddy.

'This is two days in a row,' Elsie was saying now. 'You're about as much use as a chocolate teapot. Get thyssen home and sleep it off.'

Teddy, who had plainly met his Waterloo for the umpteenth time, sneaked away, his head bent against an icy wind and the even cooler countenance of his irate partner.

Theresa waited for the huddle of gossips and customers to clear, then she wandered over to Betteridge's Ironmongers Established 194—, the last digit having been blown away by weather or ripped off during one of Teddy Betteridge's alcoholic tempers.

'Hello, love? Looking for something special? Nice tea set to brighten up your winter days? A set of cut-glass fruit dishes? And I've all the buckets and bowls you could ever want, love.'

Lying was becoming so easy. Yet Theresa found, to her utter amazement, that she was taking to Elsie Betteridge. There was a weariness about the eyes, humour in the thick, mobile lips, suffering in the woman's stance. She was about to do Elsie a favour, she told herself firmly. If the man wouldn't work, his wife could do very well without him.

'Browse if you want to. I think I'll have a sit down.' She pointed to a figure in the distance. 'That's what I call me little bit o' th' 'usband, useless lump, he is. Look at the cut of him,' she mumbled, almost to herself. 'His dad killed himself with booze, tore his liver and kidneys to pieces. At the finish, he were nobbut a raving lunatic. Now, my soft bugger's bent on going the same road as his father.'

She was so open, so generous. 'Have you two chairs?' Theresa asked.

'Stools. Here, get at the back of the stall with me. We can have a sup out of my tea-flask and put the world to rights.'

Theresa sat next to her victim. No, no, she wasn't going to hurt Elsie Betteridge. Elsie would be steering a new course, following a better map.

'There's sugar in it,' said Elsie. 'Do you take sugar?'

'I don't mind. I can take it any way it comes.' She sipped pensively at the over-sweetened brew.

'You do your best,' Elsie sighed. 'Stood out here in all weathers while he props a bar up, then you're washing and ironing at home, feeding the family. And he's swilling all the profits down the lav at the Commercial.'

Theresa placed her beaker on the stall. 'I came here to see Mr Betteridge,' she said. 'It's a matter of some delicacy.'

'You'd be as well off talking to the wall,' replied Elsie. 'At least the bloody wall stands still, doesn't keep falling down on the floor screaming for a flaming Aspro.'

'Your husband seems to have a problem with alcohol, then.'

'A problem?' shrieked Elsie, laughter trimming the words. 'A problem? Nay, it's no problem for him, love. He's as happy as a hog in shite as long as he's drunk.' She adopted a more serious tone, lowered her voice. 'It's me what's got the problem. Two kiddies to raise, a house to keep, a business to run. And on top of all that, there's him. His legs keep letting him down, then his eyes. Can't walk, can't see proper, can't keep his food down some days. I'm that mithered, I could spit.'

Theresa tutted her sympathy.

'There'd be nowt in the bank if it weren't for me. I've hidden some.' She took a loud swig of tepid tea. 'I call it me running away savings.'

'Don't run away,' said Theresa. 'You stay where you are.'

The large woman shook her head, causing a prematurely grey strand of hair to slip from beneath the tea-cosy hat. 'Funny. I don't know you, but you're right easy to talk to. See, I'm not sure how much more I can put up with. It's his house, so I either stop there or I go.'

Theresa dived in head first. 'Mrs Betteridge, I've been working in Liverpool for some years.'

'Oh yes?'

'With street girls.'

'What? You mean prostitutes?'

Theresa nodded. 'I think that lady wants serving.'

Elsie dashed off to sell a bucket and a long-handled mop. 'Well?' she asked as soon as she got back.

'It's advisable that you should see your doctor, Mrs Betteridge.'

The woman's face wore a puzzled frown. 'Eh?'

'We try to get the girls off the streets, but we don't always succeed. One of them slipped the net quite recently. She was due to come into the clinic for treatment, because she had contracted a nasty disease.'

'And what's that got to do with the price of flour cakes?'

Theresa steeled herself. This was a powerfully built person, and God alone knew how she would react to the news. 'She got as far as Bolton before seeing sense, then she travelled back to Liverpool and came in for treatment.'

Elsie was very still. 'Go on.'

'She gave me the names of those she had associated with in Bolton. One was called Teddy Betteridge. He told her that he had a business on the market, so I thought I'd better warn you. The illness is very contagious.' Like tuberculosis, thought Theresa. What a complete fraud she was. How many people had she infected with her coughing and spluttering?

Beats of time passed while Elsie Betteridge remained motionless in her seat.

'Are you . . . all right?'

Elsie turned her head and looked directly at her companion. 'No, I'm not. I'm . . . Oh, I don't know what I am, to be honest. You think you've seen it all

when you live with a drunk. He's like a baby sometimes, doesn't always get to the lav in time, if you take
my meaning. There were blood in it once. Little
broken veins all over his face, doctors going on at
him to stop before it's too late.'

'It must be awful.'

'Aye, you can say that again, with knobs on. And
now, we've got this.' She stood up and stretched her
back, as if making herself firm. 'It's bad enough for
my kiddies living with a drinker, but we can't have
me ill as well.' She paused. 'Mind, now as I think on,
he's been too drunk to . . . you know . . . for ages, so
I'll be in the clear. I will see the doctor, but there's
no danger.'

Theresa felt terrible. She had created this situation, had planned it with a precision that had been
almost military. Hurting those who had injured her
was one thing; causing this woman unnecessary pain
was a different matter altogether.

'Ta,' Elsie Betteridge said before reclaiming her
seat. 'It were coming anyroad, love. Don't be worrying
yourself over me, 'cos you've done the right thing.'

Theresa swallowed her guilt and it tasted vile.

'Will you be going back to Liverpool?'

'No. I'm from round here originally, then I got a
job and stayed over there until just before this
Christmas.' She was planning to kill the woman's
husband and two other men. 'I'm moving soon, but
it'll be in Bolton. I've been staying with a friend.'
Elsie's children would have no father. They'd be
better off without a drunkard in the house, as would
Elsie.

'It's curable, isn't it?' asked Teddy Betteridge's
wife.

'Yes,' replied Theresa. He didn't deserve this

388

rough-edged, big-hearted woman. He was an alcoholic, a rapist, a ne'er do well.

'Well, I'm grateful to you, love,' declared Elsie. 'It's a good thing you told me and not him. He'd have drunk another cartload of ale and forgotten all about it.'

There was no more to be said. Theresa bade Elsie goodbye and began the walk towards Derby Street. Tonight, Teddy Betteridge would feel the edge of his wife's tongue. The others, Chorlton and Hardman, had already been informed of their condition.

She stopped at a newsagency, bought a few toffees for Jessica and a packet of Weights for Ruth. Ruth needed sweetening while Maggie was with her. Even at her sweetest, Ruth displayed all the qualities of spilled battery acid. Within the next few days, Theresa would be visiting a lawyer. He would finish the process of buying the house, then there was the will to write. If Theresa could do anything at all to keep Jessica away from Ruth, then such action would be taken now, before it was too late.

A car screeched to a halt. She looked over her shoulder, saw that no-one was hurt, prepared to continue her journey. The car reversed, stopped next to her. Strangely, Theresa was not surprised to see Stephen Blake. He ran to her, stood in the middle of the pavement, eyes wide, hands fidgeting. 'Theresa?'

She exhaled. 'Dr Blake,' she said, looking levelly at him. 'How nice to see you again.'

THIRTEEN

Jessica had got her own way at last. It hadn't seemed much to ask, just her mother for Christmas, then her mother for life. Mam had arrived with two new people, one of whom had returned to Liverpool. Monty Sexton had been a great boon. What Monty couldn't do with a pack of cards wasn't worth knowing. He was a magician, an entertainer who had brought the festive season to life. He could produce coins from nowhere, flags from an empty box, silly paper flowers from his hat. Jessica missed Monty.

She didn't miss Auntie Ruth, though. Auntie Ruth, who had refused to cook, had come with Monty and Maggie to spend Christmas Day at Auntie Eva's. While everyone had played games, the miserable woman had hugged the fire until her legs had reddened, had smoked and smoked until the whole house had reeked of tobacco.

Well, now there was just Auntie Maggie. Auntie Maggie was all right, but she was a bit prim and proper, something of a Holy Josephine, never missing mass, her bedroom filled with statues, dried crosses from umpteen Palm Sundays, missals, a bible, the Blessed Virgin on a plinth, sanctified water in a dish. And she always wore purple, as if every day was a day of mourning, like Lent.

Eva was making bread. The dough queued in a row of blue-rimmed enamel bowls in front of the fire, each container covered by a piece of white muslin. Jessica sat in a fireside rocker, her eyes fixed to the nearest bowl of dough, her thoughts several miles away.

'A penny for them?' Eva was preparing her one-pound and two-pound loaf tins.

Jessica turned her head slowly, as if she were in a dream. 'What's going on, Auntie Eva? What's happening with Mam? She's never in and she looks . . . she looks angry.'

Eva was in no two minds, though she could say nothing. Theresa had enjoyed Christmas, had been pleasant to everyone. The woman was flagging – on that score, there could be little room for doubt. But underneath the party spirit, another spectre had lurked, the ghost of knowledge, a soul fed by new and unpalatable discoveries. 'It's just all the change,' replied Eva. 'You know – coming home, giving her job up, looking for a house.'

Jessica swallowed. 'Is she going to die, Auntie Eva?'

For the mother of a young girl to die was terrible, unthinkable. But for that girl to wait, watch and ruin her own life while expecting the event was a million times worse. 'No, Jess. She's tired and she's—'

'Got TB.'

Eva clutched at straws and caught one. 'Eeh, she'll have had that checked while she was in Liverpool. They'd not have let her work with old folk if she'd been infectious. As for her heart – she's come this far, so she could go a lot more miles. Did I ever tell you about Sammy Pickering?'

Jessica nodded.

Eva carried on regardless. 'Nobbut twenty-four, he were, when they told him his heart were nigh on its last beat. When I laid him out, that man had skin like a baby's and hair as black as coal. Looked after himself, he did, and he lived to see ninety-seven. I'm not saying your mam'll get that far, but if she slows down, she'll have a few more years.'

Jessica had heard her mother's coughing, especially during the nights. 'Auntie Eva, I've done a terrible, terrible thing.'

Eva put down her tins and sat opposite Jessica.

'Spit it out, lass.'

'Mam's been the spitting one, always coughing and spluttering.'

'Go on.'

'And she asked me if I was immune. I told her the doctor had said I'd built up a resistance to TB with having had a mild dose. She was satisfied with that, but she pushed her bed across the room and slept under the open window. In this weather, too. So I thought about it and . . . oh, Auntie Eva.' Tears threatened.

'Tell me, love. Please.'

'I followed her.'

'Oh.' Eva paused, waited for more.

'To the market. She was chatting to Mr Walsh on the fish stall, then they went outside to talk privately.'

Eva felt a cold, closed fist inside her stomach. 'Just a chinwag, Jess.' Just a chinwag about a stolen baby.

'She went for a walk, then back to the market.'

'A walk? Where to?'

'Looking at things. Man and Scythe, the Olde Pastie Shoppe, the war memorial, Town Hall. Historical places. Like she was saying goodbye.'

'She's been away a while. She was enjoying her home town.'

Jessica gazed into a roaring fire. 'Mam spent a lot of time with Mrs Betteridge. She runs a stall on the open market – pots and pans.'

'I know the one.'

'They drank tea, then talked. I came home.'

'And what's so wrong about that?'

The girl gulped back a sob. 'He was driving his car up Derby Street. He stopped and asked me where my mother was.' She bit her lip, bit back the frustrations. 'I've always said I'd no idea, Auntie Eva. We've both told him lies about not knowing where Mam was. With all the coughing and the running about buying a house, I was worried. So I told him the truth. For the very first time, I said I knew where Mam was. He went looking for her. What'll happen when he finds her?'

In Eva's unspoken opinion, Theresa should be found. For a start, it was obvious that she was still pursuing the three men who had raped her. What on earth had she been saying to Elsie Betteridge? Elsie was a rough and ready type, a woman who liked a jar of ale, a natter and a dirty joke. But she had a big heart. More than once, Eva had been on the market when Elsie had shown her true colours. 'Here, love, take this one off me hands, will you? I've had it that long it's taking root.' And some old girl had walked off with a free long mop and a big smile.

'I didn't mean to hurt Mam,' said Jessica.

'Of course you didn't. Stop your worrying.' Then there was the TB. Dr Stephen Blake, who had visited Eva over the years, had often said that a spontaneous remission was not unheard of, but Theresa had been living in a city, not in the Swiss Alps. The woman wanted examining.

'He was going to drive up and down until he found her.'

Eva smiled. 'Eeh, you do talk lovely, sweetheart. That school's turning you into a right nice young lady. Now, listen to me, Jessica Nolan. What will be will be. She needs help. Dr Blake'll give her the once-over, make sure she's fit. Leave it to him.'

Jessica inhaled deeply, as if trying to summon up courage. 'He loves her, doesn't he? Even after she ran away, he carried on loving her.'

'Aye, I think you're right there.'

'She might marry him. I could be a bridesmaid.'

'We'll see.' Eva checked her bowls and decided that the mix had risen sufficiently.

'Who's my real father?'

Eva steadied her hands and carried on with the job. 'I don't know,' she said truthfully. Jessica didn't look like any of them. Whoever had fathered her, this lass was Nolan through and through, good features, Irish skin, her mother's eyes.

'Everybody has a dad.'

Everybody came from an egg and a microscopic piece of male flotsam, and the woman was the nurturer, the incubator. Most men, good men, hung around to raise their children, working hard, caring for their wives, playing daft games with the young-sters. Dads were usually proud of their offspring, interested in their progress, their schooling. But sometimes, a child came from a hurried, cruel act, from a streak of slime left by an uncaring ogre. Such a child had only a mother. Theresa Nolan had separated herself from this poor girl, had gone after money on which a foundation might be built for Jess.

Jessica had enjoyed little parental love. Even the female, the one who should have been close, had abandoned Jess.

'Who was it?'

Eva kneaded and rolled, kneaded, divided, and set the dough in her tins. 'That's not a question I can answer.'

'Why?'

'Because it's not my place and I can't tell you what I really don't know, can I?' It was probably Chorlton. According to Theresa, he had been the first. But who could say which of those creatures had produced the fastest swimmer, the winning ticket?

'Will she tell me one day?'

Eva didn't know the answer to that one either.

Jessica went out into the lobby, pulled on her hat and coat, wandered into the street. The snow had almost melted, leaving in its wake a few slag-heaps of greyish matter piled against walls. There were no children playing, no doors open. Everyone had remained inside to enjoy the fireside and indoor games. Most had sisters and brothers, most had someone who would listen and share a table to draw or make a jigsaw.

Irene hove into view, her pale, expressionless face framed by a red woollen scarf. She stopped and looked at her beautiful cousin. Mam liked Jessica. Jessica was pretty and clever and she never got told off for being a little rat. 'What are you doing?' Irene asked.

'Nothing.'

Irene wiped a dewdrop from the end of her nose. 'I'm going to see her.' She nodded towards her mother's house. 'I don't know why I bother, like. She couldn't care less about me.' She pondered for a second or two. 'We've not been lucky, have we, me and you? Mine knocking seven shades of the rainbow out of me, yours leaving you to Eva Know-it-all.'

Jessica shrugged. 'Mam went to earn money and save up.'

'She left you.'

'She couldn't help it.'

Irene shrugged. 'Your mam ran away from the hospital. They'll drag her back there. She can't go piking about with TB. Folk with TB gets locked up.'

Jessica decided that Irene might know things. She had the sort of eyes that knew everything, glassy but wise, empty but hiding a huge store of secrets. 'Who was my dad?' she asked.

The older girl stared blankly at Jessica. 'It were rape,' she answered eventually. 'That's what your mam said, anyroad. Grandad didn't believe her, so he threw her out. Mam says your mam was held down and forced, if you get my meaning.'

Jessica got her meaning. In a girls' convent school, a rich seam of gossip seemed to develop about forbidden topics, dark whispers in grey corners of hallowed halls. While nuns floated along on a sea of prayer and self-denial, their charges investigated life to the full, bent, it seemed, on avoiding nunhood at all costs.

Irene was enjoying herself. She watched her cousin's face, saw the pain and bewilderment. 'You haven't got a dad,' she explained. 'Mine's no good, but I do know who he is. Mind you, we don't know where he is. Good job, because Mam would kill him if she could catch him.' The older girl delivered as near a smile as she could manage before marching off to do battle with the harridan who had borne her.

Jessica saw Irene going into the house, noticed the

statutory entrance fee of ten Players clutched in Irene's disappearing hand. 'Oh, heck,' muttered Jessica. Dr Blake had probably found Mam. Mam would be hauled back to Williamson's, would be prodded and photographed and shoved in a freezing room.

The whole concept was terrifying. Had Mam travelled home to die? Was there really no dad to come along and rescue Jessica from Ruth McManus's clutches? Alive, Mam had a say in where Jessica stayed, but . . . No, it didn't bear thinking about.

Jessica Nolan went back to Auntie Eva's to comfort herself with new bread, plum jam and a roaring fire. When a person was only twelve, she had no real say in anything important.

Drinnan's was at the top of Cannon Street, a corner building, slightly wedge-shaped. A row of tables flanked the Derby Street side, affording occupants a view of the road and its ongoings. Theresa gazed through steamy glass and watched a brewery horse on his way home after carting beer. Soon, there would be no horses on Derby Street. Lorries were all the rage these days, noisy, rattling monsters spluttering and backfiring all over the place, blue smoke pouring from exhausts.

She turned slightly and looked at Stephen Blake. He was tidier, scarcely older, quite handsome. There was a slight cleft in the square jaw, while his eyes remained as cloquent as ever. Whatever she had felt for him during her stay at the sanatorium remained very much alive. Was this love and did it matter? Still clumsy, he rattled coins in his pockets, jangled a spoon in its saucer, almost upset the cutlery tray. Smiling in spite of everything, Theresa looked through the window again, watching another horse slip-sliding its way to stables on the icy road. She must not think about Stephen Blake. The man was too close for comfort and she longed to touch him, to make sure that he was real.

He was buying coffee and biscuits, was probably preparing the inquisition. It was no longer of any consequence. She should keep her mind on Jessica and on . . . the other business. A gun in her handbag. She was sitting in the best ice-cream parlour for miles with a pearl-handled, loaded lady's gun. She calmed herself by thinking about her savings. Even if the three men didn't pay up one last time, Theresa had enough to buy the house, enough to leave Jessica in reasonable comfort. Katherine was fine. Katherine was a member of a proper family. She was loved, educated, well dressed and well fed. Theresa continued to fantasize about murder. About three murders. And her insides were weak and fluttery because the one she loved was here, was struggling against the possibility of spilled coffee. Strength, firmness of resolve – how she needed those commodities.

'There we are.' He placed the cups on the table, went to fetch a plate of biscuits.

Theresa sighed, hoping that this fine doctor would give her some time, some leeway. She had to follow through what she had started, needed to stand in control in front of her attackers and . . . At this point, when she reached the 'and', her thoughts occasionally lost their clarity. She wanted to kill, to deliver three bullets into three blackened hearts. Stephen should go away. Stephen softened her, made her falter.

He sat down. 'How have you been?'

Too tired to argue, she spoke slowly and clearly. 'I have a cough, but no blood. I get exhausted and my limbs ache. Sometimes, my hands and feet are a bit blue and numb.'

He nodded encouragingly.

'I had to go.'

'Did you run from me?'

She shook her head, lowering her eyelids in case the lie showed. He had not been the reason, though he had sat on the edge of her decision, had probably tipped the scales. 'No. I wanted to work, to leave something for Jessica. I needed to make use of the years instead of lingering palely in some hospital.' Theresa raised her chin and forced herself to look at him. He remained attractive, to say the least, had probably struggled to give up the drink. 'I helped to run a seamen's mission in Liverpool – I was the housekeeper. It wasn't a terrible job and it paid well.'

'I see.' He drank some coffee, grimacing. So, she had worked, had saved every penny for the child. He frowned into his thick, white cup. 'How do these people manage to believe that we all want this stuff made with boiled and burnt milk?'

'I can't imagine,' she replied.

He cleared his throat of the thick substance. She was still beautiful: too lovely to look at. Her near-transparency terrified him.

'Will you report me?' she asked.

He thought about that. 'I don't know. You need testing again – for your own good.'

She nodded. 'Give me a month, please. I'm buying a house for Jessica. She'll be living there with a friend of mine – Maggie Courtney.'

'Oh.' He stirred the coffee, dragging off a layer of half-set skin. 'And where will you be?'

399

In prison or worse, she replied inwardly. For his ears, she answered, 'In your hospital, I suppose.'

At last, he managed to look her in the face. 'I never forgot you.'

'No.'

He rubbed a hand across his brow. 'And I never married.'

'Neither did I.'

The ensuing silence was acutely painful. Stephen sought a change of subject. 'What's wrong with Eva?' he asked. 'Hasn't she done a good enough job?'

Theresa nibbled at the edge of an anaemic-looking biscuit. All her life, she had been answerable. Firstly, her father had ruled her life. Michael Nolan, a monstrous bigot, had chased all his children, had forced them into early marriages. Theresa, deeply wounded by the rapists, had been cast off. Eva Harris had helped her and had helped herself to Jessica's twin sister. Again, Theresa had enjoyed no say, no control.

'Theresa?'

Everyone was answerable, she supposed. To bosses, to families, to God. She knew people with lives worse than her own had been. With unwelcome but familiar suddenness, her skin began to crawl. The second rein on her had been held by Betteridge, Hardman and Chorlton, who still sounded like a firm of solicitors. 'I should have sued them at the time, should have got the police in.'

'Yes, you should.'

She scarcely heard the man who had been another jailer, wished he would go away. Deadened senses were coming to life in his presence. She had always wanted love, to be loved for herself and in spite of herself. This doctor had loved her instinctively, unconditionally. His soft, gentle eyes were clouding her own vision. 'I saved most of my wages,' she told him now. 'For Jessica. Maggie will take care of her, you'll see. I'll probably die young, not of TB, but because of the rheumatic fever.'

His hand crept over the tablecloth and enclosed her fingers. Startled, she stiffened, then felt the ice thawing in her veins. Warmth crept along her arm and into her chest. This was a mess. She had no room for complications, no time for dalliance. How could one town contain such a man alongside slime like the other three? 'Do you still dream of your brother?' she asked. Her breath, already shortened by disease, contracted even further. He was so wonderful, so kind.

'Sometimes,' he answered. 'And I dream about you, too. Like my twin, you were becoming a mere shadow.'

'I'm still a shadow.'

'Very thin,' he agreed.

It was as if she had been given a pill, a sedative of some kind. Her body, unused to total relaxation, threatened to keel over. Was he a healer as well as a doctor? Could he make her well?

'Spit it out,' he said.

'For analysis, doctor? Or are you trying to relieve me of this horrible coffee?' His presence illuminated their table, trimming the hem off a dark brown day. No-one else existed. Drinnan's drifted off into a mist. The two of them were no longer restricted by mere masonry.

'Tell me,' he asked again.

Barriers between them had slipped off quietly, had gone the same way as the ice-cream bar's walls. 'It's too awful, especially for you.'

Stephen fought the urge to catch her up in his arms and remove her from an unkind world, to take her somewhere else, somewhere clean and fresh. The Alps. He could get work there among richer consumptives. A month. She had asked for a month.

'I lost someone, Stephen.'

He swallowed hard. 'A lover?'

'No. A long, long time ago. Someone was stolen from me.'

'Ah.' He waited. 'Go on.'

Theresa went on. 'After the attack, when I knew I was pregnant, I wanted to die there and then. Eva saved me, took me in, found me somewhere to stay. She blackmailed my house out of Maurice the Mole, Roy Chorlton's father. Eva and the Walsh brothers – they're fishmongers – got money out of the three families. I was grateful.'

He watched her as she remembered the gratitude, but he dared not speak. He feared that she might bolt like a frightened filly if he interrupted.

'My Jessica and Liz Walsh's baby were born on the same night. Eva was the midwife in both cases.' Theresa clung to his hand, her lifeline. 'Liz's child died. It was a little girl, small enough to be buried in a shoe box.' She placed her other hand on top of Stephen's, making sure that contact would continue while she spoke. 'During labour, I fainted a couple of times. I know now that I gave birth to identical twin girls. One was removed and swapped for a shoe box.'

His mouth opened, but the words took their time. 'By Eva?'

Theresa nodded.

'Good grief.' He shook his head slowly, as if kicking his brain into a gear that could accept such news.

'She never told me, Stephen. In all these years, she has said not one word.' The fear was gone, while the anger was damped down past embers, almost to a heap of warm ashes. 'I think Eva persuaded the Walshes to move to Liverpool. Danny, he's the older brother, keeps the Bolton end of their business going, with his wife to help him. Well, I suppose Eva got a real shock when I, too, ran off to Liverpool. She visited me, brought Jessica with her.'

'And kept your secret—'

'She kept her own secret, too,' said Theresa softly. 'Guarded it so well. Then I saw Jessica on Bold Street in Liverpool. Except it wasn't Jessica. It was Katherine Walsh, daughter of Bernard and Liz.'

'What did you do?'

Theresa smiled sadly. 'What could I do? I've not been much of a mother. I've concentrated on Jessica's future, on her adulthood. I think I distanced myself so that she would not get too reliant on a mother who is guaranteed to die young. But now, after the deception, I've decided to take Jessica away from Eva. Perhaps it's a form of revenge, because I've been very angry. As for Katherine – well, I made sure I met her. We spent about twenty minutes together in a café in Waterloo. Bernard Walsh must have been scared to death in case I spoke up. I didn't, of course. Katherine has a proper family, parents who will look after her.'

Stephen Blake found himself trembling. 'But they're sisters,' he said. 'Twins, from the one egg. They knew each other long before they were born.'

Theresa lowered her head. 'I realize that. Jessica had an invisible friend called Lucy. When I talked to Bernard Walsh, I found out that the girls have even

403

shared symptoms. Just one was ill, but the other felt the same pain.'

'It happens, believe me.'

'I need no convincing.'

His other hand came up to join hers on the table. He held tight to Theresa's fingers as he spoke. 'They must be told some time,' he insisted.

'Yes.'

'Did Mrs Walsh not offer to take Jessica, too?'

Theresa shook her head. 'She didn't accept that her baby had died. According to Bernard, she shut herself down, lost her reason for a few hours. Liz Walsh is one hundred per cent sure that Katherine is her own, that Katherine has no twin sister. I can't tell her. I can't do it, Stephen.'

'God.'

'Exactly.' Theresa allowed her eyes to close. 'My heart is such a mess, too. I need treatment to buy more time. I look into the future and I see Jessica alone. While she's a child, people will rally round, I know. But when she's grown and in her twenties, she'll have no blood basis, no relatives who want her. Except for my sister, who's as mad as a hatter. And my daughter shouldn't be alone, because she has the closest tie possible, a twin.'

This was a good woman. She had worked herself near to death to provide for her daughter, had deliberately chosen not to interfere when meeting the other girl. 'You've done your best,' he told her. 'In the circumstances, you have acted like a saint.'

Her eyes flew open. Saints did not carry guns in their handbags and hatred in their souls. 'I made my decision and details are with a lawyer,' she said. 'While talking to a solicitor about buying a house, I shall be making my will with regard to the care of

Jessica and so forth. As for the two girls, I decided that twenty-four was about the right age, not too young, not too old. Whether Liz likes it or not, my twins will have each other.'

'And Eva?'

Theresa lifted a shoulder. 'I'll forgive in time. And, of course, she may have to sign documents in front of witnesses, just to prove to the two girls that they are related. There'll be no case for Eva to answer, no kidnapping charge or whatever, because that would damage Katherine and the Walshes. Eva knows what's coming – I've seen it in her eyes. As for me, I just want everything written down tidily for the future.'

He blinked a couple of times. Having found her, he could not bear to imagine being separated from her again. She must not die, not yet. 'I've loved you for years,' he declared bravely.

Taken aback by this out-of-context statement, Theresa told the whole truth. 'I think I began to love you, too. It was frightening. I've no idea how to love a man.' She almost laughed at him. 'You've gone very red.'

He could not lose her. Even if her life was going to be short, he would be a part of it. 'When do you move?'

'In three weeks.'

'And then?'

She sighed. In three weeks, it would all be over. A smoking gun, emptied of bullets, a sick woman running to this doctor for protection. Could he be her alibi? No, he was too straight for that and, anyway, she must not abuse him. 'I'll come to see you.'

They disentangled their hands and ordered more

405

coffee, this time made with water. Over the more palatable brew, they talked about all kinds of things, about Jessica's schooling, about the sanatorium and new, exciting drugs which might just promise a speedier cure for TB. He boasted about his car, a second-hand item with no sense of decorum; described his house in the country, his washing machine with automatic mangle which actually ate clothes. 'I'm down to five socks,' he grumbled amiably. 'Thank God they're all black. I change one each day.'

She believed him. With her face beginning to glow, Theresa drew a word-picture of the old sailors in Jutland House. 'They treat a game of draughts like war. Dominoes can be fatal, and we put away the dartboard for obvious reasons.'

Stephen laughed, then glanced at his watch. He had to be back on duty within the hour. 'Promise me you won't disappear again.'

'I promise.'

'May I see you again in a few days? Nothing strenuous, just another coffee with a slice of toast.'

Theresa placed a hand to her brow in the classic pose of a ham actor. 'Oh sir,' she sighed. 'I do not think I have the strength for toast.'

He mumbled something deep in his throat.

'What did you say?'

'Nothing.' She didn't miss a trick. He would have to tread softly, because he was about to tread on her nightmares. From which poet had he bastardized that thought? 'Don't give up hope,' he advised her. Tomorrow, he would ask for extended leave. If refused, he would give notice. By fair means or foul, Stephen Blake would drag Theresa Nolan to Switzerland.

*   *   *

The table was laid. Maggie, who had had enough of Ruth McManus's company, had accepted Eva's invitation with alacrity. 'She keeps giving me these evil looks,' Maggie told Eva and Jimmy. 'If I take Jessica up to my room for a little talk, she follows us and gives me an extra evil look.'

'Aye,' replied Eva Coates. 'One of them looks could fell a rhinoceros from forty paces. I don't know what gets into her, I really don't.'

'She's insane,' opined Maggie loftily. 'A few slices short of the full loaf. Do you know, she watches me while I'm asleep. It does me no good waking up with her leaning over me. And that daughter of hers is another one, sneaking up behind me in the yard, telling me to be careful in case her mam goes strange. Goes strange? She's gone there quick smart already on the express train – and no return ticket. I can't wait to get out of that place.'

Jimmy rattled the *Bolton Evening News* into shape in order to pursue his new hobby. Each night, he read the obituaries, sometimes aloud and with feeling. 'He only does it to prove he's still alive,' Eva was often heard to say. Several years older than his wife, Jimmy considered that surviving TB was his greatest achievement.

Jessica came in. 'Is Mam not back yet?'

'No,' chorused the two women.

Behind his newspaper and still at the births column, Jimmy kept quiet. Apart, Maggie and Eva were both manageable – he even enjoyed sensible conversations with one or the other. Together, they were a force with which he would not care to contend. So he read the announcements columns instead.

'Do you think she'll be in soon?' asked Jessica.

'Yes.' Once again, the voices were united. Jimmy

reached the deaths. It occurred to him that Maggie and Eva were like a ventriloquist's act – one opened her mouth, and the same sound came from the other.

Jessica flitted about for a few seconds, smiling tentatively when Eva caught her eye. Eva understood the reason behind Jessica's nervousness. How many times had Eva herself come close to pointing Dr Stephen Blake in the direction of Liverpool? Jessica had not betrayed her mother – she had simply tried to get Theresa to face the fact that she needed treatment.

'Harry Bowker's gone,' said the voice behind the news.

'Shut up,' ordered the female duo.

'Died in his sleep.'

'So will you if you're not careful.'

Satisfied that his wife had regained the ability to speak solo, Jimmy carried on reading.

Eva placed the bread board on the table and crowned it with a nicely browned cottage loaf. Jessica was still twitching like a marionette. Jimmy was in his rightful place behind the *Evening News*, while Maggie employed her hands with a bit of knitting. Eva had tried so hard, but had failed to dislike Maggie Courtney. When Theresa's new household came into being, Maggie was going to be a part of it. Eva would lose Jessica, who had become a daughter – perhaps a granddaughter. But it had only been a matter of time. Theresa had, at last, found out about the other twin, and had taken umbrage.

'Are you all right there, Eva?' asked Maggie. Her heart bled for this poor soul. The Irishwoman had asked herself time after time what she might have done in the circumstances. But she could not discuss any part of Theresa's past, because the past belonged to those who had created it.

'I'll live,' replied Eva.

Jessica's eyes were fixed on the door, her ears alert for the sound of footsteps in the lobby.

Jimmy's newspaper shivered. 'He were nobbut sixty-two—'

'Shut up,' yelled Eva.

Maggie changed needles, tucking the left one under her arm. 'Your fascination with death is unusual,' she told Jimmy. 'You should have followed the queer one's daughter into undertaking.'

Eva suppressed a giggle.

'And you keep reminding us of our own mortality,' continued Maggie. 'We all end up in a box and in the newspaper, but we don't need telling every day that life is short.'

Jimmy lowered his guard, folded it, saved it for later.

'Thank God for that,' murmured the visitor. 'If he'd found two or three, there would have been no containing him.'

'He found four once,' said Eva. 'He was that excited, he lost his breath and nearly keeled over.'

The man of the house decided against rising to the bait. Ageing and wise, Jimmy knew his place. He was a figurehead, the one who sat at the front of the ship, but Eva was the pilot.

The front door opened. Jessica froze, hands clenched in tight fists, heart beating rapidly, goosebumps on her arms. She should not have told the doctor that Mam was home. Mam had hidden for years from doctors, never listening to Eva's pleas. All those years in Liverpool had not been without purpose. Mam had saved for a house, a place in which mother and daughter could be a family.

Mam was taking a long time to remove her outer clothing.

'Theresa?' shouted Maggie.

'I'm coming.'

The moment her mother entered the room, Jessica could see that something had happened. But Mam wasn't angry. She was pink and flustered, as if she had been somewhere interesting. Mam was far from furious. In fact, Theresa Nolan's expression was not a stranger to happiness.

'I'm sorry, Mam.' Jessica wanted to test these uncharted waters.

'What for?'

'For telling Dr Blake where you were.'

'That's all right.' Theresa sat at the table. Her appetite had never been good, but she couldn't wait to get her teeth into a nice shive of Eva's famous bread.

Jimmy looked at Maggie. Maggie dropped a stitch and looked at Eva. Eva watched Theresa. 'Have you been drinking?'

'Only coffee.'

Jimmy, uncomfortable in the sudden silence, decided to speak up. 'Harry Bowker's gone,' he said. No-one told him to shut up, so he continued. 'In his sleep. Kept a lovely plot, did Harry, best allotment for miles. He used to hang about with a girl called Martha in our street. She had a lazy eye, wore a patch on her glasses. Mind, he wed somebody else – a woman from Blackburn, I think.' His tale died from lack of nourishment, because no-one was listening.

Theresa sat with a beautiful smile on her face, a tangle of curls dangling over her eyes. When she

410

blew away these obstacles, the other occupants of the room caught sight of a new brightness in the irises, a barely suppressed excitement which threatened to spill into Eva's best china.

'Coffee, you say?' Maggie picked up her stitch.

'Coffee,' replied Theresa. 'With sugar and biscuits that had seen better days.'

'Fancy,' murmured Eva.

'Ooh, with sugar too,' added a mischievous Maggie.

Jessica gave her attention to Jimmy, the only person who was not behaving like a total lunatic. He winked at her. 'Cupid,' he mouthed noiselessly.

Maggie read her pattern aloud, listing knits, purls and passing the slipped stitch over.

Jessica, fit to burst, had to end her agony. 'Did Dr Blake find you?' she asked her mother.

Eva left the room hurriedly, muttering about some ham on the bone, her shoulders and voice shaking. Maggie relieved herself of the half-finished tea-cosy and shovelled coal into an already bright inferno. Jimmy studied the fire irons. Women worked in peculiar ways and, while he sensed the hysteria in the air, the poor man could not quite pinpoint its origin.

'Mam?'

'Yes, he found me.'

'Always asking for you, he were,' said Jimmy. 'And his interest weren't just medical, you might say. He's missed you something shocking, poor lad. After you scarpered from Williamson's, he were broken-hearted. Anyroad, he's found you now, so let's hope for a happy ending.'

Jimmy's words brought Theresa down to earth. There could be no happy ending for her and

411

Stephen, because she had a bad heart and a need for vengeance that had become a part of her essence.

Jessica, relieved beyond measure, took her place at the table. If Mam loved Dr Blake and if Dr Blake loved Mam, then that was all right, because Dr Blake was a nice man. He would be a stepfather – not a proper dad, but he would be better than no dad at all.

The meal was a procession of silences and sudden bursts of chatter. Theresa's colour faded back to normal, Jimmy wittered on about old Harry and his leeks, Maggie and Eva discussed the pros and cons of plain and self-raising flours. Jessica ate her ham, watched and listened. Mam was in love with Dr Blake, but she still couldn't manage to be completely happy.

FOURTEEN

Theresa Nolan forgave Eva Coates over a plate of tripe and onions in the UCP. Eva was the one with the tripe, a foodstuff with which Theresa had never reached an agreement. She remembered the old 'shawlies' from her youth, aged crones who usually gathered in clusters on street corners, women who had 'seen life', who sang the praises of cows' stomachs, black puddings and beef tea 'with plenty of floating fat'. 'A good plate of manifold lines the ribs against winter', was one of their favourite sayings. What had happened to all those pipe-smoking, stout-supping, snuff-sniffing women? Dead by now, Theresa supposed.

Eva shovelled the last morsel into her mouth. 'That's what I call a meal,' she announced.

Theresa bit back a tart response about the subject. It was plain that Eva was already slightly uncomfortable in her company. Eye contact was strictly at a minimum. Having finished her gourmet lunch, the older woman gazed around the café and called out to those she recognized.

'Eva?' Theresa said softly.

'Hello, Gert,' called Eva. 'Did you get that tooth out?'

By way of response, the Gert in question displayed

a gap in her lower jaw. 'He says I've got roots like dandelions. You should have seen my face.'

Eva turned to Theresa. 'Her face isn't much without the bruises – she must have looked a bugger with a black and blue gob. And her husband's a nice-looking bloke. Life's funny, isn't it?'

'It is.'

Something in Theresa's tone caused Eva to jump out of her seat. She crossed to another table in order to take a closer look at Gert's dentist's misdeeds.

Theresa placed her elbow on the table, resting her chin on the palm of her hand. Eva was taking evasive action again. But certain topics needed airing before Theresa could get on with her arrangements.

Eva returned. 'I think he very near broke her jaw.'

'Eva, I—'

'More like a bloody butcher, he is. Jimmy had to get his gum stitched at the infirmary after visiting that man. If he's a dentist, I'm a flaming brain surgeon.'

A short silence ensued. Theresa, her hand still acting as a head rest, waited for Eva to settle down. But Eva didn't settle down. She rooted about in her handbag, then in her shopping basket. She read lists, counted the money in her purse twice, checked her Co-op divi sheet, examined in great detail a pound of bacon she had just purchased.

'Have you done?' Theresa asked.

Eva froze, then placed her purse on the table.

'You must know what this is about,' Theresa went on.

Eva Coates – Harris-as-was – stared down at her empty plate, which wasn't quite empty, as it still boasted a small pool of white sauce and a few scraps of onion.

'It's about Katherine.'

'Ta-ra, Eva,' yelled Toothless Gert as she left the shop.

Eva employed a wave of her hand as response. 'I'm sorry,' she told Theresa. She could not think of one sensible sentence to add to her apology. The recently ingested tripe sat very heavily in Eva's nervous stomach.

'That was a terrible thing you did, Eva. I mean – well, you know I didn't want that pregnancy. I was grateful to you – I'm still grateful. You took me in, found me the house, did all you could for me.' Theresa paused, remembering. 'I made my mind up not to get too fond of Jessica, but she crept under my skin. Then I didn't like the idea of her needing me, so I gave her to you while I provided for her from a distance.'

Eva nodded, her teeth biting down on her lower lip.

'You got both of them, really.' Theresa leaned across the table and lowered her tone. 'I should have been told. Anybody giving birth should get the chance to see her baby. Well, I met Katherine for the first time several weeks ago. And don't worry, I sat in a café with Bernard and Katherine, and I said nothing to my daughter, the daughter I'd never clapped eyes on until she was going on twelve years of age. I was very upset, but I've no intention of upsetting her other mother.'

Eva raised her head and looked Theresa full in the face. She had to take this, had to force herself to pay the small price, to accept the tiny punishment meted out by Theresa.

'Because Liz Walsh is my daughter's mother,' continued Theresa. 'She and Bernard are doing a grand job, giving her a good life, looking to her needs. Her clothes were beautiful, Eva. I know why you did it. Don't cry, please. Don't set me off, because I reckon we could cause a flood between us. Eva, they've given her more than clothes. My girl is loved, and I'm thankful for that.'

Eva wept noiselessly into one of Jimmy's hankies.

'Life's so sad and so short,' Theresa said. 'Even eighty-odd years isn't much of a span, not when you look at history. But I won't even get that long, will I? So.' She inhaled deeply, tried to prevent a catch in her throat causing a bout of coughing. 'The terrible thing you did was also the right thing, Eva. Look at me. Look at the way I was then, too. I'm a bag of bones with a heart that carries on like a broken clock: miss a beat, tick twice. I'll stop altogether one of these days.'

'Don't say that, love—'

'I'll say what I want to say.' Theresa Nolan would be doing a lot of speaking up in the next few days. 'When I first found out about Katherine, I felt like throttling you. Then, when I came to your house for Christmas, I had to cool down for Jessica's sake. Over the past couple of weeks, I've tried to put myself in your place. If I'd been the midwife that night, I don't know what I would have done. It's all over now. All the worrying you must have done . . .'

Eva rubbed at her reddened nose. 'I persuaded them to leave Bolton, and they finished up within spitting distance of you.'

Theresa opened her bag and took out an envelope. She had to become businesslike, to make sure that Eva and the others would see to Jessica. 'This is a copy of my will. Keep it. I've paid a solicitor to deal with everything when the time comes. Jessica's guardians will be you, Dr Blake, the Walsh brothers and Maggie.'

'Right.' The sense of relief was almost overwhelming. Eva felt as if she had begun to relax for the first time in over a decade.

'The girls have to be told, Eva. They've to be introduced to one another. Even if Liz Walsh is still alive, I want my twins to know each other. I've left a bit of leeway for unforeseeable circumstances, but it's got to happen before they get to twenty-five.'

Eva, still too choked to deliver a string of sensible words, nodded again. Theresa talked like a text book, as if she'd been studying while she was away.

'Stephen had an identical twin brother.'

In spite of the circumstances, Eva noticed that her companion had not awarded Dr Blake his full title. They were on first-name terms, then. If only Theresa could enjoy better health, they might have made a lovely couple.

'It took him years to get over the war. His twin brother was blown to pieces and Stephen was the MO for that unit. He told me that identical twins have a very special relationship. He was in shock for years after his brother died, as if a part of himself had passed away at the same time. I've thought about that. If Katherine and Jessica go through life without meeting one another, we'll be denying them their birthright.'

Eva took the folder and placed it in her basket. She sniffed away her tears and broached another troublesome subject. 'If anything does happen to you, yon daft sister of yours will try to get Jess.'

Theresa nodded thoughtfully.

'She's a bad bugger,' added Eva.

Theresa swallowed. Ruth might be bad, but Theresa, all nice and gentle on the surface, was a raging river of hatred underneath the pretty manners. At least Ruth screamed out against the world. Ruth didn't go round cafés and shops with a loaded gun in her bag. So who was the real lunatic?

'Theresa?'

'Yes?'

'Are you going to get yourself looked at?'

She had promised Stephen, had given her word to the one man about whom she had managed to care. 'In time,' she said carefully.

Eva muttered something about buying a few cow heels and some pigs' trotters.

'Leave it until after I've moved out, please,' begged Theresa. 'You've eaten the tripe and I've watched you. No feet, Eva. Not just yet. I can't be doing with feet, not while I've a lot on my mind.'

They left the UCP, walked through Bolton, bought an evening paper and some stewing steak. As they passed the fishmarket, both women stopped and looked at Danny Walsh, father of a little boy, uncle to Katherine.

'Liz had a hysterectomy,' said Eva, her tone sombre.

'I know,' answered Theresa. 'Never mind, she can borrow one of my two girls for a while. But not for ever. Nothing can be for ever.'

'Bloody bitch,' roared Teddy Betteridge. His father, who had died from alcoholism, seemed to have reared a son and heir destined to follow the same route through a short existence. 'Who told her? That's what I want to know.' He glared at his partners in misbehaviour. 'She's bolted. She's taken my

418

kids with her.' A tear trickled down his beer-bloated face. 'I love my kids, I do. I've no reason to live now.'

Roy Chorlton, who had consumed two pints of bitter, had sat and watched while Teddy Betteridge made his way through eight. Now on his ninth, Teddy was becoming belligerent.

Ged Hardman flicked a beer mat off the edge of the table, caught it, repeated the exercise.

'I wish you'd stop that,' yelled Teddy. 'You've got me dizzy.'

'It's the beer that's making you dizzy,' advised Roy Chorlton. 'Slow down a bit.'

Ged stopped flicking and looked his comrades over. Here they all sat, three mismatched men thrown together because no-one else would have them. Each was being treated for the clap, but Roy Chorlton was the only one who wasn't suffering because of family. Mother had gone absolutely epileptic over the letter. Warned in writing not to use the same lavatory as her son, Lily had gone a very funny colour while tackling Ged. It was a well-known fact that venereal diseases could not be contracted from toilet seats, but Lillian had refused to be appeased. 'So you admit that you have this filthy illness?' she had screamed. 'I've been thrown out,' he told Betteridge now. 'So don't carry on as if you're the only one in trouble.'

Teddy wasn't taking that comment lying down, sitting up or standing on feet that were turning to jelly. 'You've been thrown out into a nice little semi where you can please yourself, furniture and carpets included.'

Roy tugged at Teddy's coat. 'Shut up,' he snapped. The pub had quietened; people were not looking at the trio, but all ears were at the red alert stage.

'I want my kids,' the drunkard blubbered.

Roy and Ged looked at one another. It was a universally accepted fact that Teddy had long disliked his children, his wife, her cooking, her appearance, and the neglected house his father had left him. For donkeys' years plus several, Teddy had not said two words together in praise of his family situation.

'Bad enough catching the clap off that whore without finishing up on my own, no clean socks and not a slice in the bread bin.'

The ensuing silence was painful, to say the least. Pint and gill glasses froze in mid-air, while cigarettes produced their own blue smoke rather than the usual grey, lung-processed fumes. The clientele waited for more.

'Bloody fool,' snapped Ged Hardman, his face fiery except for the white pits.

Teddy Betteridge was not going to be called a fool in public, not by anybody. 'What did you say?'

'I called you a bloody fool,' answered Ged. 'Telling everybody our business. Why don't you put an advert in the paper, make sure the whole town knows?'

Roy, who had been a witness to more than one of Teddy's drunken rages, tried to hang on to him. 'Come on, Ted,' he pleaded as the man rose to his feet. 'Calm yourself before you do any damage.'

Betteridge swept Roy aside as if dealing with a troublesome insect. 'You can all bugger off,' Teddy bellowed, the words directed at everyone in the room. 'Yon feller called me a fool.'

Roy righted himself, reached for Teddy and tried to get a grip on him, but Teddy was riled beyond reason. He lunged drunkenly across the table and knocked Ged Hardman as near to the middle of next week as he could manage. Ged, dragged from his seat and hurled to one side, felt the window smashing when his head punctured the glass. As if angered by the assault, the pane bit back, slicing into Ged's neck with a long, cold shard.

Hanging there, impaled and useless, Ged Hardman felt the life ebbing out of him. Unfortunately, Ged was sober, having imbibed no more than a whisky and a gill of Magee's. He was dying. The knowledge raced into him as quickly as the life fluid gushed out. In a matter of seconds, his eyes glazed over and he sank into a dark red abyss.

Teddy Betteridge blinked slowly, as if waking from a long sleep. Blood poured down both sides of the broken window, some falling outside onto the exterior sill, the rest dripping down the wall next to the three men's table. 'I didn't . . . I didn't mean to . . .'

Roy jumped up and supported Ged's weight. As soon as he touched the man, he knew that it was too late. A major artery had been punctured, and the man's heart, enlivened by adrenalin, had pumped hard, emptying Ged's body in a matter of seconds.

A woman screamed. Customers, who had been stilled by the loud pronouncement about venereal disease, were now stunned by the knowledge that they had witnessed a death. 'He's murdered him,' shrieked the same woman.

A man near the door shot outside, across the road and round the corner towards Bolton's central police station. The landlord dashed off into his living quarters to use the phone. Women wailed while men, shocked to the core, sank down into chairs or onto stools, some opting to place themselves on the floor. From that level, they could fall no further if they fainted at the sight of so much gore.

Roy Chorlton and two stalwart citizens lifted Ged Hardman down and laid him against the wall beneath the window. When an eyelid flickered, Roy placed his hand on the white face and bade a silent goodbye to his drinking companion. Of the two, Roy would have chosen Ged to carry on living. He rose and turned to face a shivering Teddy Betteridge. 'You'll hang for this,' he said, his tone icy.

'But it was an accident.' Frantic and almost sober, Teddy begged the crowd to stand by him. 'He called me a bloody fool,' he sobbed. 'So I hit him.'

Roy walked to the door and turned his back to the main road. 'We must all stay,' he announced. 'We're witnesses.' He spoke to the landlord as soon as the man reappeared. 'Make sure nobody sneaks out through the rear entrance.'

Teddy sank to his knees and began to slap Ged's face. There was blood everywhere, rivulets trickling between ancient flags, pools settling in uneven surfaces of the slabs. He could not believe that his friend was really dead. Not five minutes earlier, they had been talking, drinking, having a smoke.

'Leave him alone,' called Roy. 'The police will want to see him as he is, not even more messed up.'

Teddy Betteridge rose to his feet. He was still rather unsteady, though the drink played just a small role in his physical weakness. This wasn't the first man he had killed, but the others had been foreigners, had played the game of war for high stakes, had paid with their lives. Pumping bullets into Germans was one thing; killing a mate was horrible.

'Don't even think about it,' ordered Roy.

'Eh? Think about what?'

'Running.'

Teddy's head twisted and turned wildly as he looked at all the people in the bar. While women wept, men stood up and formed a solid wall in front of him. There was anger, even hatred in their faces. They didn't understand. 'It was an accident,' he said again.

'I've never seen a bloke thrown through a window by accident,' said one of the men.

'I just hit him.'

'You killed him, more like.'

The landlord broke through the ranks and covered Ged Hardman's body with an army blanket. 'His mother'll go mad,' he commented. 'He was all she had.'

Teddy sank into a blood-spattered chair. The full horror of what had happened began to sink in. He would go to prison. He might even hang. His wife wouldn't care, because she'd piked off to live with her sister up Doffcocker. His children wouldn't care because they had never even liked him.

Two policemen pushed their way on to the scene. One knelt down and felt for a pulse in Ged Hardman's wrist. He looked up at his partner, shook his head, then covered Ged's face. 'Right,' he said. 'The ambulance is on its way. What happened?'

Ruth was out. Maggie Courtney, with her hair down and her corset loosened, stretched in front of a proper blaze. Ruth McManus did not believe in overfeeding guests, herself or the fire. While her miserly host was out at work, the visitor was making the most of her absence; she had piled on the coal, spread a quarter-inch of marg on her toasted crumpets. She licked her lips, remembering the delicious taste of her recent sin. The fact that Maggie herself had paid for the margerine, the crumpets and the makings of the evening meal would cut no ice with Ruth. Ruth McManus was the female equivalent of Ebenezer Scrooge, with knobs on. Not doorknobs, though, Maggie pondered sleepily. No Jacob Marley decorated the door of Ruth's house, even if the woman did insist so firmly that her house was haunted.

The door in question flew open, then was slammed home with a vengeance, while a cold draught added its unnecessary weight to these heralds of a new arrival.

'Maggie?' It was Theresa.

'In here.'

Theresa burst into the room. Her pretty hair was sticking out all over her head like a halo created by some extremely untidy artist. She wore one of Eva's aprons over a skirt that had seen better days, and her feet were encased in a pair of greyish carpet slippers.

'Saints alive,' proclaimed Maggie.

'He's dead.' Theresa waved a very crumpled *Bolton Evening News.*

'What?' Maggie rubbed the last chance of sleep from her eyes. 'I was just drifting off nicely,' she grumbled.

'It's saved me a job, I suppose.' The visitor was walking up and down the room like a cat on hot tiles, shivering, quaking, chattering. 'It couldn't have happened to two nicer people.'

Maggie tut-tutted. 'All right, I give up. Give me the answer to the riddle, for I'll get no peace until you do.'

Theresa told herself to calm down. She had learned, of late, to control her body's mechanism by counting backwards from ten, regulating her breathing by slowing her progress through the reversed numbers. Stephen had begun to teach her about relaxation, about the use of gramophone records and soft music on the wireless. Although he was a doctor, he believed that poetry, music and sheer willpower had a lot to do with remaining alive.

'Have you done striding about like the Coldstream Guards?' asked Maggie.

'Yes.' Theresa sat at the table. 'Ged Hardman's dead,' she announced. 'It's here in the paper. Teddy Betteridge pushed him through the window of the King's Head on Deansgate. He bled to death in a matter of minutes.'

'Well now.' Maggie sat up straight. 'Isn't that two of your men dealt with already? You can throw away your gun and live the civilized life after all. Your daughter – and your other daughter – will not have a murderess for a mother. It's all been done for you, so.' Pleased with herself, Maggie added, 'See? I told you there was no murder in your cards.'

Theresa tutted her impatience. 'Don't start all that again,' she warned. 'Anyway, there's one of them still on the loose. Chorlton was the first.' Her voice was cold.

'Ah, stop that. Hasn't he lost his friends?'

Theresa decided not to pursue that particular line of enquiry. Some people deserved to lose things. 'The magistrates remanded Betteridge. He'll be charged in Crown Court with murder. It says here . . .' She wrestled with the evening paper. ' "Witnesses were horrified. Two men and five women were treated for severe shock after the event. As a mark of respect to the deceased, the King's Head will remain closed until Friday." '

'Terrible,' sighed Maggie. 'Aye, a violent end is an awful thing.'

Theresa Nolan stared blankly into the fire's depths. To her surprise, she found herself agreeing with Maggie. It was terrible. She wondered how Teddy Betteridge felt after killing his supposedly close friend. What had driven him to do that? 'It would be the drink. Like his dad, Teddy Betteridge is an alcoholic.'

'Maybe so. God rest the dead man, anyway.'

Theresa wondered whether Maggie was trying to rile her. She had a way of taking the bull by the horns just for devilment. Yet Theresa, who ought to be celebrating, felt empty now that the first flush of excitement had passed. 'I'm still going to see Roy Chorlton,' she said.

'See him if you must.'

'I will.' Unwilling to discuss any details of her intentions, the younger woman took up her *Evening News* and left.

Maggie Courtney's appetite had disappeared. The pork chops she had bought for herself and Ruth no longer appealed. Seeing Theresa so excited by the demise of one man and the imprisonment of another had made Maggie feel sick. Yet Maggie believed in Theresa. Theresa was not a bad woman, she was an angry one. Had the rapes not happened, how different her life might have been.

Ruth entered and made herself the centre of attention, as usual. 'I've had a pig of a day,' she announced. 'Bloody machine broke down four times and we'd two mechanics off sick. You've got a big fire there. Coal doesn't grow on trees.'

'Coal is trees,' replied Maggie half-heartedly.

'Don't talk so daft.'

The door opened again. Maggie began to wonder whether she was living in a house or on Crewe station. When Irene's uncomely face appeared, the Irishwoman closed her eyes and prayed to St Jude.

'Eeh, Mam,' began the unwelcome visitor.

'What do you want?' Ruth threw off her coat and claimed the other fireside chair. 'She's bloody married and I still can't get shut of her,' she advised Maggie.

Maggie opened her eyes. Irene came back again and again in a fruitless search for affection – even recognition.

'We got the body this afternoon after the police had finished with it. There weren't a drop of blood left in him.'

'She thinks she's telling us summat,' said Ruth wearily. 'We all know who you mean. Don't be coming here thinking you've a surprise up your sleeve. Deansgate were awash with his blood this morning. I reckon he'll haunt that pub from now on.'

Deflated, Irene sat in a dining chair. 'He felt funny,' she said. 'As if he were a doll, one of them plastic ones off the fair.'

After a few seconds of silence, Irene addressed Maggie. 'Well, I've done one thing right,' she said. 'I'm so glad I got out of here and got married. At least that job's a good 'un.' The implication that Ruth had been a less than perfect mother hung in the air, but no-one tried to capture it for closer examination.

Maggie nodded and tried to smile, thanking God that Irene showed no sign of wanting to become a mother. Heaven forbid that she might have children, thought Maggie, as any offspring of Irene's would be kept within this unhappy woman's reach, would never be allowed to grow and go.

Irene looked at her mother, saw hatred burning bright in those angry dark eyes. 'I know where I'm not wanted,' said Irene now. 'Ta-ra, Maggie.' She flounced out, banging her leg against the door-frame.

Ruth laughed at her daughter's clumsy misfortune, but sobered when she noticed that Maggie did not share the joke. 'Have you got a ciggy?'

'There's a packet on the dresser.'

Without a word of thanks, Ruth walked across the room to pick up the ten Players Weights. 'Is the tea on?'

The Irishwoman's paddy began to simmer. 'If you want food, prepare it yourself. I shopped for it and paid for it, so you can cook it.'

Enlivened by the prospect of a fight, Ruth sat down again and lit a cigarette. 'What's up with you?' she asked.

'You are up with me and I am done with you.'

'Bugger off, then.'

'Don't worry, I shall. Then you'll have no audience to applaud or boo you. It's been like living with a petulant child, so it has. And as for that girl of yours, you're reaping exactly what you sowed, no more, no less.'

Ruth inhaled, blew a couple of smoke rings, and smiled. 'She's took after her father. He's Irish. He beggared off back to Mayo and left me with his brat to rear and not a penny out of him.'

Maggie glowered. 'Could you blame him? What sort of a woman tells her child she's ugly? What kind of mother leaves a small girl in the house with no

428

food? But you always had your smokes, always had what you wanted.' Maggie stood up and towered over Ruth. 'Irene works with the dead because she fears the living. She gets no accusations out of a corpse. And she's waiting for you, I've no doubt. Once she has you stretched out in a box, she'll say all she's bitten back in the past. In fact, it would come as no surprise to me if she put an end to you. Not because she's evil, but because you deserve it.'

No-one had ever spoken to Ruth in this way. The whole neighbourhood knew Irene and her mother; not one single soul had come up smiling after a close encounter with the cotton carder or the undertaker's assistant. 'You know nowt, you,' snapped Ruth. 'Stuck on me own here with me dad and that little rat. None of the others bothered to—'

'That little rat was a child, a human being.'

'She's wicked,' snarled Ruth.

Maggie paused. Was there a hint of Ruth's nastiness in Theresa? Did madness run in the Nolan family? After all, the patriarch had been a tyrant of some considerable notoriety. Could insanity lie at the root of Theresa's need for vengeance? Maggie thought not. No, this one here, a being like no other, had created a monster in her own tainted soul's image. 'I pity your day of judgement,' she told the seated woman, 'because you have not one single saving grace. I pity your family and the victims who get torn by your tongue and by the wicked machinations of your daughter. I understand that many of her neighbours and even some of your relatives have received poison pen letters from her. She has neither the wit nor the wisdom to conceal her identity in spite of a lack of signature. Poor spelling and bad grammar betray her, for she got little in the way of education. Which is a pity, because her talents might have served her had she been given encouragement.'

Ruth let out a roar, leapt up and pushed Maggie away. 'What would you know, you owld bitch?'

'More than you do, and that's for certain sure.'

'Ha,' spat the dark-haired Lancastrian. 'All the same, you Irish. Fat, lazy, useless and stupid. One more brain cell and you'd be a potato in the famine.'

Maggie placed her hands on her hips, thrust her chin forward. 'I could chew you up and spit you out in a fight. Oh, you'd not care to take me on, for I've wiped the streets of Liverpool with men and women twice your size.' She wagged a finger under Ruth's nose. 'But I won't need to touch you, because your daughter will do it all for me. And when Irene does finally snap, she'll have the weight of these streets behind her.'

Ruth McManus blinked. The shock of someone actually standing up to her was almost overwhelming. Like most bullies, she was a coward, a frightened soul diminished by her father, a woman whose only satisfaction lay in the persecution of others. Needful and unfulfilled, Ruth had destroyed her own daughter because she was incapable of giving or receiving love. 'You'd best get out of my house.' Her voice was low, threatening.

'I'm going, so. I'll sleep on Eva's sofa until we move into Theresa's house.'

Ruth grinned hideously, displaying an array of tobacco-stained dentures. 'When our Theresa pops her clogs, I'll be round to collect my niece.'

'When Theresa dies, you'll be long gone,' prophesied Maggie.

'Is that a threat?'

430

Maggie walked to the door and swung round. 'That, my dear Ruth, was a definite promise. And don't forget – I have the sight.' She smiled menacingly. 'You'll die before Theresa does.'

Theresa watched the workers leaving by the back gate. There were five of them: three men, two women. They chattered in a small huddle for a few seconds, then each set off for home. Theresa needed to be quick. She didn't want Chorlton to lock the shop before she'd had the chance to get in.

Counting backwards, remembering Stephen's advice, she ambled round to the front of the shop and placed her hand on the latch, experiencing a peculiar feeling whose constituents seemed to be a mixture of fear and self-congratulation. She had timed it just right, as the workers had gone and the master had not yet locked the door. She had timed it perfectly, and her heart was beating hard in spite of all her efforts to remain cool and clear. She had no idea what she would do once inside, yet she had to go in, had to look her tormentor in the eye.

He was taking money out of the till and placing it in a green canvas bag. He looked up, then glanced down at the cash, freezing for a fraction of time before forcing himself to look at the beautiful, wraith-like woman who had entered his shop.

Theresa wandered the length of the counter until she stood within two yards of him. Slowly, she opened her handbag, lifted out the gun, then placed herself in one of the chairs provided for older customers.

Roy Chorlton swallowed audibly. He had spent several years in the company of firearms, many of which had been handled by official enemies, but he had never before seen a gun in the hands of a civilian. He dropped the bag onto the counter and gripped the rim of the wooden surface. Somebody had to say something.

At last, she spoke. 'Lock the door, turn the sign round, close all the blinds.'

After a moment of near-paralysis, he complied with the instructions and returned to his place.

Theresa nodded slowly. 'You look just right there, Mr Chorlton. Every inch the shopkeeper. Do you rub your hands together when a sale is made? Your father used to do that. Yes, Maurice the Mole was a greasy creature, too.'

He kept his eyes on the gun. It was small, but anything fired from that distance would fell a man. Three days ago, Ged Hardman had been killed and Teddy Betteridge had been deprived of his freedom. Bail had been refused. It seemed that Roy would have no chance to apply for bail, for mercy, for the right to remain alive and uninjured.

'It's my turn now,' she whispered.

He gulped again, made no reply.

'How does this feel?' she asked, as if making an enquiry about a bolt of cloth.

'Unpleasant,' he managed.

'Good.'

For what seemed like an hour, she sat there with the gun trained on him while he shivered in his shoes. How could she achieve such stillness? he wondered. She didn't flinch, didn't shake, scarcely blinked, seemed almost to have stopped breathing.

With a suddenness that surprised both of them, Theresa swung round and fired a bullet into a dummy dressed in a fifty-pound suit. The missile pierced fine worsted, sliced through the figure, then embedded itself in a wall. Smoke floated out of the broken 'man', made its way upwards and thinned away to nothing. 'That's how easy it is,' she told him. 'Just a tiny squeeze on the trigger and it's all over. My turn. My turn to have total control over you.'

Urine trickled down Roy Chorlton's leg. 'Someone will have heard that shot.' His shop was not one in a row. Surrounded by warehouses and small factories whose occupants had clocked off for the day, he held little hope unless someone passing by had recognized the report as gunfire.

Unimpressed by the man's comment, Theresa examined the gun as if assessing its performance. 'It works.' Her tone was conversational. 'Frightening, isn't it, when someone takes over and gives you no choices? Imagine how you would feel if there were three of me.'

He decided against reminding her that he and his fellows had carried no guns. The balance was about right, anyway. With a trio of attackers, Theresa had stood no chance. Here and now, in his own shop, Roy Chorlton feared a very small woman with a very small gun. He probably deserved this.

'I have a daughter,' she continued, deliberately neglecting to mention Katherine. Let Katherine survive, let her remain untouched by this. 'Jessica is probably yours. The other day, I asked for money from the three of you. With one dead and the other in jail, it's your responsibility.'

'I have your money,' he managed. 'May I get it?'

She nodded.

Roy opened the register and pulled out a Bolton Savings Bank pass book. 'Two thousand pounds,' he said. 'It's in your name and the paperwork is correct.

433

To withdraw, you will need only to confirm your identity.'

'Two thousand pounds,' she murmured. 'Very generous indeed. Tell me – is that the value of your life?'

He shrugged. 'When I opened this account, I didn't know that my life would be under threat. Some of the money is Ged's. He had it transferred the day before he died.' Humiliated by his body's weakness, he was glad of the counter, because it hid the wet patches on his trousers. Had she really felt fear as strong as this? Of course she had.

'I got hold of this gun some years ago. I had one or two vague ideas about killing the lot of you, but you and I are the only ones left. What shall I do with you?'

Roy did not move. If he ran, she might well shoot. If he stayed, would he stand a chance? 'Not a day has passed without my regretting what I did that night.'

'My thoughts exactly. If I hadn't gone visiting, if I'd stayed at home . . . "If" is such an important word.'

'I'm sorry. I've always been sorry.'

She nodded thoughtfully. 'Yes, so have I. And I've always wanted to face you just like this.' She gazed around. 'Nice shop. Doing well, are you?'

'Well enough.'

Theresa stood up. 'Take off your clothes.'

His jaw dropped. 'I beg your pardon?'

'Undress. Now.' She raised the gun.

With fingers that seemed to be made of melted butter, Roy struggled with jacket, tie, waistcoat and shirt.

'Put them on the floor. The vest, too.'

With his white and flabby upper body stripped

naked, Roy's embarrassment was unbearable. He crossed his arms to hide a chest that might have been a woman's except for the patches of black, matted hair.

'Trousers,' she ordered.

He could scarcely believe his ears. Anger bubbled, but he quashed it, removed a leather belt, undid the urine-soaked fly, stepped out of the garment.

'Go on,' she said mildly. 'Everything off. Let's see what Nature intended when she made this deliberate mistake. She must have an excellent sense of humour.'

When the last thin layer of modesty lay in a wet heap on the floor, Roy made a feeble effort to hide his droopy breasts with one hand, his lower parts with the other.

Theresa stepped forward and grabbed a bunch of keys from the counter. 'You can go now,' she said.

'What?'

'You heard me. This is the nearest a woman can come to rape, you see. You stole my virginity and I've taken away your outer wrapping so that the world can see you as you really are. Clothes make the man – isn't that so true? Underneath, you're just like a garden slug, shapeless and without any value to mankind. I can't hurt you on the inside like you hurt me. But I can make you a fool.'

'I can't go out like this.'

'I had to. I had to push a second-hand pram with your child in it. People pointed, talked about me because I was an unmarried woman with a child. If I can be a fool and survive it, so must you. The back door, I think.' She waved the gun in the direction of the workroom.

He turned and walked slowly away from her.

Theresa picked up the bank book before following the ridiculous figure through to the rear of the shop. The cheeks of his bottom flapped about as if they had no muscles to support them. The whole picture was made all the more laughable because the man still wore black socks stretched all the way up to his knees.

'Open it,' she ordered when he reached the back door.

Roy Chorlton stepped out into a biting evening. A clear sky advertised severe frost, the effects of which hit Roy as soon as he was out of doors. Behind him, the door slammed shut, a key turned and two bolts shot home. He ran into the lavatory shed and closed the door. Death would come swiftly if he didn't find some cover. She was so damned clever. His car keys were among the bunch she had taken.

Inside the shop, Theresa leaned against the door and broke her heart. She howled for the night when she had been hurt, for the Liverpool years, for Jessica, for her stolen child. Sobs racked her body when she thought about the man in the yard, because she actually pitied him. The pity infuriated her, so she wept harder. After ten minutes or so, she dried her face, rubbing the skin with a scarf until she glowed.

The Town Hall clock announced half past something or other, possibly six. Theresa had never cried like this, so perhaps the dam had finally burst. Whatever, she felt considerably better. But her feet refused to follow instructions; although she tried to walk towards the front door, her lower limbs remained on strike.

'I can't do it,' she told herself.

Still leaning against the back door, she gripped

Chorlton's keys, feeling the cut edges biting into her palm. The temperature outside was deathly cold. He might freeze. He might be found dead in the morning, his body curled against the ice, too misshapen for a coffin. 'I'm a good person,' she told the unoccupied room. Bolts of cloth lay on shelves, paper patterns on a cutting table. Three sewing machines sat idle on a bench, spools of cotton in an open box, measuring tapes and chalk on a desk.

'Oh God,' she mumbled.

A bus rattled past towards Deane Road, then another on its way to Trinity Street Station. Ten, nine, eight . . . Her breathing steadied, settled down. With painful slowness, she drew back bolts, unlocked the door with the biggest key. On a sudden impulse, she picked up a large piece of uncut cloth and dragged it out behind her.

He heard her coming, though the chattering of his teeth was almost deafening. He didn't care any more. With his skin stiffening and his extremities numb, he knew that death would arrive within hours. Perhaps she would finish him off, put him out of his misery. Whatever, it no longer mattered.

The door opened. She stepped inside, drew the woollen length across his shoulders. 'Come,' she told him.

He could not move.

With incredible tenderness, Theresa wrapped him up and led him into the yard. 'Just a few more steps and we're there,' she said several times.

Inside, he huddled in a corner away from her. There was no sign of the gun, yet he feared her unpredictability. Was the woman mad? She had threatened to shoot him, had shut him out naked in the cold, had dragged him back in. To what? To a

437

cup of tea. She had set the kettle on the ring, had lit the black paraffin stove to heat the workroom.

'It's all over,' she told him as if reading his innermost thoughts.

He shivered uncontrollably as his mechanism fought to redistribute the near-frozen blood in his veins. She piled further lengths of cloth around him, layering each piece so that air would be trapped between woven fibres. 'Why?' he asked, almost biting through his tongue with teeth that refused to be still.

She sat down while the kettle simmered its way towards boiling point. 'I had to have my pound of flesh, I suppose.'

'But you brought me in.'

'Yes.'

'Why?' he asked again.

Theresa considered her reply to what was, in the opinion of both people present, a very good question. 'You took away my dignity, so I removed yours. For many years, I felt as if you and the other two had killed a part of me. But tonight was about being in charge, I suppose, just to warn you that I was capable of fighting back. Yes, I did mean to kill you, but I've changed, grown up. I seem to have matured very suddenly.' She crossed the room and made the tea.

'We had no luck, any of us,' he said, his voice stronger. 'Ged got lumbered with his mother as well as that dreadful skin. Teddy had an unhappy marriage and a terrible drink problem. I'm just ugly. No girl would ever look at me.'

'Would you like me to contradict you, tell you that you're handsome?'

He all but laughed. 'No, not at all.'

'Good.' She held the cup to his lips and supported his head as he sipped the scalding, over-sweet concoction. 'Is it poisoned?' he asked after a minute or so.

'It isn't.' Theresa put the cup down, dragged a stool across the room and sat facing him. She took one of his hands, then the other, massaging each in turn until the blood flowed more easily.

'You could have left me out there,' he said softly. 'Thank you.'

Theresa almost grinned. 'Believe me – for ten minutes or so, you were going to be abandoned to the elements. Then I thought: No, he'll only get chilblains.'

Roy Chorlton laughed, then the laughter broke wide open and turned to tears. The girl even had humour. 'I'm sorry, I'm so, so sorry,' he kept saying until sobs claimed his breath.

Theresa allowed him to cry, simply standing in the doorway until his sobs abated. This was, perhaps, the moment for which she had been preparing all evening, or, possibly, for the past thirteen years. 'I forgive you,' she said. And although she didn't fully understand her feelings, she meant every word.

FIFTEEN

'Mam?' It was great to be able to talk to Mam regularly. Not since the days of the devil in the coal hole had Theresa and Jessica actually lived together. Williamson's didn't count. Williamson's was just a TB hospital, a place to which Mam might have to return for a month or so, but it would not be for ever. For ever was here, on Tonge Moor Road, with grocery shops, a library, chip shops, ironmongers, a big Co-op.

'Yes, love?'

'Did you know that Michelangelo died just as Shakespeare was born? On the very same day?'

Theresa wiped the sweat from her brow.

'Leave the curtains, Theresa,' ordered Maggie. She addressed Jessica. 'When was that, then?'

'Sixteenth century,' replied Jessica.

'What was the date?' Theresa asked, her fingers becoming very annoyed with brass curtain rings.

'April the twenty-third.'

'And the year?' Maggie who was moving furniture, stopped to glare at Theresa, who should have been sitting on the furniture.

'I can't remember,' answered Jessica. 'It doesn't matter – I was only saying—'

'It must have mattered to him that died.' Maggie flopped onto a sofa. 'As for Shakespeare – wouldn't that be some sort of sacrilege for you English folk? God, aren't you all supposed to know about the Bard of Avon, his birthday and all that? So Michelangelo died and your man was born. Out with the paint and in with the typewriter.'

Jessica laughed. 'They didn't have typewriters. They used feathers.'

'I suppose they walked behind the goose till one fell out.' Maggie giggled. 'Or they took their lives in their hands and had a quick pluck. Geese are terrible fierce.'

Jessica walked to the window of her new house. And it was her house, too, with deeds she had perused before leaving them to be minded at the bank. She took the curtains from Theresa and carried on with the threading of hooks and rings.

Maggie thought about Shakespeare. She could remember just one play. 'Ah, yes. Didn't your man sit there on his horse, a saucepan on his head, God for England and St George – all that kind of stuff. Then he suggested using dead bodies for the fortifications. Only the English could be so barbaric.'

'Henry the Fifth.' Theresa was very pleased with herself. 'It was a metaphor.'

'Was that with or without vinegar?' asked Maggie sweetly.

Jessica decided that she liked Maggie. The argument – whatever its subject had been – between Mam and Eva was settled, so Jessica would still be able to visit Auntie Eva and Uncle Jimmy. But Maggie was great fun. She knew loads of daft stories about goblins and leprechauns, and she could sing and dance an Irish reel at the same time with a glass of water on her head. 'Maggie?'

'That's me.'

'Did you really never go to school?'

The Irishwoman made a strange sound, something like a 'pshaw'. 'Of course I went to school. It was seven miles there, seven miles back, and not a daycent pair of boots to me name. So I went just the once – I think it was a Thursday. Oh, it tired me out, all that praying and chanting and catechism and still seven miles home at the end of it.'

'Just once?' The girl's eyes were round.

Maggie nodded. 'I left early because it looked like rain.'

Theresa exploded with laughter. 'You went once and left early?'

'That's the truth of it.'

'It explains a lot,' said Theresa. 'Large gaps in the education of a person do show, at least once a day.'

Maggie threw a cushion at her sometime ally.

'Everyone's silly at times,' said Jessica. 'I had an invisible friend called Lucy. I met her in the dresser mirror when I was about three. Of course, she was me, really. Till I met Katherine, then she was nearly me.'

Maggie dropped the other cushion. Theresa sat in a dining chair and tried not to look shocked, tried not to look at Maggie. 'Katherine?' she managed eventually, her voice pitched rather high.

Jessica blushed. 'I never told anyone. When Williamson's let me go down to the farm, I escaped.' She remembered her first real contact with nature, the sounds of birds, the clean scent of damp earth. 'She just appeared with a dog – it had a stupid name. And she went.' Such a special, precious, hurtful day that had been.

Theresa cleared her throat. They had met, yes, and Jessica had stored the memory for all time. Against all the odds, Katherine and Jessica's paths had crossed. 'She must have been pretty if she looked like you.'

Like many blondes, Jessica considered herself very pale and uninteresting. 'No, she was ordinary. The dog was crackers, though. I told Katherine lies, said I was from a big farm with loads of animals. I was jealous of her. She had lovely clothes and a dog of her own.'

At last, Theresa managed to look at Maggie. 'How do you feel about dogs?'

Maggie shrugged. 'As long as they're not over-cooked, they taste very nice with onions and taties. And the skins come in handy for slippers and gloves.'

While Theresa laughed nervously, Jessica almost stopped breathing. If she said nothing, if she held back words and giggles, she might get a dog.

'We'll get you a dog,' Theresa promised recklessly. Was she making too many of these promises? She had sworn to Stephen that she would go in for tests, had told Roy Chorlton that the bitterness was over, was offering Jessica a dog. 'There are fields nearby where you could walk a dog. I'll get you one before I go to see about my chest.'

Jessica thought she might burst. She had every-thing now – a home, a mother, nearly a dog. She had everything except a father, and she couldn't ask Mam questions about him, not while Mam had to go and see about having TB and a weak heart. Mind, there might be a stepfather in the offing . . . 'Mam?'

'Yes?'

'Are you going to marry Dr Blake?'

Theresa blushed.

'He hasn't asked her yet,' volunteered Maggie.

'She won't stand still long enough in the one place in case he does ask her.'

Many a true word was spoken in jest, thought Theresa. Her experience of men at close quarters had been limited, because she had scarcely dared to contemplate intimacy since the night when Jessica and Katherine had been conceived. The brutish cruelty of her first encounter had left her bruised mentally as well as physically. Stephen had put the physical side right, but could she live with a man, could she really trust anyone? 'One thing at a time,' she warned her daughter. 'The dog, the whole dog and nothing but the dog. So be quiet.'

After threading the rings, Jessica sought permission to go outside. When the dog arrived, she would need to know where to take it. 'Don't go far,' shouted Theresa to her daughter's disappearing back. 'It goes dark early.'

When Jessica had gone, Theresa flopped back in her chair.

'They've got to come together some time,' commented Maggie.

'I know. If I'm not around, Bernard has promised to see to all that.'

Maggie grunted. 'Make sure of that,' she said. 'Nature brought them to life at the same time for a reason. Those ties are very close.'

'I'm sure they are,' answered Theresa.

Soon, she would be very sure.

Danny Walsh sat with his wife and mother-in-law in their enlarged kitchen. The remains of a feast lay on the table, fish bones on huge dinner plates, a clutter of cups, cutlery and napkins on a tray.

'That was a very nice meal,' Danny told his

444

mother-in-law, who thrived on praise, though she never knew how to cope with it.

'A bit more salt in me sauce next time,' she said.

Pauline patted her stomach and groaned. 'I feel as if I've eaten a three-piece suite,' she said. 'Stuffed to the gills, I am.'

Danny cocked his head on one side, listening for the baby. The baby was his pride and joy; he was also Pauline's main reason for living. She had done it, had achieved motherhood against all odds.

Edna Greenhalgh started to fiddle about with the debris.

'Leave it, Mam,' said Danny.

'No, I won't. She's ate a couch and two chairs, and you've been working all day. Sit still till I make another brew.'

While Edna clattered about, Danny closed his eyes and concentrated on contentment. He was a lucky man, with a wonderful wife, a son, a lovely home and a mother-in-law who wasn't too bad. Edna kept Danny on his toes, reminded him never to take life for granted.

His mind wandered, went back to the day when he had acted as substitute for his brother, the day on which Eva had extracted money for Theresa Nolan, the golden time when he had met Pauline in Chorlton's shop.

'Do you think he'll hang?' asked Pauline. There was no need for names, because the main topic for weeks had been the killing of Ged Hardman.

'He should hang,' said Edna from her place at the sink. Edna was of the hang-them-now set, one of those who might have asked questions after the trap door had opened and the hanged man's legs had swung for at least five minutes.

'I'd say it was manslaughter,' answered Danny. 'Not planned, like a real murder.'

'Lily Hardman's heartbroke,' continued Edna. 'He'd just left home, too, had his first house. They say she's gone into one of them declines, stopping in bed, won't eat.'

Pauline spoke up. 'That won't last long. She's better at business than most men in this town.' Pauline tried to imagine life without her baby, but found the concept unbearable. 'Still, losing her son will slow her down a bit.'

Danny Walsh's thoughts strayed to Theresa Nolan, who had been the indirect cause of the meeting between him and Pauline. She had moved today. Danny had seen furniture being delivered, had slowed his car while passing to watch Theresa sweeping the short path to her front door.

'I wonder how Theresa's going on?' muttered Pauline.

Danny frowned. As ever, his wife seemed to tune into his thoughts as if she had antennae built into her head. He jerked his own head in the direction of Edna. Pauline knew about Katherine's origins, about the rape, the birth of twins, but Edna had been kept in the dark for many years. She was old, curious, full of gossip.

Edna cleared her throat. 'Right,' she said, swivelling round and planting large, slipper-clad feet well apart. 'Let's be having this straight, shall we? There's nowt I don't know, Danny. And our Pauline never told me – I just listened now and again.' She nodded vigorously while drying her hands on a tea-towel. 'I'd not be surprised if them three blokes have death wishes after what they did. Happen Teddy Betteridge lost his rag over summat to do with Theresa Nolan.'

Danny's mouth fell open.

'Shut that, Danny, there's a tram coming.' The old woman warmed the pot, spooned in some Black and Green's. 'By rights, Theresa has two kiddies. I've heard you both chunnering about it. I've said nowt to nobody, so you can talk free in front of me, not just behind me back.'

'But, Mam,' cried Pauline. 'How long have you—?'

'About three year. But I know when to keep me gob shut, which is more than can be said about yon husband of yours. Good job it's not summer, he'd be catching flies.'

Danny closed his mouth and grinned sheepishly. 'I'm a lucky man,' he said gruffly. 'There could be wasps and all.'

Both women knew exactly what Danny meant. Pauline kissed him. Edna, who never cried, wiped a bit of wetness from an eye before brewing the tea. She was the lucky one, because Danny was a saint.

Bernard stretched his legs and glared at John Povey. 'I wish you'd never got me going on this flaming game.' He pushed away the backgammon board. No matter how hard Bernard worked at it, John always seemed to have the edge. 'As for chess – give it a rest. Bloody kings and castles – I don't know whether I'm coming or going, there's that many rules.'

'Never mind, you'll get your own back on Saturday afternoon.' Saturday afternoon was golf time. Bernard Walsh had developed a near-perfect swing, while his delicacy of touch with a putter was becoming legendary at the West Lancashire Golf Club.

Bernard laughed. Both men closed their shops at one o'clock each Saturday in order to get a round at the club. John was hopeless. He wielded a five iron as if attempting to gain a part in some Errol Flynn movie, all swash and buckle. With a putter, he could miss the shortest hole, cursing and swearing at his own lack of co-ordination. What amazed Bernard was that this pharmacist, who could mix a perfect potion right down to the tiniest granule, was unable to judge a distance of five or six inches between ball and target.

'I've bought a house,' rumbled John, his voice hoarse with laughter.

'Have you, now?' The idea of John Povey moving house was a sobering one. He led a life of extravagant eccentricity, providing meals of fish, chicken and minced beef to a nomadic tribe of cats about whose number he was never certain. His house was a monument to chaos, its rooms crammed with books, bottles, bunsen burners, crates of notes. John was writing three books on various aspects of pharmacy, many pages of which were jumbled into one cardboard container. Sometimes he rescued sheets of vital information which had doubled as mats underneath cat dishes. John Povey would eventually invent a momentous formula on a piece of paper which he would lose. 'When are you moving?'

'I'm not.'

Bernard chuckled. 'I see. One house for you and *Paradise Lost*, another for the cats.'

John's laughter boomed again. His friend always referred to the unfinished and mixed-up manuscripts as *Paradise Lost*. 'No, I've bought the Corner House. An investment, I suppose. I shall let it out to young people. It needs young ones.'

Bernard agreed. The house on the corner of Crosby's Northern Road was like no other on earth.

Built in the 1920s to the specifications of a retiring sea-captain, it was a happy mix of stuccoed walls, Spanish galleon windows and Virginia creeper. 'I've never been in, you know. Liz has wanted to look inside ever since we came here, but the old man's been too ill.'

'He saw ninety-five, though,' commented John. 'With my help, of course.'

'Of course,' echoed Bernard. 'Good job you weren't teaching him golf.' He walked to the window and peered through darkness at the house across the way. Liz regarded it as some kind of magic place, the sort of house that should appear in children's fairy tales. 'I suppose it's romantic,' the fishmonger conceded. 'He loved his wife, the old chap. After she died, he drove her Humber every Sunday to keep it alive. Till he lost his sight.' He remembered seeing the captain sitting in his living room, a huge magnifier balanced in front of a fourteen-inch television set.

'Did they pull the flag down to half-mast when he died?' asked John.

'Yes, they did.' The captain's flagpole was a talking point. He had flown the Union Flag high on the King's birthdays, had lowered it for more sombre occasions. 'He liked his garden, too.' There was clematis, there were laurels, lilac trees, roses. 'So who are you going to put in there?'

'Pharmacy students.'

Bernard swung round. 'What? Folk like you but younger?'

'That's the idea.'

'We shall all be blown to kingdom come.'

'No, blowing up is chemistry.'

'Are you sure? Because it looks like there's been a

fair few explosions in your house, especially in that back kitchen.'

John wore an expression of pretended hurt. 'Listen, Bernard. It may look a mess to you, but I can lay my hand on anything I need just like that.' He snapped his fingers.

'What? You've been looking for the bottom half of your best suit since last April.'

'Anything important, I mean.' John looked at his watch, checking it against the grandfather in a corner. Liz would be home soon. She was at church, up to her eyes in the Young Wives, showing them how to sew and knit. She would also be telling them a few jokes and tales which would not necessarily conform with the teaching of the Holy Mother Church. When she came home, there would be the obligatory cocoa and chat, then John would drive home to cats, scribblings and the inevitable search for tomorrow's cleanish shirt.

Bernard heard it first, a strange groaning sound, followed by a muffled cry. He put his head on one side, listened hard. The dog lifted his chin and growled deep in his throat.

'It's Katherine,' John said.

'No, she's asleep,' replied Bernard. He got up and went to the bottom of the stairs. John was right. The unmistakable sound of sobbing floated down into the hall. Bernard ran to his daughter's side, John hot on his heels.

She was sitting up in bed, her face devoid of expression. 'So cold,' she said.

'I'll get her another blanket.' Bernard turned to leave the room.

'She's fast asleep,' said John. 'Look.' He waved his

hand in front of Katherine's eyes. She neither flinched nor focused.

'What's the matter with her?' Bernard was suddenly frightened.

John perched on the edge of the bed and took Katherine's hand. 'What's happening?' he asked softly.

Still staring straight ahead, the girl spoke. 'So cold. My ankle hurts. The grass is all slippy with the frost.'

'Did you fall?'

She nodded.

'Where are you?'

'Here. I'm here. I'll bring the dog when I get it. For a walk. My ankle hurts so much. At the bottom of the slope.'

John looked at Bernard. 'I'll bet you a pound to a penny that something's happened to the other one.'

'Jessica.' The name, whispered by Bernard, was not a question.

The chemist tried again. 'Is there a name for the place where you fell?'

'Jolly,' announced Katherine.

'It's the Jolly Brows,' Bernard said. Without hesitation, he fled from the room, two things on his mind. Firstly, he must do what he could for Katherine's sister. Secondly, he had to do it before Liz got home.

Pauline answered the phone, listened to Bernard's gibberish. 'I'll get Danny—'

'No! Liz'll be back in a minute. Just send Danny to see Theresa Nolan – she's at Eva's up View Street.'

'Danny says they've moved to Tonge Moor Road.' Pauline managed to squeeze these words in.

'Tell him the Jolly Brows. Can you remember that?'

'Yes, but—'

'I can hear Liz coming,' he said. 'Now, listen. Katherine's having a nightmare. We think Jessica's hurt and that she's somewhere on the Jolly Brows – near a slope.'

Pauline gazed at the dead instrument in her hand. This was crackers. Katherine was dreaming in Crosby, Liverpool, so her sister, in Bolton, was in trouble. This was a sister she had never known, one she had met just briefly and by accident. Was Bernard on some funny pills administered by his friend, the chemist?

Danny came in. He had been sitting by Jonathan's cot, had been watching the sleep of the truly innocent. 'Who was that? Why are you staring at the phone?'

'The world's finally gone mad.' She told him the story. 'Where are you going?'

Danny grabbed his coat from the hallway. 'It may be rubbish, but are you prepared to take a chance? What if it was our child? I'll be back as soon as I can.'

Pauline found herself staring at an empty space where her husband had recently stood, while holding in her hand a receiver dead enough to warrant burial. Edna, who remained very much alive, came in from her little morning-cum-sitting-room. 'Were that Danny going out? It's past nine o'clock.'

Pauline sighed. 'Mam?'

'What?'

'You put the kettle on while I phone Williamson's.'

The old lady staggered slightly. 'Why? Is the baby all right? Has somebody got TB?'

'No, it's nothing like that.' Pauline studied the tough old bird who had birthed her. She was a nuisance, a moan and a little devil at times. But in that moment, Pauline Walsh caught a glimpse of her mam's frailty. Edna Greenhalgh's suit of armour had slipped, the open visor revealing a very ordinary woman who feared life and its vagaries. 'I love you, Mam.' How long had it been since Pauline had said those words?

Edna gulped. 'I love you and all, Pauline.'

'I want to get hold of that Dr Blake, send him round to Theresa Nolan's. Bernard and Danny think there could be something up with young Jessica. Theresa's friendly with the doctor, so he might want to help.'

'Oh.' Seeing her daughter's confusion, Edna put the kettle on and busied herself with cups and saucers. Pauline loved her. Everything would turn out for the best.

The Jolly Brows lay between the top of Tonge Moor and Bolton's ring road, Crompton Way. It attracted playing children, courting couples, stray cows and a small cast of dubious male characters well practised in the art of displaying private parts, though these creatures tended to protect their valuables during cold snaps.

An ideal place for dog-walkers, the Jolly Brows had drawn Jessica, on that cold afternoon in February 1952, to investigate its possibilities. She had run and run until, exhausted and slightly breathless, she had made her way towards the Tonge Moor Road end. A steep slope led back to civilization, and Jessica, having lost her footing, had tumbled downwards, injuring her ankle.

She lay shivering in a crumpled heap. She tried to call for help, but the road was too far away, while her voice grew weaker as frost entered her bones. Drifting in and out of consciousness, Jessica found herself in one of her 'floating' dreams, episodes of which usually involved moving about without actually walking. It wasn't flying, though. It was a simple matter of skimming along at ground level without using her lower limbs.

She was in a room with another girl – The Other Girl – the one who looked so like Jessica. Above her head, a silvery-white figure hovered, its wings outstretched over both occupants of what appeared to be a bedroom.

'That's our guardian angel,' Katherine explained. 'We share.'

'Why?' asked Jessica.

'Because there aren't enough to go around. We look the same, so we get him between us.'

Jessica stared at the angel. He bore an uncanny resemblance to Dr Blake, who was tidier than he used to be.

'They're coming,' said Katherine. 'They're near that little hill about halfway across, the one at the edge of the path.'

'Oh.' What was this girl going on about?

'How's your ankle?' Katherine asked.

In the dream, there was no pain. 'It's all right.'

'Good. I'm glad it's stopped hurting.'

A dark mist came down, obliterating completely the heavenly visitor near the ceiling. Jessica reached out and grabbed Katherine's hand. Together, they bobbed about in space, laughing as the fog turned to warm fluid. 'This is where we began,' explained Katherine.

Jessica accepted this certain truth.

'I miss you,' said Katherine.

'I miss you, too. One day, we'll be together for always.'

'Yes, we shall.'

As suddenly as it had begun, the dream ended. Reluctantly, Jessica released her hold on Katherine's hand, felt herself being dragged upwards.

She woke on a stretcher. Dr Blake, Mam and Mr Walsh, the fishman, stood back as Jessica was carried away. Mam ran and caught up with the stretcher-bearers. 'Where's Katherine?' asked Jessica.

Theresa placed a hand on the pile of blankets that covered her daughter.

'Don't cry, Mam,' said Jessica. 'I'm all right.' Why was Mam crying so loudly? The girl closed her eyes and gave herself up to sleep. This time, there were no dreams.

'Jesus,' wept Theresa. 'What am I supposed to do?' She looked from Danny Walsh to Stephen, returned her attention to Danny. 'They're both mine,' she sobbed. 'I didn't know. I didn't give her away – she was stolen.'

Danny blew his nose. Another hour in the cold and Jessica Nolan would have been dead. He was absolutely flummoxed by what had happened. 'Liz doesn't know anything about this little lot,' he said sadly. 'What a bloody mess.'

Theresa tried to calm herself down. She had one daughter being warmed up and getting her ankle set, another with perfectly decent parents in a pleasant suburb of Liverpool. 'There is nothing that will make me hurt your sister-in-law,' she told Danny Walsh. 'But there's something going on, isn't there? Between the two girls, I mean. Look what happened tonight. I know it seems daft, but—'

'It isn't daft at all.' Stephen Blake removed his arm from Theresa's shoulder. 'I'm a twin. Even when we were separated, we were together. If he had a pain, I had the same pain. I'm a doctor, so I should dismiss all this as nonsense. But it's fact that twins can communicate by a method we shall never analyse.'

Theresa, after the initial, almost painful sense of relief when Jessica had been discovered, had dissolved into near-hysteria. Katherine had held the answer, had guided her father, that very good man, so that Jessica could be saved. The whole thing was frightening, incomprehensible, beyond all normal explanation.

'If it hadn't been for you, Mr Walsh, Jessica might have frozen to death,' said Stephen.

Theresa hoped that Katherine would not remember her dream. Nothing could be done to bring the twins together without damaging Liz, who was completely blameless. She was and always had been a good mother to Katherine – on that score, Theresa had no doubt. Liz Walsh was a sensible, humorous woman who deserved Jessica's other half. 'The girls seem to need one another,' murmured Theresa. 'When I first found out about Katherine, I was in the middle of Liverpool. I very nearly got on the train to visit Eva and give her a piece of my mind.'

Stephen Blake understood Theresa's dilemma only too well. She was ill. She had already made arrangements for Jessica's future in case . . . in case. He swallowed. Although Theresa had been back for a very short time, his love for her had grown into a huge, hopeless pain in his chest. He could not bear the idea of life without her; he might well have to cope with life without her.

'There's nothing I can do, is there?' she asked him now.

'No.' If Theresa died, one girl would grieve, while

the other could continue without any real disturbance – for a while, at least.

'Promise me?' she asked Danny.

'I promise.' One day, Liz and Katherine would have to be told.

'Before they're twenty-five, before they get too old to care.'

Both men nodded their agreement.

'It's important.'

Stephen realized just how important it was. Conceived together, born together, they should be together.

A doctor drifted down the corridor. 'Mrs Nolan?'

'Yes?'

'You can take her home tomorrow. She's a very lucky girl.'

Yes, thought Theresa, Jessica was a lucky girl. From a distance of forty miles, a soulmate had saved her life.

Jessica remembered nothing of her floating dream. She came home to a bed tucked under the stairs, a lot of fuss from Maggie, Mam, the local doctor, and Eva and Jimmy who visited almost every day. It was nice in the living room with its bungalow range, easy chairs, sideboard and table. Everyone was extra-specially kind, particularly Dr Blake from the sanatorium. He knew a man who bred dogs, and a little baby Alsatian was earmarked for Jessica. The puppy was too young to leave her mother, but would be ready when Jessica's ankle healed.

Theresa hovered, listened, waited for her daughter to say something – anything at all – about Katherine, but Jessica did not mention her twin. Were they telepathic? Was there some kind of invisible communication system in existence? If so, did it kick in only during times of crisis?

Theresa had visited Danny on the market, had been reassured that Katherine retained no memory of the nightmare which had led to the discovery of Jessica. Whenever she thought of the day on which Jessica had disappeared, Theresa shuddered. She and Maggie had searched for hours, then, after Maggie had gone for the police, Danny Walsh had arrived. The love Theresa felt for her daughter was immense; she had not expected to experience emotion of such intensity. In Crosby, another child lived, went to school, ate and slept, another girl for whom Theresa might have developed similar feelings.

'Mam?'

'Yes, love?'

'Why are you sad?'

'Because I nearly lost you.' And because I never even knew your sister, Theresa said inwardly.

'Will you have to go back into Williamson's?'

Time was closing in on Theresa. She had prepared as best she could, had invested over three thousand pounds as well as buying the house so that this precious daughter would have a head start. But Theresa wanted to be there, wanted to guide Jessica into adulthood. She was already in love with Stephen, now she was beginning to fall in love with life.

'I'm going to call her Sheba.'

'Who?'

'My dog, of course.'

'That's nice,' replied Theresa vaguely. She went off into the kitchen to wash dishes. As she rinsed cups and plates, she tried to reassure herself. Jessica had Maggie, she had Eva, Jimmy and Stephen, she had the Walsh brothers who would keep a weather eye on things. There was the house, there was money. Theresa dashed a tear from her cheek. What Jessica needed was a mother. No-one could truly replace a mother.

Roy Chorlton was a meticulous man. He shaved twice a day, had his shirts laundered by professionals, filed his clothes with military precision – black socks divided from grey socks, suits graded according to colour and weight. He sat on the edge of the bed with duster and polish, slightly breathless after a long attack on a dressing table and two wardrobes. The woman who came in twice a week did not do cobwebs or windows, while her streaky applications of beeswax fell far short of perfection.

'I should sack her,' he said aloud. But he couldn't. She had rent to pay, three children to clothe and feed, and a husband who had gone off with a barmaid from the Swan.

After weeks of treatment, the nasty legacy bequeathed by Maria Martin was beginning to clear up. He found himself grinning ruefully. How sweet had been Theresa Nolan's vengeance. She had driven three men to their doctors, had broken a marriage, had stripped Roy of clothes and dignity. He admired her logic, her ability to plan and follow a stratagem through to the bitter end.

He stretched out on the bed, dropping polish and cloth onto the bedside table. Betteridge and Hardman had not been the best of companions, but life without them was considerably greyer, emptier. Roy had been interviewed by police, had refused to be interviewed by press. Sooner or later, he would be a witness at a trial that might send Teddy Betteridge to the gallows.

Life was a grind. He worked five and a half days a week, went to the cinema alone each Saturday night, cleaned his house on Sundays. Church bells failed to summon him, as he associated religion with his father, a Sabbath-only Christian without an ounce of charity in his soul.

Roy had read press reports about Jessica's accident. They had been contained in a couple of inches of script on two consecutive nights, and they had had a disturbing effect on him. She was probably his daughter, his flesh and blood. His part in her creation did not bear thinking of, yet her safety was suddenly of paramount importance.

'Oh, God,' he groaned. 'Are You really there?'

There was no reason on earth sound enough to keep Roy Chorlton alive. He had no wife, no lover, no child to care for. Brotherless, sisterless, he owned a passing relationship to someone in the south, and another family in Yorkshire who sent a card at Christmas, usually a depressed-looking robin in a snowbound tree. Once, twice, almost totally removed, these relatives played no part in Roy's life.

He needed somebody, anybody, just a friend with whom he might have the odd meal or have a drink, take a walk. Roy was a good cook, a man who had managed to sub-divide Mrs Beeton's 'take twelve eggs' into manageable, sensible portions. His soufflés floated out of the oven, his omelettes melted on the tongue. But none of that mattered, because there was no-one with whom Roy could share the fruits of his labour.

Suicide beckoned; it grew more attractive each day. He had considered various exits, but had decided against anything involving the letting of blood. Hanging would be nasty, would leave him looking even uglier, all blackened face and protruding tongue. Gas was probably the best answer, though an explosion could occur, and he had no desire to alarm his neighbours unduly.

Tablets, then. A few pills, a bottle of whisky, a couple of towels under the garage door, car engine running, a gradual descent into the final sleep. Father had choked to death with all his ill-gotten gains spread around him, so perhaps Roy's end was destined to be similar.

He was jolted back into the present by a loud hammering on his front door. This noise was followed by a continuous ringing of the bell, a jangling that echoed the state of his nerves. He jumped up, straightened his clothes and went downstairs.

It was Lillian Hardman. She shot into the hall like a bullet from a gun, eyes wild, hair dishevelled, face devoid of its usual paint job. Frantically, she grabbed Roy's arm.

'You shouldn't be here,' he said.

Lily pushed Roy against the hall stand, an object whose carved surfaces were uncomfortable, to say the least.

'Mrs Hardman—'

'Call me Lillian. Or Lily, if you wish.'

He didn't wish. 'Mrs Hardman, I was a witness to—'

'Exactly.' She leaned forward until their faces almost met, causing Roy to lose the ability to focus. The white, blurred face spoke again. 'It was murder. He killed my son. You have to say that in court.'

'Interfering with a witness is an offence—'

'So is Ged's killing. You were there.'

'As were forty-odd other people.' Gently, he eased the woman backwards.

'You were the nearest.'

461

Roy closed his eyes, saw the blood, the shattered glass, felt Ged dying in his arms. 'You must go,' he told her.

'Not until you promise me.'

No such promise lay within Roy's reach. Teddy Betteridge, a buffoon of a man, a drunken wastrel whose intellect was limited, was still a human being. Yes, he had killed Ged Hardman, but had that attack been planned? No.

Lily sank onto a monk's bench. A clock above her head sang the quarter. 'I got a letter saying that Ged had a dirty disease.'

Silently, Roy praised Theresa Nolan for her inventiveness, her staying power.

'Did he have that filth in him?'

Roy nodded.

'So he'd been with a . . . with a whore?'

He nodded again.

'My son would never do that. He was a good, clean-living boy.'

'And you, Mrs Hardman, were a good, clean-living mother to him. Especially when he was young.'

Lillian's face blanched. She slumped, elbows on knees, head in her hands. 'I blame George,' she said, her tone quieter. 'Running off like that with a girl young enough to be his daughter. Yes, this is all his father's fault.'

'We are each our parents' fault,' Roy replied.

She raised her face. 'Are you blaming me? George was useless. I was young and I wanted affection—'

'Just as we all do. But some of us are totally inept, Mrs Hardman. Your son and I would have given our right arms to be loved, to have a companion at home. Even a difficult marriage would have been better than nothingness.'

She stood up. 'I'm going back to work tomorrow,' she said, a defiant edge to her words.

'That's a good idea,' replied Roy.

She turned on him. 'Who do I leave it to? Can you answer me that one, Roy Chorlton? Why am I trying so hard in that stinking hole now that Ged's been murdered?'

Roy pondered. 'Sell it.'

Lily stood stock still, her mouth slightly open.

'Get your money back and travel the world. If you don't need the factory, rid yourself of it, have a good time, because life is very short.'

She nodded slowly. 'You're not as daft as you look.'

'No-one could be as daft as I look, Mrs Hardman.'

'I'm . . . sorry,' she said. 'For barging in and screaming like that. I can't come to grips with Ged's death, you see. I want somebody punished.' She remained where she was, thoughts rushing through her mind and showing on her face. 'You've got me thinking. Thank you, Roy. Why should I stay here for the rest of my life? Yes, you've certainly given me food for thought.'

After Lillian had left, Roy sat in his elegant living room with its panelled walls, leather suite, inlaid desk, oak bookcases. Like Lily, he had no reason to continue here. Perhaps, once the trial was over, he would follow the advice he had so recently given away.

Theresa would be staying in Bolton, he supposed. In the newspaper, she had been photographed with Jessica and some doctor from Williamson's. They had posed like a family, and that had cut Roy to the quick. What vague expectations had been lurking at the base of Roy's brain? Had he wanted more than forgiveness, more than a truce? Perhaps he had imagined himself in that picture, one arm around the child's shoulder, the other drawing close a woman of extraordinary loveliness.

'You're pathetic,' he told himself aloud. There were some minted cutlets in the fridge, but he could summon up no appetite. 'She'd never look at you if you were the last man on earth.' Even without the rape, Theresa Nolan would not have glanced on Roy Chorlton's side of the street.

He thought back to the time when a Theresa Nolan would not have been good enough, when he had expected to marry a woman of decent trade stock, somebody with a business to inherit, with a father who knew what was what. And here he sat, into his thirties, with a small television set, a radio and two tiny, unwanted lamb cutlets for company.

The car was in the garage. He had plenty of towels to pack the cracks, enough petrol, whisky and aspirin to make a good job of it. But something held him back. What was that something? Was it hope, stupidity, instinct? He drew a hand through his hair, felt the ever-widening track running along the centre of his skull. Ordinary would have sufficed. He'd never hankered to look like Gregory Peck or Rock Hudson, hadn't wanted to be a spectacular specimen of masculinity. Something along the lines of Fred Astaire without the fancy footwork would have sufficed, an acceptable face and body, nothing remarkable. Oh, but feeling sorry for himself was becoming a hobby rather than a habit.

When she had rubbed the life back into his hands, he had felt so much joy, a glimmer of hope. She could have shot him then, after touching him. 'I can't carry on here,' he told the wall. Pictures of himself, Theresa and Jessica plagued his dreams while he slept and when he was awake. There was no future for him here, in Bolton. A fresh start was required, somewhere too far away to pop back for a day trip. America or Canada, perhaps. He had the money to begin a new life, must summon up the energy to match.

His stomach rumbled, reminding him that matters mundane must be attended to. Appetite or no, a man needed his fuel. He rose, walked to the window, looked out on a grey, wintry garden. Across the road, lights blazed in a house where a family talked, played, listened to gramophone music. Everything outside underlined the deathly silence in his own house, the home in which he had been born, where his mother had died, where his father's body had rested before burial. Yes, this was a moribund place. It was time to investigate pastures new.

Theresa Nolan's front window overlooked a fairly busy main road with some council houses on the opposite side. She liked Tonge Moor Road. It was decent without being posh, lively without being overly busy. There was a little garden under the window, a few flower-beds bordering a minute square of grass. In the summer, there could be marigolds and busy lizzies, perhaps a few geraniums if the weather held up. In the summer, Theresa would not be here . . .

He put a hand on her shoulder. 'It's our only chance,' he said softly.

She noted the 'our', put up her hand and clung to his fingers. Still facing away from him, she continued to watch this little piece of the world, Jessica's place. 'Maggie will look after her,' she said.

'Of course she will.'

A number 45 bus travelled towards Harwood, its lighted windows misted by warm exhalations against cold glass. The policeman who lived across the way closed his gate and went inside, the pointed helmet tucked beneath an arm. Four or five children whooped their way down Tintern Avenue, a dog skipping along behind them.

'You mustn't worry,' Stephen advised. Her hair smelled of springtime. 'Worry will make you ill.'

Switzerland was such a long way from home. She had been across to the library, had studied travel books. It was a beautiful country: clean, dramatic.

'And your . . . differences with the three men seem to have resolved themselves.'

Maggie had been so pleased. In fact, she had laughed for hours when told the tale of Roy Chorlton's humiliation. For Theresa, the whole thing had been an anticlimax, because the strong feelings she had held for over a decade had evaporated at the sight of that naked, vulnerable man. With the second dead and the third in prison, there remained no axe and no grindstone. 'I don't hate anyone any more,' she told her lover.

He drew her close, folding his arms across the little body whose middle section could be spanned by his long fingers. Years earlier, Stephen had been the happy recipient of Theresa's first adult kiss, had made love to her. Now, he held her, but refused to express his love fully in spite of all her pleadings. She was ill, far too ill to make love.

'Will I live?' she asked.

'I think so.' He hoped so with every fibre of his essence.

'How long will it take?'

'As long as necessary.'

She leaned her head against him. For her, he had applied for special leave from his job, had provided the money for treatment, was putting his life on one side in order to travel with her and remain near her for a while. 'I love you, Stephen,' she said. 'I loved you before Liverpool.' She needed to stay alive for him, for her daughter. The thought of a premature death suddenly angered her, though she had accepted for years the inevitable shortness of her time on earth. Now, with so much to hope for, she resented her body's weaknesses.

'They make marvellous clocks and chocolate,' he told her. 'And the views are breathtaking.'

'Breathgiving would be better.'

He laughed. 'There's plenty of air, believe me.'

After Stephen had left, Theresa stayed for a while in the quiet darkness of Jessica's front room. She listened to Maggie, who was bumbling about in the kitchen, probably putting together another batch of her famous soda bread, then she heard the large-footed puppy padding about after a ball. She watched the neighbourhood as it quietened towards night, saw the evening-shift mill girls walking home after four hours of sweat followed by ten minutes on the bus. The old lady next door clattered milk bottles; the library lights went out; a man whistled his way home from the pub.

The door opened. 'Mam?'

Theresa turned. 'You should be in bed, love.'

Jessica pushed the door home, then sat on the blue, second-hand sofa. 'I want to ask you something.'

Theresa felt the question before it arrived. She steeled herself, dropped into a fireside chair, waited.

The little dog sat, looking as if she, too, awaited answers.

'I need to know who my dad is,' said the twelve-year-old child.

In that moment, the whole of Theresa's life dashed through her head, a fast-moving film on sticky reels that created stills from time to time, photographs which stuck for a second or two before whizzing on at a silly speed. Like a drowning woman, she had to view it all.

'Mam?'

She was small and her mother had just died. Older, she listened to her father's ravings, to Ruth's verbalized black hatreds; she saw her rapists moving towards her. What had happened to her basket? Why hadn't she recalled the basket before? There had been bread in it, bread she had given away, then the empty basket had gone missing.

'Are you all right, Mam?'

'Yes, I'm just . . . Give me a minute.' The mill, spools turning fast, rings spilling, cops in a skip, the stench of oil and human sweat, ninety degrees and no shade. Fainting, being told to go home; that little job in the paper shop, weighing sweets, putting toys in the window, marking the newspapers for delivery. The munitions canteen, dinners for those who made murderous weaponry; then Jessica, sweet, hungry, needful.

Sanatorium, Stephen; living at the Mersey's edge, Maggie, the girls; a house for Jessica, three thousand in the bank until she became old enough to manage her own affairs, Maggie living here . . .

'Cousin Irene says you were raped.'

Theresa's heart beat rapidly. 'There was . . . Yes, that did happen,' she answered.

468

'So you didn't want me?'

'When I saw you, I wanted you.'

Jessica sighed heavily. 'What is the name of my father?'

It had to be Roy Chorlton, Theresa told herself silently. He had been the first. One of the others was dead, one in prison. And Chorlton was now a strangely decent man. Were she to choose a father for Jessica, it would have to be Chorlton. Nevertheless, the easiest route had to be followed now. 'The man who was your father is dead.'

'In the war?'

Theresa's next lie was a simple nod of her head. Lying was so, so easy. She moved across the room and put an arm about her daughter's shoulder. 'None of this was your fault. Out of a bad thing, the finest thing came. You are the best person in my life, the sweetest child and the most wonderful friend.'

'I'll miss you, Mam.'

Jessica's questions about her father's identity had probably arisen out of sudden insecurity, Theresa thought. 'I will be back. It's only a rest and fresh air.' It was slightly more complicated than that, but Jessica did not need the full truth.

'Can't you get better up at Williamson's?'

'It would take longer.'

Leaning against her mother's shoulder, Jessica blinked away the selfish tears. Poor Mam had to go away to a foreign country where no-one spoke much English. The mountains were always snowy and so bright that they were almost blue. It was a pretty prison, prettier than Williamson's, but Mam would still be jailed.

Theresa felt her daughter's breathing as it slowed

towards sleep. The danger was passing; the questions were finished.

'Mam?'

Oh, no. Not again. 'Yes?'

'What was his name?'

'I don't know.'

'I wonder whether he had another daughter, one who looked like me. Still, we can't find out now. It's too late.'

The fire dwindled. Maggie came in with a cup of tea, saw the two of them together, a strawberry-blonde head resting against a mop of paler, golden hair. Feeling like an intruder, Maggie backed out and took herself and Sheba back to the range.

She picked up her beads, kissed the crucifix, blessed herself. Beginning her own private novena, Maggie Courtney prayed for the twins, for their mother who had to travel towards a half-promise of a future, for herself, for Eva and Jimmy. She even prayed for Theresa's sister, Ruth, whose wickedness was renowned. Maggie offered up thanks for the Walsh brothers, for Stephen Blake, for all those sent by God to iron out the paths of Theresa and Jessica.

'Bless us all,' she begged. 'Bless the man in prison, the one he killed and the one who remains. Amen.'

She stared into the fire, moving only when the clock showed ten. It was time to get mother and daughter to bed, time to set the table for tomorrow's breakfast. Whatever happened, whatever befell mankind, daily rhythm and ritual must continue.

SIXTEEN

Teddy Betteridge took his own life in May 1952. He hanged himself in prison and was buried within its grounds.

Maggie read the reports, cut them out and saved them for Theresa. She considered posting them, but decided against it. Theresa was fighting for her own life; there was no point in worrying or exciting her about the demise of a man who had abused her. Maggie said her beads for the suicide and discussed the event only with Eva. Jessica thrived; beyond that, nothing was allowed to matter.

Jessica found that life without Mam was not quite as bad as she had expected. For a start, there was Sheba, an Alsatian whose humour and gentleness combined to make a wonderful companion for her young mistress. After early teething troubles involving a certain amount of destruction, Sheba became dignified indoors, a raving lunatic in the fresh air. Her devotion to Jessica was obvious, though the young bitch had a soft spot for Maggie, the bringer of food.

Jessica had probably got used, over the years, to being motherless, yet it was Maggie Courtney who made the biggest difference this time. Auntie Eva was lovely, but Maggie was imaginative, colourful and very funny.

She taught her charge how to knit, sew and crochet, but none of this was boring, because the Irishwoman told hilarious stories throughout the lessons, tales of leprechauns, drunken uncles, a priest with an unfortunate lisp, the nun who kept walking seven miles in an effort to get Maggie and her siblings to attend school.

'How did you get rid of her?' Jessica would ask, though she knew the answer off by heart.

'We let the bull out. Sister Imelda ran off like an overweight crow trying to get off the ground. Have you ever seen a nun leaping over a stile?'

'No.'

'That's just as well, because it was a desperate, mournful sight, so it was. And didn't she get stuck halfway over? Flapping away, she was, with her wimple up her nose and the head-dress off up the lane somewhere. She never came again.'

'I'm not surprised.'

The other thing was that the items designed and created by Maggie never turned out as expected. Had the goal been missed by a mile, then perhaps an undoing session might have been appropriate – unravelling, rewinding, starting again. But Maggie's tea-cosies had spout holes that were only just too small, handle holes slightly left or right of centre. She constructed jumpers for the unfortunate, those with one arm slightly shorter than the other, socks for folk with ill-matched feet. The coat she made for Sheba – 'It'll keep her warm in the winter' – was quickly disposed of by the dog, who, after being subjected to a trying-on session, simply dragged the offending item outside and ragged it to bits in the yard.

'This doesn't seem to fit,' Maggie would say as she forced a cosy over the teapot. 'And didn't I have it measured just right?'

Jessica loved her guardian. As spring turned to summer, the two grew closer, playing together on swings at the park, entertaining Jessica's friends from school, girls who came to share in the feasts of scones, soda bread, home-baked ham, home-made jams. All who visited were impressed by the eccentric Irishwoman who dressed mostly in purple, whose earrings all but brushed her shoulders, whose stories were an impossible mix of common sense and an almost certifiable insanity.

Postcards arrived regularly from Switzerland, pictures of chalets perched on hills, of ski-slopes, of people clothed in national dress, beribboned plaits dangling from strange, fly-away hats. 'They look like the Sisters of Charity in miniature,' Maggie would remark on seeing these odd items of headgear.

'They're Dutch,' explained Jessica. 'If you read the back, it's a festival of dance with people from different countries. See – a group of Irish dancers in daft frocks.'

'They're not daft at all. Your English morris men are what I'd call daft. And would you look at your man here – leather shorts. Ah, well. As long as some of these funny-looking folk are mending your ma, they're good enough for me.'

It was the banter that kept Jessica going. But when she was alone, or when lessons at school were boring, she thought of Theresa, worried about her, wondered when, if ever, Mam would come home. Latin was the worst. During Latin, the poor girl often had her mother dead and buried after ten minutes of declensions. Four months was a long time and, even

473

though all the letters and postcards reassured their readers, Jessica wondered whether Mam and Dr Blake might be hiding something.

Dr Blake's extended leave had been extended further. His post at Williamson's was safe, because the man had taken no holidays in five years, so he was staying by Theresa's side for as long as possible. They loved one another – of that, Jessica was absolutely certain. She would like him to be her stepfather; most of all, though, Jessica wanted her mother back in one piece, reasonably healthy and with many years of life in front of her. TB was one thing; a heart damaged in childhood was far more serious.

Since moving from Eva's house, Jessica had used buses to get to school. She took the 45 to town, then the 39 to school, walking across the civic centre to make her connection. Often, the man who owned Chorlton's Fine Tailoring was standing outside when Jessica passed by on her way home. At first, he nodded at her, then began to say hello. He was a funny-looking fellow, with eyes that bulged rather like those in the face of Toad of Toad Hall. He was smallish, roundish and his hair was black, with a wide section of white-skinned skull showing in its centre.

After a month or so, Jessica responded when he greeted her. Trained by her mother and by Maggie not to talk to strange men, Jessica began to file Mr Chorlton in the 'not strange' compartment. He was just a nice, ordinary chap who spoke to people as they passed by his shop. He wasn't always there; sometimes, he would be inside helping people to try on jackets or pick out shirts. Even then, he would wave at her through the window.

The weather grew warm as Bolton Holidays

loomed. Jessica's school did not observe the local wakes fortnight – the girls at The Mount worked right through to July, then took a long rest until September.

When the Holidays arrived, the mills closed, and the town was quieter, almost deserted at times. Her relationship with Mr Chorlton began in the second week. He took to sitting outside with a small table on which was placed a jug of lemonade, real lemonade with fruit floating in its depths. Another chair arrived, and Jessica found herself quenching her thirst in the company of this quiet, rather sombre man. They talked about the weather, about how crowded Blackpool, Southport, Morecambe and Rhyl would be, about the lack of trade, about Latin.

'You'll need it for university,' Roy informed her. 'One ancient, one modern, a good mark in English and in maths.'

Jessica laughed. 'I've never got past *Julia ad oram ambulavit*. I mean, who talks Latin?'

'Priests – the mass,' he answered.

'That sounds different. It's like another language all over again. Anyway, I shan't need it, because I'm going to teacher-training college. I'd like to work with young children.'

He thought about that. 'You could do worse. Getting children to read and count must be very rewarding.'

Jessica decided that Mr Chorlton was all right. He treated her like an adult, as if her ideas counted.

'Where do you live?' he asked on the Thursday.

'Tonge Moor Road.'

'With your parents?'

She shook her head. 'My mother's in Switzerland trying to get strong. My dad died in the war, so I live

475

with a lady called Maggie. She's Irish and very funny.'

So Theresa had consigned him to a coffin. Was this his daughter, though? Could the seed of such a hideous man produce the fresh loveliness of Jessica Nolan? She looked like her mother. She didn't favour Hardman or Betteridge, either, so Theresa's genes must have made the larger contribution in the creating of Jessica.

'Thank you for the drink,' she said. 'I was very thirsty.'

He took the plunge, though he had no intention of swimming at the deeper end. 'You know, I think I remember your mother. She used to work for a short time in a newspaper shop, then in a canteen at the munitions factory.'

'Yes, that's right,' she answered. 'But with being ill when she was little, she hasn't been able to do really hard work. That was why she went to Liverpool, because the job was easy.'

'She's a lovely lady,' he said.

'Yes,' answered Jessica. 'I wish she'd get well and come home.'

When his possible daughter had made her way towards the Trinity Street bus station, Roy took himself and his furniture back into the shop. The place was so empty that the chairs echoed when he put them down. A few items of clothing remained, a dozen shirts, a rack of ready-made suits marked down for clearance, some socks, underwear and ties.

Canada. Or New Zealand, perhaps. At home, he had books galore about these two beautiful if rather differing countries. Canada was huge, wonderful, with cold winters and summers that played fair in most parts. The English were often cheated, because

476

seasons were sometimes difficult to define, each blending into the other, each producing grey skies and drizzle. In the climate of Britain, there were few dramas.

Then there was New Zealand, smaller, back-to-front, with Christmas in the heat, New Year spent in the garden or on a beach. So green, so clean, an idealized version of the British Isles. Of the two places, he currently favoured the Antipodes.

He would perhaps buy some sort of business at the other side of the world: he was playing with the idea of a small restaurant. Everyone had a God-given talent, he supposed, and his was the ability to make a good meal and to improvise successfully when cooking.

He locked and bolted the door, then carried the jug of lemonade through to the workroom. Sewing machines and other tools had been sold; his workers had placed themselves elsewhere and the lease had been taken by a man who intended to sell shoes.

Roy sat down and drank the last of his lemonade. He would miss Jessica. She was his nearest, most certainly his dearest. As for her mother . . . He looked round the area in which she had tended him that night, gazed at the chair she had used, at the door she had locked, bolted, then unlocked. 'Just a few more steps,' she had said.

Bolton was his home. Lancashire had been his lush, green playground, the place where he had walked as a child, the area which would pull at his heartstrings for ever. The moors, the farms, little villages of stone cottages, the lake at Barrow Bridge, the town with its bustle and noise. Yet he had to go.

'I can't stay,' he told a drinking glass. 'I would try to claim her eventually.' He must never tell Jessica that he believed himself to be her father. Desperate for someone of his own, he might weaken in later life, might say words that would hurt so many people.

There was no-one else, no chance for him here. Perhaps some woman from foreign parts might take pity on him, marry him, nurse him into his dotage. As for his friends in Bolton, both were now dead. Ged Hardman had bled to death in the King's Head; Teddy Betteridge had strung himself up with bed-sheets while remanded in prison. Roy was the only one remaining of the King's Head trio. Since the night of Ged's death, Roy had not entered that pub, preferring to drink alone in his large, empty house.

He rinsed jug and glasses, leaving them to drain. Tomorrow, the clearance sign would go up and he would sell off the few remaining items, leaving no reason for him to return to the shop. If he really was going to emigrate, he would need to empty the house and leave the shell in the hands of agents.

A loud hammering at the front door made him freeze. He glanced at his watch and realized that he had closed rather early. After drying his hands, he went to let in his customer.

Dressed almost exclusively in purple, Maggie Courtney pushed the man to one side and entered the shop.

'May I help you?' asked Roy.

She slammed a deep-mauve dorothy bag onto a plate-glass counter. 'I'm Maggie Courtney,' she announced. She was in high spirits, completely ready for the fray. 'And I want a word with you. Several words, in fact.'

Temporarily confused by the accent and the sheer colourfulness of his visitor, Roy awaited further explanation.

478

'What game are you playing?' she asked.

'I beg your pardon?'

'Well, you'll not get it. There's no pardon granted to the likes of you, Mr Chorlton.'

He took a step away from her. 'I don't understand—'

'Indeed, and nor do I. You shouldn't be accosting young girls on their way home from school. Not with a reputation like yours.' She tried to envisage him naked and on the run from Theresa, socks up to his knees, his little legs dashing away from that pearl-handled gun. Having seen many men without their clothes, Maggie was not impressed by her imaginings in this particular case.

'You mean Jessica, I take it?'

'Exactly. If you have any notions in your head, clear them out now before I pick up a broom and do the sweeping for you.'

Roy Chorlton found himself backed up against one of the counters. He mopped his brow with a handkerchief and wondered how he might explain himself. This woman in her purple dress, purple cardigan and gaudy make-up was truly terrifying. She made Lillian Hardman seen a quiet soul, Theresa Nolan a gun-toting angel. 'I'm leaving the country,' he achieved finally.

'Now, isn't that the best news for a decade or more? With the other two dead and gone, you'd be the only rapist left.'

He felt heat arriving in his cheeks.

'That child is not yours, Mr Chorlton.'

'But I didn't mean—'

'She's Theresa Nolan's daughter, nothing less, nothing more. She has been nurtured and cared for by Eva Coates and by me, because her mother has never been well enough. The rapes took away any chance of good health, because she didn't care about herself after you had used her. Stay away from that child.'

He nodded.

'Was that a yes?'

'Yes.' He would have agreed to almost anything to be rid of this person.

Slightly mollified, Maggie took a closer look at him. 'Jessica is nothing like you. She's like her mother, the Lord be praised.' He was uglier than sacrilege. 'So. Why did you start talking to Jess? She tells me everything, you see.'

He gulped. 'Just lately, when she was passing, I started to say hello. I'm going to Canada or New Zealand and I wanted to . . . To be honest, I have no sensible answer to your question.'

Maggie understood. She also understood Theresa's newborn near-pity for this unfortunate creature. It was a terrible thing to be born into a world in which your own kind would have no time for you. Looks should not matter, but they did. Artists through the ages had produced wonderful images: paintings of Adonis, statues of David, all kinds of beautiful men and women. And here cowered a gargoyle. 'Well, as long as you mean no harm.'

'No harm at all.'

'Good. And don't talk to her again, or Theresa would have a fit over there in Switzerland.'

'How is she?'

Maggie studied the man quizzically. 'Ah, I see. She's wrapped herself around your heart. Isn't that just the pig's backside? And there you were, just a needful boy taking what was rightfully his – the body of a beautiful girl. Well, that's what dogs and cats do, so where's the difference? Then, years later, you realize that she's lovable.' Yes, she did feel a bit sorry for him. He looked like a man who had suffered and repented.

'Is she improving?'

Though she felt a sight sorrier for Theresa. 'She's on the mend, or so they keep saying. Dr Blake's with her. I think they might just settle down together when Theresa gets home.'

'Good.' He was surprised to recognize that he meant it.

'I'll give her your best wishes.'

'I really do hope she has a good life and a long one.'

Maggie exhaled slowly. She had to be getting back, because she didn't like leaving Jessica on her own. 'Mr Chorlton, I trust you'll have a safe journey.'

'Thank you.'

'And that life will treat you kindly. I think you have punished yourself for years because of what happened that night.'

He made no attempt to reply.

'Well, I must away.' She turned, stopped. 'Those men's socks – are they really that price?'

He nodded. 'It's a clearance sale.'

Maggie opened her purse. 'I'll take two pairs. They'll come in handy with my winter boots in a few months.'

Roy grabbed a handful and pushed them at her. 'Keep your money,' he begged. 'Please.'

Maggie did not need telling twice. 'Listen, son,' she said as she grabbed the free socks. 'I think I have you worked out, so.' Her experience of men spanned almost three decades. 'There are rapists, then there are men who make just one horrible

481

mistake and regret it for ever after. You don't need me to tell you which parcel you belong in. What you did was terrible, but she has forgiven you. Hang on to that knowledge and say your prayers.'

He watched her leave. Alone again, he sank into a chair and closed his eyes. But eyelids proved a poor dam against the tears. He sobbed until he was empty of emotion, just a shattered shell in an empty room, in an empty life. There was no forgiveness for Roy Chorlton, because he would never forgive himself.

Irene was laying out a Mr Thornton from Noble Street. At ninety, he had a mop of silver hair and a gentle face, the sort of face a real grandfather should have.

As she smoothed his shroud and added a little colour to his skin, she spoke to him as if he were alive. 'I can tell you're a nice man,' she told him. 'And you've worked hard, too, right up to the end.' With a small wooden tool, she cleaned the underside of his nail-tips before applying a coat of clear varnish. Irene prided herself on her corpses. They all went out of the preparation room looking a damned sight happier than when they came in. Well, most of them did. Sometimes, Irene got a body she didn't like, often a dark-haired woman with a shrewish face. Such folk reminded the young woman of her mother, a creature who had caused Irene almost unbearable pain.

Such a woman lay across the room from Mr Thornton. Irene went over to deal with her once Mr Thornton was up to scratch. She was a Mrs Entwistle, a youngish woman who had died of a stroke. Irene washed her, performed all the necessary offices, combed the hair, cleaned and painted the nails. 'One day,' she told the still form. 'One day, she'll be lying there where you are, nicotine up to her elbows, stinking of Woodbines. I bet she'll sit up and ask for one last smoke before we put the lid on.'

Irene found some hairpins to make Mrs Entwistle a bit tidier. After all, it wasn't Mrs Entwistle's fault – she hadn't asked for a face like Irene's mother's. 'You don't look like her now, with your fringe fastened back.' She applied a little more rouge, a tiny smear of lipstick. 'The worst of it is, I love her. She's me mam. I really tried to make her love me back, but she never. I was only naughty so's she'd notice me. Nobody likes me. You look a lot less like her now. Yes, you're pretty.' Irene lifted the woman's hands again, found no cigarette stains. This one had fed her children rather than her own habits. This one hadn't locked little girls in houses while she went to work. Irene forgave the lady on the table and went on to make her gorgeous.

When all her silent clients were prepared for their final journeys, Irene sat down and took her break. It was so peaceful here, so quiet. The work she did was important and she was often congratulated by grieving families. No-one shouted at her; no-one told her she was too ugly to deserve attention or affection. She had received gifts galore from grieving relatives, while several other undertakers had tried to lure her away. Even an extra pound a week from the Co-op had not tempted Irene. This was where Mam would come. This was where Irene would spend that last hour with Ruth McManus.

Mr McRae came in. Irene had taken some getting used to, because she talked to the deceased while preparing them. But that was an integral part of her talent. Communicating with her charges was one of the factors in the young woman's resounding success. 'The Wilkinsons sent you this.' He handed her a pound note. 'They said their dad looked better dead than he did alive, as if you'd ironed the pain out of his face.'

Irene smiled, the uncomely face made slightly more acceptable by the small grin. 'I talked him better,' she replied.

'Well, whatever you do, it works. I'm putting your wages up by ten bob.'

The smile disappeared. 'Co-op offered a quid,' she advised him.

He sighed. 'All right, Irene. A quid it is.' Shaking his head, he left the woman nicknamed 'the queer one' to her tea and her imaginings. Sometimes, he wondered what she thought about while she sat so composed, as still as the other occupants of the preparation room. Of her intelligence there could be no doubt. She could calculate the cost of a funeral in ten seconds flat, was a wizard with the books, with measurements and any other task that required a level of reasoning.

He lit candles in his chapel of rest, rearranged a few flowers so that visitors could say goodbye to a cherished member of their family in decent surroundings. Mr McRae sat down to wait for the chapel doorbell. He never allowed Irene much contact with relatives. She had a way of staring at people, never blinking, seldom smiling, as if the marble eyes sought to drill right through to the soul of a person. It was her mother's fault, he believed. Her father hadn't been much use, either, having buggered off back to Ireland at the first sounding of a war siren. As for her grandfather – well, Michael Nolan had done the world a favour by dying after a dozen false promises.

The doorbell rang. Mr McRae donned white gloves and an expression of sympathy. Life and death had to go on.

Ruth McManus had been dealt a terrible hand in life. Her self-pity, carefully nurtured throughout childhood, youth and adulthood, was now in full glorious flower.

She hunched herself over the meagre fire, hitching up her skirt in order to gather into herself as much heat as possible. It wasn't her fault. Yet again, things had turned on her, the usual ill luck conspiring with those around her to cause limitless, bottomless pain. Everybody smoked in corners at the mill. Everybody sneaked out now and then to have a crafty drag on the stairs, in the lavs, in a corner of a shed when the boss was out.

But the boss had come back early. After several verbal warnings, Ruth had received a letter of dismissal. Nobody would back her up. Colleagues, some of whom had received similar verbal diatribes about smoking, had ignored her. They were glad to be rid of her, she supposed, just because she spoke her mind and didn't suffer fools. Three Woodbines left. When they ran out, she would have to go on the scrounge, to neighbours who didn't care two straws, to Irene who hated her, to shops where her poor reputation caused owners to refuse her credit.

She lit a cigarette. 'What did I ever do to her?' she asked aloud. 'She got what she needed, never went without.' Ruth was blessed with a brilliantly selective memory, a talent which shielded her, helped her to ignore the blacker days in her past.

The rent hadn't been paid. Her sisters and brothers would not take her in, neither would her daughter.

That little rat had fallen on her feet, was being praised halfway to glory because she knew how to dress up a corpse. 'Her's in the right bloody place,' breathed Ruth through a fug of smoke. 'They can't see her ugly mug, can't tell her where to get off.'

Well, where was Ruth going to end up? Down the Sally Army with all her possessions in a paper bag? She thought briefly of Eva, but dismissed the idea within seconds. Eva had pulled no punches when describing Ruth's incompetence as a mother. They all had it so wrong. Ruth was the victim. Ruth had been born one of the middle children in a huge family. After the death of her mother, Jessica, she had dragged herself up. Dad, God rest him, had done his best, but he had worked in a mill, had concentrated on his younger children and on teaching the older end how to cope. Stuck in the centre of all that, Ruth had been deprived.

Giving no thought to the rest of the 'middlers', she saw only her own misfortune. The rest had married decent men, anyway. They were all comfortably placed in council houses and . . . The Woodbine-bearing hand froze in mid-air. Their Theresa wasn't in a council house. Oh, no, their Theresa was off in Switzerland having the life of bloody Riley. In fact, the house was in Jessica's name. Surely a niece would not want to see her Auntie Ruth on the streets?

Ruth placed the two remaining cigarettes on the mantelpiece. She would get herself dressed up in her nice red two-piece, would use her last few pennies for bus fares. It was time to go visiting.

Jessica opened the door tentatively. Behind her, Sheba, who sometimes disgraced her kennel name, Roncott, Queen of Sheba, bared her teeth in a fashion that was rather less than regal. When the dog really didn't like someone, she forgot her manners and left little space for negotiation.

'Please wait while I put the dog in the yard.' Jessica closed the door in Ruth's face and went to tend to Sheba. Maggie was in Liverpool again, because she wanted to visit an old friend who had been taken into hospital after a bad fall.

When the front door was reopened, Ruth smiled, though the action seemed to cause some difficulty. It was clear that her face was happier when frowning. 'Jessica?'

'Yes?'

'Can I come in?'

The girl hesitated, Maggie's words ringing in her ears. 'Don't let anybody in,' she had said.

'Well?' The stiff smile was fading fast.

'I'm . . . I'm not supposed to let people in. Maggie's gone to Liverpool—'

'I'm not people, I'm your Auntie Ruth, your mother's sister. A cup of tea would be good.' She brushed past Jessica and strode into the house. 'Very nice,' she said, peering into the front room and taking note of the tiled fireplace, blue sofa and chair, carpet, handsome rug, pictures on the walls. 'That's a lovely tea-trolley,' she remarked.

In the living room, Ruth was similarly impressed. It was all right for some: new sideboard, decent table and chairs, a square of good carpet, some rockers, a chaise longue under the stairs. 'A bit fancy for a terraced house,' she muttered. 'Is there a bathroom?'

'Yes,' replied a bemused Jessica. Auntie Ruth was behaving like someone intending to buy the place.

'How many bedrooms?'

'Three,' was the reply. 'One for Mam, one for Maggie, then I have the attic with windows on the roof.'

'Doing well, aren't you?'

Jessica ran into the kitchen to make tea. Being near Auntie Ruth had always made her cold, almost shivery. Irene had much the same effect, though Jessica had a small corner of pity for her cousin. Ruth McManus looked as if she might be cruel, as if all or many of Irene's stories had been true. Mam and Maggie were always going on about not talking to strange people, but the strangest people of all were already known to Jessica.

'Kitchen's nice, too.'

Jessica all but jumped out of her skin. The woman had crept up right behind her, was standing so close that her breath moved the small hairs on Jessica's neck. 'Do you take sugar?'

'Aye, I do. Would there be any ciggies in the house, love?'

Jessica shook her head. 'Maggie doesn't smoke any more. She said she couldn't afford it.'

Ruth gazed round at the electric cooker, electric kettle, a little Hoover washing machine in a corner. 'Everything right up to the minute, eh? Have you got a television?'

'No.' Jessica warmed the pot and spooned in some tea.

'Have you got any money? Just for a few ciggies. The outdoor licence is open – I could go down and be back before the tea's brewed.'

Jessica lifted a ceramic cottage from the window sill. All Auntie Ruth's questions began with 'have you got?' She took out a pound note and handed it over. 'Eeh, love,' gushed Ruth. 'Your blood's worth bottling.'

Jessica emitted a breath of relief as her aunt dashed off to buy her cigarettes. What had she said about blood? Auntie Ruth seemed the sort who would take anybody's blood, anybody's anything. With her spending money all gone, Jessica sat and waited. It had taken ages to save a full pound. A nice man at the Co-op had swapped all Jessica's coins for a note. That pound had been earmarked to go towards a new summer frock.

Ruth McManus returned with forty Woodbines and two pints of stout. The stout was for her nerves. 'I'm bad with me nerves,' she explained. 'Anybody with a daughter like mine would be bad with their nerves. She's drove me mad all her life.'

Jessica, feeling very uncomfortable, offered her aunt a cup of tea.

The front door slammed. 'Sorry I'm late,' yelled Maggie. 'It took longer than I thought, Liverpool and back. Poor Ada's all wound up like a mummy, both legs in plaster, bandages on her arms.'

Ruth raised her eyebrows quizzically.

'It's Maggie's friend,' Jessica explained. 'She fell and broke her legs.'

Maggie entered. She was wearing a purple suit, purple hat, purple shoes. In the doorway, she ground to a halt. The devil's wife had arrived, then. 'Hello, Ruth.'

'I've bought you a bottle of stout,' announced the visitor.

Jessica opened her mouth, closed it immediately. She had paid for the beer, but manners forbade her to speak up.

Maggie placed her garish handbag on the sideboard. All her purples quarrelled today, each being of a shade that played havoc with the next. 'I'm off the drink, thanks,' she replied.

Jessica poured tea for Maggie.

'No smoking, no drinking?' Ruth laughed shrilly. 'Are you thinking of taking the veil?'

'If I did, I'd be a better candidate than some.' What the hell was this woman doing here? Ruth wasn't the sort to bestir herself to come halfway across Bolton unless she was after something. 'So,' said Maggie as she settled into a chair. 'To what do we owe the pleasure of your company, Ruth?'

The intruder plastered a very sad expression across her face. 'Get me a glass, love,' she asked Jessica.

Jessica went into the kitchen.

'I've lost my job,' Ruth moaned. 'I've no money and the landlord's going to throw me out.'

Maggie tut-tutted. 'That's terrible. What are you going to do?'

Ruth grabbed the glass from Jessica. 'Get me a bottle-opener,' she commanded.

Jessica left the room again. As she searched though a jangle of implements in the cabinet drawer, the reason for her aunt's visit became clear. The woman wanted to move in. As her hand closed over the bottle-opener, she suddenly felt sick. She didn't want to live with Auntie Ruth.

'Ta,' said the aunt in question when Jessica handed over the opener. Ruth removed the cap deftly, poured the stout like an expert, running the black fluid down the glass's side, topping it with a flourish to create a creamy head.

'You'd soon get a job as a barmaid,' suggested Maggie.

'I don't want to be a bloody barmaid.'

'But beggars can't be choosers.' Maggie sipped at her tea, a little finger crooked outward while she played the lady. 'A job's a job. With rent to pay and food to buy, you'll have to take whatever you can get.'

Jessica felt utterly miserable. The thought of living with Auntie Ruth was awful. Auntie Ruth's anger showed in her face. It didn't just visit her features occasionally, wasn't a temporary guest, it was more a long-term resident, a fully paid-up member.

'I thought I might move in here for a bit.'

Jessica swallowed. This was her house, her very own place, paid for by Mam on Jessica's behalf. But how could she, a twelve-year-old girl, forbid an adult to stay here?

'No,' said Maggie firmly.

Jessica's heart soared. Maggie was here. Maggie was her shield, her guardian, her saviour.

'You what?'

Maggie did not flinch. 'I'm sorry, Ruth, but we aren't able to allow that, not without Theresa's permission.'

The clock ticked. Two or three large vehicles clattered by, probably buses or lorries. Jessica picked at the sleeve of her cardigan. Ruth sat like a statue, the glass of milk stout frozen mid-air, as if the bearer intended to propose a toast. Maggie, wearing her no-nonsense face, kept her eyes fixed on Ruth.

'Who the bloody hell do you think you are?' asked Ruth.

'Maggie Courtney,' was the tart reply.

'You've no right talking to me like that. This is my sister's house, not yours. I've got rights, I've—'

'You can't live here without Theresa's permission,'

insisted Maggie. 'Just as Theresa couldn't live in her father's house without his say-so.'

'That was me dad – he wouldn't let her in.'

'And after he died?'

Ruth's eyes became harder than ever. 'He's still there.'

Maggie made an improbable sound that was half laugh, half snarl. 'Well, I never saw him. I wish I had, because there might have been someone to talk to, someone who didn't come out with a load of rubbish about spooks and how horrible her daughter is. Monty pretended to see your ghost, of course. He's a great joker.'

Jessica wished with all her heart that this argument would stop. Trouble frightened her, and she knew how colourful Maggie could be, how her speech could become as purple as her clothing.

Ruth jumped to her feet, spilling half of her Mackeson's on Theresa's new rug. 'Our Theresa's never coming home,' she screamed at the top of her voice.

For a heavy smoker, this one had good enough lungs, thought Maggie. 'I beg your pardon?'

'Our Theresa. She'll not be coming home no more. Her's been on the way out for donkey's years. Switzerland's just somewhere nice for her to die with her fancy man on the spot.'

It was Jessica's turn to freeze. For several seconds, she remained motionless while Ruth's words echoed in her head. Mam not coming back? Mam dying in a foreign country?

'You black-hearted bitch—' began Maggie. She stopped in her tracks when Jessica leapt to life. 'Jessica—' But it was too late. The sweet, well-educated, well-behaved child had just delivered a blow to her aunt's upper body, a punch that sent Ruth McManus reeling backwards onto the chaise longue. There was black beer everywhere.

'You are a very bad person.' Jessica's voice was quiet. 'No wonder Irene was always in trouble. You can't stay here. I won't let you stay.' She leaned over the woman. 'This is my house. My mother went away to work so that she could buy this house for me. She's lovely, my mother. And she isn't going to die.'

Ruth was thoroughly shocked. Few had stood up to her in years, and here she was, flattened by the one member of her family who was receiving a good education with emphasis on manners, decorum and religion. Where grown men had flinched and shivered, this girl had stepped in and said her piece.

Jessica, appalled at what she had done, fled out of the room and up two flights of stairs until she reached her attic. This pretty, oversized room was twice the length and width of the other two bedrooms on the first floor, as it covered the whole house, with dormer windows front and back. But Jessica didn't notice the pretty pinks and golds. She lay face down on the bed and sobbed. The tears were born out of fear for her mother's health and disgust with herself. Maggie's temper had been on hold. Maggie, who had a habit of speaking her mind, had kept her dignity; Jessica had disgraced herself.

Downstairs, daggers were unsheathed and getting sharper. Maggie, who had not budged an inch, said not one word as Ruth McManus struggled to her feet. Would a bit of vinegar lift the stains from upholstery? Maggie wondered. Would Jessica be pacified? Would this awful woman bugger off back to hell, the place from which she had obviously originated? But Maggie's silence was not a sign of defeat. Each woman recognized that the other was gearing up, preparing for the fray.

Ruth rubbed ineffectually at her ruined best red suit.

Maggie picked up an apple and bit into it.

'Well?' The intruder's voice was shaky.

'Well what?'

'Aren't you going to clout that little madam?'

Maggie shook her head vigorously, dislodging henna-dyed curls and a handful of hairpins. 'I don't believe in it,' she mumbled through a mouthful of orange pippin. 'See, the way I look at it is – well, if you batter a child, it grows up to be a child-batterer. I mean, look at your own case. You're selfish, power crazy and a freak. So you've made your daughter into the same thing, but probably worse, because she has a brain. God help your grandchildren.'

Ruth did an impression of a stirred-up snake, almost hissing before she struck back. 'You bloody bitch,' she spat, furious because the cleverer words had not yet arrived.

Maggie continued to gnaw at the apple, a feat made no easier by the dull edges of old dentures. 'Say what you like – you're out of here.'

Ruth hesitated. As hesitation did not form a part of her usual repertoire, she was further annoyed. Angrily, she lit another of the cigarettes provided by her niece. 'When our Theresa dies, all I'll need is to talk to the right people – doctors, welfare, our Jessica's schoolteachers. When they find out my niece is living with an owld woman with no blood-ties, there'll be a right cartload of ructions. Then I'll get her.'

'You?' laughed Maggie. 'With no job and no house? And no legal papers signed by Theresa to

494

nominate you as guardian? Not a cat in hell's chance, Ruth.'

'We'll see.'

Maggie shrugged, the movement designed to conceal panic. What if they tracked her back to Liverpool and discovered her past? 'Do your worst, and I shall do mine. I am the legal guardian of Jessica Nolan. Nothing you can do will alter that, especially once your character has been investigated by the so-called powers.'

'Just you wait,' snapped Ruth.

'Oh, I shall. Bye-bye for now. You know where the door is.'

Ruth was beside herself. The rent collector had been shouting abuse through the door, and Maggie bloody Courtney had sent a solicitor's letter to do with the guardianship of Jessica. With her hands tied by the letter's implications, Ruth was red-raw angry with the whole world. Suffering from nicotine withdrawal and a dearth of milk stout, food and coal, she was bordering on the hysterically dangerous.

No-one in the immediate vicinity seemed willing to employ Ruth McManus, which fact had delivered a blow to her ego, as Ruth saw herself as the greatest, the fastest, the most competent. She was going to try a big hotel in town, a place where she was less well known. There were no cigarettes, the tinned food was running out and the weather had turned. Although July was only half over, Ruth sat in her living room wrapped in two jumpers and a shawl.

No-one had visited her since God alone knew when. Irene seemed to have given up. She'd gone and got herself a second job collecting money from people who bought clothes and furniture through a loan club. So Irene worked a normal day in the funeral shop, then did her other job in the evenings. Irene would have money. Irene wouldn't miss a few bob, a couple of quid for bread and ciggies.

She threw off her shawl and donned her unhappiest coat, a grey thing that had accompanied her to the mill for years. Noxious emissions from Bolton's various industries seemed to have seeped into the coat, lending it a patchy, gun-metal sadness. Ruth's favourite colour was red. Like Maggie, she had a tendency to combine inappropriate shades, her outfits ranging from orange right through to burgundy, the resulting mixed marriages often turning out less than ideal. But today was a grey day, a day for looking homeless and starving.

She left by the back door in order to avoid direct confrontation with the rent collector. She wasn't herself, hadn't felt right since Jessica's tantrum. As for the solicitor's letter – that had kicked the rest of the belly out of her. She was even getting headaches, pains in her back, a bit of sciatica down her left leg.

Dodging in and out of doorways, Ruth made her way down Derby Street until she reached the funeral parlour. Irene would be round the back doing things with cotton wool and face powder. After negotiating a narrow side alley, Ruth found herself at the back door. This was locked against prying eyes and strange kids who liked looking at the dead. Irene had been one of those queer children in her time.

Uncomfortable when in the vicinity of death, Ruth tapped at the door. Irene opened it. She was dressed all in white, her dun hair bundled into a mob cap, a plastic apron tied over the bleached overall. 'Oh, it's you,' she said in her usual monotone.

'Can I have a word?'

496

Irene stepped back and made a gesture that invited her mother in.

Ruth paused, took one last, deep breath of air and entered a large room filled with the sickly-sweet aromas of disinfectants and preservatives. 'Are you on your own?'

'No.' Irene pointed out four sheet-enveloped figures. 'Mrs Hardcastle, Mrs Charleson, Billy Mayer from John Street – he were only twenty-one, motorbike accident – and Elsie Shipperbottom.'

'Elsie?'

Irene nodded.

'What happened?'

The younger woman shrugged. 'She just went to bed and died. I've not seen her death certificate. I just clean them up and pass them back to their families.'

Ruth perched on the edge of a chair. Her daughter seemed so efficient, so adult. It suddenly occurred to Ruth that she had no tangible power over this girl. Married and with two jobs, Irene seemed to be the older of the pair. 'Erm . . . I thought I'd walk down and see how you're going on, like.'

Irene whipped the sheet off Elsie and started to wash the body.

Ruth turned her head slightly so that she might avoid the sight of a dead working colleague.

'Thirty years in the carding shed doesn't half show,' commented Irene. 'Poor woman's hands are wrecked.'

The visitor bit down against a remark about Elsie Shipperbottom's hands now being beyond repair and redundant.

'I hear you lost your job,' Irene remarked.

'Aye. The house and all. I've got no money, nowhere to live and nowt to eat. There's been an eviction notice.'

Irene brushed Elsie's silver-streaked auburn hair. 'Still, you're better off than these in here, eh? This one's next address'll be Tonge Cemetery. Makes you grateful for every day, working here.'

Ruth's patience was gossamer thin at the best of times. 'You'll have to lend me some money,' she said.

'Lend?'

'Aye, that's what I said.'

Irene placed the hairbrush on the edge of Elsie's table. 'You don't know the meaning of the word, Mam.' She paused for thought. 'No, that's not true. If you lend something – and, let's face it, that doesn't happen often – you expect it back within half an hour. The whole town knows if you've not been paid back quick smart. But as for paying back what you owe . . .' Irene shrugged, her hands wide apart. 'What's the money for?'

Ruth tried not to grind her teeth. 'Food, rent, gas.'

'What about your ciggies?'

'If you can spare enough.'

Irene covered up a lady who had raised four children, a lady whose husband, crippled in a war accident, worked from his wheelchair mending shoes on a last in a cold, outdoor workshop next to the lavatory shed. Elsie had often given the neglected Irene a jam butty or a piece of pie.

'Well?' Ruth's dander was up and preparing to operate.

Irene sat down. ' "Eeh, Dad, isn't she ugly?" ' she began. 'I can see you now, telling me there were nowt to eat, but oh, you had your smokes. No shoes to go to school in, no chance of a place at the grammar school for me, because you had to have your ale and your Woodbines.'

Ruth jumped up.

'And don't start telling me I shouldn't talk to you like this, because it's time somebody did. See, I'll leave a box of food on your doorstep, because I'm not as wicked as you, not quite. But you can find a job and pay your own bloody bills, Mam. We're moving soon, going to buy a house with a garden and a garage. There's no car yet, but there will be.' Irene nodded thoughtfully. 'Here's me, refusing you ciggy money so that I can live a normal life. But you refused me living money so that you could smoke.'

It occurred to Ruth that she had spoken no more than a few syllables since arriving here, on Irene's patch. She should have found neutral territory, somewhere away from the funeral place. In this white, spotlessly clean room, Irene was queen.

'You might as well go, Mam. You know you don't like dead bodies.'

Ruth's mouth opened, but no words emerged from her mouth. She was suddenly like a dictionary with most of its pages ripped out.

Irene walked past her mother, opened the door wide and waited.

'It's all right, I'm going.' Ruth picked up her slender, empty handbag and stalked out. Just before the door closed behind her, she spun round. 'I said you were ugly because you were. And you still are. Do you keep an extra pillowcase for him to put over your head before he touches you?'

The door did not slam. It was eased home with a gentleness that served only to infuriate the outsider even further. She threw herself at the door, kicking and pounding until she had exhausted herself.

Mr McRae parked the hearse in the side alley, climbed out and came up behind Ruth. He placed a hand on her shoulder. 'Mrs McManus?'

She spun round. 'What? Bloody what?'

He studied her. The wildness in her eyes was so bright that it seemed to send out small sparks of fire. She was shaking from head to foot, and her hair, newly streaked with fine strands of grey, stood out around her face like the mane of some jungle animal. 'You should see a doctor,' he said mildly.

'I don't need a flaming doctor. I want a gradely daughter, one as'll see to me when I need help.'

Mr McRae nodded slowly. 'She's the best worker I've ever had. Irene has a gift, a very special talent. She treats the deceased with a great deal of respect.' It was no wonder Irene worked here, he thought. The preparation room was so peaceful, an ideal escape from this virago of a mother.

'But what about me? Me? I'm her mother, I'm the one who saw to her when she were little, gave her a roof, food, clothes.'

The undertaker remembered Irene, recalled chasing her on several occasions. Even then, years ago, Irene had talked to the dead, had touched them, had loved them in her own, very peculiar way. 'Mrs McManus, we provide a service for people who are grieving. They visit, come to see their loved ones in their coffins. We can't have you kicking doors and screaming, not here. Please go.'

Ruth eyed him speculatively. 'I came for money – she owes me two quid, but she can't pay me till she gets her wages off you.'

He drew a black leather wallet from a pocket, took out a five-pound note, closed the wallet.

Ruth's mouth watered as she thought of Capstan Full Strength, fish and chips, a pint of beer.

'Promise me you'll stay away,' he said.

She nodded vigorously, snatched the money and made to leave.

He grabbed her arm. 'Any repeat performances and I'll get the police.'

She ran. For the moment, Ruth McManus had all she needed. It did not occur to her to pay her back rent or to pursue the chance of work in town. She had money, so she spent it.

Back in the house where she had no right to be, Ruth lit a Capstan, leaned back in her chair and patted a full belly. She would manage. Everything would turn out all right, said her ale-softened brain. All she needed now was a decent daughter . . .

The letter arrived at the end of August. Edna, who had just served breakfast to her daughter and son-in-law, collected the mail from the doormat. 'More bills, I shouldn't wonder,' she remarked as she placed the envelopes next to Danny's cup and saucer.

He opened a gas bill, an account from a roofer, a couple of receipts. The last item was bulkier, so he poured another cup of tea before looking at it.

'What's up?' asked Pauline as she watched his face changing while he perused several sheets.

'It's from a firm of lawyers,' he said eventually. 'Roy Chorlton sold his house last month. It says he's thinking of emigrating permanently. It doesn't even tell us where he's going.'

Edna clicked her dentures. 'What's that to do with us?' she asked.

Danny laid down the letter and took a deep breath. 'He's put aside twenty thousand pounds. For Jessica.'

SEVENTEEN

The deterioration in Ruth McManus was swift. By mid-September, she was up before the Bolton bench for shoplifting and for causing an affray. Her daughter, Irene Mott, sat in court, ate a quarter of a pound of treacle toffee while listening to the case, then paid the fine imposed.

Outside, she walked swiftly away from the magistrates' court and towards the only peace she had known. But even her peace offered disquiet today, as one of her clients was a young mother and another was that young woman's child. The job was all right until it came to children. Perhaps she would ask Mr McRae to prepare the three-year-old boy. Suicides were never pretty, but this one had gassed her son as well.

'Hang on!'

Irene stopped in her tracks, but did not turn her head. It was Mam, of course. Mam, who had lost three jobs for stealing, for drinking, for slacking. Mam, who had battered a shopkeeper for trying to retrieve his own property, Mam, who had just cost Irene the price of a new carpet.

'You've got to help me, Irene.'

Irene, the rat, wanted to desert the sinking ship,

but she stopped, waited. There was no point in trying to escape anyway; the ubiquitous Ruth McManus would find her sooner or later.

The younger woman glanced down at the hand on her sleeve, saw nicotined fingers, raised her eyes until she was looking straight into her mother's dark brown irises. It worked. The hand withdrew, joined its fellow in a search for smokes. Items in the handbag rustled and rattled until they made way for Woodbines and matches.

Ruth lit up, calmed down.

'I have to get back to work,' said Irene mildly.

'Lucky for some. I've no work to go to.'

Irene nodded. 'That's not my fault.' Mam believed that the world owed her a living. She had always thought that she was possessed of some divine right to easy money.

'I've got to come and live with you. What's going to happen when I don't pay my rent?'

Irene studied her shoes for a moment, then allowed her gaze to travel round the crescent-shaped civic buildings. Finally, she gave her mother full attention. 'I've got to lay out a baby boy today. His mother killed him, just like you tried to kill me.'

'I never—'

'You battered me, threw me against doors. When that didn't work, you tried to kill who I am inside. I told you a few weeks ago, Mam, that I don't want anything to do with you. We're not going through all that again. You've got a nice little room to live in, and all you need to do is get a job and keep it. It's simple.'

'Simple? You little rat . . .'

The little rat walked away in the direction of those who truly needed her. Irene knew that she had not been a good person, that she had invested time and energy into trying to bring others down to her level of misery. With shame in her heart, she recalled interfering between man and wife, spying, sending nasty, filthy and unsigned letters. She had broken lifelong friendships, had divided neighbours, had set street against street, sister against brother, house against house. But now, strangely, the dead had taught her how to live.

Ruth stood with her mouth agape, then sat on the library steps and smoked three or four Woodbines. When her mouth began to taste like an open sewer, she made off towards Deansgate and a cup of tea. She needed to think. With three shillings and fourpence in her purse, there was no chance of paying rent, of feeding gas or electric meters, or of feeding herself.

She tapped her fingernails against a plastic table-cloth, drank her tea, smoked another two or three ciggies. Her family didn't want her any more, especially now, since her troubles. The Nolan sisters and brothers, all long married, many with over-large families, had neither time nor patience for their Ruth. Ruth was the bad apple, the one who should be avoided whenever possible. Just lately, when trying to visit members of her family, Ruth had seen curtains twitch, had listened while mothers 'shushed' their children, her nieces and nephews.

Niece. Jessica. She hadn't tried Jessica's household for a while, not since receiving that snotty letter about guardianship. Ruth worked on the erroneous assumption that people forgot after a while, that her sins would be buried beneath the layers of life's other happenings. It was Jessica's turn, she decided as she left the café.

Ruth's room was in a terraced house near Tonge Park and not far from the house in which Jessica lived with that terrible woman and a stupid dog. Ruth threw herself onto the bed and stared at a stain on the ceiling. It bore a passing resemblance to a leg wearing a long boot, like Italy. None of the furniture was her own; she had sold her dad's bits and pieces for a measly twenty quid, that lovely dresser, the sofa, rockers, tables, beds.

Here, she had the use of a narrow bed that sagged in the middle, one easy chair, a rickety table with a couple of mismatched diners, a wardrobe, a meat-safe and a sink which had to double as a washbasin. There was a shared bathroom on the floor below, and the whole house stank of boiled vegetables and fatty bacon.

She was fed up. Just a few months ago, she had lived in a decent house, had held down a job in the carding shed. Now, she was reduced to a smelly bed-sitting room in a place that housed people who were practically vagrants. Her next-door neighbour, an Irishman of indeterminate age, with a beard that looked like a matted carpet, was wont to sing all kinds of maudlin songs right through midnight and into the early hours. Ruth didn't know how to deal with him. Not long ago, she would have flattened him with a word, a glare or a crack with the yard-brush, but uncertainty had taken hold. She was losing her grip.

There was a hole in one of her curtains. The view wasn't worth looking at, just a back yard complete with dustbins, a clothes line, a brick shed that used to house a lavatory. Across the cobbled alley, another row of houses blotted out the sky, chimney stacks poking their noses upward and emitting smoke of various shades. Then, on top of all the other pro-blems, there was the gas cooker, which had a mind of its own. Mottled blue in colour, it squatted on bent legs next to the sink and had two settings: too low to cook, and too hot to manage.

This was not meant to be. She should have been a grandmother by now, ought to have had a decent husband, a couple of gradely children, three or four grandchildren. And what did she have? Nothing. Just frayed curtains, threadbare rugs and an oven that fought back.

She sat up, lit a cigarette. Irene had moved into a two-bedroomed house on the road to Harwood. It was a semi-detached with gardens front and back, room for a garage, a nice, Accrington-brick finish, leaded bay windows. Irene didn't need her mother any more. All through childhood, adolescence and into adulthood, the girl had been Ruth's shadow, looking for attention, depending completely on her sole parent. Even when newly married, Irene had sought out her mother at least three times a week. 'She's got past herself,' Ruth said through a perfect smoke ring. 'A long way to fall, so she'd best watch out.'

The clock on the mantelpiece showed a quarter to three. It was an alarm with greenish fingers that glowed in the dark. Because it would not work in the correct, upright position, it lay on its side like a drunk after a heavy night. She could not stay in here. There was a cleaning job at the Starkie pub, so she would wander up Thicketford Road, have a look at the landlord and then make her way to Jessica's house. After all, even bad luck had to run out at some stage.

'I thought you were leaving the country.' Danny Walsh looked Roy Chorlton up and down. 'That's what it said in the letter, anyroad.'

Roy shuffled on the spot. 'I just wanted to make sure that the money was safe and that it would be accepted.'

Danny raised a shoulder. 'How should I know? As guardians, me and our Bernard and the others will hold onto it, but Theresa might not want it.'

'It isn't for her. It's for my . . . for Jessica.'

Danny put down his skinning knife and glanced about. There weren't too many customers hovering, not at this time in the afternoon. He lowered his voice. 'You think she's yours, then?'

Roy shook his head. 'No, she's Theresa Nolan's. I just couldn't go off without making sure that I'd done all I could.'

Danny felt a bit sorry for the chap. His two best mates were dead, and he was not the sort of man who attracted women. For a split second, Danny played with the idea of mentioning Katherine, but he dismissed it instantly. Bernard would not approve. As for Liz – well, the whole of Bernard's life had been dedicated to keeping Liz in blissful ignorance. 'When do you go?' he asked.

'In a few weeks.'

'Where to?'

'I'm off to New Zealand. It looks so clean, very fresh, a bit like England, but so much prettier. They've given me the all clear to open up a little restaurant in Hamilton. It's not a huge town, not by our standards, but people have to eat and, though I say so myself, I'm a bit of a dab hand in the kitchen.'

Danny waited. There was obviously more to come.

'Will you write to me?' the man asked.

Danny's reply came swiftly. 'Of course I will. I'm not a great one for letters, but I'll let you know about

Jessica. Don't worry, because there's a few of us keeping an eye on her.'

Roy nodded thoughtfully. 'Do you know how Theresa is?'

'No. She's still in Switzerland with Dr Blake. It's the TB. When she went off like that to Liverpool, she risked her life, you know.'

Roy knew all right. He knew that she had almost died in childhood, that the damage to her heart had not been improved by rape and childbirth. She had fought for money from the three putative fathers, had developed tuberculosis, had worked in Liverpool for the sake of her child. 'She's a wonderful woman.'

'Aye, she is,' answered Danny.

'If I could go back in time . . .' Roy's voice faded away.

'We'd all do things differently given half a chance,' said Danny.

Roy inhaled deeply. 'She got hold of a gun, you know. I think she wanted to shoot holes in all three of us, but Ged was already dead and Teddy Betteridge was in prison. He killed himself a few months later. So I was her only target.'

'Good God,' exclaimed the fishmonger.

'She dealt with me very well. It was an unforgettable experience, to say the least. And I'm still alive and kicking.'

Danny noticed that the man was almost smiling. 'She had her moment with you, then?'

'Frightened me halfway to hell,' replied Roy. 'And I don't blame her, not one jot.'

The men shook hands, then Danny watched as Roy Chorlton walked out of his life. From the back, he looked about sixty, and tired – not quite finished, but well on his way.

'Oi,' yelled a customer. 'Are you selling that plaice or saving it for the museum?'

Danny eyed the old man, an adversary for many years. 'Here,' he said, throwing two plaice onto a sheet of paper. Deftly, he folded the parcel. 'Have these on me.'

'Bloody hell,' exclaimed the man. 'What's the world coming to?'

'Not another word,' warned Danny. 'And no heart attacks, please. I can't be bothered with ambulances and the like, so hop it.'

The old man hopped it.

Roy parked his car at the top of Scafell Avenue and sauntered down Tonge Moor Road. He was a free spirit; there was no shop to run, his house was sold and he was able to wander wherever he chose. Often, he chose Tonge Moor Library. Not because Jessica Nolan might be an occasional visitor, he told himself repeatedly, but because it was quieter than the big central library.

Just beyond the squared-off area where librarians lurked, there were tables on which were spread all the national and local newspapers. Beneath the terrifying glare of an almost female staff member, Roy perused *The Times*, often glancing up to stare back at the tweed-clad, iron-haired monster who presided over the building. Behind her, revolving doors admitted other rate-payers who had the effrontery to read within the dragon's sphere.

His heart leapt ridiculously when the child walked in and offered her book for exchange. The Evil One grabbed the volume, searched for marks and scribbles, studied the date stamp in case a penny might be owed. This woman would not have looked out of place had she stood in the proud and perfect ranks of Hitler's SS.

Jessica saw him, remembered chats and lemonade, ran to him. 'Hello,' she said.

The librarian's face became uglier.

'Hello, Jessica.'

'Silence!'

Jessica giggled and went off to find another book. Roy folded his paper, leaned back in his chair and played a staring-out game with the hideous keeper of the word. Anyone would think that she owned the books, that she had written, edited, printed and published the damned things. Reading was a source of information and pleasure; a right, not a privilege. This was not a free service; patrons paid their dues in rent or in rates.

She glanced away. Roy congratulated himself silently. Until recently, he might have cowered beneath such withering looks, but the throwing off of shackles seemed to have given him new confidence. He had made the right decisions at last. His only regrets embraced two people, one of whom was taking a rest cure in Switzerland while the other, behind a pair of glazed doors, was picking out a book to read.

Roy decided that the gargoyle in no-man's land was probably a Beryl. There was a Beryl in every workplace, an officious, self-righteous creature whose sense of self was defined by her job description. Not all Beryls were female; Roy had, in his time, been a Beryl, had cursed his tailors and cutters for a crooked seam, a bit of fabric wastage. His father, Maurice, had definitely been a Beryl. Why Beryl? he wondered. Why not Edna or Frances? Then he remembered Mrs Foster. Mrs Beryl Foster had been the Chorlton housekeeper many years ago, had ruled the house with an iron fist clad in a feather duster. So that was why his subconscious had landed on that completely innocent name.

Still musing, he stared at his feet, waiting for Jessica. The woman behind the counter was furious. Roy was taking up a chair and he was not reading. He wondered where she kept the sackcloth and ashes.

At last, Jessica emerged, a triumphant grin plastered across her face. When the stamping and card-filing ceremony was completed, Roy followed the girl outside, pausing in his travels to growl at the tight-faced librarian. One day, there might be a riot in this branch, because everybody hated her. Perhaps he should organize a petition before leaving for new pastures.

They sat side by side on the wall. 'I got it,' she cried happily. 'The book I wanted.'

He told her about New Zealand and she told him about Auntie Ruth. 'She wants to take me to live with her,' said Jessica. 'She says that my mother will die, then she'll get me.'

'Why does she want you?'

Jessica considered the question. 'Because she thinks Irene's ugly and she thinks I'm not. She's been in court for stealing. Maggie keeps the doors locked, because we think Auntie Ruth came one day when we were out and stole fourteen shillings and sevenpence.'

'Oh dear.'

Jessica raised her library book. 'I hid this one and Miss Atherton didn't find it,' she explained. 'You can only get one book each day so, if you find two, you try to hide one behind another row. So it's there next time. She didn't find it. *Swallows and Amazons*.'

Roy scarcely heard the child. He was still thinking about Ruth McManus, whose reputation was depreciating by the day. If Theresa died, would that dreadful aunt have a claim on Jessica?

'Colin Duckworth did a wee in her wellies,' Jessica was saying now.

'I beg your pardon?'

Jessica jerked a thumb over her shoulder towards the library. 'Miss Atherton, the librarian. When we had the bad weather, she left her wellingtons in the lobby and Colin did a—'

'My goodness.' It looked as if the local children would see their day with the ogress inside. He switched thoughts, returning to the unpalatable subject of Ruth McManus. 'Doesn't your cousin Irene work with the undertaker?'

Jessica nodded. 'She likes dead people. My mam said it was because Auntie Ruth always screamed at Irene and the dead ones don't scream.'

'I see.' And he did. Lately, Ruth McManus seemed to have fallen off her rocker completely, stealing, clouting shopkeepers, getting herself sacked, evicted, written about in the *Bolton Evening News*. Surely such a woman would not be allowed to raise Jessica?

'There she is now.' Jessica pointed out a figure hurrying along on the other side. 'I suppose I'd better go home, because Maggie might start. She doesn't like Auntie Ruth.' Jessica jumped off the wall and dusted herself down. 'I hope you'll be happy in New Zealand.'

He wanted to embrace the girl who probably had his blood in her veins. Instead, he shook her hand and wished her success in all she undertook. She walked away, leaving in her wake a man she did not truly know, a man who had divided his assets with her, who had invested in her prospects.

Inside the house, Jessica put down her library book in the hallway and entered the living room. She only had to follow the sounds to know that the two women were in the back of the building.

'I'm moving in and that's that,' Ruth was saying.

'Over my dead body,' came the swift reply.

'That can be arranged,' spat Ruth.

Jessica entered the room.

'Tell her,' yelled Ruth. 'Jessica, tell this Irish witch that I'm your real auntie and that I can stay.'

Maggie stepped between the two of them. 'Do not use the child. I am in charge until Theresa returns and—'

'It's all right,' said Jessica. 'Sit down, Maggie.'

Maggie sat.

'Please go,' Jessica begged her aunt. 'There would be trouble if you came to live here.' She swallowed. 'I'm sorry I pushed you last time, but you have to go. My mother wouldn't want you here.'

'Why?' asked Ruth. 'What have I done to her?'

'It's what you did to Irene,' replied Jessica.

Ruth planted her feet well apart and placed a hand on each hip. 'What I did? What I bloody did? It was her dad that buggered off and left me to see to her, no money, never a penny off him for her keep. You don't know what I've been through, none of you.'

Maggie could not contain herself. 'We do know, but. You've made sure that the whole of Bolton, Lancashire and probably the British Isles know what a sad life you've had. Why don't you broadcast it on the BBC Home Service?'

Ruth glowered. It seemed that her level of control

was being depleted on a daily basis. She turned her back on the sender of solicitors' letters and concentrated on Jessica. 'You should see where I'm living, love. There's no proper cooker, the bathroom's shared and it's filthy. I've got a job starting Monday. It's at the Starkie, right on your doorstep. All I want is a bed and a butty for a couple of nights.'

Maggie simmered, heated up towards boiling, but managed to keep her lid on, just about.

'No,' said Jessica quietly.

Maggie's heart leapt; Ruth's jaw sagged. Maggie, prouder than ever of her young charge, recognized that Jess was developing into a woman who would stand her ground. Ruth, confused, hurt and hopeless, dropped into a chair and sobbed.

'Crocodile tears,' yawned Maggie. She'd seen plenty of those before, usually running down the faces of working girls whose lives had become a little too adventurous.

Ruth continued to weep copiously.

The owner of the house, a girl with too little experience in the wiles of female adults, was perplexed. Auntie Ruth, who had no money and no proper home, was in a real state. Maggie, who had the full trust of Theresa Nolan, was in charge. Jessica glanced from one to the other.

'Don't give in,' Maggie pleaded. 'Remember the fourteen shillings.'

'And sevenpence,' added Jessica vaguely. And the pound had not been repaid, either, the savings for a new frock had never been returned to their rightful owner. But Auntie Ruth was so sad.

The door burst inward. Irene, who looked as if she had just been dragged through a hedge backwards, entered the room. 'I knew it,' she said. 'I knew you'd be next.' She waved a hand in Jessica's direction. 'I had a feeling,' she continued, 'so the boss gave me some more time. I went round with food for Mam, then I caught sight of her on the way to the Starkie. When she came out, I followed her. And here she is, crying and carrying on.'

Ruth's tears dried like a shallow summer puddle beneath a flawless sky.

'Come on, Mam,' said Irene. 'You can't stop here. The only way we can all manage is if you live by yourself.'

Ruth exploded. It was an experience that would be remembered for ever by each person in the room. Firstly, she jumped up and swept everything off the table – cups, plates and cutlery which had all been laid nicely for the evening meal. Secondly, she threw herself on her daughter, raking her nails down the younger woman's face before sending her crashing into the sideboard.

Temporarily dazed into immobility, Maggie and Jessica watched while Ruth McManus kicked and ripped at her daughter.

Maggie jumped up, took hold of Ruth from behind and lifted her across the room. A pair of matching vases leapt to the floor and smashed to smithereens as Irene finally hit the ground. Ruth screamed words that were filthy, the sort of language Maggie had heard during her early career on the streets. Irene got up, blood pouring from a wound near her left temple.

Jessica, whose legs had become decidedly wobbly, sat in the nearest of the rockers. Ruth, still held in Maggie's vice-like grip, did an imitation of a beetle turned on its back, all clawing tentacles and panic.

'You should get that cut seen to,' Maggie advised Irene.

'I've survived a lot worse,' replied the shaken young woman. 'Now, you've seen her at her best. She's the one who should be in hospital, in a padded cell and a straitjacket.'

Foam appeared at the corners of Ruth McManus's mouth. Fascinated and horrified, Jessica clung to the arms of her rocking chair. Auntie Ruth looked for all the world like an over-excited dog who was whipping himself into a lather. As if reading her mistress's thoughts, Sheba began to bark underneath the window, her large head appearing and disappearing as she leapt up and down in the back yard.

The sequence of events that followed became hazy, dreamlike. It was as if a film were running slowly, evenly, but at the wrong speed. Ruth went limp, slumping forward over Maggie's joined wrists. Maggie, believing that this was a ploy to gain freedom, continued to hold onto her prisoner.

'Her face has gone funny,' said Jessica, her voice high-pitched.

Irene put a closed fist against her own bruised mouth. 'Bloody hell,' she breathed. 'Put her on the sofa – she's having a stroke.'

Ruth McManus was placed on the chaise. Her eyes, frantic and fear-filled, tried to focus. No sound emerged from the mouth, the lips seeming to be twisted into a rigid, crooked shape. Irene, neglecting her own injuries, dashed out of the house to seek help.

Maggie knelt beside the prone figure under the stairs. 'Can you hear me?' she asked. 'God, Jessica, run and fetch a damp flannel. Ruth? Can you hear me?'

Jessica returned with the cloth and watched while Maggie wiped her aunt's face. Ruth looked terribly old, terribly white. Irene leapt back into the room, Roy Chorlton hot on her heels. 'The doctor from next to the library's on his way,' he said.

Maggie looked up, saw a man who should not have been there, felt glad that he was there. 'What'll I do?' she asked him.

'Loosen her clothes, stand back and give her air.'

Maggie unfastened Ruth's cardigan and blouse, then drifted to the other side of the room.

Roy checked the breathing, felt the pulse. The woman was hanging on, but the heartbeat was weak and erratic. He patted the patient's hand. 'Good girl,' he told her. 'Keep calm and you'll be fine.'

After what seemed like hours, the doctor arrived. He had sent for an ambulance after Irene's description of the symptoms. 'Did she fall heavily?' He nodded in the direction of shattered cutlery.

'No,' answered Irene. 'But I did after she attacked me.'

Jessica stared at her cousin. There was no grief in her voice, no pain, no sorrow. Irene did not care, it seemed. Irene was so calm, so nerveless.

The doctor hovered over his patient like a black bird of prey, as if waiting for the moment when he could fall upon a newly deceased animal. Jessica, suddenly missing her mother more acutely than ever, blinked back the tears. Maggie fingered a rosary in her apron pocket, repeating in her mind words of ancient prayers, pleas she had learned at her mother's knee almost half a century ago. Roy stood well back, in the kitchen doorway, observing the grief in his daughter's face. His arms ached to comfort her. With Betteridge and Hardman both dead, the identity of the original seed no longer mattered – Jessica was his. Irene picked up bits of pottery and placed them on the sideboard. Her wounds had stopped bleeding, but her cheeks were streaked with blood, as was her right temple.

The doctor glanced at Irene. 'I'll see to your injuries later,' he said.

She shrugged. 'I'll look after myself,' was her reply. 'I've been doing it all my life.'

Maggie stopped in the middle of a Hail Mary. There was a glint in Irene's eye, an expression that was not a total stranger to triumph. What was this young woman thinking? A shiver ran the length of Maggie's spine, a frozen finger trickling downward from the neck and touching every vertebra in its path. Evil was visiting the room. Evil had arrived in the form of Ruth McManus, but Irene had delivered something else into the climate, an element that had magnified and solidified the earlier atmosphere.

The Irishwoman inhaled, suddenly aware that she had been holding her breath. She remembered Theresa back in Liverpool, poor Theresa who had planned revenge, who had seemed to live simply to pay back those who had hurt her. Theresa Nolan's anger had been nothing, a pale shadow of real, malicious hatred. Hatred was here, now, in this house. It crackled in the air, bounced off walls, embedded itself in the woman on the sofa, travelled back to the patient's daughter, magnified itself, returned to Ruth McManus.

Maggie blessed herself, brushed past Roy, went into the kitchen where she retched violently until her stomach was empty.

A hand touched her shoulder. 'Are you all right?' asked Roy Chorlton.

'You know,' she said between gasps, 'we are looking at the edge of madness. God help us all.'

EIGHTEEN

Christmas loomed again, its proximity advertised by chill winds and small flurries of snow that failed to settle.

On the walls of Jessica's huge attic bedroom, postcards from Switzerland punctuated buttermilk-painted walls, while photographs of Mam stood on a chest of drawers. Dr Blake had never been home. He was working in Europe, was moving from one TB hospital to another while writing a book on the various treatments available to sufferers of the disease.

Although Mam's letters were always full of fun and promise, there was no mention of a date when she might come home. Jessica had a tendency to read between lines, and was reaching the conclusion that Theresa would never return. Being twelve-going-on-thirteen was a bind, too, because Jessica could not obtain a passport without the permission of parent or guardian. Who would help her visit her mother? No-one. So she had to sit and write falsely cheerful letters in response to similar messages.

She immersed herself in school work, gaining high marks in subjects she loved, mere passes in areas which did not interest her. Apart from Latin, geography was the worst. She stared for endless hours at lists of capitals, tried to remember the outlines of countries too far away to be accessible, places she would never consider visiting in a million years. What was the population of Calcutta? Who cared? Only the folk who lived in India might need an answer to that one.

Although her mother remained absent, Jessica was well cared for. There was Maggie, who kept house and earned money by cleaning, then Eva and Jimmy, who always welcomed Jessica into their View Street home. Schoolfriends had an open invitation to Tonge Moor Road, many staying at weekends and during holidays, most envying Jessica her parentless state, because Maggie was such a card. She sang for them, danced for them, gambled with them. Many a shilling's worth of copper was lost or gained on Friday nights in front of a blazing fire where toast incinerated itself on the end of a forgotten fork, where Maggie's scones baked in the bungalow range oven.

On an unusually friendless Friday, Jessica sat on her bed surrounded by shoe boxes. She reread her mother's letters, arranging them in order and packaging them into ribbon-tied bundles. On a wicker chair, the dog snored in spite of hailstones battering the windows. Jessica looked into the fire, an interesting construction which sat right in the centre of her floor. It was simply a hole in the chimney, a grate that could be viewed from either side of the room. It was romantic, Jessica thought, to be able to curl up and look through the fire. She imagined that lovers would like to sit here and watch flames dancing in the middle of a room. Mind, romance would soon fly out of the window for whoever had to cart the coal up two flights of stairs.

Maggie was coming. Jessica could hear the heavy treads on the narrow, steep staircase that led to the attic.

The door bounced inward. 'We'll be needing a lift,' breathed Maggie. 'I'm all of a fluster.' She threw herself onto the spare bed. 'And I wish we'd never had that telephone plumbed in.'

Jessica grinned. Plumbed in?

'I've had a phone call.'

Jessica had gathered that much already.

'From Monty. He thinks the Liverpool Mafia has an eye on him. Even though his nephew's up high in the police, he still fears for his safety.' She studied Jessica for a second. 'You don't need to know the details, just that Monty's a good man.'

Jessica noticed a glow in Maggie's cheeks. 'Are you blushing?'

'Indeed and I am not,' snapped the Irishwoman.

'You are.'

The older woman tutted her impatience. 'Whatever, Monty's coming. I said he could stay in your mother's room for now. Do you mind?'

Jessica giggled. She did mind in a way, wanting to keep the room as it was for her mother's return, but Monty was lovely and Maggie needed company her own age. 'Maggie and Monty,' she pondered aloud. 'You sound like a pair already.'

For answer, Maggie threw a pillow across the room.

'He probably wants to marry you,' said Jessica loftily. 'Although I can't imagine why.' Another pillow hit her full in the face.

'I am not the marrying kind.'

'And I won't be a bridesmaid to a person who throws things at me.' Jessica stood up. 'Come on, then,' she said. 'Let's get Mam's room aired.'

They went down to the first floor, stripped the bed, switched on a little two-bar electric fire. 'Maggie?'

'What?'

'Will Mam ever come home?'

Sighing, Maggie sank onto Theresa's newly undressed bed. 'TB's a terrible, troublesome thing, Jess. It comes and it goes, or it comes and it stays. Put the business this way, pet, if Stephen Blake can do anything at all to make your mammy well, then he will. Isn't he among all those specialist fellows? Well now, between the lot of them, they've got to come up with some ideas. She's in the best place, all mountains and lakes, beautiful fresh air and the loveliest food.'

Jessica sniffed. 'Can't I go and visit her?'

'We'll see.'

We'll see. It was always 'we'll see' and 'be patient' and 'don't worry'. It wasn't good enough. Sometimes, Jessica got really angry with people. She was young, but she knew about life and illness and misfortune. 'There's something you're not telling me.'

Maggie groaned. How many more times was she going to be accused of withholding information? She, too, had had enough. 'Jessica,' she began, barely held patience etched deep into the syllables. 'I love you more than anyone on God's good earth. I never had children, so you've got all the love I have. On your life, I tell you now that I don't hold anything back from you. On your life, not mine.'

Jessica swallowed. 'I'm sorry.'

'Ah, it's no matter. But.'

'But what?'

'If you carry on in front of Monty about him

and me being an article, you'll suffer. It'll be porridge and peas. You know how much you love porridge and peas.'

Jessica giggled. 'Can't I even ask him if he likes you a little, tiny bit?'

'No, you can't.'

'Can't I just—' A pillow flew past Jessica's head. 'But I was only—'

'Shut up.'

Jessica uttered not one more word.

Irene opened the door, allowing Maggie and Jessica to enter before following them up the hallway. It was a pretty little semi with two small living rooms and a kitchen downstairs. The front room had been given completely to Ruth McManus. Disabled by her stroke, the woman lay in a narrow bed near the window. A fire danced merrily in the grate, the flames looking incongruous in the sad, dark room. Next to the bed, a small table supported a spouted cup, a spittoon and the remains of a mashed-up dinner. There was no ashtray. It appeared that Irene fed her mother and gave her drinks, but she had obviously drawn the line at holding a cigarette to those narrow, wordless lips.

Jessica sat in one of the two upright chairs, Maggie in its twin. The only other seat in the room was a commode, a wooden item bought second-hand in a Bolton junk shop. Beneath the hinged lid was Ruth's toilet onto which she had to be helped by her daughter.

'How are you today?' asked Maggie, her tone made higher by false geniality. 'You look a bit brighter.'

The woman who 'looked a bit brighter' tried to

speak. The resulting sound was guttural and incomprehensible.

Jessica fiddled with her gloves. In the hall, three parcels containing Christmas gifts had been placed on a bookcase. There was a tie for Albert, a purse for Irene and a bed-jacket for Ruth.

Irene came back. 'I've made a brew. Would you like to come through? Albert's working, so it's just the three of us. Come on,' she insisted. 'The back room's much nicer than this.'

It certainly was. Red carpet, dark grey suite and floral curtains, pleasant pictures on the walls. A gate-legged table had been opened and set with crockery, cutlery, cakes and biscuits. 'What a pretty room,' exclaimed Jessica.

'It gets the sun in spring and summer,' replied Irene. 'And there's French windows leading out to the lawn.' Except for the accent, she might have been a middle-class lady describing her middle-class life.

Maggie sat, accepted tea and a fruited bun spread with best butter. 'Is your husband doing two jobs?' she asked.

'Yes.' Irene bit through a cake and gulped it down, grabbed for another.

The woman had been starved, Maggie reminded herself. In childhood, Irene had been deprived of love, of food, of attention. To compensate, she had married a man she could control, had made a pleasant home for herself, was stuffing food into her mouth at a rate that would result in obesity at some stage. She was dedicating her whole life to the care of her mother, had lost status and income to mind her sick parent. Food was both consolation and compensation.

Jessica gazed round the room, noted the huge difference between this and the dark space in which her aunt lay. There were no pictures in Auntie Ruth's room, and the floor was covered in brown lino. It was as if the two places were in separate houses, one new and clean, the other old-fashioned and neglected. She bit into a slice of fruit cake and kept her thoughts to herself.

'Do you bring your mother in here ever?' asked Maggie.

Irene swallowed another large lump of food. 'No,' she replied.

'It might cheer her up a bit,' suggested Maggie.

Irene shook her head. 'For one, she stinks and for another, she doesn't notice where she is.'

'I think she does,' said the older visitor.

Irene eyed Maggie. She did not brook contradiction, especially from a guest who was eating her food. 'I know what she needs. I've looked after her ever since she came out of hospital, even gave both my jobs up. It makes no difference where she is.'

'She can see and hear,' insisted Maggie.

Irene simply stared at her guest.

Maggie shivered and asked for another cup of tea.

While pouring, Irene kept her eyes fixed on the Irishwoman's face.

Jessica, aware of the tension, pointed to a photograph on the mantelpiece. 'Is that my grandad?'

'Yes,' answered Irene. 'He were a bad bugger and all, but he couldn't hold a candle to my mam.'

Maggie felt sick. She had heard the tales of this young woman's journey into adulthood, remembered Eva's words as clear as day. 'She told one man that his wife was going with the window cleaner,

526

then she told the wife a story about the husband sleeping with another neighbour. The street was practically in flames. As for Irene – she went with anybody and everybody . . .' Irene was grabbing at love, love in the shape of food, a new house, in the form of any man who would lie down with her.

Irene stuffed another small cake into her mouth. Her face, never handsome, was gathering a layer of lard over poor bone structure, making her moonlike appearance even more expressionless. She never smiled, seldom frowned, had few lines on her skin. Maggie lowered her gaze and looked at plates almost emptied by her hostess. The grim harvest reaped at the end of Irene's childhood was clearly illustrated by her behaviour this evening. 'Irene, if you ever need help with your mammy, I'll come.'

'That's very nice of you,' replied Irene. 'But I like to look after her myself. It's very satisfying.'

Maggie's spine went cold. She lifted her head and looked into eyes as empty as green glass marbles. This young lady had already paid for her mother's funeral. For years, Eva Coates had ruminated on what would happen when Ruth's body finally fell into the open arms of her daughter. 'Maggie,' Eva had been wont to say. 'That Irene's waited for ever to tell her mam where to go. I'd not want to be a witness when Ruth gets carried in at the back of that undertaker's.'

Irene's hands were steady as they gathered up plates.

'Shall I wash those for you?' asked Jessica, needing something to occupy her.

'He'll do them when he comes in.'

Maggie closed her mouth with a determined snap, told herself to lock her tongue away. The man was doing two jobs, was working like a veritable Trojan, yet this little madam had him right under her thumb. So the abuse continued, was passed along the generations like a tightly wrapped parcel whose outer layers thickened and increased with time. Would it ever unravel, would it ever finish?

The Irishwoman cleared her throat. 'Irene, she needs . . . she needs things around her, sounds, colours, anything that would stimulate her—'

'We all need things. I never got nothing off her, not even dinners.'

'So, it's your turn now.' Maggie recalled Theresa's account of her famous showdown at Chorlton's Fine Tailoring, a naked man in a chilly back yard, a pearl-handled pistol, a need for control, for equality. Hadn't Theresa Nolan said those very words to Roy Chorlton? Hadn't Theresa said, 'It's my turn'? And now, it was Irene's turn to wreak a vengeance whose taste must have been far from sweet.

'Exactly,' replied Irene. 'If we wait, we all get our turn.'

Maggie shivered again. The woman in the next room was not dead. She was worse than dead. A living corpse with no chance of managing the simplest bodily function, Ruth McManus existed in a dark brown world where she could hear, where she could see, where she could not express herself. Irene's dream had come better than true, because she tended her mother's corpse daily, spoke words of hatred and knew that her victim's chances of responding were negligible. How paltry Theresa's stab at justice appeared now, in the face of true obsession and real madness.

Jessica cleared her throat. 'I'll go and see Auntie Ruth again,' she said.

'Please yourself.' Irene shrugged. 'You'd be as well off talking to the wall.'

Maggie followed her charge into the other room. She sniffed the air, found the smells of sickness lurking beneath a liberal spraying of perfume. 'Find the bathroom,' she told Jessica. 'And a nice flannel and a towel. I'll just wipe the poor sick one's face.' Maggie waited until Jessica had left the room, then she pulled back the bed covers. These were tucked in tightly, but the Irishwoman persevered until what was left of Ruth McManus displayed itself.

Gagging heavily, Maggie staggered back.

Ruth's lips twisted, tried to mould a sound. 'Rat,' she managed.

The stench of gangrene had sent Maggie spinning towards the door, but she gritted her teeth and returned to the bedside. Ruth's body was filthy. The source of the worst smell was not visible, as it probably came from unwashed and untreated bedsores on Ruth's back. A greyish undersheet had not been changed in days, possibly in weeks. Streaks of dried faeces had impregnated the flannelette, mingling with patches of urine and food. 'You've some pain, girl,' said Maggie. Blood supplies to Ruth's back had probably been cut off, mostly because she had never been turned. The odour of dead flesh must have been emanating from that source for weeks, at least. There was not the slightest doubt in Maggie's mind – this was severe, criminal neglect.

Jessica and Irene entered the room simultaneously. Maggie swung round and faced Ruth's tormentor. 'Take those things back upstairs,' Maggie told Jessica. 'I shan't be needing them.'

Irene hovered in the doorway, her face as flat and

unresponsive as ever. 'Do you want another cup of tea?'

This, decided Maggie, was insanity at its peak, evil at its worst. Yes, Irene had been ill treated as a child, but no human being in God's world should be in Ruth McManus's current state.

'I told you she stinks,' said Irene. 'They do after a while. You can keep them too long, you know.'

'Does a nurse come in, ever?' Maggie fought to keep her tone level.

'She doesn't like anybody near her except me.'

You can keep them too long. It was clear that Irene fed her mother, yet she treated her like any of the other corpses she had handled over the years, saw Ruth as something dead, yet alive. Maggie felt a trembling deep in her bones, as if she had become the sudden victim of some neurological disorder. She didn't know what to do. If she left Ruth in this state, she would be doing less than her humanitarian duty. But, if she took on Irene, the outcome might be terrible, especially with Jessica in the house. 'Ah well,' she said after a few seconds' thought, 'you can only do your best, Irene, no more and no less.'

Maggie and Jessica bundled themselves into coats, scarves and gloves, bade their hostess goodbye, then went to wait for a bus.

When the vehicle reached Tonge Moor Library, Maggie told Jessica to get off. 'I'll be back soon,' she said. 'Go in the house, close the door and don't let anyone in unless it's Monty. You never know when he'll turn up.'

With her mind set on her immediate goal, Maggie Courtney carried on into town. It was time to get the police.

* * *

Maggie held onto Monty's arm. It was Christmas Eve and she should have been elsewhere, should have been with Jessica. Jimmy and Eva were staying for the holidays, would be sleeping in Jessica's attic while Jessica slept downstairs on one of the sofas. Monty had Theresa's room, and Maggie thanked the Lord for Monty's presence. Without him, she would have felt a sight worse.

They walked away from the bus stop, through a pair of heavy iron gates set into tremendously high walls. This was where the ill people lived, those poor, often forgotten souls who had been badly treated by life, folk who simply didn't have the strength of mind or the power of soul to cope with a world that could be forever cruel.

'Come on, girl,' chided Monty. 'We don't want to be here till Easter, do we?'

Maggie smiled at him. He was taller, straighter and younger than before. Since the trial, Monty had pulled himself together, had become proud of his achievement in helping to close down a business whose roots lay in man's need for filthy behaviour and filthier lucre.

A porter stopped them at the main door and asked to see their pass. 'Ward Seven,' he advised them. 'Doors will be locked and you'll have to knock.'

It was grim. The corridor, painted a heavy cream above the dado and a sad green beneath, led Monty and Maggie past several doors, each bearing a number. When they reached 7, they paused, drawing breath in unison before Monty raised a fist. The door opened and a cheerful nurse grinned at them. 'Going to break my nose, are you?'

For answer, Maggie gave her the pass and a covering letter.

The young, fresh-faced woman sobered. 'So you've come to see our Irene, have you?'

Maggie nodded. 'How is she?'

The nurse shook her head. 'Well, she's eating. She's eaten everything except her bed so far. And she's so . . . so calm.'

'Especially for someone who killed her mother,' concluded Monty softly.

Maggie staggered against the door-jamb. 'I should have stayed. But I thought if I faced her out with Jessica there, it might have got unpleasant.'

'You did what was right at the time,' said the staff nurse. 'This was an incident just waiting to happen. But the doctors can't work out whether she's fit to stand trial. On the one hand, she was treating her mother like another corpse, but on the other, she fed her and finally killed her. Yet she's so rational. Ask her anything about anything and she'll give you a perfectly acceptable answer. Ask her about her mother and her childhood, and she glazes over.'

Maggie nodded. 'There's a woman called Eva Coates – she's staying with us at the moment. Eva has lived almost next door to Ruth and Irene since Irene was born. She knows more than I do, so ask her. But I suppose only the doctors can decide whether or not Irene can be prosecuted as a sane person. Myself, I have doubts.'

The nurse drew Maggie and Monty into the ward. It was not an open ward. It was another corridor, narrower than the outer one, with doors along each side. 'The cells are padded,' said the nurse. 'And I must warn you that everything you say will be overheard by a doctor. Are you willing to visit in view of that?'

'Yes,' replied Maggie immediately. 'Whatever it takes, she must be treated fairly.'

Irene's room was empty except for a bed on the edge of which she was perched, a magazine in her hand. Monty stood with his back to the handleless door, an item that was upholstered as thickly as the walls. Although he knew that the nurse was right outside, he felt claustrophobic and found himself pulling at his collar.

Irene looked up. 'You get used to it,' she advised him.

Maggie sat next to the patient. 'Are they treating you well?'

The younger woman lifted a shoulder. 'Food's all right, I suppose, but there's never enough. They let me read books.' She paused, chewing thoughtfully on her lower lip. 'I never had books. Nowt to read, no toys, no food.' She was silent again for a second or two. 'How's my mam?'

Maggie sighed heavily. 'Dead, love. She died three nights ago. You were with her.'

Irene nodded. 'I laid her out. I washed her. I paid for her funeral, saved up for years.'

The Irishwoman closed her eyes, caught the scent of death in her nostrils, remembered the dirt, the panic in Ruth McManus's eyes. 'Irene, you killed her,' she said clearly for the benefit of whoever was listening. 'When Jessica and I left, you put a pillow over Ruth's face until she stopped breathing. You had been feeding her, but she was not clean.'

Irene turned her head slowly and stared dispassionately at Maggie Courtney. 'Oh no,' she stated. 'I'm the murdered one. My mother killed me years ago. I still walk about, but I'm dead.'

'Dead?' Maggie's voice, squashed by a drying throat, had raised itself in pitch.

Irene nodded. 'That was why I worked with them. I understood them and they understood me.'

Maggie allowed a few beats of time to pass. 'You killed Ruth, Irene. You took a pillow and pressed it on her face until she stopped breathing. She had been neglected so badly that her bedsores had gone gangrenous.'

'I washed her.' The tone was not defensive. 'Like I washed all the others.'

Maggie took hold of Irene's plump, flaccid hand, felt no response, no resistance. 'She wasn't like the others. Ruth was alive. You made her dinners, you fed her.'

'Yes. I was good to her.' She pulled her hand away and turned a page of her *Woman's Weekly*. 'You can go now,' she said. 'I want to finish reading this.'

Back in the company of the plump young nurse, Maggie wept quietly for a few minutes. 'She's as cracked as an old cup,' she managed finally.

'Yes,' answered the nurse. 'That's what we all thought.'

In a bed in Crosby, Liverpool, a young girl twisted about until the covers were in knots. The dream was weird, all shapes and swirls, a mountain, birdsong and a woman in white. The lady had shoulder-length hair in a pale blond colour with a tiny hint of red. She stood on a balcony and laughed as if watching a comedy act in an outdoor theatre.

The man with her was a blur, darkish hair, darkish clothes and a booming laugh. 'Jessica,' the lady said, a hand outstretched in Katherine's direction.

'I'm not Jessica,' replied a very young child. The

534

teacher came and dragged Katherine away. 'You should stay in your chair,' said Miss Brown, an expert in being cross.

Katherine, who was six again, kicked the angry teacher.

'I'm going home,' called the lady on the balcony. She floated heavenward, arms outstretched like the steady wings of a great wandering albatross. The man followed her, a giant bat outlined against an ice-blue sky.

Katherine sat up in bed, her mind clinging to the frayed edge of a dream that refused to knit together again. At least she was almost thirteen once more, not a victim of one of Miss Brown's tantrums. The other woman's hair – she had seen it before, but she could not remember where or when. The lady on the balcony had shouted a name, the name of a girl who lived on a farm. It didn't matter. Dreams came, dreams went, but today was Christmas. And anyway, men and women could not fly.

Katherine Walsh straightened her bed and lay down again. As sleep reclaimed her, a very silly thought skittered across her mind. Was it possible, she wondered, to have someone else's dream by mistake?

Jessica woke with a start. There was something different about today, something special. She was downstairs, but she had been sleeping on the ground floor ever since the arrival of Jimmy and Eva, so there was nothing new in that. She yawned, and remembered. It was Christmas Day. No. Well, yes, it was Christmas, but that wasn't the really special bit. What else was special about today? she wondered idly.

She turned over and faced the back of the chaise. There had been a dream, only she could not recall any of it. Closing her eyes, she courted sleep, but it drifted away from her on a draught of sage and onion accompanied by the clatter of utensils.

'Sorry,' said Maggie, emerging from the kitchen. 'Still, it's just as well that you're awake, because I want to use the range as well. Electric is all right, but I'd sooner have my coal oven any day of the week. Anyway, happy Christmas and would you like a cup of tea?'

Jessica nodded, sat up and rubbed the remnants of night from her eyes. Sheba barked, licked her mistress's face, then lay down again on the rug. 'Happy Christmas, but it doesn't seem right,' Jessica told Maggie. 'Having Christmas while Irene's in hospital and Auntie Ruth's dead.'

'Life goes on.' Maggie grappled with a string of sausages that seemed to have a will of its own. 'These English sausages aren't up to much,' she grumbled.

'It's in the sideboard,' said Jessica.

'What?'

'Your present.'

Maggie sniffed, picked up a sausage that had fallen by the wayside, rubbed it on her apron. 'No presents until after lunch,' she reminded Jessica. The defluffed sausage was placed in a pan with its brothers. 'That'll teach you to try and make a break for it, English pig,' chided Maggie.

Jessica sat up in her makeshift bed, sipped her tea and thanked her lucky stars. She had Maggie, that lovely, humorous lady who would give her a big hug once the sausages were sizzling. She had Monty, the wonderful old sailor who had managed to make geography interesting, who had painted word pictures of far-away places with magical names.

'Your present's too big to wrap,' said Maggie with her head in the oven.

'A bike?'

'Wait and see,' advised the Irishwoman. She stood up, pushed the dyed hair away from her eyes, opened her arms wide and demanded Christmas kisses.

Physical contact often brought tears to Jessica's eyes. She missed her mother every minute of every day, even while thinking of other things, even when playing with her dog, listening to the wireless, or doing her homework. Maggie's touch, though gentle and full of love, served only to remind Jessica that Mam was away, that she might die.

Monty came in, newly shaven and wearing a white shirt with a dark tie and navy trousers. 'They're on their way,' he announced, a thumb jerking towards the ceiling. 'She's been yelling at him for half an hour – he's lost his tie-pin, cufflinks and God knows what else. Happy Christmas.' He kissed Jessica first, then Maggie.

'No presents till after lunch,' grumbled Jessica.

Offstage, Eva's voice floated none too gently down the stairwell. 'A shave? Call that a close cut? What did you use – a butter knife? I've seen shorter bristles on a bloody hedgehog.'

Jessica laughed. She was safe. There was Eva, there was Jimmy. She had Monty and Maggie, she had friends at school, her beautiful, devoted Sheba. Yes, she had many blessings to count.

Katherine Walsh rode her brand-new bicycle up and down the Northern Road. Wrapped tightly in a new scarf and an old coat several sizes too small, she tried to come to terms with gears, bigger wheels, a taller saddle. She reached Moorside Park, turned, and set off homeward again. Mam was up to her eyes in stuffing and gravy, while Dad, newly immersed in carpentry, was testing his Christmas tool set and making a great deal of noise in the garage. With one thumb already bandaged, Bernard was also trying out some interesting language.

When the bicycle skidded, Katherine steered into the swerve, her reaction instinctive and completely correct. But the bike hit a small stone and sent Katherine hurtling against a garden wall. She had read about people seeing stars, but had never taken the meaning literally. She blinked, sat up, found herself worrying about the new bicycle, which must have cost a good fifteen pounds. Houses across the way wobbled, steadied themselves, then shook like inanimate victims of a huge earthquake.

People walking home from church hove into view. They clustered round the fallen girl, identified her, sent one of their number to fetch the Walshes. Then a path opened and John Povey bent over her. Katherine remembered that he had been invited for Christmas dinner. 'Katherine?' He placed a hand on her forehead. The girl moved her lips to speak, but her tongue felt thick and stupid. Colours merged, voices echoed, sleep beckoned.

'Katherine?'

She opened her eyes and smiled up into a beautiful face. The angel in white spread her wings and folded them over Katherine's prostrate form. There was birdsong, there were mountains poking snow-tipped crests into a sky of palest blue. 'Come home,' whispered the angel. 'Come home to me.'

*   *   *

Jessica seldom had headaches, but she took an aspirin and went to lie on Maggie's bed, well away from the hustle and bustle of giblet gravy and mince tarts. Eva and Maggie were arguing the merits of brandy butter set against the more traditional appeal of white sauce. Jimmy, after failing to find his tie-pin, cufflinks and new handkerchief, had dragged a willing Monty out to the Starkie for a pre-lunch pint. Even here, on the first floor, Jessica caught snatches of a heated discussion about flaky and shortcrust pastries. Too many cooks? One would certainly have sufficed.

She closed her eyes and spread a cold flannel across her forehead. Maggie's answers to a headache involved a cold compress over head and eyes, a hot water bottle on the stomach. 'This will send the blood away from your head and stop the pain,' she was wont to say. 'Drawing blood to the stomach aids digestion, too.' If the aforementioned remedies did not work, syrup of figs was the next port of call. Headaches, in Maggie's ever-changing book, had two sources of origin: the eyes, or the bowels. Jessica was quite lucky, as her occasional headaches were blamed on studying. Which was just as well, because syrup of figs had been known to make way for the dreaded castor oil, a curse which should never be visited upon any God-fearing child. Iron jelloids and spoonfuls of malt were bad enough . . .

'My head,' said a voice like Jessica's own, though the vowels came out a little bit squashed. Jessica walked down a street she had never seen, one of those posh places with grass verges and trees. There were telegraph poles, too, and a red phone box outside one of the houses. Jessica looked inside her little handbag and searched for a tape of Aspros.

Someone else needed the aspirin, cold head and warm tummy treatment, it seemed.

This was a special place. This was a special day. A giant seagull bounced along on air currents; it came closer. 'Hello, Jessica,' it said before flying off down the road. Even while asleep, Jessica knew that she was dreaming. Seagulls did not speak; they certainly sounded nothing like Mam. Seagulls squawked and hovered about looking for fish and scraps.

She woke refreshed, with the headache just an unhappy memory. Eva hovered with a cup of tea. 'Bossy Boots says if you don't want your dinner, she'll plate one up for you and keep it for later.'

Jessica grinned. 'I don't know why you two keep arguing,' she said. 'Really, you're the best of friends.'

Eva sniffed. 'He's arrived home medicated. Monty's all right, but my daft bugger's been at the whisky. Jimmy and whisky are not what you might call compatible.'

The girl in the bed heard Eva's words, noticed a quiver in the voice. 'Don't be upset, Auntie Eva. He'll get sober when he eats something.'

'Aye, well, he'd bloody better.'

When Eva had left the room, Jessica tidied the bed, washed her hands and began to walk downstairs. Everyone stopped talking. The cuckoo clock did its job, announced three o'clock before letting the bird re-enter its nest. There had been a bird in the dream, hadn't there? Why could a person never remember dreams properly? Why had Eva's voice shaken? Was there bad news? Why was the house so quiet?

In the rear living room, Maggie was leaning casually against a sideboard that almost groaned beneath platters of meat, plates of mince pies, an enormous Christmas cake. Eva, Jimmy and Monty were seated at the table.

Jessica looked from one to another, saw faces that were deliberately impassive.

'We've decided you can have a quick look at your present before we start,' said Maggie.

Jessica smiled broadly. There was a new bike in the front room, a red one, she hoped. 'Are you sure?'

Eva nodded. 'But hurry up. I'm that clemmed, me stomach thinks me throat's been cut.'

Jessica laughed and went off to claim her Christmas surprise.

'She's all right.' John placed Katherine on the sofa. Bernard and Liz hung back, coats still fastened, scarves hanging from their necks. 'They would have kept her in if they'd been really worried,' John added.

Liz had forgotten all about dinner, but the smells reminded her. 'Can she eat?'

Katherine didn't want food. Getting out of hospital had not been easy. People in white coats had wittered on about concussion, had taken X-rays, had thumped her knees with little hammers. Now, she had to be watched for symptoms like vomiting or falling asleep suddenly. Her bike was leaning against the table and it seemed to be in fair condition – of the two of them, the bicycle had come off best.

'I'll . . . er . . . go and make the gravy,' said Liz. Christmas had to happen. She didn't want it, would have preferred to sit with her beloved daughter, but there was a guest and Christmas was, after all, a fixed feast.

John poured sherry for Liz, whisky for himself and

Bernard. 'I'll keep an eye on Katherine,' he promised. 'You two go and do whatever needs doing.'

Bernard, who had had enough of carpentry, decided to help his wife in the kitchen. Within ten minutes, he had been expelled with a grim warning about interfering where he wasn't wanted.

The chess board came out and war was declared at one minute past three o'clock. Katherine watched and listened, smiling when her father cursed after losing a precious piece.

She leaned back and closed her eyes, found herself drifting again.

'Katherine?' Bernard's voice was full of concern.

'I'm not asleep,' she replied. She watched the angel as it glided past, its wings outstretched in a perfect line. The darker figure floated along, a guardian angel to the guardian angel. They were both going home, onward and upward.

'We're there,' said the female, pale hair streaming in her wake like silk highlighted by sunset. 'Bye, bye, Katherine.'

Katherine sat up, opened her eyes and smiled. Everything was all right at last. 'I'll have some dinner, please,' she called.

'That's my girl,' whispered a voice from somewhere else. 'Oh yes, that's my girl.'

Jessica pushed open the door and stepped into the front parlour. In an effort to conceal Jessica's gift, heavy curtains had been closed to shut out the meagre light of a December afternoon. She felt her way past the sofa, pulled back the curtains and found a red bicycle leaning against the window-sill. 'It's beautiful,' she called to the people in the living room.

She squatted down to look at bright, spoked wheels, felt the saddle, counted three gears. No-one had followed her right into the room, yet she suddenly felt someone's eyes on her. It would be Maggie, she decided, picturing the Irishwoman standing in the doorway with a self-satisfied smile decorating her face.

In an easy chair by the fireplace, Theresa Nolan allowed silent tears to wash her face. This was the daughter she had abandoned, the one she had tried not to love right from the start. A new bicycle, a nice house, twenty thousand pounds invested by a man who might have been her father. What use was all of that without closeness?

The tears slowed. Lucky to be alive, lucky to have Jessica, Theresa calmed herself. For months, she had deliberately widened the already spacious chasm between herself and Jessica. This child was so wonderful, so lovely, that she must never grieve for a dead mother, must never feel hurt. Now, here Theresa was, alive and kicking after sailing through surgery so new, so dangerous, so innovative . . .

'Oh, it's wonderful,' breathed Jessica. 'All shiny and new.'

Theresa, too, felt shiny and new, just like her daughter's bike. The TB had righted itself, but the heart had finally threatened to stop, turning Theresa into a frequent visitor at Death's dark gates.

Jessica spun a pedal, pressed the brake lever, ran her fingers along a spoke.

'Jessica?'

The girl remained perfectly motionless until the pedal stopped spinning. 'Mam?' she gulped.

'Yes, it's me.'

Slowly, almost afraid for her sanity, Jessica turned

543

and looked at the figure in the chair. She swallowed twice and remained where she was, steadying herself by holding on to the edge of the sill.

'It's really me, love. All mended, no TB and my heart's a sight better.' The child was so beautiful: tall, straight. And that hair – a film star would kill for it.

Whitened knuckles were pressed against the child's even, perfect teeth. 'You didn't die. Every day, I prayed that you wouldn't die.' It occurred to Jessica that she might still be asleep, that the bicycle and Theresa could be parts of some very intricate dream.

Unable to speak, Theresa shook her head. After clearing her throat, she managed an explanation of sorts. 'I had an operation on my heart. They sewed it back together again. I've even come home in an aeroplane. You have to be well to fly.'

'Oh.'

Theresa smiled tentatively. 'Dr Blake was there during the operation. He helped out.' How many men could say that they had literally touched the heart of their beloved? 'I have missed you so much, Jessica.'

The girl dashed across the room and threw herself at her mother's feet. 'I can't believe it. Oh, I can't believe that you're here.'

The door was closed softly by someone in the hall. For several minutes, mother and child simply held one another, sometimes touching, sometimes pulling or pushing away to examine a face, a hand, a pair of eyes, the fall of a lock of hair. They talked then about the missing months, about mountains, convalescent homes, algebra, Mother Olivia's temper, Auntie Ruth, Irene.

'Will you be my bridesmaid?' Theresa asked.

'Oh yes. Oh yes, please, Mother.' Jessica grinned. 'I'm a bit too old to call you Mam.'

'Then Mother it is.'

'When will you get married?'

Theresa shrugged. 'There's no hurry. I don't have to go at anything in a rush, because I have time. Before we went away, we didn't know whether . . . Never mind. Stephen found someone who would perform this operation.' She laughed aloud. 'Trust me to be special, eh?'

Jessica nodded mutely. Mother had always been special. 'Are you my Christmas present?'

'Yes, love. Too big to wrap, like the bicycle. I'll never know how Eva and Maggie kept this secret.' She paused. 'Just as I expected, you're turning out to be a grand girl. You've never given anyone the slightest amount of trouble. How many girls would accept the idea of a new stepfather just like that?' She clicked her fingers.

'Well,' replied Jessica, speech slowed as if by deep thought. 'Somebody has to keep him clean. And he has a lot to answer for, like making my mother talk so posh.'

They fell about in the manner of two schoolgirls with a fit of the giggles, nothing to laugh at really, yet tickled to the marrow by the sheer silliness of themselves.

The door opened softly. 'Are you two daft buggers going to have some dinner? Only my Jimmy's that starved – he's halfway through his tie.'

The result of this statement sent mother and daughter into further peals.

In the doorway, Maggie Courtney and Eva Coates clung together, each acting as life support to the other. They cried and laughed, watched the antics of the mother and the daughter.

'Like two puppies,' Eva managed.

'Exactly,' said Maggie. 'Young and happy. Exactly as they should be.'

APRIL 1965

The Corner House waited at the junction where it had sat for almost forty years. Because of its position in life, the title was correct, yet the building's frontage had no corners. Its 'eyes' were positioned where right angles were the norm, as if a pair of giant knives had dropped from the heavens to slice off the usual joints, making rooms a slightly crazy shape because of this odd positioning of windows. The square bays twinkled, each tiny oblong of leaded glass throwing off the sun haphazardly, the old, flawed panes attempting to do impressions of faceted diamonds.

One eye was closed, the other open. The winking window, created by a dropped blind, sat at one side of an arched porch, while its wide-awake brother overlooked a rose garden. Buds were erupting on almond and cherry trees, laurels continued to drop and grow their everlasting foliage, blackbirds fussed in the branches of a white lilac, tulips nodded, daffodils curled and folded their petals to make way for the gaudier emblems of summer.

Inside, a small feast had been prepared behind the blind-covered window of the dining room. Platters of sandwiches queued alongside cakes, tarts and quiches. A salad bowl rested between silver servers, while jelly and cream took pride of place. The new ones, the expected invaders, were each a quarter of a century old, yet their passion for childish puddings had not abated.

The sitting room, dust-free and contented, boasted an almost intact crystal chandelier, a collection of comfortable seats, an open fireplace and a TV. Wicker chairs with plumped-up cushions furnished a small, sun-filled conservatory. In the kitchen, a clock dropped confident ticks into near-silence. The damped-down coke oven sighed softly into its chimney; rows of ill-matched plates covered a dresser; pans hung from a pulley line.

At the top of the stairs, an oriel bay soaked up light and scattered it across the landing and down the flight. At peace with itself, the house creaked gently, waiting quietly, its breath held against a future that had always been uncertain. But they were coming. The red carpet was down, the flag had ascended its pole, paint and wallpaper were present, correct and new. Soon, soon, there would be laughter and noise.

On the erosion at Blundellsands, two men gazed across water over which Viking ships had once travelled to invade and populate the land just north of Liverpool. They turned simultaneously and walked south, each with his hands clasped behind his body in the manner of the Queen's husband.

John Povey, the already wild grey locks made crazier by a skittish breeze, took the part of pacemaker; Bernard Walsh, whose trilby had already made several breaks for freedom, wore the hat pulled so severely downward that it looked like an integral part of his facial structure. 'They might not like each other,' he mumbled. 'They could be opposites by now. Mind, opposites are supposed to attract.'

'What?' roared John, back-pedalling to look at his slower friend. He saw Bernard's lips moving, but heard nothing. Bernard's words had travelled off towards Formby, while John's hearing was muffled by mobile air scuttering in from the water.

Bernard gave up talking. Speech got whisked off in weather such as this. But his mind continued active. It was amazing, truly amazing. The twins were both teachers, were both engaged to marry teachers in June. Jessica's wedding was scheduled for the nineteenth, Katherine's for the twenty-sixth. Jessica and her fiancé had applied for jobs in Liverpool. It seemed that Jessica had fallen in love with the city years ago, when visiting her mother.

Theresa. Bernard sighed, strode over a stranded jellyfish. She had fallen asleep in 1959, had slipped away unexpectedly in her bed. Stephen Blake, OBE, renowned worldwide for his expertise in the field of tuberculosis, had found his beloved dead by his side.

John touched his friend's arm. 'Don't,' he mouthed. 'Don't think sad thoughts.'

Bernard took no notice. All in all, Theresa Blake had been a wonderful woman. She had never approached Katherine again, had lived her short life to the full in a wonderful farmhouse on the moors. Aye, she had been a good person, that little mother of twin girls.

Well, today was the day, the meeting time. Bernard wondered briefly about the forthcoming weddings. How would those two young men react when Jessica and Katherine came together? Twins were always close, even when geographically separated. The girls were both teachers of infants, members of the same union, had joined the same political party. They had marched, albeit separately, for the cause of nuclear disarmament, had taken up cudgels against fox-hunting, hare-coursing, racial and sexual discrimination. What had Theresa Nolan-as-was released into this unsuspecting world? And could those two young men play a real part in the lives of this perfectly matched pair?

The windblown walkers climbed into John Povey's untidy car. 'Poor Theresa,' remarked Bernard, vocal chords tightened by emotion.

'Stop it.' John peeled a shrivelled banana skin off the gear stick. 'She got six good years, six extra years. Without the op, she'd never have got home from Europe.'

'Katherine dreamt about a woman in the air. She didn't remember it until I told her the truth. It was her angel dream. That Christmas, after she fell off her bike, Katherine thought she saw Theresa going to heaven. But Theresa had been flying in reality, though she did use a plane.'

John nodded. 'Have you seen my car keys?'

'In your hand.'

'Ah.' The pharmacist started his motor. 'Everything will be fine, you'll see. Life moves on. Its components remain the same. In the long run, few catalysts have a truly lasting effect.'

Bernard groaned. 'Don't go all pharmaceutical on me.'

'That's a big word for a fishmonger.'

'And I've dealt with bigger fish than you.' The car stank of cats. Word had spread among the feline world, and John was inundated with the creatures. 'Have you started letting moggies sleep in your car, John?'

The chemist frowned, considering the question. 'It's not a case of allowing, not with cats. They arrive, they commandeer, they leave.' He didn't notice the smell; he was surprised when others did. 'I need to increase my order for fish heads.'

They remained stationary, each staring out into the estuary, each steeped in his own thoughts.

Katherine had taken it well, Bernard mused. In a way, she had seemed unsurprised. After half an hour of total silence, during which she had neither wept nor smiled, she had made her pronouncement. 'There was always something. She was in the woods that day and Chaplin seemed to know her. He tried to keep us together, as if rounding up a couple of lost sheep. I needed to find her, but I didn't know how to. There were some dreams . . . and I felt I shouldn't mention anything to my mother.'

Bernard had remained silent, had listened.

'The woman in the Mustard Pot was our birth mother.'

'Yes.'

'She was very beautiful.'

'And very brave.'

Bernard scratched his nose, saw seagulls swooping, diving, rising again. Roy Chorlton continued to correspond with Danny, though the letters were sporadic. He had married a widow, had reared stepchildren, had made a success of his restaurant in New Zealand. The other two, Betteridge and Hardman, were long forgotten. Ged Hardman's mother had sold the tannery, had gone abroad and married a titled Italian. Elsie Betteridge, slimmer, quieter, was the mother of two educated children and the owner of a rather smart dress shop.

Life did go on, though its components remained the same, just as John had recently declared.

'The day I told her about Jessica, Katherine just went out into the garden and threw the ball for Charlie,' said Bernard. 'After she'd thought it through.' Charlie was Chaplin's replacement. He was old now and quite stiff, but he still retrieved for his mistress. 'It was as if nothing unusual had happened.'

'Quite,' replied John Povey. 'You know Stephen Blake's opinion on the matter. He's a true scientist, ear-marked for a knighthood, yet he still upholds the identical twins theory. It's weird, yet it seems to be true.'

'Stranger than fiction,' concluded Bernard.

'It is. It is indeed.'

'Katherine flicked through all our photo albums that day. She said that Liz would always be her mother.' He missed Liz. After five months, Bernard still wept in his lonely bed. 'Thanks for encouraging me to do what needed doing,' he told his friend. 'God knows it took me long enough to speak up.'

'Let's go,' suggested John.

Bernard drew a hand across his chin. 'They both like jelly and cream.'

'And that's as good a starting point as any,' answered John.

John Povey's car drew up outside number 1, its nose turned inward, tail slewed outward. The chemist's parking left much to be desired and was invariably unparallel. Bernard had got used to John's driving, inured to the knowledge that a passenger inevitably suffered premonitions of life after death. John was John. 'Why didn't you marry?' Bernard asked on a sudden whim.

'Nobody asked me.'

'You're supposed to do the asking.'

John Povey clicked fingers and tongue. 'So that's where I went wrong. Why did nobody tell me?' The strong affection John had felt for Bernard Walsh's wife would never be discussed by him. His love had gone to her grave and the secret would go into his when the time came. He had loved just one woman, and she had never known about his feelings.

They glanced across at the Corner House. It looked so smug with its newly trimmed beard of Virginia creeper, with its shiny black and white paintwork, shaped hedges, flag flying at full mast. Bernard and Katherine still lived opposite in the semi Bernard had bought at the end of the war. The Corner House, bruised and battered until recently by a series of students, was now the property of Katherine Walsh and Jessica Nolan. They could share it, let it, sell it, use it for weekends, do with it whatever they chose.

'They'll be all right,' said John.

'I hope so.'

Inside Bernard's house, they fed Katherine's dog, had several cups of tea, tried, with a terrible lack of success, to concentrate on backgammon. Upstairs, a pair of feet padded about; the bathroom door closed; water gushed; Katherine sang.

'I know you loved her,' said Bernard when his pieces had all been blotted out of existence. 'You cheated,' he told his friend.

'I beg pardon?'

'Just now, at backgammon. Never with Liz. It's all right, you know. She never noticed, but I did.'

The dog yawned.

'The Corner House,' Bernard continued. 'So

553

much for you to give away. These are wealthy young women.'

John raised his shoulders. 'What would I do with it? The students wrecked it and. if I lived there, it would end up condemned. Katherine favours it as a meeting place, somewhere for herself, her sister and their fiancés to get to know each other.' He paused. 'When did you realize how I felt about Liz?'

It was Bernard's turn to shrug. 'It came on gradually, like a dose of flu. And it doesn't matter.'

'Neither does the house.'

'OK. Pour another cup and pass the biscuits.'

Upstairs, Katherine Walsh lay flat out in water, nose peeping through bubbles in search of oxygen. Starting with her feet and working upwards along her body, she relaxed and allowed the warm fluid to encompass and embrace her. It was like a place in one of the recurring dreams, something from another time, a time when she had scarcely existed. In that dimension, she had not been alone. She had never been alone, had always been a part of . . . of whatever.

She sat up and dropped a dollop of shampoo on her head. 'I am stolen goods,' she informed the wall. For stolen goods, she had certainly enjoyed a happy life, so she wasn't going to start complaining. With the shower adaptor, she rinsed her hair, heaved herself out of the tub and grabbed for towels.

What should she wear? Her mind flicked through the wardrobe, cast aside the Paco Rabanne copies, her famous chain-mail mini, some geometrically correct skirts and a Quantish white dress with a huge orange flower on the front. She would wear the blue suit, little make-up and her fashion boots.

In the mirror, a solemn, space-age child faced her. At twenty-five, Katherine managed to look eighteen, an asset which she failed to appreciate at this juncture in her life. Thick, wilful hair, cut severely into the nape, flowed longer onto her jawline. 'A sixties chick,' she told the reflection. Many men had remarked on her beauty, yet Katherine judged herself to be merely OK, a blank page easily improved by eyeliner and mascara. 'It's like painting by numbers,' she advised the mirror. Fortunately, her fiancé, Martin, had seen her undecorated and had not dropped dead from shock.

Today, Katherine Walsh would be smart, because she was about to meet a very significant person. But why did she need to be smart? Surely Jessica should meet her as she wanted to be, bright, breezy, plastic earrings and jangle-bangles? 'What does it matter?' she enquired aloud. A broad grin visited her face. Who was she, anyway? And did the answer to that question have any value? Liz and Bernard Walsh had done a great deal for her. As a result, she needed no framework, no knowledge of her so-called father, no point of reference. She was Katherine. She was her own security.

The East Lancs seemed to be the longest road in the world. Slowed by traffic through Leigh and Lowton, Stephen Blake picked up speed along the carriageway that linked Liverpool and Manchester. On each side, scrubby land was punctuated by groups of houses here and there, then the odd factory, a glimpse of a distant steeple. 'It's all the same,' commented Jessica. 'Like some dried-up place in Africa.'

'No hills,' replied her stepfather. 'That's what makes the difference.'

Jessica was not nervous. In a strange way, she was going home, because her twin was there. Also, Jessica and Luke were both going to live in Liverpool, perhaps in the Corner House, perhaps elsewhere.

'You mustn't neglect your husbands,' remarked Stephen. 'Twinness is very close, but don't make it exclusive.'

'OK. Anyway, Luke and I are thinking of buying a place in Woolton,' she said. 'And we could all use the Corner House as a place for special occasions or holidays. Perhaps Katherine will live there full time, opposite her father. It doesn't matter, not yet.'

Jessica had not always felt so calm, but her initial annoyance on discovering Katherine's existence had died of neglect, as she had ceased to feed it. The subject at whom Jessica's anger had been directed was a woman approaching seventy. Yes, Eva Coates had acted high-handedly, but who should judge her? Auntie Eva had done her best at the time, had seen Mother's weakness and had removed the second born. Katherine had grown up privileged, but so had Jessica, as she had lived with Mother, had spent a particularly happy evening with Theresa and Stephen just before Mother had died.

Jessica glanced sideways. Blake had done a wonderful job, all things considered. Devastated by the death of his beloved, Dr Stephen Blake had carried on being a father to Jessica, had continued to live with her at Beacon Farm out on the moors, had carried on with research day and night. He was a great man, and his country was finally recognizing that fact.

'A penny for them,' said Stephen.

She laughed. 'Tell me all about my sister again. Tell me the bits you left out.'

'Which bits?'

'If I knew which bits, there wouldn't be any.'

'And what if there aren't?' He enjoyed bandying words with his stepdaughter. 'If you know there are bits, then you must also know—'

'Shut up, Blake.'

'All right.' He made a movement that zipped up his lips, then relented. 'She's a teacher, as you already know. She likes wild music and tame six-year-olds. According to her Uncle Daniel, she's a bit of a card. Many of her jokes would not bear repeating in the staffroom of a Catholic school.'

Jessica, an infant teacher with a mid-blue sense of fun, smiled to herself. 'You've told me all that before.'

'She likes dogs.'

Jessica's ageing Sheba was at home being dog-sat by Maggie and Monty, who continued to live together in Jessica's Tonge Moor house. 'So do I.'

'She's a raving socialist, like your good self, and she once bumped into John Lennon in a fish-and-chip shop.'

Jessica gulped. 'Did she speak to him?'

He nodded. 'She gave him a chip. Apparently, the wrappings of that meal are framed on the wall of her bedroom. She adores him. She goes very strange when he's on TV. Of course, with you being a McCartney devotee, there could be quarrels.'

Jessica all but glowered. 'I like John as well. Did you know they used to come to Bolton before they were famous? Even after they were famous.'

'I was not aware of that fascinating fact,' replied Stephen.

'Well, they met some girls at Butlin's and they stayed in touch for ages. The Beatles called Bolton

Bedrock because everything closed at eleven o'clock.'

'Not cosmopolitan enough for boys from the rarefied atmosphere of Liverpool.'

Jessica dug her dear stepfather in the ribs. 'Stop mocking me, Blake.' She twiddled her thumbs. 'What's going to happen?' she asked. He was a twin. He should have a few answers.

He pondered for several seconds. 'Well, you'll meet a precious stranger today. There won't be any tension after ten or so minutes, because you'll . . . you'll just reach out. By tomorrow, you'll be comparing backgrounds and finishing each other's sentences.' He nodded sagely. 'Be careful not to shut out Martin and Luke when they arrive at the weekend.'

Jessica howled with laughter. Luke was the sort of fellow who could never be shut out. He was noisy, vibrant, idiotically funny and he played a guitar loudly and not too well. When he wasn't twanging, Luke messed about with wood and screws. One day, he might build a bookcase that could sustain itself and a couple of paperbacks. 'He's bought a pink pressing of Elvis Presley's hits, Blake. A pink LP. It's all "Heartbreak Hotel" and "Jailhouse Rock". And, of course, he wants to build a record cabinet.'

Stephen nodded. 'We'll have the area cleared, Jess, alert the bomb squad. Where on earth did you find that boy?'

'Under a blackberry bush.' This was the truth.

'Ah yes. After he wrote off his scooter.'

Jessica wondered aloud about her sister's fiancé.

Her stepfather filled in a couple of gaps. 'I regret to inform you that Martin's a drummer.'

'Oh, God.'

'Exactly.' Stephen stopped at a red light. 'Shall I turn back?'

Jessica considered the suggestion. 'Katherine can play the piano, I believe, so she can do the keyboard bit. And I'm an excellent singer. If Cilla Black can do it, I can.'

Genuinely in the dark, the driver looked at his passenger. 'Who? Who's Cilla Black?'

She punched him. 'Drive on,' she ordered. 'My future awaits.'

The door swung inward. Katherine Walsh loitered near a fireplace above which a mirrored overmantel filled the chimney breast right up to the picture rail.

Jessica Blake stepped into the room, pausing fractionally on the threshold, holding her breath. At last, she was slightly nervous. How many years since the adventure in the woods? Nineteen, twenty?

A stair creaked, settled. Upstairs, rooms prepared for this day listened contentedly, waiting for life to begin again. Light softened by evening's gentle shades trickled lazily down the stairwell into the hallway. The refrigerator hummed; a clock struck a quarter to something or other. Whatever the time, the time was now.

Outside the open-eyed window, shrubs settled as the wind resigned suddenly and without notice. In this microscopic corner of a tiny planet, all was still. Birds rested; the flow of traffic abated; bell-ringers ceased their practice.

The mirror reflected two girls in blue, one with a modern haircut, the other with a sensible French pleat. Both wept silently, happily. Whispered words crept over floorboards, under doors, up the stairs. Differences, similarities, opinions and hopes were all discussed in damped-down, stilted tones that almost matched.

The sun sank into the river, leaving behind a sky that was magnificent, especially for spring. Dappled golds melted into graded blues, each colour vying for attention and praise. The day's end was celebrated by a vision fit to grace any canvas painted by Turner and his peers.

Near a rockery, the sea-captain's flag lay listless against its support. The winking window saw the young women eating together; the kitchen soaked up sound and movement while the new arrivals brewed and poured tea.

The girls cried again, laughed, told tales of two mothers and two fathers. The awkwardness was over. Now, they talked more clearly, more easily. For them, this was a beginning, a first time, a starting point.

The wise house settled itself down for the night, unspoken knowledge etched into brick, layered into plaster. There was no beginning, no end, not for the Corner House. It sat at the junction where it had existed for almost forty years, continuing its vigil, listening, learning.

The children of Theresa Nolan talked until dawn, packing the moments with their own history, their own dreams. The house dozed. Soon, it would be morning.

THE END